Destiny of the Fireblood
By Kathe Todd

Warning: contains graphic depictions of sex.

I0658296

Destiny of the Fireblood (The Fireblood Chronicles, Volume 1) by Kathe Todd. Copyright © 2015, 2016 by Kathe Todd. Published by Kalefaction Press, an imprint of Rip Off Press. All rights reserved. No portion may be reproduced by any means without the permission of the copyright holder. Visit KatheTodd.com for contact information and the full list of titles available. First print edition March 2016. ISBN: 978-0-89620-024-1

Chapter 1: Arrival

Bernadette Bouchard stopped to catch her breath at the top of the hill and looked behind her, to the border outpost straddling the road to the south. She had actually done it, she was here! For most of her life, since she'd been a small child, she'd dreamed of traveling to the wild and wooly province of Iscandia. There, she was sure, she would find fame, fortune, glory, and the chance to meet some real men – not the clumsy farm boys she'd been rolling with since the age of fifteen back home in Auverne.

Bernadette had never felt as if she belonged in the rural environs of her home village. Women there got married, popped out a few babies, got fat, got old, and died. They never went anywhere, saw anything, or had any adventures. Better to die in a flaming battle than to wither away like that! So with little more than the clothes on her back and a rusty iron dagger (long since polished and honed to razor sharpness), she had left home and set out for the road north.

The land and climate on this side of the border was little different from that in Auverne, she realized. But somehow the air was electric with promise. Here, she would prove herself as a warrior. Though Iscandia was a province of the Reman Empire just as Auverne was, it had been added much more recently and was considerably wilder and more lawless.

Iscandia had need of adventurers like her, skilled with bow and blade, who could beat back marauding bandits and the depredations of rogue mages and others who preyed on its citizenry. From all she'd heard, the Reman troops stationed here had their hands full keeping the peace in the cities, and putting a lid on Norse partisans who though Iscandia ought not to be part of the empire at all. Outright war had not erupted, perhaps because for the most part the citizens of Iscandia already *had* home rule. While the eorls of the nine marches paid tribute to the emperor and were subject to his decrees, they ran those marches with little or no actual interference.

Up ahead, Bernadette noticed a little encampment set up beside the road. There were a couple of hide tents and a campfire, and a horse grazed nearby while a Gatti, one of the fur-covered, humanoid race who traveled throughout the empire as nomadic traders, rummaged through the contents of a wooden cart. She had a few coins in her pockets, and decided to stop and see what the trader might have to offer. She was going to need supplies for her journey, as there were many miles between here and Waterdon.

A female, dressed in a blouse and skirt as if she were a human woman – but with a slit cut behind to allow her long, well-furred tail to move free – looked up as Bernadette approached the camp. "Good morning, mistress," she said politely. Throughout the empire, which covered nearly the entire continent of Agena and its surrounding islands, the *lingua franca* known as Common was spoken and written. But the woman could tell from Bernadette's accent where she had come from, in case the fact she was walking north on the road leading from the border crossing were not enough.

"Just up from Auverne, are you?" the trader asked, her chatoyant golden eyes assessing the taller woman. Not that Bernadette was all that imposing. She stood not quite five and a half feet tall, her body on the slim side beneath the leather traveling clothes she wore. The Gatti on average were shorter than humans, the quasi-human alfar (collectively referred to as elves) taller.

"You're right," Bernadette said with a self-deprecating smile. "And I'm heading for Waterdon, so I'm going to need some supplies. What do you have for sale?" The Gatti woman smiled slightly, showing small pointed teeth, and gestured her to step within the bounds of the campsite and approach the cart.

The traveler had already gotten a crash course in dickering during the walk up here from Pied de Puce, which nestled in a stretch of farmland some two hundred miles to the south. She'd picked up a basic wooden bow and a quiver of iron-tipped arrows, and had been able to feed herself on game most days during the journey across Auverne. Even in childhood she'd been a good shot, and had often brought down squirrels and rabbits in the wooded hills surrounding the valley in which her home village sat.

Now she applied her skills to beating the Gatti woman down on the price of a couple of leather water skins, a small tent, and some non-perishable foodstuffs. Who knew what conditions she would find as she set off along this ancient road? From the look of the surface, it had not seen any maintenance in decades so there were probably going to be many lonely stretches with no inns at which to buy food or put up for a night under a roof.

Their transaction concluded, Bernadette asked "Is there a town or village of some kind along this road nearby?" The trader's face took on a quizzical look.

"You don't have a map of the province?" she asked in surprise.

The traveler looked embarrassed. "At the border crossing they told me I only needed to turn west at the fork, and that road would take me all the way to Waterdon. It didn't occur to me to ask about places along the way."

The Gatti woman showed those pointy teeth again. With fur completely covering their faces it was hard to tell the cat-people's ages, but Bernadette guessed this one was probably at least as old as her mother. She felt utterly foolish for a moment. She was an adult, twenty-two years old. Most of the girls she'd known growing up were married and mothers by now. Yet she, the bold adventurer, had not thought to bring along such items as a tent and a map? At least she'd brought along a winter cloak and a bedroll. They said it got *cold* here in Iscandia.

The trader was rummaging in a box that sat near the front of the cart, and in a moment she produced a folded piece of paper and handed it to Bernadette. It looked like paper, but it didn't really feel like it. It had a slightly slick texture, as if it were waterproof. When she opened it up, there were no creases where it had been folded. Perhaps it was some sort of cloth, too fine-grained to see the weave?

It was the most beautiful map Bernadette had ever seen. The whole of Iscandia, and a few islands to the north of it, was laid out before her eyes in glorious detail. There were the roads, the rivers and lakes, and a scattering of cities interspersed with triangular marks she took to indicate mountains. And far over to the right, though nowhere near all the way east, was a marker for Waterdon.

"I must have it!" she blurted, cringing inside at losing her cool. Her supply of guilders, everything she'd saved during years of doing odd jobs around Pied de Puce, was dwindling fast. She dropped her gaze, face coloring like a sunset to match her ruddy hair, and murmured. "I don't have much money left. I can only pay you two guilders for it."

"Done," the trader replied shortly, and held out her remarkably human-looking hand for the coins.

In a daze, Bernadette handed over the money and thanked the woman, then stepped off a few paces to study her new acquisition. According to this, there was a village called Milburn located near the crossroads where this road joined the major road running east and west. To the west, not that far away from the crossroads, was the fabled dypalfar city of Alfenstein.

She definitely hoped to see the place someday, but she was eager to reach Waterdon first and enroll with the Brave Company – a legendary band of heroic adventurers who performed daring feats (for pay) all over the province. With them she'd have a roof over her head, meals and equipment covered, and a steady source of income while she learned her trade. The real adventuring stuff, the chance to make her name, would come after she'd improved her skills.

Tucking the map into a pocket inside her tunic, Bernadette set off along the road north. "By the way," the Gatti woman called to her before she'd gone two steps, "that's a magic map. I'm sure you'll find it helpful to you in your travels, dear." Bernadette turned back and smiled at her, then giving a little wave of thanks she continued on her way. Magic map? As if…

Chapter 2: The Road North

Bernadette continued up the ancient stone-paved road, her heart swelling with feelings of freedom and joy. She was on her way at last, here in Iscandia and walking into a world of possibilities. She yanked a somewhat stale hunk of bread out of her pack and gnawed on it as she continued on her way. The area on either side of the road here was forested and hilly, and she found it lovely. The region where she had grown up had been flat and agricultural, but here the landscape had a wildness that appealed to her sensibilities.

She kept her bow strung and near to hand, along with the couple of dozen arrows she had left. Considering how flat her purse was becoming, it might be better if she could catch some game along the way to this Milburn place. She expected there would be a market for any hides she could gather, and possibly she could trade some extra meat for other things she needed.

There was little stirring in the woods as she walked along, but she did spot a stag darting in and out of the trees ahead and fell into a crouching stance. She successfully stalked the enormous, hugely antlered beast, her soft boots moving soundlessly over the forest floor, and sent an iron-tipped arrow driving into him at the point right behind the shoulder nearest the heart. He didn't fall immediately, but he was mortally wounded and Bernadette tracked him for a while longer before ending his agony with two more well-placed arrows.

Lifting the carcass to bleed it in the approved fashion was beyond her. The deer of Iscandia were huge, weighing (she judged) more than 500 pounds. But Bernadette skinned the creature for its hide, and sliced off as much meat, with her new steel dagger, as she felt she could reasonably carry. The rest she left as a gift to the foxes and ravens. She made a small fire and toasted a couple of steaks over the flames, wolfing them down. She was a woman of appetites, an athlete who needed to pack away plenty of food on a daily basis and deeply enjoyed doing so.

After butchering the stag, she felt grubby beyond belief. Bernadette had been raised to believe that cleanliness was a virtue (though one often ignored at need), and when she came upon a small stream crossing the road she stepped aside and walked up it a few dozen yards to a small, crystalline pool. Peeling off her leather tunic and trousers and her linen underclothes, she stripped naked and went into the stream to wash the blood, sweat, and dust from her skin and hair.

By the gods, the water was cold! Refreshing, though, on this afternoon in early summer. She sat in the pool and let the running water sluice the grime from her body. Bernadette's skin was smooth, pale, and spotted with small freckles, overlying a body that was slim-curvy but becoming increasingly muscular as her active lifestyle had required more and more from her.

She ran her hands through the wet, dark auburn hair surmounting her pubic mound, and let her fingers dive down between her labia, spreading them and allowing the cold water to carry away the stickiness. Mmm, that felt kind of good. Having been busy trying to stay alive for most of the past few weeks, she'd had very few opportunities to relieve the desires that came as naturally to her as the hunger for food, or for adventure.

Perhaps there was some citizen of Milburn who would provide her with some relief. At the moment, naked as she was, she yet wore the amulet she'd received from Selene, the Wise Woman of her village – back before she'd (eagerly) surrendered her maidenhead to that first clumsy farm boy some seven years previously. It assured that no seed would take root in her womb, and protected her from the various infections one was likely to pick up while spreading one's favors around. On occasion, Bernadette thought it was her most valuable possession. Keeping alive with bow and sword were all very well, but keeping her freedom was of equal value to her.

Refreshed, Bernadette let her body air-dry before putting her clothing back on – wishing she had some clean underwear – and continued on her way. She came upon a farmhouse in the midst of the woodland, seemingly deserted, and raided its garden for some potatoes and other vegetables. Only a little further along the road she spotted an ominous-looking figure blocking the path ahead. It was a woman, but unlike any she'd seen before. She was just standing there, not walking along like a fellow traveler; and by her rough appearance, leather armor, and collection of weapons she was probably a bandit.

Part of what had drawn Bernadette to Iscandia was the knowledge that here, women could partake of all the same opportunities as men. A division of labor between the sexes was strongly encouraged in tradition-bound Auverne, but here women could be soldiers, smiths, even eorls. And apparently, bandits.

She decided it might be a better idea to avoid a confrontation, and slipped into a screen of bushes beside the road intent on sneaking past the highwaywoman – if that was what she was. She was nearly past when suddenly an arrow came whistling past her head to embed its steel point, quivering, in the tree behind her.

"Come out and hand over your money!" the female bandit called in a harsh voice. Shit, she'd been spotted! Bernadette ducked behind the tree, an oak more than three feet in diameter, and crouched as she nocked an arrow to her own bow. "Don't think you can hide from me," the woman called, as she began making her way through the underbrush up from the road.

Bernadette moved silently around to the north side of the tree as she heard the bandit coming toward the south. She'd slung her bow behind her back and was wielding a steel short sword, apparently planning to run her quarry through. The young Galise took two quick, silent steps and put an arrow into her attacker's throat at point blank range.

A look of surprised horror came across the bandit's features as she crumpled to the ground, blood spurting. Most of it seemed to be leaking inside rather than out, and Bernadette stood there in consternation as she listened to her antagonist noisily choking to death on her own blood. There wasn't anything she could do, not that she would have wanted to. The bitch got what was coming to her!

When the body lay still Bernadette lived up to her name. In Old Galise it meant "bold as a bear," and she quite ruthlessly set about stripping the corpse for its valuables. In her simple moral viewpoint those who made a living harming innocents forfeited any consideration. This was the first human being she had killed, but she expected it would not be the last. After all, she intended to be an adventurer!

The bandit's purse had contained a handful of golden guilders and some smaller coins as well – enough, Bernadette hoped, to get her a night's lodging in Milburn. Furthermore, the armor she'd been wearing looked like it could be made to fit Bernadette with a little alteration. After considering the perils of the journey, and the fact that this woman likely had a gang, Bernadette slipped the armor's central piece, the breastplate, on over the top of her leather shirt. She unstrung her own bow and slung the bandit's bow, a superior recurve type with a heavier draw, over her back.

Here she'd been nearly unencumbered on leaving home, and already Bernadette was starting to feel like a pack mule as she continued up the road. Dusk had not quite faded from the sky when she came upon the gates of Milburn. They stood open, but were well-patrolled by city guards. That a village with only three streets to it had gates across the road leading through it was further indication of how dangerous things might be in this part of Iscandia.

By now Bernadette was feeling tired, hungry, and footsore. Not to mention, a bit horny. It was clearly too late for her to visit any merchants, so she made a beeline for the inn, located only a few paces inside the gates at the southern edge of town. She was looking forward to a drink and a hot meal, and perhaps a little male companionship.

Bernadette walked into the inn, welcomed by the warm glow of hearth fires, and approached the bar at the far end of the room. It was kept by a severe-looking Reman woman. Bernadette introduced herself, and was able to sell her the remaining cuts of venison, still fresh enough, along with the raw potatoes and vegetables she'd liberated from that farm garden.

Inquiring about a room, Bernadette was told that the price was five guilders. Not a fortune, but a bigger chunk of her current fortune than she cared to part with just for a bed. Passing her hand briefly over her amulet, she ordered an ale instead. That was only fifty pence. Then she took a seat at one of the long wooden tables that ran down either side of the room.

Bernadette was young, not hard to look at, and a stranger in these parts. She had not been sipping at her tankard of ale for longer than a minute or two when she was approached by a young Norseman. He seemed eager to make her acquaintance; but he was a local, he didn't appear to have two guilders to rub together, and he reminded her all too vividly of the succession of clumsy farm boys with whom she'd vented her teenage lusts back in Auverne. She brushed him off with a smile.

A little while later the inn's bard approached her. He'd been making some pretty but unremarkable background music and was now on break. "Hi, I'm Donatien," he said with a winning smile. "I don't think I've seen you before?" A fellow Galise! But she didn't mention the coincidence.

"I'm Bernadette. Just passing through. You're the bard here?"

Truth to tell, Bernadette had a big weakness for bards or musicians of every stripe. They might be a bit deficient in the martial arts, another area that was important to her in her assessment of a man, but they had that certain *something*. Donatien was good-looking, with blue eyes and dark blond hair pulled back in a ponytail. He was dressed in gold-trimmed finery and carried a beautifully-polished lute.

He filled her ears with tales of his alma mater, the Bards' Academy in Sylvanian – where she absolutely must go if she had the slightest interest in becoming a bard. Bernadette liked music but didn't see in herself any particular talent; nor did the lifestyle seem more appealing to her than that of the warrior-adventurer. But she hung on his every word. He began buying her ales, in between returning to his duties as entertainment for the inn's patrons.

By the time Donatien was finished playing for the evening, most of the locals had gone on their way back to their snug homes. Bernadette was feeling quite buzzed, and her horniness was rising. "You have a room here at the inn?" she asked, stopping just short of batting her eyelashes. He smiled at her rakishly, nodding. Clearly he imagined he had been fighting some kind of a battle, and had just won it. Since her goal from before they met had been to get him (or someone equally suitable) into bed, it was less of a victory than he thought.

"What do you say we go there and have a drink?" he suggested, though no further drinks were required or desired. Bernadette agreed with a smile, and he took her arm as they made their way down past the tables to a door at the far end, opposite the bar. "Good night, Lucia!" Donatien sang out to the innkeeper where she stood behind the bar. He wanted to be sure it was known around the inn that he'd scored with the hot young visitor.

The room wasn't much: just about big enough for a double bed, a hearth, and a small table with a couple of chairs. "It's lovely!" Bernadette exclaimed, taking a seat on the bed and bouncing on it suggestively. It didn't take Donatien long to hang the lute in the corner and join her on the bed.

"You are absolutely stunning," he murmured, moving in for the kill.

She smiled demurely and pushed him off slightly, playing hard to get. But her intentions for the balance of the evening were aligned with his. She usually preferred to know her bedmates better, to establish a bond of friendship if not something deeper; but in this case, after all that she had been through earlier in the day, all she really wanted was a hard cock inside her and a warm bed to sleep in afterward.

Donatien planted a deep kiss on Bernadette's lips, and she responded. Then he began unbuckling her armor. She helped him peel it off of her, then removed her own undergarments and soon sat naked on the bed. His eyes widened. This girl was not just attractive, she was beautiful! Provided you didn't mind a few freckles, which as a Galise he emphatically did not. Her cheekbones were high –the alfar ancestry all Galise were supposed to have showing mostly in facial structure and the slight tilt of the deep blue-gray eyes. Her body was lithe and sculpted, her breasts full and firm with erect pink nipples, her limbs long for her height.

Aroused, Donatien hastened to pull his fancy tunic off over his head, then shed his boots and hose. Bernadette admired him in turn. He was surprisingly well-built for a guy who spent his days sleeping and his nights hanging around an inn playing a lute. It must be natural. His slim but muscular body was very lightly sprinkled with dark blond hairs matching the hair on his head in color if not texture, and the hard cock she'd been hoping for earlier sprouted, rigid and practically pulsing, from a nest of matching pubic hair at his crotch.

All right! This was more or less exactly what she'd had in mind. Her brain fuzzed by the ale, but nowhere near enough to mute her desire, Bernadette reached for him. As she continued to sit on the bed, she beckoned him near and found that rigid member jutting practically in her face. She started by stroking it, then took it in her mouth and began applying suction. He moaned, thrilled to discover that this chance-met beauty was talented as well.

Bernadette had the thought that a guy like this probably saw a lot of women in the course of his daily life. She wasn't the only woman in Iscandia drawn to pretty bards. So she expected he might be good for a bit more than the old in-and-out. She was not mistaken. She released him from her mouth, his cock quivering, and drew him down to kneel on the carpet beside the bed. She put a hand on the back of his head and pressed him close, her thighs spread wide. And he obliged with tongue and lips.

It *had* been a long time. He had been at it, licking and sucking, for no more than a couple of minutes before the feeling within Bernadette burgeoned into a rising wave of wet heat and she climaxed. Ah! Oh, that was good! Her affection for her chance-met lover was rising, and she welcomed his satisfactorily stiff cock into her dripping slit only moments later. He was young enough yet to lack a great deal of control, and had plunged into her hot and slippery depths only a few times before he spasmed in ecstasy and deposited his load of semen deep inside her. With no consequences, thanks to the amulet.

Donatien fell atop her on the bed, then shortly wriggled around so that they were lying entwined with their heads on the

13

pillows. "Bernadette! You're fantastic! I... love you!" Yeah right, she thought. I'll bet you say that to all the girls. He wasn't quite the action hero she'd envisioned between her legs, filling her cunt with a cock somehow magically endowed with the power to send her to the moons; but he was definitely a cut above the clumsy farm boys – and for tonight he would do nicely.

In fact Donatien's youthful sexual energy proved to be more than Bernadette had hoped for. I've got to start sleeping with older men, she thought blearily after the third time he had awakened her for more passionate heaving. She had been feeling a need for sex, and that need had now been fulfilled several times over. The need for some sleep was now starting to dominate her thoughts, and it was a great relief when he finally appeared to be sated and let her drop off for good.

Fortunately, bards sleep late. At some point warm sunlight was streaming in through the window and Bernadette awoke to find Donatien snoring beside her, lost in slumber. Good. She kissed him gently on the brow, not hard enough to wake him, and slipped out of bed to find her clothing. She wasn't quite walking bowlegged, but not far off. Whoo, she thought, I guess I can check *that* one off my list. She left the breastplate off, tucking it into her pack, as she had plans for some modifications before she left town.

Bernadette emerged from the inn into mid-morning sunlight, another lovely day in the southern regions of Iscandia. She wandered up the street and soon found a general store, where she went in and sold what small loot she had acquired that was not immediately needed. The prices that she got were not what she'd hoped. Seemingly, she would need to spend some time in Iscandia familiarizing herself with the people and learning how to work her wiles on the shopkeepers, before she would be able to bargain for fair prices.

Bernadette continued down the town's main street and spied a smithy. She went in and introduced herself to Liam, the powerful middle-aged blacksmith. He offered to give her smithing lessons, but the price he wanted for training was beyond her means. She had already put in some time at the smithy of her childhood friend

14

Louis' father, Reynard, during her adolescence; so she knew her way around the forge a bit. She sold him the deer hide, which he quickly got up onto a tanning rack. A hide that size was almost enough to make an entire set of armor.

Next Bernadette bought some already-tanned leather strips from him and used them to improve the two bows she was carrying, thus enhancing their value and utility. She sold the old one to Liam, and got his permission to use his equipment to refit the dead bandit's armor so that she could wear it herself. The boots were too big, and those she sold as well. The sword was decent steel, a fine blade, and by the time she left Liam's and turned east she had honed it to a razor edge and was wearing it at her side. She now had a tidy little nest egg, some reasonably good armor, and some weapons that were not completely useless. With those and a decent supply of food and water, she felt ready to pursue new challenges.

The next village marked on her map was Underhill. Milburn had proved to have a small stream powering a sawmill, so Bernadette guessed that Underhill would likely be found against the backdrop of a hill. Was Waterdon beside a river, and Sylvanian in the midst of a forest? Perhaps one didn't need to visit every town and city in Iscandia to know what they were about.

Chapter 3: Underhill

The morning smiled, a light breeze ruffling Bernadette's long, auburn hair as she strode along the road leading to Underhill. She tied it back with a strip of leather to keep it out of her eyes, enjoying the cool air on her face. The sun was warm, a few puffy clouds added some character to an otherwise boringly blue sky, and the woods seemed to be full of game. Not all of it harmless, she knew, but the awareness of threat lurking at every hand failed to dampen her spirits. She was naturally a carefree person, the most pressing of her burdens in her former life having been restlessness and dissatisfaction with the *boredom* of that life, in the rural village where she'd grown to womanhood. Now that was behind her, she felt ready for anything.

Well, almost anything. Bernadette was still feeling a bit sore from those frolics with the bard that had interrupted so much of her intended good night's sleep. She vowed to avoid such encounters for the foreseeable future. Or, at least until she was well and truly horny again. Which, she sighed, wasn't likely to be very long from now if past experience was any indicator. But then, in a strange new land among unfamiliar people and creatures, the future wasn't all that foreseeable was it?

Another activity Bernadette firmly decided to avoid for the time being was the exploration of any mysterious ruins, bandit lairs, or likely-haunted caverns she should chance across. The fight yesterday had made her only too aware of her limitations. She needed to figure out a way to earn the money for some training, and to befriend someone who could act as a battle companion and watch her back while she was still developing her skills.

As Bernadette walked along she managed to bring down a couple of foxes with her bow, and took their pelts. The little creatures seemed insufficiently shy of humans for their own good. Stalking deer would have required time for sneaking up on them and more time to butcher the carcasses, and Bernadette was anxious to reach Underhill before night fell; so the foxes were all she caught during the journey.

Despite her intentions, Bernadette had not yet reached her destination when darkness fell. She threw her fur bedroll down on the soft ground in the shelter of a pine tree, hoping it would be safe enough. There she passed the night unmolested, sleeping quite soundly after her day's walk and her short sleep the previous night.

The next day, by the greatest good fortune, she made it to the small and scenic hamlet of Underhill without being attacked by any bears, wolves, smilodons, trolls, bandits, or other unspeakable creatures. The sun was even still well up in the sky. On the other hand, other than the acquisition of the fox pelts, she had not found anything of value on the trip and her store of guilders was sure to dwindle.

Bernadette first made her way to the inn. It was called the Hungry Hunter, and she headed right for the bar to chat with the Norse barkeeper. She pumped him for information, while avoiding offering to purchase anything. In short order she learned that there was a local love triangle among some people named Staeven, Florein, and Carlotta. She also picked up a broadside, issued by the eorl, that offered a reward for cleaning out a gang of bandits from a local mine.

As it turned out, Staeven was to be found right there in the inn's common room, nursing an ale and eager to tell his troubles to anyone with a sympathetic ear. He was quite good-looking, tall and muscular with dark blond hair and up-tilted blue eyes. Here we go again, Bernadette thought – then nope, not going to happen. In any case, Staeven was clearly smitten by this mysterious Carlotta – whoever she might be. Carlotta Vendici, Bernadette soon learned: the sister of one Luigi Vendici, owner of Underhill Trading. This was the town's general store, and only a short distance from the inn.

Bernadette listened to his tale of frustrated love, making sympathetic noises as she sipped a glass of water. But she was surprised when after the briefest of conversations Staeven asked her, a stranger, to deliver a letter to his lady-love. His plan was simple, and seemingly the work of a simpleton: the letter was purportedly from his rival, and informed Carlotta that she and

Florein could never be together. Bernadette had only to deliver it to Carlotta and Staeven's path to her heart would be free of encumbrances. Or so he imagined.

Bernadette accepted the letter, left the inn, and continued on down the town's dusty main street. The entirety of the village sat between the main east-west road and a nearby mountain range, and there were indeed hills in view. She shortly found Underhill Trading, and the aforementioned Carlotta and Luigi, in the midst of a heated discussion about a robbery the store had recently suffered. Apparently an ancient artifact, a statuette of a dragon crafted of solid gold, had been the only item stolen.

Carlotta was indeed lovely, and it was easy to see why she would have suitors fighting over her. Not the sort of life Bernadette wanted, mind you, but… She handed over the letter and told Carlotta it had come from Florein, as Staeven had requested. Bernadette had not expected this ploy to work, but apparently Carlotta was taken in. She said she would not be seeing Florein anymore.

Carlotta thanked Bernadette for the information. Meanwhile, her brother Luigi (a typical Reman, money foremost in his thoughts) told Bernadette that he would be most grateful if she could recover the stolen statuette. She pulled out a little notebook in which she'd begun keeping a journal, and recorded the information. Clearly she was going to have to start keeping track of such things. Luigi directed Bernadette to nearby Deadfall Barrow (an ominous name if ever she heard one) as the likely hideout of the bandits he believed had stolen the statuette.

Bernadette continued exploring the village. It didn't take long. There was a smith, and she sold him her fox pelts but didn't buy anything. Then she returned to the Hungry Hunter to report the good news about Carlotta to Staeven. He was delighted, and hugely grateful. Could he do anything for *her*? "Could you help me out?" Bernadette asked. "There are a couple of things I need to do that would be a lot easier with a big strong man along."

Was she laying it on too thick? As much as she hated to admit it, more than anything she needed somebody to watch her back during her adventures. Her newfound resolve to remain celibate was safe with him, she hoped, since he was so head-over-heels for Carlotta. He agreed happily, as enthusiastic for adventure as she, and they soon departed the inn. He'd brought along a bow and a dagger, similar to the equipment she'd started out with a couple of days ago. Bernadette could only hope he knew what to do with them.

Chapter 4: Among the Undead

Bernadette and Staeven had not been on the road very long before the sun dipped low and it seemed night would soon be on them. But above the road, Bernadette spotted some stone structures that were clearly man-made. Now that she had some back-up, it was time to actively approach some adventures – and perhaps garner some loot. "That's Deadfall Barrow," Staeven informed her.

"Perfect," she replied. "This is where Luigi told me to go to find his golden statuette."

Bernadette strung her bow, and the pair crept carefully along a dirt path leading up the hillside. Halfway up they encountered a stone tower manned by three bandits, whom they swiftly killed. Staeven seemed to have some battle skills to go with his good looks. After dispatching these enemies, the pair continued up the monumental stone steps leading to the looming edifice's entrance.

Bernadette was pleased to learn that in addition to his abilities with a dagger, Staeven was a skilled archer. Between the two of them they picked off the bandit sentries, lurking in the area outside the door, while they were still some distance from the front of the building. The ominous-looking carved wooden doors opened on an enormous chamber, shrouded in darkness. At the far end they could see the glow of a campfire and hear voices murmuring. Creeping closer, they saw the bodies of shria lying here and there around the room.

Bernadette shuddered a bit. Shria were nasty creatures like rats the size of small dogs, but with the sharp teeth of shrews. Aggressive, vicious, and often running in small packs, they would attack anyone who came near them. Fortunately they were not too difficult to kill.

Bernadette and Staeven were eventually close enough to the bandits' campfire, still undetected, to make out their conversation. "Where does Andalo think he's going with that golden statue?" asked one.

The other replied, "Who cares? He can be the one to risk the spiders."

"But what if he gets out the back way and takes the treasure for himself?" the first complained. "I want my cut!"

"Just zip your lip and keep an eye out for trouble," the other responded.

So, these *were* the bandits that had stolen Luigi's treasure. And seemingly, one of them had carried it deeper into the ill-omened barrow. The other two would have done better to have heeded their own advice and kept an eye out; but it was already too late for them. Firing their bows simultaneously, Bernadette and Staeven were soon the only living beings in the chamber.

Bernadette searched the bandits' bodies and campsite, coming away with some coin and a few other useful items. She and Staeven were both getting tired, so they decided to rest here, using the bandits' fire and their sleeping pads, until they'd recouped their energies and were ready to continue in search of Andalo and his stolen treasure.

Arising some hours later, Bernadette went off into a corner to relieve herself. Then she got some provisions out of her pack. Staeven soon joined her at the campfire, and they shared a light meal before heading out. He was surprisingly taciturn given his garrulousness earlier, but had certainly proven a brave enough companion and an effective fighter.

They were soon wandering a series of rock-hewn corridors that occasionally opened out into small chambers, with curious-looking dark wood furnishings. Bernadette was repulsed to find that the place was infested with shria, which kept popping out of nowhere to attack them. Why the hell don't they just run away, she wondered?

After some minutes of picking their way through the building's corridors they found the passageway blocked by spider webs. Uh oh, hadn't one of those bandits mentioned spiders? Bernadette cut her way through, only to be confronted by a spider the size of a small horse! She used sword and shield (the latter item a recent acquisition from the belongings of the late bandits) to attack it while Staeven shot it full of arrows, and in a few heartbeats it collapsed and died – fortunately without having managed to bite her. These oversized arachnids could be found in deep, dark places throughout Agena, and their venom mimicked the symptoms of freezing.

Bernadette heard a voice calling out weakly, "I need help!" She approached a webby mass hanging from a doorway at the far end of the chamber, in among the strands of which she could just see the features of an elf. Could this be Andalo, the guy the other two bandits had been talking about? The figure said, "Thanks for killing that spider," he said – voice muffled. "Quick, cut me down before any more of them come!"

Andalo or I'm a shri, she thought, demanding "Where's the golden statue?"

His muffled reply confirmed Bernadette's suspicions. "It's in my pocket. We'll need it to get through the door to the treasure room!" What was all this blather? Wasn't the thing just a valuable golden art object? Whatever the bandit was on about, Bernadette judged that he couldn't be trusted.

"Give me the statue first," she told him.

"I can't move my arms!" Andalo protested.

He had a point, so Bernadette cut him down. She wasn't totally surprised, though, when he immediately bounded to his feet and ran off down the corridor. She was after him in a heartbeat, and had brought him down with a couple of well-aimed arrows before he'd gone fifty paces.

Bernadette rifled his body, and soon recovered the fabled statue along with a few other items of loot and the elf's journal, which told her everything Andalo had known about the statue and its uses. The statue *was* an impressive-looking thing, solid gold and more than eight inches from nose to tail. The dragon stood with wings and rear claws spread, as if stooping on prey, and there were three symbols embossed along its back. Lured by Andalo's tale of treasure, she and Staeven continued on their way, deeper into the labyrinth.

The pair proceeded with considerable trepidation, as they now found themselves in an area of catacombs. The walls were lined with stone tombs, many of which held skeletons or mummies.

They had not gotten very far in when one of those mummies abruptly sat up, eyes glowing red, and put its feet on the floor. Then it paced slowly forward to attack them. Its clothing and armor were shredded rags, its sword of an ancient Norse design though still sharp and free of rust.

"By the gods!" Bernadette cursed. "What in all the hells?"

As she and Staeven struggled to return the creature to the death it had somehow escaped, Staeven panted "Aptrgangr!" After it lay unmoving at their feet he added, "Some say that they are the ancient servants of the dragon worshipers, cursed to serve them in death as they did in life."

"Ugh, really?" she muttered in reply. "I just hope it'll *stay* dead now..." It did. Indeed most of the mummified corpses they found along the way were already permanently unmoving.

They came to a room with its exit blocked by an iron gate, flanked by three pillars. Each side had a symbol carved onto its surface, and you could rotate the pillars to show one or another of the sides. Up a flight of stairs on the right side of the room was a gallery with two fixed carvings, showing similar symbols. Between them was an area where there had been a rock fall, and back downstairs Bernadette realized that the chunk of rock which had fallen from the gallery was still lying on the floor. It had a plaque showing another symbol.

Correctly surmising that the fixed plaques were a clue to the settings needed for opening the gate, Bernadette rotated the movable pillars until they were showing symbols matching the fixed ones. Then, cringing a little at the thought of the lethal trap she might spring if she'd guessed wrong, she approached a lever in the center of the room and pulled it. No arrows shot out to impale her. Instead, with a rattle, the gate lifted into a slot above the doorway.

Continuing further and killing a few more aptrgangr, Bernadette and Staeven came to a small cavern with a little stream flowing through it. A pull chain opened a small iron gate and they picked their way through the ankle-deep water until another tunnel opened up to the right. They were forced to dash past swinging, razor-sharp blades in two passageways, kill more aptrgangr, and climb stairs to cross a bridge that led to another door as they continued on their way. Bernadette was pleased to find that, faced with *real* adventure at last, she was avid for more. She felt so alive!

Inside the door, they found a broad, deep room carved from the native rock. There were bas-relief carvings of what Bernadette took to be myths or perhaps historic events along either side of the room. And at the far end, the way was blocked by an odd-looking circular stone door. It had three concentric rings surrounding a central circle with two clusters of three familiarly-spaced holes in it.

Bernadette pulled out the statuette. Sure enough, the holes fit the dragon's hind feet's talons precisely, so it must be a key of some kind. But it did not turn. Then she took another look at the statue's back, and realized that the symbols embossed on it matched carved representations on the three stone rings of the door. She tried rotating each ring until the carvings on the door matched up with the images on the statue, starting with the neck and working toward the tail. Then she reinserted the talons in the holes, and this time it turned.

Bernadette heard a low grinding sound as some mechanism began operating, the door sinking slowly out of sight. She backed off a little, unsure as to what would happen next. But nothing leaped from the shadows to assault them. They entered an enormous space, a natural cavern it seemed, with a rock ceiling far above. Though no sky was visible, the cavern was suffused with what looked like wan daylight.

Across a narrow stone bridge was a stone platform, and beyond that a semicircular rock wall carved with elaborate ornamentations and some kind of runes. Bernadette approached it curiously, wondering at the strange writing. Within the wall's arc sat an ornate black chest, and off to one side was a stone platform. On it rested an ominous-looking black stone sarcophagus, and as they drew nearer to the chest the sarcophagus' lid shattered and a large, particularly mean-looking aptrgangr emerged wielding a deadly ancient Norse greatsword. Uh oh.

The aptrgangr they had encountered in the catacombs had been silent except for the occasional grunt or warning chirp as they came out of their tombs; but this thing let out an ear-piercing, raucous cry that nearly stopped Bernadette in her tracks. Rebuffed, she raised her shield and then attacked it with her sword. She was becoming more familiar with the use of the shield, and getting better at fending off attacks with it. But swinging the sword was wearing her out in a hurry. Panting, her arm feeling like lead, she finally dealt the creature a blow that drove it to the ground. Then Staeven provided the coup de grace with his dagger.

Bleeding from several small cuts and shaking with fatigue, Bernadette sat and rested until the natural resilience of youth and her athlete's body had put her on the mend. She had only a few healing potions, and she wanted to save them for emergencies. Given a few minutes, she would soon recover her strength without the need for chemical intervention.

When she was feeling better, Bernadette searched the now doubly-dead aptrgangr. Among the items he carried was an odd-looking rune-carved stone, which Bernadette suspected was valuable. She pocketed it, planning to hold onto it until she could consult with someone about what it might be. Then she turned her attention to the chest.

Ooh, loot! *Good* loot, at that. There were weapons and items of armor superior to anything she was currently carrying, gold coins of an antique design (but spendable as any modern guilders, she was sure). And right at the bottom was a glittering, bright blue gem the size of a pigeon's egg. Despite the dim light in the cavern it glimmered, and she thought she heard a wordless chorus in her mind. A glance at Staeven convinced her she was hearing things.

As she bent over the chest to retrieve the stone, the sound climbed to a crescendo. And as she seized it in her hand one set of runes on the wall behind her glowed blue for a moment, brightening quickly to white. Holding the gem in her palm she turned to stare at the phenomenon – and then looked down to see

what she had taken for a sapphire melting into her skin –
penetrating her body as if she were made of mist.

There was no pain, and the skin of her palm remained
unblemished after the gem had disappeared beneath it. For a
couple of heartbeats a blue glow emanated from her palm, then it
faded. And deep within her mind she felt she had just gained some
understanding of what the runes meant. But she had no idea what
to do with the knowledge.

Staeven's eyes went wide as he stared at what had just
happened. "Fireblood!" he murmured, involuntarily taking a pace
backward as if Bernadette had threatened him somehow.

"Fireblood?" she asked. Where had she heard that before?

"From the days of the dragons!" he said, in tones of awe. Oh
right, he'd mentioned the dragon worshipers earlier. Since it was
Iscandia where they'd once ruled, it stood to reason that children in
Iscandia would have been raised on all those old tales. Nobody had
seen a living dragon in millennia, though their bones could still be
found here and there. Bernadette guessed that most of what was
said about them was so much made-up stuff based on speculation.

Correctly analyzing his companion's expression, Staeven said
"No, no, it's true history – not just legends!" She eyed him
questioningly. "There was a line of humans with something of
dragons in them, the so-called Firebloods. The dragons worked
their spells through jewels created within their bodies, and only the
Firebloods had the ability to absorb those jewels into their own
bodies and use the dragon spells."

Bernadette's obvious lack of excitement was beginning to get
to Staeven, and he finished lamely, "That was all thousands of
years ago, of course. They say the Fireblood line continued long
after the dragons were all gone, but without any dragons to give
them jewels I guess the magic was dead."

"Um, thanks for the information," she replied – doubting it all.
She couldn't exactly explain what had just happened. Maybe the
"sapphire" was really a chunk of ice? Whatever, she didn't feel any
different. And now, it appeared to be time to start looking for a
way out of here.

As they climbed the stairs toward what looked like it might be an exit Bernadette spotted another, plainer chest in the shadows off behind the staircase. This, too, offered some gold and armor, and an enchanted circlet. Her heart surged with glee. They were alive, and she was finally getting real treasure to show for her efforts!

Around a few more bends they came to a dead end; but there was a pull switch mounted on a stone pillar and when she activated it a section of the rock wall before them slid out of sight. They found themselves walking into weak sunlight high up on an otherwise featureless, snow-covered mountain slope. "How do we get out of here?" Bernadette wondered aloud. The way down looked steep and dangerous. She pulled out her map, studying it with some faint hope of figuring out just where they were.

Bernadette was surprised to discover that the map now showed Underhill, where it had not before. Furthermore, Deadfall Barrow was marked as well. How was this possible?

Staeven, looking over her shoulder, said matter-of-factly, "Oh, good. You have a magic map."

"Okay, it's magic… how do you use it?" she asked, puzzled.

"As long as you can see the sky," he explained, "and if your mind is completely calm, all you have to do is touch any marked place on the map where you've been before and wish to be there. And it takes you there. One of the Hungry Hunter's customers showed me one a couple of months ago, and explained how it works. That was how he got to Underhill."

Bernadette gaped at him. Oh, really? This was going to be a huge help! Of course she'd have to walk to anyplace she hadn't previously visited first; but she still said a silent apology to that nameless Gatti trader for having doubted her. She wanted to return the statuette to Luigi, so she touched Underhill on the map and the next thing she knew, she was standing at the gates just outside town. Amazing! She looked around her and was pleased to see that the map had brought Staeven, as well. She was not finished with his help, as yet.

Chapter 5: Building Skills

Bernadette and Staeven walked on into town. It appeared that some time had elapsed locally since they had been standing on the mountainside, but it was hard to tell for sure. The sun was moving on toward late morning. The smithy was the first place they passed, and there seemed to be no one at the forge. She had some looted weapons and armor she wanted to work on before selling them, so she stopped off. He'd given her permission to use his facilities on her last visit.

Bernadette was concentrating on her work and was startled by a deep voice saying, "Not bad. Maybe I ought to hire you to help at the forge." She turned to see Heimdal there – the tall, full-bearded smith with his cinder-smudged leather apron, leaning up against one of the roof's supports.

Heimdal was impressed with her work, and told her, "You should keep practicing, and some day you'll make a master smith." Bernadette thanked him, and continued improving her collection of looted weapons and armor until she had run out of materials. She felt enormously pleased with herself.

But while she was still learning the craft, it would be hard for her to afford to buy smithing supplies – she needed to be "scavenging" them. Bernadette knew there were mines in the area, and most smithies (though not this one) had a smelter where one could make one's own ingots from ore. She needed to get her hands on a pickaxe.

Bernadette sold most of her improved items to Heimdal. Then she and Staeven headed for Underhill Traders. Luigi was overjoyed to see his golden statue back where it belonged, and gave her 400 guilders as a reward. She got more of his gold by selling a few gems (the ordinary kind, which did *not* melt into her skin when handled) she had acquired during the trip through the barrow. Her nest egg had soared to over 2,000 guilders, and she was beginning to feel a little more comfortable. No more hopping into bed with bards to avoid paying for a five-guilder night's lodging, at least!

"There's one more thing I'd like your help with," Bernadette told Staeven.

"Sure," he said, with a boyish grin. Gee, he was cute…

"Any idea where this Lodestrike mine is? I can earn some money if I kill the bandit gang there."

"It's a little way down the road west of here and back in the hills a bit" he told her. "The place always seems to be infested with bandits, since the mining company closed down."

The mine's entrance was at the top of a short dirt path sloping up from the main road. As they approached, weapons drawn, a woman sentry commanded them to halt. Bernadette had no problems ignoring requests from bandits, and instead she dropped the sentry with a couple of arrows. After this, the deadly pair (as she was now coming to think of herself and Staeven) entered through the rough wooden door of the mine.

They soon found themselves in a dimly-lit corridor hewn from the native rock, with supply crates lying here and there. Ahead, there was a wooden bridge and they could hear voices murmuring from an area down below it and to the right. Bernadette crept closer to peer over the bridge railing. There, in a campsite, two of the bandit gang were quietly conversing by torchlight. She could not make out what they were saying; but a quick arrow into each of them soon put an end to the discussion.

Knowing there would surely be more bandits hereabouts, Bernadette sneaked down a ramp to search the campsite for useful or valuable items and strip the dead bandits. She found herself admiring their hard-muscled bodies regretfully, and it occurred to her that her determination to remain celibate might be getting a little wobbly already. She and Staeven returned up the ramp and down another stone corridor.

Up another corridor to the left, they found a wooden walkway leading back further into the mine. They continued their stealthy progress, and as they came to ore deposits Bernadette stopped to mine them using a pickaxe she'd liberated from the bandit campsite. Oof, the stuff was heavy – but if she wanted to keep improving her smithing skills she needed supplies. It was becoming clear to her that here in Iscandia, the best way to get good quality equipment was to make it yourself.

The duo encountered the occasional luckless bandit as they crept through the branching mine corridors, along with some pretty good loot in a storeroom. Then they came around a bend and discovered a vast cavern with elevated ramps on either side, and a smithy area right down below them. Bernadette put an arrow into the bandit who was working the forge, dropping him in his tracks. Her bowshots were getting more deadly with practice.

After exploring the area below and looting some weapons from the armory, they tiptoed up the ramp on the left side. While Bernadette was peering into the dim recesses at the top of the ramp looking for a target, the bandit leader suddenly bolted upright from where he'd been sitting, having a meal at a small table nearby, and ran right past her in the darkness to close with Staeven.

Well *that* was unexpected. By the time she had hurried down there and spent a moment trying to get in a shot without hitting Staeven, the bandit was lying dead at his feet. That took care of the assignment that had been set out in the broadside. But what else might they find here? Bernadette and Staeven took the elevated walkways back toward the rear of the cavern and thence to a winding corridor that eventually deposited them at a door leading outside. By then she'd accumulated a goodly pile of iron ore and a few small gems.

"That seemed worthwhile," Bernadette remarked to Staeven. She was beginning to puff from the exertion of carrying all that loot and ore, and asked him to take some of it. "What do you want me to carry?" he asked politely. Such a nice boy. Actually, she was probably little older than Staeven herself. But she felt as if she'd already logged a lot more experience.

After leaving the mine their path ran along beside a pleasant small stream, and Bernadette was feeling awfully grubby after mucking about in the mine for an hour. Hot, too, as the afternoon was warm. Bernadette eyed Staeven speculatively. "What do you say we take a little break, and go for a swim?" she suggested.

He was amenable, and soon they had both stripped down and waded into the water at a spot where a small crystalline pool contained pretty little darting fish no bigger than her longest finger joint. The water felt marvelously refreshing, and Bernadette was enjoying herself splashing around and catching them, then flinging them onto the bank. These little guys, she knew, were one of the more valuable chemia ingredients to be found in the wild.

When any fish as yet uncaught had beaten a retreat downstream, Bernadette lay back in the water (which was no more than waist deep) and relaxed for a moment, letting some flow into her mouth and quench her thirst. She gazed at Staeven, feeling a thirst of another sort, and observed that he was looking back at her with a haunted expression – and a rising erection. My, what a nice body he had. Golden complexion, firm muscles, broad shoulders… His shoulder length hair was hanging in wet strands and his dark blue eyes were burning in a way that suggested internal torment.

Ah, Bernadette realized. Carlotta. He's been in love with her for ages and has only just cleared the path for them to be together. Then in a moment of youthful enthusiasm he goes off questing with a pretty stranger; and now he's discovering that he has urges he wasn't prepared to deal with. Once again she felt the old, wise woman to Staeven's boyish innocent. But she also had a sharp desire to feel that nice cock inside her, out here in the lovely afternoon air.

She swam over to where he was sitting, trying to hide his erection under the rippling surface of the water. "Staeven," she said gently. "It's okay, I mean, if you want to… I wouldn't mind." His face turned bright red.

"I can't," he stammered. "Carlotta… it wouldn't be right… I mean, you're beautiful and everything but I just can't." As he spoke, she could see through the clear water that his erection was beginning to subside as embarrassment and shame took over from lust.

"It's okay, I understand," Bernadette said. Then she kissed him on the brow and dived back under the water for one last chilling dip before getting out and back into her clothes. The cold

31

water helped, somewhat. But she made a mental note to herself to go looking for some more appropriate male companionship as soon as she'd gotten settled down in Waterdon. She expected that the famous mead hall of the Brave Company would be a great hunting ground.

They returned to Underhill and visited Heimdal once again. Smelting the ore she'd gathered would have to wait, but Bernadette was able to sell off the loot she'd captured on the visit to the mine – lightening her pack while enriching her purse. Then she and Staeven strolled back down Underhill's main street to return to the inn.

"Thanks so much for your help, Staeven," she said. "I hope you and Carlotta have a happy life together." She gave him a chaste hug, biting her lip. She'd hoped to add the bounty for killing the bandit gang to her already bulging purse, but learned from the bartender that she would have to apply to the steward of the Eorl of Westmarch – at the eorl's palace in Alfenstein. Well, *that* wasn't going to be happening for a while.

The afternoon was wearing on, and it seemed too late to begin walking east again. "You're heading for Waterdon?" the bartender asked, and she nodded. "Why not put up here for the night, and catch the carriage tomorrow?" he suggested.

"Carriage?" Bernadette asked. Now that she had a decent supply of gold, her options were expanding.

"Sure," the barkeep said. "One runs between Alfenstein and Coldstein once a week, and you're in luck since it stops here on the way east tomorrow."

Elated at the prospect of riding instead of walking, Bernadette didn't even ask how much the fare was. She would spend the balance of the day exploring Underhill, have a comfortable night in a snug bed at the Hungry Hunter; and tomorrow, she would be on her way.

Chapter 6: The Ride East

Up early and fortified by a hot breakfast, Bernadette climbed up into the carriage as the sun was rising toward mid-morning. She hadn't known what to expect, and was somewhat surprised to see that this form of transport was nothing but a rough-hewn buckboard wagon constructed of wooden planks, to which a plank bench seat had been added along either side.

There was storage beneath the seat for her pack and other belongings, but if there was rain (as it seemed likely there might be at this season) she and her fellow passengers were just going to get wet. I'd be getting as wet walking, Bernadette told herself. And at least this way she was saving her feet – not to mention the exertion of hauling all that iron ore.

There were four other passengers on the wagon, which was pulled by one very large and sturdy-looking horse. It reminded her of the plow horses she'd known in the farming region surrounding her home village. The wagon lumbered and creaked along the much-weathered road, rocking the passengers as it hit potholes. Before long Bernadette's ass was starting to complain about the hardness of the seat, and she got out her bedroll to make a fur cushion. Much better!

The passengers chit-chatted among themselves as they rode along, there being little else with which to occupy their time. Three of them appeared to be a family – husband, wife, and their adolescent daughter. None of those were likely to be of much help if they had to fight off bandits, though the wagon driver looked competent enough.

And the fifth passenger seemed like he'd be a good man in a fight, as well. He was a grim-looking fellow, in his middle 40s at a guess, with a long scar down one side of his face and wearing leather armor heavily augmented with steel plates. He had an enormous battle-axe at his back, and seemed a bit forbidding.

He soon warmed up to Bernadette, though. "You're an adventurer?" he asked, eyeing her in her martial garb with the hint of a suggestion that he didn't regard her as all that formidable. Considering he was easily as old as her father and had probably been adventuring in Iscandia since before she'd been born, she reckoned he was entitled to that view.

"In training," she replied with a self-deprecating grin. He cracked an answering smile, a rather frightening expression.

"Name's Gunnar," he said, holding out a meaty paw.

She shook it, and replied "Bernadette Bouchard. I've been in Iscandia less than a week, but I plan to make it my home. I'm going to Waterdon to join the Brave Company."

Gunnar raised an eyebrow. "A group with a noble past," he remarked noncommittally. She didn't miss the unspoken comment.

"And now?" she asked. If there were things she ought to know about the Brave Company before signing up, this might be her opportunity to learn them. The old warrior gave a lopsided grin.

"Far be it from me to say anything bad about the Brave Company. They were great heroes in the time of Sigrandil. And I think they've tried to preserve the traditions. But there's no real need for them in today's world. And I've heard some rumors that..." Bernadette was staring at him, eager to hear what he had to say yet fearing it.

"Better you should just go to Waterdon and see for yourself," Gunnar concluded. "It's not for me to say whether the rumors are true, but you should be careful. Spend some time learning what they're like, what they do, before you sign up with them. It might be just the place for a young adventurer starting out, who can say?" That was as much as she was going to get out of him.

The carriage stopped at another village along the east-west road near sunset, and everyone repaired to the local inn for a hot meal and a bed. Bernadette eyed the inn patrons as she sat eating her venison stew, but spotted no likely prospects for bed-warmers.

In the morning they continued, and camped that evening at the side of the road. What with the carriage's slow pace and occasional stops for calls of nature or feeding and watering the horse, they were moving not much above a fast walking pace. Bernadette had to console herself with the notion that she was saving her feet, and that so far at least they had not been molested by bandits or bears. She doubted she'd have fared so well as a woman on foot, alone.

Slow the pace might be, but each day they moved closer to Waterdon. In late afternoon on the third day they pulled up at the village of Plainview, spread north of the road in an area of slightly rolling plains. The wagon had not yet slowed to a stop when there came a loud roaring, like a big cat proclaiming its territory. Bernadette realized she had been hearing it as a background noise, obscured by the creaking of the wagon and the conversations that were going on among the passengers, for some time.

Now it was right on top of them though – and Bernadette's heart stopped in her chest as she realized that an enormous scaly monster was dropping on them from the sky! It was gigantic, perhaps forty feet from hard-scaled nose to spike-tipped tail – the leathery wings so big it didn't seem possible that it could land within the confines of the village's main street. And there was no doubt in her mind, as impossible as it seemed – the creature was a dragon!

As the family who were sharing the wagon screamed in terror, Gunnar was the first to react. In a trice the old warrior was over the side, pulling out his battle axe and running down the street to where the flying monster was coming in for a landing atop the village inn.

"Take cover!" Bernadette cried to the family, as she pulled out her bow and strung it. As an afterthought she buckled on her sword, though that didn't seem like such a great weapon to use against something that could eat you in one bite.

Like everyplace in Iscandia Bernadette had seen so far, Plainview had a contingent of uniformed guards despite its small size. They, and various other members of the local citizenry, were converging on the inn with bows at the ready. Before she could reach it the wagon driver, also armed with a bow, came running up behind her. The two of them skidded to a stop as the thing took a deep breath and released a jet of flames at least a foot across and thirty feet long, crisping everything it touched. Then, as arrows began raining on its seemingly impervious hide, it launched itself into the air again.

The extra weight as the dragon pushed itself aloft caused the roof of the inn to collapse partially, splinters flying. The close quarters were clearly giving the impossible creature some trouble, and likely the village didn't have any structures strong enough to support its weight for long. It came in for a landing out beyond the main street, then folded its wings and stalked forward ponderously on its four clawed feet.

As the dragon came down the narrow street, taking up more than half its width, its lashing tail was breaking chunks out of buildings on either side of the road. It roared its defiance, then shot another gout of flame before continuing on its way. Bernadette and the wagon driver, along with the rest of the defenders armed with bows, stood well back and peppered the dragon with arrows. Many of them bounced harmlessly off the tough scales, but a few stuck. Nothing more than a pinprick to creature this size, no doubt, but it seemed enraged at the attack.

Gunnar and half a dozen villagers with edged weapons charged, hoping that by spreading out they might get around the snapping jaws and have a chance at actually injuring the monster. Bolder than most, the axeman brought his weapon down hard on the right side of the horny snout, snapping off some protrusions and drawing blood. The dragon roared in fury, and with astonishing speed turned its head to seize the old warrior in its jaws. He shook the man like a terrier with a rat, snapping his neck, and then flung him to land like a rag doll twenty feet away.

Oh, no! Tears came to Bernadette's eyes as she saw the brave warrior brought down. Blinking them aside in a fury, she raised her bow again. She'd picked up a lot more arrows during her recent quests, but even so her quiver was almost empty again. The villagers with blades got in a few more hits, and it seemed the dragon had had enough.

The defenders scattered before him like chaff in the wind as he bulled his way down the village street to where the wagon stood – the terrified horse frantically trying to escape its traces. Realizing its peril, it bolted down the main road – wagon and all. But as soon as the dragon was out in the open again it spread its wings and took to the sky. Moments later the screaming horse, ripped from the harness, was being borne off to the north as the stunned villagers watched in a peculiar mixture of horror and relief. The village was safe – for now.

Chapter 7: Waterdon

Dozens of villagers had been injured, and there were not enough healing potions to go around. These marvelous products of chemia, in use throughout the continent, could heal wounds in a matter of minutes. Bernadette donated what few she had, and the most seriously injured people – including several with third degree burns – were treated. There was no mage in the village, not even an herb witch or hedge wizard, to provide magical healing.

Many others received standard first aid, and would likely recover well enough in a few days. But for Gunnar and three of the village men, it was too late. As they were laying the bodies out for burial, the village headwoman came to speak with Bernadette. "I am Gilda Berenson," she said, holding out a hand. The blonde woman with many streaks of gray in her hair was several inches taller than Bernadette and had an air of command about her.

"Bernadette Bouchard," the traveler replied politely. "How can I assist you, mistress?"

"You have already been a big help," the woman said, "and I hate to ask this of you as dusk is coming on. But you were heading for Waterdon on the carriage, were you not?" Past tense. *That* was for sure. That wagon would probably have to be broken up for firewood now, and even if it were intact there was no horse to pull it.

She could guess what was coming, and was more than willing. "You want me to head for Waterdon on foot, and alert the eorl of the dragon attack?" Gilda smiled grimly at her, but there was a pleased look around her eyes. She'd hoped it would take no convincing to get the intrepid young adventurer to help.

"Yes, please," she said with a nod. "He needs to send some troops to us to help us defend the town in case the dragon decides to come back."

After rescuing her pack from the wreckage of the carriage and retrieving as many arrows as she could from the scene of the fight, Bernadette made sure her water skins were full. Gilda handed her a big, fresh bread roll cut in half and laden with slices of cold beef as she was about to set off. "It looks like you might not be the only one missing their hot supper tonight," she said apologetically. "You have the thanks of everyone in Plainview."

It was full dark by the time Bernadette set off on the road east. But the largest of Terris' three moons was already well up over the horizon, and nearly full tonight. There was more than enough light to see by, the remaining white paving stones of the road glowing faintly in the moonlight. She'd sadly left her collection of iron ore behind, in the interests of being able to get to Waterdon as quickly as possible. Soon she had fallen into a lope she thought she could maintain for miles.

Bernadette kept her bow strung, but it was her sword she used against a pair of wolves that attacked her as she was jogging along. They never laid a tooth on her, and she regretted only that there was no time to skin them out. Wolf pelts would be great for winter clothing, which she was sure she was going to need here in another few months.

Despite the trauma of the day's events and her desperate push to reach aid, Bernadette found herself feeling almost cheerful. *This* was the kind of thing she had longed to experience, during those years of interminable boredom in Pied de Puce. When she began to feel winded she slowed to a fast walk, then picked up the pace again after she was rested.

Three hours later she could see the walls of Waterdon rising ahead and to her left, dotted with tiny lights. The city, seat of Waterdon March, sat on a steep hilltop that rose above the plain. A few miles beyond that one of Iscandia's many towering mountain ranges sparkled in the moonlight, snow wreathing the peaks even in summer.

The main road she was on continued to the east, eventually going all the way to the eastern seaport of Coldstein. She turned left at a much better-paved path and wound her way up the hill to the city walls, where she found the gates closed and barred – and flanked by a pair of guards.

"The city is closed for the night," the one on the left told her sternly. By now it was past four in the morning, and the eastern sky was already beginning to lighten. The sun rose early and set late in these latitudes, so close to midsummer.

She replied, "There's been a dragon attack in Plainview! I've been sent for help!" They let her through right away.

"Go all the way up to the top of the street, then turn left and climb the stairs to the eorl's palace," she was told.

Urgency driving her on though she was nearly wilting with exhaustion, Bernadette climbed up through the city. She passed a sprawling building of classic Norse design she was sure must be Ynglingar, the famed mead hall of the Brave Company. Supposedly it predated the city itself.

She felt a trace of regret as she barreled past it. Recent events, and Gunnar's lack of enthusiasm for the ancient order of heroes, were beginning to erode her original enthusiasm for joining up. Eh, that was something she could consider after she'd fulfilled her mission, had something more to eat, and then slept for a week.

Once again Bernadette was challenged at the entrance to the eorl's palace, which more closely resembled an ancient Norse longhouse than the sort of stone castle one could find here and there in Auverne. In the historic past, kings had been scattered as thickly as trees around that relatively small province.

Arriving before dawn, Bernadette had expected to find no one stirring except perhaps the kitchen staff baking bread. But in fact there were many guards milling around – and a man she took to be the eorl was sitting in an ornate chair atop a dais at the far end of the room. She came up panting, and the discussion broke off as all there turned to stare at her.

Ormund, Eorl of Waterdon March, sat on his throne looking tired. He was a tall, somewhat spare man who looked to be in his early 50s, with silver-sprinkled blond hair and beard – a classic Norseman. At his side stood a balding middle-aged Reman, his steward. He too looked as if he hadn't had enough sleep lately.

The eorl spoke. "You appear to be in some distress, young woman," he said in kindly tones. "Tell me what brings you here at this hour." Bernadette dropped her still-heavy pack to the floor and heaved a sigh. Then she took a deep breath. As she told of the dragon attack on Plainview, the eorl's face darkened.

"Another one," he said with a sigh.

"This dragon has been sighted before?" Bernadette asked, anxious to satisfy her curiosity.

"It virtually destroyed Horvirstead, south and east of here, two days ago," he said sadly. "and now it has come north." He turned to a tall and rather fearsome-looking nachtalfar woman in heavy armor, who stood at his side like a watchdog ready to defend her master. "Miralis, assemble a force at once and dispatch it to the aid of Plainview."

"Thank you, your, uh, grace," Bernadette said. She had never met anybody of higher rank than the mayor of Pied de Puce, and had no clue about correct courtly address. "They could use some more healing potions there, or perhaps a mage with healing abilities. Many were injured in the attack."

"See to it," the eorl commanded Miralis, and she nodded before leaving.

The old man peered at Bernadette with concern. "My dear," he said, "You appear to be wilting. Can I offer you something to eat or drink?" She smiled wanly at him.

"I ran here from Plainview all night," she explained. "What I could really use is a bed."

"Certainly!" he cried, and in short order the exhausted Bernadette found herself being led off through the kitchens by a motherly-looking woman wearing a floury apron over her skirt and blouse.

"You just tuck yourself up here, dear," she said kindly, gesturing to a neatly made-up bed. It was probably the cook's own, but she would have no need of it for the next several hours.

"Thank you," Bernadette said, stifling a yawn, and began peeling off her armor.

She awoke some hours later feeling much rested. A few more hours might have been nice, but the smells of food from the kitchen had penetrated her consciousness and would not let her sleep any more. She slipped out of the bed in her underwear, making it up again, and put her armor back on. It seemed somehow inappropriate to be thus clad here in the palace kitchens – but the only other garb she owned was the worn leathers she'd had on when she arrived in Iscandia. Besides, a lot of the people she'd seen when she got here earlier had been heavily armored.

The kindly cook was working on preparations for tonight's supper, lunchtime having gone past. But she sat Bernadette down at the kitchen table and demanded that she eat her fill of warmed-up beef stew and still-fresh bread rolls slathered with butter. Mmm! The young adventurer washed her meal down with room-temperature ale and felt 100% better. She supposed she had better go check with the eorl again, to see if he needed anything from her before she set about exploring Waterdon. That long-anticipated pleasure was calling to her like a siren, the utterly unexpected dragon threat an unwelcome interruption.

She walked out into the central hall and found Ormund on his throne once again. He seemed a little more rested than he had at dawn, and she guessed that he too might have caught a nap. He smiled at her and said, "Feeling better, I see! I don't believe I caught your name." Bernadette performed something halfway between a curtsy and a bow.

"Bernadette Bouchard, recently of Auverne, sir." A half-smile touched his lips.

"Come to seek your fortune in Iscandia, have you?" the eorl asked with a twinkle.

Bernadette's face went pink. That was the accursed problem with being a redhead, there was no hiding your feelings. "Yes, sir," she said, eyes downcast.

"Well you're doing an excellent job of it so far!" Ormund boomed. "The March of Waterdon owes you a great debt for your selfless service in bringing word of the attack on Plainview. As a token of my gratitude, I am presenting you with a suit of steel armor from the palace armory. You can pick it up downstairs, and my armorers will see that it is fitted for you."

As she made to thank him, he went on. "I have another task I hope you can aid me with. You need to speak with Garimund, my court wizard." He arose and walked off the dais, Bernadette trailing him, down the stairs and to a room off the east side of the main hall. There she met Garimund, a mysterious (and presumably powerful, if he was the eorl's court wizard) figure shrouded in mage's robes and a cowl that nearly hid his face. From his voice, though, he was neither that old nor that ominous a fellow.

Garimund said that he was studying dragons (given recent events, no doubt a popular pastime among the scholarly), and needed a certain stone, small and shaped like a tile, that his research led him to believe would be found somewhere in Darkfall Barrow many leagues to the west. This, he hoped, would give him information about the locations of dragon burials. That sounded to Bernadette a lot like the mysterious object she'd looted from the dead aptrgangr a day or two ago. "Oh, this old thing?" she asked with a smile, pulling the very dragon tile in question out of her pack.

Garimund was stunned and delighted. "You already found it? That's wonderful!"

Just then Miralis burst in on them, to report that a dragon had been seen attacking the guard outpost along the main road west of the city – only a short distance away from the walls of Waterdon itself. She asked the eorl, and Bernadette as well, to join her in the strategy room up a flight of steps on the eastern side of the dais. Shortly after they had gathered there, Ormund instructed Miralis to assemble some soldiers to go investigate the watchtower. He told Bernadette to meet Miralis there too, as she was now considered to be their local "dragon expert." Bernadette's expertise had so far convinced her it was best to stay the hell away from them. But she seized on the challenge.

Miralis, gathering guards as she went, trotted for the main entrance and down the steps. Bernadette, trailing behind them, had the presence of mind to pull out her magic map. It had certainly gotten her and Staeven back to Underhill. She had passed what looked like a watchtower of some sort during her run from Plainview. Would it work again?

In moments she found herself looking at the same watchtower. But it looked far different from what she'd seen of it by moonlight. It was now partially ruinous, the scorched bodies of Waterdon guards lying here and there on the turf. Above, she could see a dragon circling. But in the bright light of mid-afternoon, she could see it was *not* the same creature that had attacked Plainview.

That dragon had been far larger, spikier, and dark gray in color. This one was no more than two-thirds the size, and a sort of medium tan color with bronze glints reflecting from its scales as it turned in the air above. It was roaring in the same way the other one had, as if it were a large wild animal proclaiming its territory. Weren't dragons supposed to have been sentient? From the stories Bernadette had read in her youth, the dragons were in some way like gigantic scaly people, with a language and culture of their own. Hadn't they ruled throughout Iscandia back in the time when men were dressed in furs and just learning to forge iron?

Whatever the true nature of dragons, the fact that there was more than *one* dragon abroad was a cause for concern. Had she arrived in Iscandia just in time to help that province fight an invasion of giant scaly monsters out of legend? It was too weird to contemplate.

Moving to the tower, bow at the ready, Bernadette spoke to a guard. The man appeared to be in a state of shock and terror. "It just swooped down and took Jorgen and Alfmund before we knew what was happening!" he cried, distraught. "Watch out, it will get you too!" He seemed paralyzed with fear, so Bernadette pushed past him and ran up 2 or 3 flights of spiraling stone steps to the tower's roof. She had hoped for a better shot at the dragon from here, but by now Miralis' contingent had arrived and the creature was spending more time near the ground, attacking them.

Bernadette raced back down the stairs and out onto the grounds, where she was able to get a few shots into the beast. Not just a beast, though, she realized. The old tales were true. It was speaking in a chilling bass voice, words she presumed were in the dragon tongue and some that sounded as if they were in the common tongue as well.

As it attempted to rise again, she was suddenly seized with a wave of indescribable emotion. She felt a searing heat in her core, as if the blue gem that had vanished into her palm days ago had suddenly flared to life. Glory, exultation, anger – and as loud as she could, she cried out a single syllable: "Kraf!" The dragon was buffeted back, as if the air pushed from her lungs had been a powerful gust of wind. Then as she fired a last arrow into its breast, just below where the left wing joined the body, it fell to the ground dead.

By the gods, what a creature! From its roughly scaled, horned head to the tip of its serpentine tail it was as long as three large horses end-to-end, and its leathery wings stretched nearly as wide. Yet now, thanks to the efforts of a few puny humans, it was broken and bloody on the ground. Bernadette approached to examine it more closely, drawn as if by an irresistible force; and as she touched its scaly hide it began to glow. Then its flesh seemed to dissolve, as if it had been mist.

Where the bloodstained body had been, only bones remained. And on the ground beneath those bones a heap of items was left behind. Ignoring the weirdness of the situation, she pushed in between the ribs to examine them. There were some weapons and pieces of armor, quite a few arrows, and even some gold! And she heard that chorus of voices again, sounding as if they were singing a celestial chord over and over.

Ah, there it was. Lost at the bottom of the pile of valuable items was a glowing gem. The last one had been blue. This one was orange, and looked nothing like any natural gem Bernadette had ever seen. Not that gems had exactly been thick on the ground in the region surrounding Pied de Puce…

Staeven's words came back to her as she reached for it, unwilling to do so but unable to resist. As she held it in her palm, it sank into her skin and within moments all trace of it was gone. But now, more attuned to her inner self, she could feel its power within her. He was right!

Two of the Waterdon city guards stood gaping at her in wonder. "She's Fireblood!" one cried.

"Fireblood? But that's absurd!" Bernadette declared. If she was a member of an ancient draconic lineage, wouldn't she or others of her family over the generations have noticed something? And how was it that even city guards, presumably young men with little or no education, knew what she did not? Maybe it was an Iscandia thing.

The guard went on, "It's not absurd, it's the prophecy coming true! The dragons are coming back, and now here *you* are. It's said that only a Fireblood will be able to use the dragons' spells. That gem is proof!"

"It just… sort of vanished," Bernadette said weakly. After all the years when she'd longed to be exceptional, suddenly she just wanted to be ordinary, normal – like everyone else.

"It went into your body!" the guard insisted. "It's there to give you power to use dragon spells. Look what it did to this one," he gestured. "You need to go back to Wyrmshalla and talk to the eorl!"

She did so shortly, fast-traveling using her magic map. Wow, it worked amazingly. Inside, Eorl Ormund was excited and extremely grateful to Bernadette for slaying the dragon. She pointed out that she'd done so only with help from Miralis and her squadron of soldiers, but he still declared that he was hereby naming her Warden of the March, as a reward for her services. She now had the right (though at this juncture, not enough coin) to buy property within the city, and he was assigning a woman named Lifa as her body servant. An enchanted sword, symbol of her office, was also included in the deal.

Warden of the March! That wasn't quite like being raised to the nobility, but it definitely put you above ordinary citizens. Along with the privileges were responsibilities, of course. If the eorl commanded you help in defending the march, you were expected to step up. As Bernadette was coming to terms with this latest turn of events, the two guards who had watched her kill the dragon came puffing in.

They saluted the eorl but didn't want to interrupt his conversation. He could see, though, that they were burning to tell him their news. "Excuse me, Warden Bouchard," he said. "Ulaf, what is it?" "We saw her kill the dragon, my eorl," the young man said respectfully. "She used a dragon spell on it, we saw! And later when she touched the body all the flesh just kind of… vanished!"

Ormund looked at his newly-minted Warden speculatively. "You used a spoken spell?" he asked her. Of all the magic known throughout Agena, only the spells of the dragons were spoken aloud.

"Y… yes," Bernadette stammered. "I didn't know it was a spell, I don't even really know any magic at all except a fire spell I use for lighting campfires."

"This spell just came to you, without study?" the eorl asked, probing.

Bernadette looked down at her feet, then up into Ormund's eyes. "When I was in Deadfall Barrow, where I found that funny stone your mage was so interested in, I found a jewel in a chest. And when I picked it up it melted into my hand. Then some runes carved into a nearby wall flared up. I think that's where the word came to me."

"She took a stone from the bones of the dragon, too," Olaf averred. "And that one melted into her palm too! She's Fireblood, has to be!"

"Thank you, Olaf. You may go now," the eorl dismissed the guards. He was sitting up very straight on his throne, hands on his knees and an expression of relieved amazement on his face. Bernadette eyed him questioningly.

Finally he spoke. "Of course," he said, "It's the prophecy…" He trailed off, wondering at this discovery. Then he suddenly jumped to his feet. "You must go to Eberburg immediately!" he said. "You are the one prophesied, the Fireblood who will come when the dragons return. You will need the Old Ones to train you, for surely the return of dragons to Iscandia means that the end of the world is at hand."

Bernadette gulped. "End of the world?" she asked. She'd barely gotten started living, and there was no way she was ready to check out yet.

"The ancient prophesies say that when the dragons appear again, our doom is at hand," the eorl explained. "But they also say that one who is Fireblood will arise, who holds the power to save us all from that fate." Whoa. Fame, fortune, adventure, and plenty of hot studs sounded fine. Having the future existence of the entire world in her hands wasn't what Bernadette had had in mind. But if that was her destiny, she supposed she had better step up.

Ormund explained that the Old Ones were a group of old holy men who made their home high atop the largest mountain in Iscandia, a little to the south and east of Waterdon. She had not heard of them before but the eorl seemed to regard them with reverence, and a visit to their headquarters of Eberburg as a holy pilgrimage.

Bernadette thanked him for everything and returned down the steps from the dais. Her mind was reeling with the events of the past couple of days. From near-penniless adventurer to Warden of the March, just like that? And the eorl claimed that she might be one prophesied to (maybe) save Terris from destruction? It was a lot to take in. Now she had a journey to take, but first she needed to make some preparations. It appeared that her thorough exploration of Waterdon, and investigation of the possibilities with the Brave Company, had been put on hold.

She pulled out her map and found Eberburg on it, though she was certain it had not been there before. Seemingly just having its owner be told about a place's existence would trigger the map's magic. A pity, she thought, it wouldn't also just transport her there. That would certainly save a lot of shoe leather.

Eberburg appeared to be right near the top of an enormously high mountain, with no roads leading to it from here. Likely Bernadette would have to travel all the way around to the far side of the mountain, then up it on what appeared to be a goat trail from a town that showed on the map as Bohrsstead. It was going to be a long trip. And if this Lifa person could come along and help her, she ought to be able to get there in one piece.

While considering her route, Bernadette spotted something on the map called the Bathing Maiden. She assumed it must be an inn, but what was it doing out there all by itself – and how had it made its way onto her map? Still, it sounded interesting. With as much coin as she had, perhaps she could have a little rest and recreation in pleasant surroundings before going off to be eaten by smilodons, dragons, and bears.

Bernadette found Lifa waiting for her near the front doors of the hall. She was a handsome young woman, in her middle twenties but with an air of gravitas that made her seem older. She was heavily armored and had a stern expression that suggested humor was not in her vocabulary. "Greetings, my warden. How may I serve you?" she asked obsequiously.

"For starters," Bernadette responded, "you can explain to me what a body servant does."

"I am here to do your bidding, carry your burdens, and fight in your battles," came the reply. Hmm, serious stuff.

"Lifa, do you know the Bathing Maiden?" asked Bernadette.

"It is a popular inn on the road that leads north, east of Waterdon," Lifa replied. "I haven't been there, but I know how to find it. People visit there from all over Iscandia."

"I tell you what, then. Why don't you gather whatever you need for a journey and meet me there?" suggested Bernadette. Lifa agreed, and shortly Bernadette made her way out the door and left Waterdon behind. Exploration would have to wait, but she did stop long enough to collect her new armor from the armory below the palace. She had the feeling she might be needing it soon.

Chapter 8: The Bathing Maiden

The Bathing Maiden proved to be a large and handsome free-standing wooden building situated a little way off the road overlooking the Brightwater River from which Waterdon took its name, perhaps five minutes' walk from the stables. It had decks all around the outside, a small building for guards' quarters in the back, and a swimming pool and soaking pool set into the rear deck. The colorfully-painted wooden sign hanging out front showed a very buxom girl in a shift, lifting the hem of it above her knee as she put a toe into what looked like a pool of water.

Very charming, Bernadette thought. Inside, she found its charms even more impressive as she walked in the front doors and discovered a large sunken bathing pool in the middle of the ground floor common room. Relaxing in it were a couple of extremely good-looking young men, in the buff. Now *that* was something you didn't see in Auverne, or at least the parts of it she had visited.

Bernadette had a feeling she was going to like this place. She approached a man wearing an apron, who seemed to be the innkeeper. "Can I use the facilities?" she asked. "Certainly," he replied. "Take any bed you like, and feel free to use the pools. Clothing is optional here."

Now where was that Lifa? She ought to have been here by now, but there was no sign of her. Shedding her travel-stained gear and parking it in a corner, Bernadette headed for that central bathing pool and stepped down into it, to sit on a bench that ran along the long edge. Oh! The water was hot, and it felt absolutely wonderful! She rubbed her limbs and ducked her head, sluicing her long auburn hair, then sat back to enjoy a soak.

Seated across from her, on a bench lining the opposite side of the pool, was possibly the most beautiful man Bernadette had ever seen. He was older than her by a few years, some laugh lines crinkling the corners of his glowingly warm brown eyes. His hair was shoulder length, a blond-streaked light brown; his body hard-muscled beneath smooth, lightly tanned skin. His face was somewhat long but perfectly proportioned, with a firm, clean-shaven jaw and a half-smile of amused pleasure that seemed to wreath his mouth whenever he looked at her.

And he was gazing at her now, very appreciatively. Her pale skin glowing from the hot water, her full breasts bobbing on the surface of the pool with the nipples pert and pink, she made a fetching sight. Bernadette couldn't help but notice that his member, which was already quite generous in size, seemed to be getting bigger beneath the water. "Do you come here often?" she asked inanely, and flushed to her hair roots. He was so outrageously gorgeous, she felt tongue-tied.

"I'm almost always here," he said with that slight smile, those warm eyes drinking her soul. "But I haven't seen *you* before."

She smiled in turn, shoving aside her embarrassment. "I'm Bernadette Bouchard," she summarized. "I recently discovered I'm 'Fireblood' and I have to leave for Eberburg in the morning. It's been quite a day."

"Fireblood? You? By the gods! I'm honored to be sharing a pool with you." His smile told her he was teasing her. "My name is Andrion Lamonte."

"Oh, you're Galise?" she asked.

"Yes," he replied. "And you as well?" he asked.

"Yes, that's right…" she murmured.

They continued to enjoy the pool, talking idly about the weather, local gossip, and so forth, as others came and went. When her fingers and toes were beginning to shrivel Bernadette said reluctantly, "I suppose I'd better go get myself a bed. I'm not sure how it's done here."

"Oh, you can just take any that's not occupied at the moment," Andrion said, those warm eyes glowing. "Or one that is, if the occupant is willing. Would you like a bed-warmer?" Once again his gaze was filling her with a warmth that seemed to spread from her face down to at least crotch level.

People in these parts were certainly direct! Quite a difference from Staeven and his shamefaced shyness. Now Bernadette *knew* she was going to like this place. With a smile and a nod she stood up and took Andrion by the hand, leading him out of the pool. She collected her gear, and they continued up the steps to the sleeping loft, where most of the inn's beds were to be found. Many were small, but there were not that many visitors at this time and they found one big enough for the two of them.

Towels had been left around the pool and they took a couple of those along. They stood on a carpet near the bed and rubbed each other down, drying off their bodies still glowing warmly from the hot water. Andrion was now sporting a towering erection, and he pressed it against her belly as he put a hand behind her damp head and kissed her firmly on the lips.

The heat of that rigid rod sent an answering heat down through her core and then back up to her heart, which was pounding with excitement. Stalking through mine tunnels in search of bandits to slay had not gotten it racing as hard as it was now, with anticipation of the things she was planning to do in the near future with this amazing, sexy man.

Without releasing Bernadette from his embrace, Andrion backed her toward the bed until they both sat down on it. Then he continued drinking her mouth with deep soul kisses, while his hands massaged her breasts gently until the nipples were hard before stroking down her flanks, her hips, the hot moist crevice between her legs. She was on fire! He moved his lips from her mouth to her neck, at the spot where it joined her shoulder, sending shivers down her spine that returned in a rippling wave of hunger and delight.

Meanwhile Bernadette's own hands were not idle. She stroked his chest and arms, loving the feel of the smooth, resilient skin overlying those powerful muscles. They next wandered along the side of his waist and flat belly, running fingers like an angel's kiss over the sensitive skin of his groin, then seizing his stiff cock with a firm grip and squeezing it rhythmically. Andrion groaned.

He turned her body in his arms so that she was lying beneath him, and she spread her legs to receive him as he slowly lowered himself into her. Aaaaah! The sensation was exactly what she had been hungering for, seemingly forever. He had more endurance than that young scamp Donatien, and made love to her caressingly yet passionately – building to a fever pitch and then easing off again, over and over. Bernadette came half a dozen times while he somehow managed to hold off until, finally, he could contain it no longer and they exploded in unison. He continued thrusting for another few seconds, both of them enjoying the hot gush – before subsiding, motionless, as he held her tight to him.

Bernadette's hair was still damp, not yet dried from the bath and now moistened with perspiration as well. He brushed a lock out of her eyes and slowly covered her face with soft kisses. "Berni," Andrion murmured. This unexpected treasure had fallen into his arms, and he could hardly believe his luck. They both sank into a doze, exhausted from their efforts, and slept for a time. Bernadette awoke some hours later and stroked Andrion's cheek, which caused him to awaken as well.

"I'm hungry. And I need to pee," she told him.

Andrion smiled lazily and sat up, leading her across the room to show her where the privy was. When she returned he had put on a robe, and had one for her – as well as some apples, fresh bread, and smoked salmon on the room's small table. They devoured the food like ravenous wolves, surprised at how truly hungry they had been. Then they took another dip in the bathing pool before returning to bed. Andrion was thinking about another round, but Bernadette begged off.

"That was fantastic," she said regretfully, "but I'm leaving on a journey of many leagues in the morning. I *really* need some sleep." Disappointment welled in him as he remembered she had mentioned leaving earlier. Would she slip out of his grasp so soon? But he just smiled, kissed her tenderly, then lay down and snuggled her into his arms as they both dropped off once again.

As morning was beginning to light the Maiden's downstairs windows, Bernadette awoke feeling a bit overwhelmed. She was entwined in the arms of her new lover, and would much rather stay right there than go trekking off to Eberburg to report to the Old Ones. Whoever they were, they didn't sound very appealing. But she sensed that her newly-discovered status as Fireblood came with responsibilities.

As Bernadette slipped out of bed, Andrion sat up too. "Breakfast?" he suggested. There was always food to be had downstairs, any hour of the day or night.

"Yep," she yawned. They put on robes and went down, his arm around her shoulder as he planted a firm kiss on the top of her head.

Downstairs, they sat and ate at the bar. Bernadette asked Lev Ciabalo, the handsome barman, "Did a heavily armored, dark-haired woman come in last night looking for me? Name of Lifa?" Lev shook his head.

"Haven't had any dark-haired women of any description in a couple of days." Bernadette's face fell.

"What's the matter, Berni?" Andrion asked sympathetically.

"She's my body servant. I just got made Warden yesterday after the dragon attack, and she was supposed to come and watch my back for me while I go to Eberburg. Now I don't know what to do. I don't think I'd stand a chance out there by myself," she admitted reluctantly.

His heart leaping at the prospect, Andrion turned his warm smile on her full force. "Want *me* to come along instead?"

Bernadette's heart skipped a beat. She would like that more than anything. "Are you sure?" she asked, gazing up at him with concern.

"I'm a journey-level mage, and I'm not a complete slouch with a blade," he replied matter-of-factly. "I would *love* to watch your back. And your front, and any other parts you think need watching," he leered.

She threw her arms around his neck joyfully. "Oh, *thank* you! I love you!" As she said it, it was something that one says casually to express gratitude or appreciation. But as she thought about it, she knew that deep inside she meant it in another way. She was rapidly falling in love with this Andrion Lamonte, even as little as she knew about him.

Not that she was about to marry him, settle down, and start having his babies. But Bernadette knew that she wanted to be with him, and fight at his side, and share her adventures with him. So far she had only seen him in a robe or his birthday suit, and a fine suit it was. But he was going to need something that offered a bit more protection if they were to survive the wilds of Iscandia together.

Fortunately it turned out that he already possessed a decent suit of armor, and a few weapons that weren't completely useless. Furthermore, she'd acquired an enchanted hood that would enhance his magical abilities, and she gave it to him to wear so that his battle magic spells would have more power.

As the sun rose above the mountains to the east, Bernadette and Andrion set off on the road they hoped would eventually lead them to Eberburg and her destiny as the Fireblood. And to whatever the future held for the two of them.

Chapter 9: The Road to Bohrsstead

Initially, Bernadette had regarded the eorl's command that she go to Eberburg, along with the revelation of her Fireblood status, as more of a nuisance than a blessing. But as she and Andrion strode out into the Iscandia countryside together, the morning sunshine peeking out at them from behind puffy clouds, she felt as happy as she ever had in her young life.

Even the frightening unknowns ahead of her now seemed to be a grand adventure. She kept stealing glances at Andrion, his handsome profile thrilling her. She recognized the symptoms, though, and took this head-over-heels infatuation with a grain of salt. Likely, this exciting stage of first love would pass before long and it would be back to business again.

"Business" found them before they had gotten very far in their journey. As they turned to the east along the course of the Brightwater they spied a strange-looking creature lurking ahead of them, and it appeared as if it might be hungry. Andrion leaned close to Bernadette's ear and whispered "Draco Gryphon. Very bad news."

They sneaked a little closer to it, and she was able to do a considerable amount of damage to it with a couple of arrows. The pissed-off creature looked like a cross between a smilodon and a small dragon and was about half the size of a horse. But fortunately, before it was able to sink its fangs into them, Andrion finished it off with a couple of lightning bolts (a spell she wished she knew) and his sword.

Bernadette was impressed, and thankful that Andrion's claim to fighting prowess had been no idle boast. His qualifications as a lover were beyond doubt, and it now seemed his battle skills were a match for them. They soon continued on their way. Studying the map, which had very little to show them in this part of the world, she decided that they should cross the river and try to pick up a trail on the other side of it. The water was clear and sparkling, like all of the streams she'd encountered in Iscandia so far, and not very deep.

Bernadette waded across the stream, then continued up the bank and soon struck a road. Andrion was right on her heels. To the east, on this side of the river, was a tall stone tower with an air of ruinousness about it. It might be manned by imperial troops, but she had the feeling it was probably infested with bandits instead.

She saw this as another deficiency in the Remans' governance of the province. Not only were the roads falling apart, but the countryside was full of abandoned structures that had been taken over by human predators. It was most definitely *not* safe to travel around here unless you were armed to the teeth or accompanied by a small army.

Directly ahead of them, though, was a broad dirt path leading up the hillside. They were on the lower flanks of the north side of the Hochstein, the mountain where Eberburg was located, and this path appeared to be going in the right direction. They had not been climbing it for long, however, when they came to some stone steps. What looked to be mammoth bones were scattered on either side of them. Mammoths had long been extinct in the parts of the empire to the south, but they still lived here in Iscandia.

Andrion reached out and grabbed Bernadette by the shoulder, pulling her back firmly and hissing in her ear: "This is a giant encampment!"

"Giants?" she whispered back at him. "I thought those were mythical or extinct or something."

"Uh huh, just like dragons, right? Let's get out of here," he said firmly, brooking no argument. They sneaked off to the left, where some large rocks formed a wall of sorts on the north side of the area. From this safe distance, Andrion gestured for Bernadette to look, and see what was standing within the rock bowl to the south of them.

By the gods, they were real! They looked like men, somewhat. But coarsely constructed, rawboned and misshapen men standing what appeared to be 12-15 feet tall. They were minimally dressed in rough-tanned animal skins, the pair of them (both male, from a lack of any breasts) standing idly staring into a huge bonfire. Each of them held a primitive club made by tying a large rock to a tree branch that was at least 4 feet in length. They seemed to be less aggressive than most of the creatures she'd met so far in Iscandia, but Bernadette definitely did not want to tangle with them.

"Thank you! I'm an idiot," she whispered to him before turning and picking her way back down the slope to the road. When they arrived there he enfolded her in an embrace and kissed the top of her head, speaking in normal tones now that they were out of earshot of the giants. "Don't say that," he said. "How long have you been in Iscandia?"

She stepped out of his arms and looked into his eyes. "A little over a week," she confessed. "And you?" He suddenly felt a thousand years old. It had been nearly a decade since he had first come here, at a time when this fantastically desirable young woman (with whom, he feared, he was already hopelessly in love) had likely been a barely adolescent child. What did he think he was doing?

"A bit longer than that," Andrion replied suavely. "Let me be your guide."

They stepped apart, beaming at each other. "Berni," he went on, "I think you should know that there's a very good chance we are going to have to fight some bandits in the near future."

"I figured as much," she said with a quirking half smile, unshipping her bow. "Let's be about it, then."

As they crept closer, though, there were no bandits in sight. Bernadette was just starting to hope that they might be able to sneak past unnoticed when a young Afran woman clad in fur armor suddenly emerged from the brush near the tower's side. She was on the alert, and seemed to have realized intruders were approaching. Bernadette didn't think they'd really been seen, though, and she fired her bow hoping to take the woman out with a sneak attack. No luck. Then Andrion let fly with his favorite ranged attack, dual blasts of lightning, and the woman was blown off her feet to lie crumpled near the door of the tower facing them.

As Bernadette was checking the bandit sentry's corpse she was nearly skewered by an arrow fired from the top of the tower. Looking up, she spotted a bandit bowman up there – moments before he went flying through the air, knocked off the tower top by Andrion's battle magic. Wow!

Now the companions crept closer, and quietly opened the wooden door leading into the tower. Without consultation, the two had decided to finish the job and clear out this bandit nest before continuing their journey. There was the rattle of feet coming down a wooden staircase to their right, and she picked one bandit off with her bow while Andrion set a second on fire.

Leaping over the bodies of their fallen comrades, two more bandits came down the stairs and the two intruders found themselves in hand-to-hand combat. Bernadette used that same dragon spell she'd used on the dragon (was it only yesterday?), knocking their opponents off their feet. Then she ran forward and drove her sword into the throat of the one with the axe, while Andrion bashed in the other's face with a steel mace. Neither got back to his feet.

The two stood panting, eyes wide and hearts beating fast, as they listened for the sounds of any more bandits. Unless one was hiding, they were now alone in the tower. As the adrenaline subsided, they began methodically searching the corpses. Then they worked together, hauling the bodies away one at a time and heaving them into the river before searching the tower.

The ancient edifice stood some four stories tall, and the top of it was ragged where stones had fallen away over the centuries. But it offered some reasonably snug living spaces. And right here on the main road between Waterdon and Coldstein, it was no wonder it had been taken over by bandits. They could just sit back and wait for victims to come their way – and if the pickings got lean, they had a river full of fish a few paces away.

By the time the two had finished disposing of the bodies and raiding the place for valuables, the sun was not far off the horizon. Standing atop the tower admiring the view, Bernadette asked Andrion, "how about if we stay here for tonight? It looks like there's plenty of food and drink, and a pretty nice bed."

He gave her a significant look along with that slight smile of his, and said, "Seems like a good idea to me." They retraced their steps down two levels, and sat at a table to enjoy a meal of bread, cheese, smoked ham, and roasted nut confections from the deceased bandits' stores.

After eating they sat talking for a while, just enjoying each other's company. Soon it was full dark, and they got up from the table and headed over to the dead bandit chief's bedroom area. Aside from the large bed, there were a couple of nightstands and a chest of drawers, with a chamberpot under the bed.

They helped each other strip off their armor. Then, standing there in their underclothes, they embraced and kissed. What Bernadette had thought a slight gesture of affection Andrion took a great deal more seriously, and his tongue went into her mouth as his hands pressed gently but firmly against her shoulders, easing her backwards until she had her back pressed against the stone wall of the tower.

The stones were still warm, holding the heat of the departed day. Andrion bent to his work, kissing her fervently, pressing himself up against her so that she could feel his stiffening member through their underclothes. Soon Bernadette was panting with excitement. "I have an idea," she murmured breathlessly, and unfastened his knee-length linen bottoms so that they slid down over his rump. She squeezed and kneaded his firm buttocks, pressing his now-freed cock up against her body as she did so.

Next Bernadette unbuttoned his shirt so that his bare chest was exposed, and pulled her own underdrawers down to about knee height. He growled and moved in, pushing up her undershirt to expose her breasts. While continuing his deep kisses, he massaged her right breast and gently squeezed the nipple between thumb and forefinger, eliciting a gasp; while with his right hand he directed his throbbing cock into the barely-accessible opening of her cunt.

Bernadette's legs unable to part farther because of the constricting undergarments, the fit was snug. Andrion was not able to push all the way in because of the angle, but it was very tight and slippery in there and the proximity of his cock to her clit sent powerful sensations of delight pulsating through her. "Aaah, ah!"

she cried, her head to one side of his as he applied his lips and tongue to her neck. He rumbled in reply.

This was glorious agony! But they both wanted more, wanted that big cock to thrust deeper, all the way inside her. By mutual consent they moved away from the wall to the bed, where she knelt and presented her rounded but well-muscled rear to him, the underpants still bunched up around her knees. He kicked his own off onto the floor, so that he could assume a wider stance and put himself at the right height to plunge, at last, to his full length within her spasming cunt.

Andrion usually had better control, the more so after a tiring day of hiking and fighting bandits; but this enchanting vixen had gotten under his skin and he was seized with an excitement that could not be held back. Thrusting, thrusting, feeling as if he were caught in an ocean tide of passion, he emptied himself within her as she screamed out her own ecstatic climax.

They collapsed to the bed for a while. Then, some decorum restored, they removed the rest of their clothing. After they had washed up a bit, they lay down in bed together with Bernadette tucked in the crook of Andrion's arm. A tremendous sensation of peace had washed over them, and as they were not really all that sleepy yet they talked quietly, filling each other in on their early lives.

Andrion had been raised in a part of Auverne on the far side of that land from her little farming village, near a city that had afforded him the opportunity to serve as a mage's apprentice. Like her, he had felt dissatisfied with the slow pace of life there and had traveled to Iscandia on reaching adulthood – the better part of a decade before she had.

Bernadette told him of her dreams and ambitions, and together they mused about the possibilities that might arise after she went to talk to the Old Ones. Was it fame and fortune in her future, or just hardship and death by dragon? To herself, she wondered how much of her future was *their* future. At the moment she felt as if she were completely in love with Andrion. But they had known each other such a short time, and experience told her there were many things that could yet come between them. Not the least of which was her tendency toward hopping into bed with just about every hot guy she met. Time would tell.

Eventually they made love again, slowly and quietly. It went on for a long, blissful time before they finally slept.

Chapter 10: Perils along the Way

The morning dawned cloudy, with light rain falling.
Bernadette and Andrion arose feeling well rested, both of them
anxious to resume their journey. They breakfasted on leftovers
from the bandits' stores, then continued east along the road they
had been following yesterday.

Trying to find a path that would take them in the direction of
Bohrsstead, Bernadette kept checking her map. Other than
Bohrsstead and a few other points of interest, it currently had very
little to tell her about the part of Iscandia lying east of the
Hochstein. Whenever they came to a fork in the road, she led them
to the right – hoping they would eventually be heading south and
to the eastern slopes of the mountain.

Before they had been hiking for long the trail became a stone-
paved road, with steps leading up gradually, passing through a
series of stone archways. "This looks official," Bernadette
remarked to Andrion. "Have you ever been this way before?"

"I don't think so," he replied, his straight brows knitting
slightly. They drew up shortly in front of an ominous-looking
stone structure, a barrow of some sort – Bernadette guessed from
its architecture.

Just on a chance, Bernadette checked her magic map. Sure
enough, there was now a marker in this spot that resembled the
building's general shape – and some lettering, as well:
"Hjalmond's Tomb." As usual in the morning Bernadette was
feeling strong and confident and ready for some adventure, so she
said "We may as well see what's in there." She and Andrion
pushed on the double doors, and they opened.

In a stone anteroom just inside, they found a young blond
Norseman – more like a boy really, tall and gangly. He was
dressed in ill-fitting antique steel armor and carrying a notched
iron greatsword. As Bernadette and Andrion came inside, he
whirled to face them – brandishing the weapon. He had the
strength to wield it, at least.

"Whoa, it's all right!" Bernadette said, holding up empty hands. "We were just curious to see what this place is." He relaxed and let the sword's tip fall, resting on the stone floor.

"Oh," he said. Then he appeared to have a thought. "I don't suppose you could give me a little help?"

"Help?" Bernadette asked. The young man blushed and looked a little shamefaced.

"I was just trying to work up the courage to go inside," he admitted.

"Afraid of aptrgangr?" she asked sympathetically. Those things had scared the crap out of her, the first time she'd encountered them.

"Not exactly," he replied. "Let me explain. My name is Grindor, and this is my family's tomb. My grandpa sent me to retrieve *his* grandpa's sword. He wants me to have it, and coming here to get it is supposed to prove I'm a man and ready to wield it. But there are a lot of dead walking, too many of them. I think something's wrong here, and I don't know if I can face it alone."

Knowing Andrion well enough by now that she didn't bother to consult with him, Bernadette offered "We'd be glad to help." The kid's face brightened considerably.

"You will? That's great. Let's go!" He led the way to the doors connecting the anteroom to the rest of the barrow, and the three of them were soon within the tomb complex.

Not very far along they came to a middle-sized room with two large, shut wooden doors in the far side, as well as a couple of motionless aptrgangr lying on the floor. "Grandpa said our family didn't have nothing to do with the dragon cult," Grindor averred, gesturing at the corpses. "So why are my ancestors walking around instead of resting in their tombs?"

"This was as far as you got?" Bernadette asked, and the youth nodded. "Those attacked me as soon as I came in, and after I got them down I ran out like a rabbit with a fox after it," Grindor admitted shamefacedly. "I had just talked myself into going back inside about five minutes before you showed up, uh…"

"Bernadette," she said. "And this is my friend Andrion." Hand squeezes were exchanged, then the young man led on.

He tried the leftmost door, but it was firmly shut. "This one's barred," he said. "But Grandpa said there was another way around." As he spoke, Bernadette was trying the other door – which indeed led to a long and winding stone corridor heading deeper into the barrow.

Bernadette's bow at the ready, all of them moving stealthily, the trio wended their way down into the catacombs. Most of these corpses had been long at rest, many of them nothing but dry bones; but from time to time they would come to a room with one or more aptrgangr prowling. Bernadette was glad to have two strong young men backing her up, as she couldn't really fight more than a couple of them at a time by herself.

After many minutes of this, they passed through a hole in the back of an empty standing sarcophagus, and down a narrow passageway. They met another aptrgangr, this one tougher than most, hiding in a recess a few feet further on. Then they came to a set of massive double doors, which Grindor said led to the main burial chamber where his ancestor's sword was supposed to be standing in a place of honor.

They opened the doors and crept inside. The place was cavernous, with a broad flight of steps leading up and an even wider staircase off to the left, at the top of which Bernadette could dimly see a black-robed figure that did not appear to be one of the undead. The three huddled together, conferring in whispers.

"That is probably why your ancestors have been going walkabout," Andrion opined. "He's probably a necromancer."

"A necromancer!" Grindor gasped. Of the many magical arts, the raising and enslavement of the dead for one's own purposes was considered most abhorrent throughout Agena. It was outlawed in several provinces, but not here in wild and wooly Iscandia.

The mage on the far side of the room had not yet become aware of their presence, and Bernadette had half a hope that a sneak arrow shot would put an end to him. No such luck! As soon as he was hit, the black-robed figure spoke a command and two aptrgangr burst from stone sarcophagi flanking the main staircase. In twos and threes, still more aptrgangr began emerging from their sleep in coffins all around the room, attacking the three intruders. At first the loathsome creatures were distracted by Andrion and Grindor, and Bernadette – still unnoticed – was able to drop several of them with her bow.

As her two companions' energies flagged, however, the undead warriors ignored them and turned their attention to her. Bernadette slung the bow behind her and went to work with sword and shield, trying to block their attacks while striking out at them. She just didn't have enough stamina for a prolonged fight, though. As her right arm tired, and her attacks weakened, four of them were closing in on her. Oh, hells! was her last thought. Then her world went black.

Andrion and Grindor, momentarily out of the battle, soon recouped enough energy to resume fighting. With spell and blade they attacked the remaining aptrgangr and their wounded, black-robed master; and after a minute or two of ferocious effort the last of their enemies had fallen. Andrion stood, eyes wide and chest heaving, as the aftermath of the adrenaline surge hit him. I'm alive, he thought, halfway in surprise. Then he looked around, and spied a small, steel-armored figure sprawled in a heap on the floor a few yards away.

His heart froze in his chest. "Berni!" he shouted, rushing to her and kneeling beside her on the hard, cold stone floor. "Berni," he repeated prayerfully. She's all right. She *has* to be all right… He placed his fingers alongside her neck and felt for a pulse. Praise the gods, there was one! Weak and thready, but her heart was definitely still beating. He scooped her up off the floor in one swift motion and cradled her in his arms, pressing his lips to her forehead with tears stinging his eyes, as he carried her out of the burial chamber and through some doors at the back to a smaller chamber with a large table in it.

Supporting Berni's weight on the table, Andrion removed her pack and rummaged around in it. There *must* be some healing potions in here – there! He grabbed a handful. They were only the smallest size vials, each affording a slight boost to health. Holding her upright with his left arm, he held a potion vial to her lips, urging her to drink. She nearly choked on it at first, still unconscious; but as some of the potion made its way down her throat her eyelids fluttered and then opened. There was a swelling lump on the back of her skull, a bloody gash on her cheek, and her left arm was bent in an unnatural position.

"Keep drinking, love," he urged her. As each potion was drained Berni became more alert and drank them with more alacrity. As she finished the fifth potion, her arm straightened, the gash on her face had closed leaving scarcely a scar, the swelling on her head had gone back down, and she was now sitting upright without his help. She still seemed awfully dazed, though. "Andrion... thank you," she murmured.

His warm eyes radiated the intensity of his relief, and he broke into a big grin. "You're all right! I was afraid..." he didn't finish the thought. It was a thought he hoped never to have again. He swept her into his arms and covered her face with kisses, which Bernadette found sweet but a bit overwhelming.

"I'm fine, love, I'm fine." She didn't know what else to say.

As the emotional moment passed, and she was feeling a lot better than she had moments before, Bernadette hitched her butt off the table and stood on the floor. Then she gathered her pack and weapons, and she and Andrion took their leave of Grindor. "I'm glad you're all right," he told her with a grin. "Here, I want you to have this." He handed her a fistful of guilders.

"Were you able to find your ancestor's sword?" she asked, curious. The lad proudly held it out for her inspection. It was a blade worthy of his quest, she thought – a slender sword with an ornate hilt crafted out of the lightweight but strong, gleaming black metal called sablium. They wished him well, and made their way out a back door that returned them to the tomb's inner chamber from where they'd started.

Andrion had received a battering in the ferocious aptrgangr fight too – and once Bernadette had recovered her presence of mind she had him drink a couple of health potions, too. She wished they had some more powerful ones; but such items were expensive and not often to be found just lying around. The two of them were still resting near the entrance to the tomb, and Bernadette mused "I kind of wish now that we hadn't left without Lifa. It seems like we could use a little more help on this trip."

Andrion nodded. Then a look of wild surmise crossed his face. "I'll bet you'd like a bath, too," he said. Bernadette laughed wryly.

"Of *course* I'd like a bath, and a hot meal and a soft bed, and…" She looked at him wide-eyed, then slapped her forehead. Her hand came away with flakes of dried blood on it. "The *map*! Now this place and the Maiden are both on the map, we can go back to the Maiden to pick up supplies. And Lifa too, probably, if she ever showed up. Then come right back here and continue our journey. Why didn't I *think* of that before?!"

Chapter 11: Reboot

Bernadette bounced into Andrion's arms and threw her legs around his waist, giving him a squeeze. Clearly, she was feeling better by the minute. "You, my love, are a genius!" She planted a big kiss on his lips, then hopped back down and pulled the map out of its hiding place.

A few moments later, they found themselves standing outside the Bathing Maiden in what appeared to be the later part of the afternoon, local time, on a warm and mostly sunny day. To Bernadette's mind, no sight had ever looked sweeter. Not counting, perhaps, the sight of Andrion's face when she had come to a few minutes previously.

They went inside and greeted Lev, who was tending bar. And there in a chair a few paces away was Lifa – wearing her steel armor and looking as if she'd probably been sitting there like a stone for hours, waiting for Bernadette's return. Bernadette considered taking the body servant to task for her failure to be here when expected, but she thought better of it. Instead, she just said, "Good, you're here. Come on." Lifa stood to attention and fell into step behind her at once.

Bernadette was not just here for extra help, though. She had a lot of business on her mind. First thing though, that bath. She and Andrion stripped off and set Lifa to cleaning their armor and rustling up some clean underclothes for them while they soaked away the blood, dust and perspiration of the day's battles.

Her near-brush with death and subsequent recovery had Bernadette feeling pretty high and more than a little randy; but on the other hand she'd been getting laid a lot more regularly of late and there *was* a lot of work to do. So after the bath, she and Andrion returned upstairs and put their clothes back on.

There was a chemia station and an enchanting table side by side within a few feet of the double bed where the two of them had slept the previous night. She recognized both apparati for what they were, having seen similar tables at the house of Selene, the village Wise Woman in Pied de Puce.

Potions, with effects ranging from healing to fortification of one's abilities in a specific discipline, were half magic and half chemistry. Magic was everywhere in Bernadette's world, and the reputed alfar heritage shared by natives of Auverne was said to increase their aptitude for using it. Anyone could learn to use magic, but only those with inborn affinity for it could become truly powerful at it.

Yet there'd been little opportunity for the village girl Bernadette to learn any magic. She had spent many hours in Selene's company, seeing the old woman as a sort of grandmother figure – and from that she had picked up what little she knew. The chemia station and enchanting table were enchanted items in their own right – imbued with the power to transform certain ingredients into valuable potions, and use the magical essence captured from living beings at the moment of death to apply magical effects to ordinary items like jewelry, clothing, armor, and weapons.

Some of those effects could be amazingly powerful, though Selene had told her that the more practice one had at using the apparati the more powerful would be the results. Bernadette didn't know how that worked, since seemingly the real magic was supplied by the tables themselves. Perhaps one's own magical energy, the well of spiritual force that enabled one to cast spells one knew, somehow contributed to the results?

Bernadette now set about trying to teach herself how to make potions. She had acquired some enchanted bracers as loot in one of her recent excursions, and she found that wearing these while doing chemia helped to increase the strength of her potions. If her theory was correct, the bracers must have been enchanted to enhance her abilities.

In the course of her adventures so far Bernadette had picked up quite a few items that she knew were chemial ingredients, and she even knew what uses some of them had. She found that if she ate a little of an unfamiliar ingredient, she could sense its properties and guess what potion it might be used to create; though the physical effects of ingesting some of those ingredients could be unsettling. By trial and error, then, she managed to craft half a dozen potions (using the vials that were supplied with the chemia station). Some of them might even be useful.

Next, to try her hand at enchanting. It seemed like a skill that would be worth acquiring. Imagine being able to make your own super-powerful enchanted weapons and armor! Before she could start enchanting things, though, she needed to learn some enchantments. If you placed an enchanted item on the table, and the enchantment on it was one you didn't yet know, you could absorb the understanding of that enchantment into your being as the table converted the item into its component molecules – leaving behind only dust.

It was like learning a spell, and this knowledge would never be lost. Thereafter, one would be able to apply this enchantment, this magic spell, to any item capable of being enchanted – while using an enchanting table and a vial of magical essence. The larger the vial, the more essence used in applying the enchantment, the more powerful it would be.

Though, Selene had also told her, until she had practiced the art for some time the strength of her enchantments would be as nothing compared with the strength of those same enchantments on the items she had destroyed in the learning process. So she was loath to part with anything particularly useful.

Bernadette did have a few things that she was willing to let go of, though. She'd collected an enchanted mage's robe that caused one's essential supply of magical energy (which would be drained by casting spells but quickly rebound on its own) to regenerate 75% faster, and she burned it to learn the "Magic Recovery" enchantment. She picked up another 4 or 5 additional enchantments, including a useful one for weaponry: the Flaming Blow enchantment.

That was step one. But she didn't have any vials of the magical essence needed to make enchantments work. Besides, if she was going to enchant anything, it would probably be a good idea to improve it at the smithy first. From what she'd been told, bearing an enchantment tended to make items resistant to further handling. Only the most skilled smiths could work with them

71

without damaging them, and once an item had been enchanted one could not lay additional enchantments on it.

"I guess we'll have to go to Waterdon, so I can use the smithy there," Bernadette told her faithful crew of two. She had passed a place called Valkyrie on her way here from town yesterday. It was right down by the city gates, and the smith was a woman perhaps seven years older than she was. She'd been busy at her forge, and the traveler hadn't stopped to talk. But she looked forward to meeting her.

"Oh, there's a smithy in the basement here," said Andrion off-handedly. "You don't know about it?"

"I didn't even know there was a basement," she replied. Was there no end to the wonders of this place? He led his two female companions down the stairs, then behind the bar to a trap door in the floor.

They crawled through the opening and down a short ladder to find themselves in a large, stone-lined room running the length of the building. There was a little bedroom area at the near end, with a double bed, nightstand, and bedside cabinet. The rest of the room was given over to crafting, with a smelter in the far corner, grindstone, crafting table, forge, and even another enchanting table. Still more amazing, the entire near wall was lined with shelves stacked high with every sort of ingot, ores, even the vials of magical essence needed to enchant objects!

"But... who does this all belong to?" Bernadette asked Andrion.

"It's, um, sort of a perk for guests," he replied lamely. She had the feeling that he was not telling her everything, but why look a gift horse in the mouth? She was not a person who did well at intrigue and plotting, or questioned the motives of everyone around her. She trusted Andrion with her life, and if he had some reason for not revealing the full story behind this hidden treasure cache, why should she worry? Just take the ingots and run.

Bernadette helped herself to every steel ingot on the shelf and a few of other types as well, though creating arms and armor using materials like sablium and dypalfar metal were still far beyond her skills. Then she told Andrion and Lifa to strip. Both of them were soon standing there in their underclothes. Andrion's powerfully muscled body was a familiar sight to her by now, but Lifa without her armor was quite a surprise. By the gods, she was built like a prentice boy's wet dream! From a narrow waist, her hips and buttocks exploded to spherical perfection, while her globular breasts, through the thin linen fabric, looked to be damn near as big as her head. She made Bernadette look like a 12-year-old by comparison. Only her stern expression spoiled the effect.

Bernadette cast a covert glance at Andrion to see if he had noticed the body servant's extremely voluptuous build. She was secretly pleased that his gaze passed over the other woman as if she were no more interesting than the furniture, then returned to look at her expectantly. He'd like his armor back, no doubt, since they were *not* just now about to hop into bed.

Bernadette set to work with a will at the forge, using the metal from her (borrowed? pilfered? gifted?) ingots to bolster the strength and protection value of the breastplates, bracers, boots, and helmets each of them wore. At the grindstone, she honed swords, maces, and daggers. She strengthened bows and gave them more killing power.

Next she took a few of the items to the enchanting table, using up some of the essence vials she'd liberated from the shelves. Such things were costly and hard to come by, and Bernadette couldn't believe her luck at stumbling onto this treasure trove. She improved and reinforced the bows she and Andrion were using, then enchanted them to set the target on fire for a while after the arrow hit. This enchantment was not only devastating to the enemy, but made it easy to see in dim light that the arrow had found its target. Plus, she enchanted a steel helmet with Magic Recovery for Andrion, so that he would be even more effective using his battle spells.

They all put on their newly improved gear, ready to face the next challenge. Or were they? Bernadette decided she must really lighten her load, and remarked "I suppose I'll have to go to Waterdon to sell off my surplus?"

She wasn't enormously surprised when Andrion answered the question: "No, Lev upstairs is a merchant. He'll likely take anything you want to sell." She was not sure what was going on with this place, but she liked it more all the time.

They went back up the ladder, and Bernadette swapped her burden of excess weapons and armor for enough coin to put her over the 6,000 mark. She could now afford to buy a house in Waterdon, from what she'd been told at Wyrmshalla. But did she need to? Perhaps she could just make this place her home base – it seemed to have everything except, perhaps, privacy.

"Why don't we get a fresh start in the morning?" Andrion suggested. Bernadette could hardly believe that it had only been yesterday morning when they had left here, full of energy and enthusiasm for the adventures ahead. Now here she was again, after having nearly been killed, taught herself the rudiments of chemia and enchanting, improved her skills in smithing, and picked up another companion to help her in her battles. That seemed like a lot of progress only to find herself back in the same location again.

It's hard to get used to that map, Bernadette mused. Distances that would take days of arduous travel could be traversed in a few heartbeats, after one had visited them on foot just once. She envisioned a future when the entirety of Iscandia would become her oyster, and she could command any part of the province with a thought. Then she blinked. Enough megalomania for one day, she told herself. "Yes dear," she replied to her lover. "That *would* be a good idea." It appeared they could have saved the trouble of putting on all that armor, after all.

The three headed to the bar and Lev served them a hearty supper of beef stew and fresh bread, washed down with some decent wine. Then they all went upstairs and Bernadette instructed Lifa to bed down in one of the single beds in another area of the loft, away from the master bedroom area where she and Andrion planned to sleep.

They helped each other remove their armor. Without a companion, one practically had to go around armor-clad at all times, so difficult was it to reach all of the straps and buckles. They were both feeling pretty tired, if now in perfect health and clean from the bath they'd taken earlier. As they stood there in their underclothes Andrion gathered Bernadette close and tucked her head beneath his chin, just holding her. He had known her barely 48 hours, and already the thought of losing her was more than he could bear. Her arms wrapped around his waist, Bernadette murmured into his strong chest "I expect having Lifa along is going to cramp our style when we're on the road, dear…" He took a slow breath, then she felt his diaphragm spasm as he suppressed a laugh.

Andrion stepped away from her a bit, to look into her eyes. "No doubt you're right," he said, lips quirking in a not-quite smile. Then, more seriously, "But I think we're both going to appreciate having her sword along."

Bernadette reached up and kissed him tenderly, in silent assent. Then she said, "Let's get to bed." She set about taking off her underwear.

"You always sleep in the nude?" he asked, watching appreciatively.

"Whenever I can," she replied. "Unless it's too cold or I'm likely to be attacked in the night. You wouldn't attack me, would you?" she twinkled, taking a breath that caused her full breasts to bounce appealingly.

He growled low in his throat, his eyes lighting at the sight of her. "It's hard to say," he replied. Then he removed his own underclothes. Bernadette was both unsurprised and delighted to see that his member was well on its way to monolithic status. This might be their last chance for uninhibited intimacy for quite some time to come. They both lay down in the bed and pulled the covers over themselves, feeling a bit of a chill to the air in the room. Then as if choreographed they turned to the lamps on either side and wound down the wicks until they sputtered and died, plunging the room into near pitch darkness. Immediately thereafter, they sought each other beneath the sheets.

They pressed their bodies together in the darkness, sharing warmth. Andrion's now fully-risen cock was pinned between them, a pulsing hot presence against Bernadette's belly. An answering warmth spread between her legs. They locked mouths, falling into each other as if into a dream. Then they began stroking one another slowly, pressed together, almost as if they were seeking to merge into one being. They were lying on their sides, she to his right, and she lifted her right leg up over his hip so that her moist sex was pressed against his shaft, enflaming her clit.

The kissing and stroking continued for a while longer, building heat until neither of them could stand it anymore and he shifted his body down slightly so that his long, hard shaft could find its way into her eager cunt. "Mmmmm!" came her involuntary cry as his cock slipped within her. Oh, yesssss. They made love for what seemed like an endless moment, savoring every sensation as they slid together in a sort of half-dreaming, prolonged ecstasy. Then the sensations became more urgent, until finally they crested a peak and plunged together into shuddering climax.

Shortly thereafter they lay in perfect warmth and harmony, encapsulated in each other, and gradually abandoned consciousness for sleep.

Chapter 12: The Journey Resumes

Before dawn's light had begun to color the Maiden's downstairs windows, Bernadette was awake. She had always been an early riser, and the excitement of her new, adventurous lifestyle had her even more eager to leap up and seize the day. She rolled over for a look at her bedmate.

Andrion was lying on his back, snoring faintly, his beautiful features in repose. He was beginning to get a bit of stubble, having not had time to shave recently. Slugabed, she thought fondly. She rolled toward him, nestled her head on his chest and licked his right nipple, wrapping the tip of her tongue around it. That got his attention.

"You..." he murmured, eyes still closed, and reached for her. Bernadette wriggled out of his grasp, however.

"Rise and shine, love! Old Ones to meet! Monsters to slay!" He opened an eye and looked at her questioningly. Then, sighing, he opened both eyes and sat up. By then she was standing on the floor at the side of the bed.

"I don't suppose you'd care to come back here and give me a blow job, first?" he asked wistfully.

"Later, dear, I promise. But we need to get moving." She was already slipping into her underclothes, and soon they were helping each other on with their armor.

Andrion produced a razor from his pack and set about giving his chiseled jaw and finely shaped chin a shave, while Bernadette was adding some supplies to their packs and getting Lifa out of bed. Actually, it turned out that Lifa was already up and had somehow managed to get into her armor without help. Unless maybe she'd slept in it. Lifa was punctilious, Bernadette would give her that; even if she was not exactly the life of the party.

By the time the landscape outside the Maiden was glowing with rosy light, the three of them were standing outside in the road that led north and then east to Coldstein. Bernadette pulled her precious map from its resting place and wished them all back to Hjalmond's Tomb. She noted as their new surroundings appeared (after a few seconds of darkness and disorientation) that it had returned them to a spot right outside the front doors they had originally come in by, rather than the area around the side of the building they had departed from.

"Onward, troops!" Bernadette cried jubilantly, her night's respite from the rigors of questing having restored her in mind, body, and spirit. "Old Ones, here we come!" Andrion glanced at Lifa to see if she might be reacting to their "general's" overblown enthusiasm, but the woman remained absolutely impassive. Interacting with her was like interacting with a dypalfar automaton. Well, he thought, smiling slightly to himself as his affection for Berni overrode his annoyance, adventure ho.

Bernadette led them around to the east side of the building, and they soon found a pathway down to a stone-paved road that led in approximately the right direction. After they'd traveled this around to the east side of the Hochstein, the encountered a path leading off to the right, exactly as she'd hoped. She felt sure that miles could be cut off their journey to Bohrsstead, and thence to Eberburg, if she could just find the right trail.

The trail she'd chosen soon began to climb sharply, and conversation was kept to a minimum between Bernadette and Andrion (conversation with Lifa was, as near as Bernadette could tell, *always* at a minimum) as they huffed and puffed their way up the steep mountainside in their heavy armor and packs. There seemed to be many wild goats here, and Bernadette was tempted to shoot a few of them for their hides and meat. But she was also anxious to reach Bohrsstead before night fell.

Goats were not the only creatures in the wild region. Twice, they were attacked from ambush by predators that seemed to prefer human over goat. Not the wisest choice on the part of the predators, as goats are notably lacking in swords, bows, battle spells, and steel armor. Her burden increased by a couple of fresh smilodon hides and a wolf pelt or two, Bernadette soldiered on.

The trail now ran beside a pleasant and sparkling mountain stream, clattering over stones on its way to some unknown destination. Then the trio rounded one last bend and abruptly found themselves on the outskirts of the village of Bohrsstead. "We're here!" Bernadette informed her companions, relief in her voice. "Here" reminded her all too vividly of her home village of Pied-de-Puce, truth to tell. The environs of Bohrsstead, nestled at the foot of the Hochstein, were much more scenic. But the size of the town and the resources therein were similar.

They walked up the main (only) street of town heading for the inn. As neither Andrion nor Lifa had ever been up the mountain before, Bernadette hoped to ask for directions as well as any local information the innkeeper might be willing to impart. Most such acted as wellsprings of local lore, gossip, and the odd broadside offering rewards for the apprehension of bandits or other public menaces.

Bernadette quickly spotted the inn, which bore the appellation of "The Pilgrims' Rest." That seemed a hopeful sign, and she and her companions made their way inside. The place looked almost identical to nearly every other inn she had seen so far in Iscandia.

Bernadette approached the bar and met the Norse innkeeper, one Holmund by name. Bald and 50ish, he was happy to tell her all he knew about Eberburg and the Old Ones, and directed her to a bridge – a little further up the road through town – that would lead her to the path they would need to take to reach Eberburg.

The day was still young by the time they approached the stone bridge crossing the stream, which was the starting point for the trail that led, over thousands of steps carved into the mountain's bones, up the Hochstein to the Old Ones' place of refuge near the peak.

The three crossed the bridge and headed up the first of what were, apparently, to be many flights of stairs. The weather appeared to be absolutely wonderful, by local standards. The sky was mostly occluded by puffy gray-white clouds, but no snow was falling and visibility was excellent. This was very useful for the three companions, as it enabled them to spot danger a long way off.

Bernadette was beginning to wonder if, other than butterflies, goats, rabbits, foxes, squirrels and such, there were any creatures in Iscandia that would *not* attack you on sight. As they picked their way up the steep mountainside, they were repeatedly assaulted by tundra wolves, smilodons, and *things* that defied categorization. Again, she was very glad of her companions and their fighting abilities.

Along the way shrines were sprinkled here and there, each with a stone tablet bearing a few couplets of a poem that explained how Ehrgeizig (whoever that was) had taught men how to use the language of dragons to escape draconic domination. At a couple of these shrines, Bernadette and her companions met pilgrims. She had trouble understanding why some should see this whole experience as a spiritual journey. To her, with her no-nonsense attitude, it appeared that they were combining a stiff hike with Story Hour, punctuated with "fight for your life or get eaten."

As they approached what Bernadette felt must surely be at least the 6,000th step, her danger sensors went on full alert. Ahead of them, she spied a shallow cave. And peering into the dimness, she thought she glimpsed a larger-than-man-sized shadow. "I think there's trouble ahead," she warned Andrion and Lifa. "I'm taking the high road." More agile than either of her companions, Bernadette scaled the rocks lining the road on the left side of the broad trail.

Bernadette had gotten perhaps ten feet up, hopping from rock to rock, when an enormous, white-furred anthropoid form suddenly emerged from the cave's shadows and threw itself upon her companions. What in all the hells? From its overall shape, she guessed it must be some type of troll. But it was nearly twice the size of the trolls she'd read about, and the wrong color. Same bad attitude, though. Bernadette began peppering it with arrows from her enchanted bow, each of which set the creature on fire for a second or two. Down on ground level, Lifa was attacking with blades while Andrion fired bolts of energy at it.

This triple attack had the creature down and out after only a few seconds of intense fighting. Bernadette hopped down from her rocky perch, grinning in relief, and told her companions "Good work." Then she took a few moments to explore the corpse, retrieving a few of her arrows if nothing else of value. "Was that some kind of troll?" she asked Andrion.

"Snow troll, I think," he replied. "I've never actually seen one before, but the description fits."

"Here's to not seeing any *more* of them," she said; and they moved on.

They were delighted, on rounding a few more bends in the snow-covered trail, to find the edifice of Eberburg looming before them. The place was larger than the eorl's palace in Waterdon, it seemed. How could the monastic order keep themselves supplied with food on this frozen mountaintop, if there were as many Old Ones as the size of the building seemed to suggest?

Then it occurred to her that no doubt she was not the only person in Iscandia with a magic map. She checked hers, and found Eberburg now clearly marked. She could now come and go from here whenever she wanted, and would never have to climb those steps again. Thank the gods! And that Gatti trader…

They approached the grand-looking front doors and rapped, but there was no response. Boldly, Bernadette tried the handle of the one on the left and found it unlocked. They stepped inside. Within, they entered a hall and found half a dozen old men, dressed in hooded robes, converging on them.

One of them stepped forward. "Welcome, pilgrims," he said. Bernadette guessed that normally only pilgrims would be motivated to make this climb, so it was a natural mistake. "I am Aethelred, the signor of our order. My brethren are under a vow of silence, but I will answer any questions you may have. You may guest with us overnight if you wish, for a suitable donation, though women must stay separately from men."

Bernadette could only assume that this gang were also sworn to celibacy. Not that they'd be likely to have any trouble keeping such a vow, up here in the middle of nowhere and given they were a bunch of grizzled old curmudgeons. She kept such thoughts strictly to herself.

She faced the old man. "Thank you, Signor," she said. "But we are not here as pilgrims. I was instructed by Eorl Ormund of

Waterdon to come here, that you might train me in the use of dragon spells. He, and others I've met, have told me that I'm Fireblood."

Aethelred went rigid for a moment, staring down at her. From the wrinkles in his face he was ancient, yet he seemed hale and unbowed by his years. "Give me your hand, child," he commanded. She pulled the leather gauntlet from her right hand and reached out to him. He turned it face up and peered at the palm (which looked no different than it ever had to her, if perhaps a bit more callused than it once had been), then gazed into her eyes.

At last the old man spoke. "You do indeed appear to have the fireblood, but we must be sure. Demonstrate your spell." As she had done at the Western Watchtower,

Bernadette gathered her breath and her will and shouted "Kraf!" This spell had blown two bandits off their feet, but the old men facing her were made of sterner stuff. They were staggered, but remained standing.

"Clearly you have learned the first word of a dragon spell," Aethelred said. "And I assume, from your youth, that no study was involved. It seems likely that you are The Fireblood, prophesied to come at this time."

"I still don't completely understand," Bernadette said. "Can you explain what this Fireblood business is about?"

The old man nodded sagely. "Millennia ago, when first the dragons ruled Iscandia and the northern parts of Darkreach, there arose a line of men – and only men, for this heritage was never among the alfar – with an inborn ability to use the magic of the dragons. Dragons are magical creatures in and of themselves, essentially immortal and resistant to most ordinary spells used by men and elves. But they possessed their own spells, spoken with the voice and powered by the stones they formed within their bodies."

Bernadette stood patiently drinking in his words, and he hurried along. "Men such as we can learn the dragon spells and the voice with which to speak them through long study, and these can be powered by dragon gems held in contact with the body. But one with the Fireblood has the ability to absorb these gems within, to make the power for dragon spells a part of his or her being. And that power is recharged by the Fireblood's own life force, by your mana. When we use dragon spells the power of the gems is soon exhausted, and there have been no new ones made since the dragons died out. You are the only fireblood alive in this time, that we know of. So you are *The* Fireblood. Do you see?"

Bernadette's face was a study, as she searched within herself. The runes that had glowed on that curved wall in Deadfall Barrow had been a spell, and the blue gem that had vanished yet lay within her, enabling her to *use* that spell! "I absorbed another gem after killing a dragon near Waterdon," she told the old man. "But I only know one spell. Do extra gems just give you more power?"

"A good question," Aethelred replied. Though he was presumably an ancient mage of great and arcane power, he seemed to her a bit like a kindly grandfather – or maybe great-great-grandfather. At 22 she'd thought 40-something Gunnar an old man, but these Old Ones were *really* old. "When you learned the first word of the Gale spell you absorbed a blue stone, not unlike a sapphire – am I right?"

"Yes, I did!" Bernadette exclaimed, excited. It seemed she had come to the right place to find out what she needed to know about her newly discovered powers.

"And what color was the gem from the dragon near Waterdon?" the ancient mage asked. "A kind of luminescent orange color," she said. "I've never seen a natural gem that looked anything like it."

"Ah," Aethelred said, considering. "Each spell has its own unique gem, which powers only that one spell. I assume you found the first spell word carved in runes on a rock wall?"

She nodded. "It was deep inside an ancient Norse tomb complex, with a lot of aptrgangr guarding it."

"That particular word appeared to you, probably because of the proximity of the gem," he told her.

Bernadette cocked an eyebrow. "You said '*first* word.' Does that mean that dragon spells can be added onto?" Andrion looked fondly at her. This was truly a woman after his own heart, hungry for knowledge.

Aethelred nodded in turn. "Each spell, in its fullest effect, has four words. They are in the ancient tongue of the dragons, of course, and while you can produce an effect using only the first – or only the first few – the spell grows and achieves its fullest power with all four."

"And the same gem provides the power, whether you use the whole spell or just part of it?" she asked. "Yes, but it will take longer to recharge of course." Fascinating!

Now he directed her to another of his order, Beren. The wizened old man spoke a single word to her, "Luft!" which Aethelred said was the second word to the Gale dragon spell. This single syllable sank into her consciousness like a live thing burrowing for sanctuary; and she now found that when she used the dragon spell it was twice as long – and twice as powerful.

"Excellent," Aethelred said. "Your quick mastery of the dragon spell shows that you are ready for more training. Your next lesson will take place outdoors, in our courtyard," said Aethelred, leading the way out the back of the hall to a large flat area behind the sprawling building. There were a set of pillars off the left, and beyond them some iron gates.

Beren gave her the first word of a new dragon spell: Stasis. "Time will slow around you, so that you seem to move far faster than anyone else," Aethelred explained. "Cast the spell, then run between the pillars. To you, it will seem that you are moving at normal speed. But to us, you will be a blur of motion as only a fraction of the time the run would take will actually have passed."

An odd spell, Bernadette thought. She guessed that from her end of things, everyone else would appear to be motionless. She lined up in front of Aethelred and spoke loudly and firmly. The tone of voice one used when speaking the spells seemed to be a component of their effects. "Wirb!" she cried, then ran forward past the pillars. She turned to look back at the other people in the courtyard, and they did seem to be motionless for a heartbeat – her vision muted, as if the very passage of light had been halted. Then suddenly the world brightened again and everything was normal.

The Old Ones looked unsurprised, no doubt having seen the effects of this spell many times before. But Andrion was amazed. "Wow!" he exclaimed. "It's as if you just vanished here, and reappeared over there!" Aethelred seemed pleased, though he didn't appear to be one for smiling much.

"With this particular spell, the effect is the same however many words are used," he said. "Each word of the spell will extend the duration of the effect for an additional period of time – from a few seconds to a full minute."

Hmmm, that could be useful, Bernadette thought. Especially while trying to get through a dungeon trap with razor-sharp pendulums swinging back and forth, as she and Staeven had recently experienced. Now Aethelred instructed her, "This stage of your training is complete. Only one thing remains before you are fully accepted as The Fireblood. You must retrieve the Staff of Zauber."

"Was this Zauber person a fireblood like me?" Bernadette asked. She wanted to pry every scrap of information she could out of these Old Ones, as long as they were willing to give it to her.

"No," Aethelred said ponderously. "He was the first of our order, the first our founder Ehrgeizig taught to use dragon spells the hard way. Eons ago he was killed by the remaining dragon worshipers, and his staff taken. It is believed that only a fireblood can find and recover it."

Bernadette accepted his commands without quibble. She had had her doubts about this strange group of secluded and mysterious old men; but clearly, they had knowledge she needed and offered power she wanted. The Old Ones wandered off at that point, having delivered their instructions, and she and her party returned inside through the monastery's back door.

Bernadette pulled out her map and spread it out on a tabletop. This business of having inborn psychic powers was a new idea to her, but she was willing to give it a try. What was the worst that could happen? Closing her eyes, she said, "Staff of Zauber, show me where you lie." Believing this mumbo-jumbo would actually work was something she was having a little trouble with; but her faith took a giant leap forward when she opened her eyes again and saw a big black arrow almost pulsating on the surface of the map, way up beyond a city called Normarsh.

Holy crap, it worked! Andrion and Lifa were flanking her, watching in fascination as she seemingly did the impossible. She turned to them and said, "It looks as though we're going to be heading far to the west and north. I'll take us to the guard outpost where the dragon attacked. But we'll have a long walk ahead of us."

Neither Andrion nor Lifa had any objections, though in the latter case none were looked for. Lifa's mission in life, evidently, was to fulfill her duties to her Warden, and that was the end of it. Andrion was along for the ride, for the adventure of it, and perhaps for love of the young woman who, in a very short space of time, had moved in like a hurricane and swept away his heart.

Chapter 13: Heading North

Bernadette, Andrion, and Lifa materialized outside the guard outpost. It stood not all that far from where a road went north, according to the map, and would cut their travel time compared with going to Plainview. The dragon was long gone and the fires were out, but with the stones of the tower scattered around it looked more like a long-abandoned ruin than a place that had been an active outpost of the Waterdon City Guard a few days earlier.

The three were nearly exhausted, after their travels and battles of the day. Furthermore, dusk was settling over the rolling plain west of Waterdon. Bernadette wondered idly if they ought to go back and spend the night at the Maiden, but she resisted the temptation. Get used to a warm, comfortable bed with a warm, comfortable man in it every night, and three square meals a day, and she'd soon be useless. Instead, they tossed bedrolls down on the stone floor of the abandoned watchtower, which at least offered them a little protection from the night and its creatures, and supped on bread and cheese before lying down to sleep.

Morning came all too soon, and as usual Bernadette was the first to arise. After spending the night sleeping on stones with only a thin fur bedroll beneath her, she felt positively eager to get back on her feet and moving. The three had been traveling only a short while, heading west, when another large stone structure appeared before them. "Fort Altiplan," the map announced. But it showed no signs of being manned by any military force. What were the Remans thinking? It seemed as if bandits occupied twice as many strongholds in Iscandia as did the military might of the great empire.

Despite a few aches and pains, Bernadette's youthful exuberance had as usual been renewed overnight – and she was up for a bit of plunder. So the trio approached stealthily with weapons drawn, and had soon slaughtered the four or five bandits that had been left to guard the fortress's walls. Then they moved inside and stalked silently room to room, leaving death and destruction in their wake. The trio worked well together, managing to avoid hitting each other with their spells or weapons when in close combat inside cramped quarters.

Her pack laden with the bandits' spoils, Bernadette and her team left Fort Altiplan behind: silent now, with only bloody corpses to guard its walls. She suspected it wouldn't be long before the place found new tenants. Its proximity to major roads running east-west and north-south made it an ideal home base for highwaymen.

On reaching the road heading north, the group settled into a steady movement that would carry them leagues toward their destination in the course of a few hours. Their progress was interrupted by attacks from smilodons and more indescribable monstrosities that neither Bernadette, Andrion, nor Lifa could put a name to. Then they came to a sprawling stone building that ran athwart their path.

"Do you know this place?" Bernadette asked Andrion. They'd spoken relatively little over the course of the day, Lifa's presence and their focus on their immediate goal seeming to suppress casual conversation.

"What does the map have to say?" he asked in reply. She checked, and it was now showing a symbol shaped like a yurt (the meaning of which she had yet to decipher) and a name: "Gundir's Tomb." She reported this information, but neither he nor Lifa had anything to add.

They wanted to explore the ruins for treasure, but soon discovered that it was patrolled by walking dead. Compared to the upper level aptrgangr however, or even a smilodon, animate skeletons armed with ancient Norse bows were not much of a threat. The three companions attacked with a will, and soon the site's guardians were nothing but scattered dry bones. Bernadette retrieved some loot from a chest, and discovered an enchanted helmet behind an iron grate. As it appeared to enhance one's magical power, she immediately gave it to Andrion.

They pushed on, finding another Norse ruin the map called "Dengier's Cairn." This was of a curious construction like a beehive sunk into the earth: concentric rings of stones above, a cylindrical bore within, and stone steps leading down to a flat earthen floor. At the bottom, a wooden door blocked an opening in the ground at one side. Within they found a single large room guarded by three aptrgangr, containing various items of value.

By the time they came back up the steps dusk had fallen, and they were beginning to get pretty tired. They had stopped only briefly at midday, to eat a few trail rations and drink some water, before moving on. The land was rising, and they seemed to be coming into a heavily wooded upland leading (so Bernadette hoped) to a pass that would take them to the northern marshlands and their goal: an ancient Norse ruin called Grabentief.

Just as Bernadette was concluding that they were going to need to camp for the night, the three of them were alarmed by a ferocious roaring. Overhead, a dragon had spied them and was attacking! She, Andrion and Lifa all burst into furious action, hurling arrows and battle spells at the creature. It seemed a bit reluctant to close with them, though. Tall trees were all around and it would not have an easy time getting at them with its teeth and claws. As it veered off and flew further away, Bernadette spotted a trail through the woods and followed it to the north, Andrion and Lifa trailing behind while keeping an eye out for the dragon.

It was not heard from again. They continued to follow the trail as full darkness came on, still in a heavily wooded alpine forest. Then abruptly Bernadette spotted a cabin off to the left of the trail. Could this be the shelter she was hoping for? Camping out was all very well in dry weather, but the wilds of Iscandia were *not* safe. She gave the door a push and it opened. Before she could speak a word, a man she took to be a mage (judging by his garb and actions) appeared on a loft above them and without so much as a word of warning began attacking them. Three against one was not much of a contest though – especially as Andrion was as adept at battle magic as any mage she'd yet encountered. Without Bernadette firing a shot, the mage (presumably the owner of this snug cabin) was soon lying dead on the floor.

Regret stabbed Bernadette as she looked down at the man's crumpled body. She hadn't intended to invade his home or rob him of his life, but there didn't seem to have been any choice about it once she'd opened the door. Too bad; but now they were here, they might as well take advantage of the cozy refuge. They ate the dead mage's food, warmed themselves by his fire, and Bernadette and Andrion folded themselves into his narrow bed while Lifa slept on a bedroll spread before the hearth.

They were all tired after a long day of hiking, with the odd fight to the death thrown in for variety; and Bernadette was still feeling as if were wrong for them to be here while the owner of the place lay stiffening in the forest outside. He'd probably be eaten by shria before long. With those concerns and Lifa's proximity, sleeping downstairs no more than a few paces away from their bed on the loft, she wasn't feeling very romantic – even if a certain hunger was already starting to grow within her.

Andrion sensed her mood, and though he would have been up for some fun despite the circumstances, he didn't try to persuade her. Instead, as they lay down in the single bed, he enfolded her in his arms and gave her a few tender kisses. Then he just held her as they both slid off into sleep.

Chapter 14: Chasing the Staff

Bernadette awoke to the sounds of Lifa stirring downstairs. How the woman managed to be always up and fully armored before she, Bernadette, had even slipped out of bed, she did not understand. She and Andrion were tightly entwined in the small bed, and as she stirred against him he tightened his grip and turned her to face him, locking his lips on hers. When they came up for air she took a breath, intending to tell him that it was time for them get up and on the road; but he placed his fingertips gently on her mouth, gazing into her eyes with languor and something more hungry; and said "Shhhhh."

He took her hand and brought it down between them to where his cock was rising against her belly. Bernadette kissed him again and squeezed, feeling it throb in her hand. So hot! She still felt a bit sleepy and distracted by the lack of privacy, but she also wanted him badly at this moment. He reached his fingers down between her legs, pushing into her crevice, and found her soaking wet.

Quietly, Bernadette guided his now fully stiffened member inside her, and they began fucking in slow motion. Biting her lip, trying to not to cry out, she shortly found that the tension of trying to take it slow and not make any noise was adding to her excitement, sending her over the edge. Her vaginal muscles tightened, gripping him inside her with a rippling motion as she came with a stifled whimper.

Andrion too was feeling sleepy if horny, and might have happily gone on making love to her like this, extending the ecstasy, for hours. But the rhythmic clamping as she writhed in silent orgasm took him by surprise, and he came too. They continued their gentle, quiet motion for a while, then lay still again. "I love you," he murmured in her ear.

"Me too," Bernadette replied so quietly that even he, inches from her lips, barely heard it. Then louder, "but we really need to get up and dressed now."

He sighed and squeezed her one last time before releasing her. "I know…"

They were, shortly, up and dressed. As they came downstairs, Lifa gave them a look of disapproval. She's just jealous of us enjoying ourselves, thought Bernadette. With that body, she could be having all the fun she wants – if she'd ever lighten the hell up. The three of them ate a light breakfast; then, before leaving the area, Bernadette went out to where they had left the body of the unfortunate mage. Luckily, the corpse was as yet untouched. She found a shovel lying near the back of the cabin, and took the time to dig the man a grave and bury him in it. She felt it was the least she could do for him.

The trio resumed their quest, traveling toward the location the map said was the resting place of the legendary staff Bernadette had been sent to find. While moving in that direction, they found themselves on the outskirts of a medium-sized town. "This is Normarsh," Andrion informed her. For all Bernadette knew, Lifa might be the world's foremost expert on Iscandia geography; but she never volunteered anything. "They have an eorl, here," he added. "And I've heard there's a skilled chemiast."

It was still pretty early in the day, with their destination not much further ahead. So Bernadette decided they would explore the town. She paid a courtesy visit to the eorl, an older woman who seemed nice enough even if her expression was forbidding. And she happened to bump into the chemiast, a young woman, out walking on one of the town's wooden sidewalks. The place seemed to have been built over a swamp, and there was water everywhere between the rows of houses. I'll bet they don't get much carriage traffic here, Bernadette thought.

The chemiast, Helga, gave her a friendly greeting. She had a decent selection of potions and ingredients, and Bernadette was able to pay her for some lessons in chemia. She left the town feeling as if she had really learned a few things. There was still a long way to go, though, before she could claim expertise. Shortly after they left Normarsh heading north, they came to an area of fens, spotted here and there with little hummocky bits of higher ground. Progress became slow as they had to climb these, then wade through the shallow water lying between them.

Bernadette checked her map and directed their path slightly more to the east. Only a few more minutes' travel saw them standing before the entrance to Grabentief, an ancient Norse ruin that Bernadette suspected would probably be crawling with aptrgangr. After her initial horror at discovering such things existed, she was now getting almost nonchalant about taking them on – in reasonably small numbers. That horde in Grindor's family tomb had nearly recruited her to the ranks of the dead.

Bernadette got a good grip on her bow and checked to make sure Andrion and Lifa were following, then led the way through the ominous edifice's front door. They crept in quietly, senses on the alert for danger, and soon found a few aptrgangr patrolling the corridors. Bernadette was surprised to discover that there was a group of renegade mages inhabiting the ruin, seemingly in conflict with the aptrgangr just as they were. But in this case, the enemy of their enemy was *not* their friend. Team Fireblood took down several of these, as they encountered them.

Eventually the underground labyrinth opened into a chasm with trees growing inside it, a waterfall and bridge visible far below. What was such a place doing deep beneath the wetlands of Midmarch? They had to kill several walking skclctons, each of them wielding ancient Norse bows but easy enough to eliminate with a shot from hiding or a blast of Andrion's battle magic. Bernadette was happy to claim the arrows in their quivers, as they were of a better quality than the ones she was carrying.

Down in the forested area below, Bernadette spotted a familiar-looking semicircular stone wall, which she hoped would teach her a new dragon spell word. She made her way down there with some difficulty, flanked by her guardians, hoping for great things. But though a nearby chest contained valuable loot, there was no spell gem – and nothing on the rune-carved wall lit up. They soon returned back up the narrow stone pathway to explore deeper into the ruins.

Ahead of them was a passageway blocked by a series of three iron gates. As she approached it, the stones below Bernadette's feet depressed slightly into the floor with a clicking noise, and the nearest gate opened. Another few feet, and the second and third gates opened in succession. But within seconds, as she was no longer standing on the trigger, the first gate had closed.

Bernadette considered her options, and decided to try out her new dragon spell. Freezing time for a few moments after the third gate had opened, she sprinted forward. And on the far side of the third gate, she spotted a lever on the wall that locked all three of them in the open position.

"Okay guys, you can come through now," she called to her companions. And added moments later, as they approached the next obstacle, "Watch out through here. I think this section of floor is trapped." The stones were laid out in a checkerboard pattern, with ominous looking holes in the center of each one. What would issue from those, arrows? Spears? These, she soon discovered, belched forth fire if you stepped in the wrong spot.

"Ow, shit!" Bernadette exclaimed, quickly hopping off the stones and onto a low area of rock that fringed the path, jumping from one such outcropping to another as she worked her way through the passage. Behind her, Andrion and Lifa could be heard cursing as each of them got toasted as well. Then, as soon as she'd cleared that danger and was standing catching her breath at the entrance to a large stone-lined room, a spider the size of a horse descended on a silken thread that must have been as strong as a steel chain, to land on the floor in front of her.

It had not spotted her yet, and Bernadette froze in place – hoping her cohorts were going to finish their fire walk and get here to help her out before it did. When they arrived she dashed to the side, firing her bow, while Lifa and Andrion mounted a frontal attack. "Ugh! I hate those things!" she declared. She got no argument on that subject from her teammates.

Smaller spiders also infested the room, but they were soon as dead as their mistress. Bernadette harvested some eggs from the spider nests scattered around the room, shuddering. Spiders' eggs, and their venom as well, were valuable chemial ingredients… but yuck! Then they pushed ahead to a much larger (and blessedly spider-free) room ahead.

As they entered it, there was a grinding noise and four enormous carvings, stylized dragons, rose suddenly out of pools of water on either side of a central walkway. Were they about to be attacked? Bernadette crouched at the ready, but there was no further movement. She and her companions proceeded cautiously down the walkway, toward what appeared to be a stone altar.

This looked to Bernadette to be exactly the sort of spot you might find a fabulous ancient artifact displayed, and she was not disappointed. Well, perhaps a little – the staff lying there looked not all that different from other magical staffs she'd seen. But was that glowing stone mounted in its head perhaps a dragon spell gem? Better not touch it. Gripping the staff by its wooden shaft, she tucked it as far into her pack as it would go – gem down.

Andrion grinned at her. "That went pretty well," he said. "Back to Eberburg?"

"I guess so," Bernadette replied, opening a passage that led to a shortcut out of the dungeon. "But first, what do you say we go to Sylvanian? On the map it looks like it's not very far from here, and I'd really like to see the imperial city." Sylvanian, one of the northernmost of Iscandia's cities, was also the imperial armies' main strongpoint in the province.

"The Old Ones didn't give you a time limit," Andrion observed. "Why not? I haven't been there in years."

As usual, Lifa's response was "You lead and I'll follow, my warden."

Chapter 15: Detours

Bernadette, Andrion, and Lifa were soon out of doors and heading nearly due west. They continued picking their way among scrub-covered patches of land, interspersed with pools of clear, shallow water. Bernadette harvested many chemial ingredients as they went along, including various mushrooms and a pretty purple flower that grew a couple of feet high, with the ominous name of "corpse bringer." She wasn't eager to sample it.

As was the case with most of the unpopulated regions of Iscandia, this area harbored a number of hostile creatures. Once again Bernadette was glad of her companions and their fighting ability, as they were attacked by a pale, eyeless thing that resembled a gigantic flea; a tall, humanoid creature with elongated arms tipped with razor-sharp claws; and something that looked like a hairless bear.

As they moved into an upland area away from the marsh they found another ancient Norse ruin, half-buried in a hillside. The same trident symbol that marked Grabentief appeared on the map for this, and the name "Mordenfell." Perhaps it was her unfamiliarity with the ancient Norse tongue, or its association in her mind with aptrgangr in the ruins she had so far visited; but Bernadette found that just the name of the place gave her the shivers. She figured they could always return another time to explore, now that it was on the map; and she led the group past it without going inside.

Abruptly they emerged from amid rocks and scrubby islands to behold a major river before them, wooden ships moored at docks on the far side. Above those, an enormous granite bluff ran parallel to the shore standing hundreds of feet high, forming a natural stone archway to the right side. There, it bridged the river's estuary where it gave out into the sea to the north. Atop the bluff, from one end to the other, rose the stone walls and towers of Sylvanian, seat of the empire in Iscandia.

Bernadette stood there on the shore, gawking like a bumpkin who had just fallen off the turnip wagon. Nothing she had seen in her travels so far approached this. "Wow," she said, "wow…"

Andrion, an amused smile playing across his lips, stepped close to throw an arm around her and kiss her on the cheek.

"Close your mouth dear," he said quietly. "You don't want any fireflies to fly inside it." She gave him a half-smirk and a glare.

"Just another big city, I suppose," she said with a casual air. "Let's get across, shall we?"

The river required a bit of swimming to cross, but Bernadette was in no mood to trek leagues out of their way on the off chance that there might be a bridge somewhere upstream. She removed her armor and underclothes and wrapped it in a bundle with her pack and weapons, then tied that to a driftwood log before plunging in, towing her possessions across with her. The water was damn cold, this far north.

Andrion repeated her maneuver and soon joined her on the far bank, on a footpath that ran along the base of the bluff. Bernadette's pale skin was bluish and horripilated, her nipples painfully erect, and she was shivering uncontrollably. Andrion admired the effect, and stepped closer to enfold her in a chill embrace; but his sex was shriveled from the cold water as well, his scrotum tight. Aside from that, it was broad daylight and they were standing out in public. No time for fun and games. By the time Lifa had made her own way across, Bernadette and Andrion were back in their clothing and armor, and ready to start up the path leading to the city gates. They left it to her to catch up with them.

The two shortly passed some extensive wooden docks, which signs told them were owned by Imperial Trading. This firm was Iscandia's biggest shipper of goods, with offices in all of the major ports. A little further along the road bent to climb a steep hill, and they passed a small farmstead that appeared to offer horses for sale. Down along the riverside to the west, a sawmill could be seen. The hills north of it were heavily wooded.

Around another bend near the top of the hill, they passed through a set of gates with guard towers on either side. Bernadette assumed this was part of the Reman army's presence here, or perhaps barracks for the City Guard. After moving through this area she and Andrion came to the city's main gates, just as Lifa caught up with them.

What an amazing place this was, easily twice the size of Waterdon! A large stone inn stood on their left, and several shops lined the street on either side beyond it. Bernadette spied the universal sign for a chemiast's shop a few paces up the road, and led her companions inside. The place was fairly large, and packed with potions and ingredients.

Moments after walking in she was greeted by the proprietress, a 60ish looking, well-kept woman who introduced herself as Agna and welcomed them to Agna's Perfumery. She was not really a chemiast, she said, more of an herbalist who made scents; but she did have a chemia station on the premises and Bernadette was free to use it.

Bernadette's pack now held a far larger and more varied store of ingredients. She had been stopping to collect anything that looked likely, whether recognized or not, during their travels. Her ambition was to get good enough at this to make her own health potions, and with some experimentation she managed to make one that not only gave you back more health than the ones she'd been carrying, it increased your overall vitality for a couple of minutes. That was useful!

Some other potions, the formulae for which she stumbled across during this session, seemed less useful and a nuisance to carry around, but she had no need to – Agna was pleased to buy everything she made that she didn't want to keep for her own use. As Bernadette and her companions left the shop, she felt that she was well on her way to the skills that would someday let her craft whatever potion she could desire. Hmmm, how about a love potion, she thought to herself with amusement – though I hardly seem to need one. So far, the part of her girlish dreams that involved exciting love affairs with gorgeous, manly hunks was coming true without any assistance.

From the street outside the shop, Bernadette spied a smithy perched atop a tall stone wall off to the left. A long stone ramp with a switchback in it led up there, and they headed that way. The establishment proved to be standing right outside the gates to Castle Grey, the Reman army's Sylvanian fortress; and the smith, Balthur, was the official armorer for that army.

"I guess the empire must keep you pretty busy," Bernadette remarked.

"Aye," he replied. He seemed to be content to be doing this, rather than out fighting battles. She begged the use of his facilities and improved some of the spare items she had accumulated as loot since they left the Maiden. She then sold those to Balthur, lightening her load while enriching her coffers. At this rate, she thought, I'm going to need to lead a pack mule around with me.

From their vantage atop the wall, Bernadette gazed out over the city. "This place is huge," she remarked to Andrion. "I feel like I could spend a week here just getting to know my way around." While she enjoyed the out-of-doors, especially in nice weather and an absence of attacking wildlife, Bernadette found that there was something enormously exciting and appealing about a city like Sylvanian.

"It might be more like a month," Andrion replied. "I lived here for half a year not long after I came to Iscandia. But shouldn't you take that staff back to the Old Ones?"

Bernadette sighed. "You're right. Maybe we can come back here after all this business is done with." Without further discussion, she pulled out her map, placed a mailed fingertip on the marker for the alpine monastery, and wished them there.

Chapter 16: Recognition

Bernadette, Andrion, and Lifa hastened in the front door of Eberburg, and had to go searching for Aethelred. Two of his brethren were in the front hall, but they of course would not speak. Bernadette found him around several corners in the sprawling stone edifice, apparently worshipping at some kind of shrine. This place was huge, and looked like it would hold dozens of dedicants. But only six Old Ones yet lived, along with their master Ehrgeizig (who had been mentioned as living up at the very top of the mountain). And they all seemed as if they were ready to die of old age at any moment.

Bernadette handed over the staff to Aethelred first thing, earning his thanks. "Follow me," he said. "It is time for us to formally acknowledge you." She dutifully followed him back to the main hall. "Fandgeir will now teach you the final words of the Gale shout," Aethelred told her. She stepped close to the incredibly wizened-looking old fellow in his dark robe, and he intoned "Struung, Wund!" As had happened with the other two words she had learned, the sound somehow entered her being and lodged there, becoming a part of her mind.

"Now, stand between us," said Aethelred, "and we will officially welcome you as The Fireblood." As Bernadette stood in the central square of the hall, with an Old One before, behind and on either side, their voices filled the air with words spoken in the dragon tongue, physically shaking her without doing her any harm. Off to the side, Andrion watched this exchange with tension, looking as if he stood ready to jump in and attack them if any should threaten her.

When the chanting had ceased, Aethelred announced that the ceremony was complete. "What was it that you said?" Bernadette asked, curious.

"We bestow on you the crown of the Fireblood, the dragon of the North. Wear it in wisdom." She twinkled at him

"What, no actual crown?" The old man nearly cracked a smile.

"Your crown is within you, your Fireblood heritage. And the gems of that crown are the spell gems that you have absorbed. As you acquire more, so will your overall power increase."

"If I'm going to save the world," Bernadette remarked lightly, "I suppose I should be out looking for some more spell stones. Any idea where I could search for more of them?"

"Do not try to develop your powers too quickly," Aethelred warned. "You are young, and there is time yet." But after seeing her pleading look, he caved in. "I sense that this location holds a Spell Wall where you may find another word, another stone," he said, marking the spot on her map.

"The walls will only light to teach you a word, or sometimes an entire spell, if the stone is nearby – or if you have already absorbed it," he explained. "Each time you are present at the death of a dragon, its flesh will dissolve. At that moment you are taking, not only any spell gems it may house, but its mana and soul as well. And just then, your powers will be at their greatest. But they will soon fade." Odd, Bernadette thought. It was like over-filling a bucket, she supposed. How could her tiny mortal frame be capable of holding, and using, the mana and soul of an ancient creature so much larger? It left her feeling profoundly small and insignificant.

Bernadette felt in need of some time to rest and think about everything that happened recently. But she still had so many questions! Of course, now that she had this place on her map, she could return here to pump the Old Ones for more information whenever she liked.

"Just one thing before I go," she said to Aethelred. "Eorl Ormund said that I was the fulfillment of a prophecy, that I might be able to stop the world from being destroyed." Aethelred's kindly demeanor was replaced with a frown.

"Of that," he said coldly, "I may not speak. Go forth and learn, Fireblood, but do not be too hasty. I repeat, there is yet time for you to master your powers."

Bernadette and her companions stepped out the front doors of Eberburg into the chill air, and she immediately pulled the map from its resting place. Suddenly, out of the swirling snow, a fur-clad figure appeared. It was small, a woman little larger than she herself was. "Fireblood," she said. "I have waited for your return. We must talk."

"We were just going home," Bernadette told the strange apparition. "Can we do it there? It's a lot warmer, and not that far off..." The woman's teeth chattered involuntarily.

"W-warmer sounds good!" she declared, "Let's go!" Moments later the four of them found themselves standing in summer sunshine outside the Bathing Maiden.

They climbed the porch and stepped inside, shedding packs and excess garments as they walked. The fur-clad figure proved to be a handsome-looking blonde woman somewhere between forty and sixty years of age, clad in leather armor. "Nice," she said, looking around and taking in a few nude people soaking in the nearby pool with the flicker of a raised eyebrow. "Where is this place?"

"Waterdon's just right over there," Bernadette said with a gesture. She seated herself at a table on the mezzanine and waved to Lev to bring them some food and drink. When everyone was seated, she addressed their mysterious guest. "All right, who are you and why were you waiting for me?"

The woman extended a hand and shook hers firmly. "Giselle Ondine," she said. "I'm the owner of the Laughing Herdsman inn, down in Forestville. We're neighbors, to some extent." Forestville was a medium-sized village some hours south and west of Waterdon, and part of Waterdon Hold.

"Pleased to meet you, Giselle," Bernadette said politely. Her questioning look prodded the woman into further explanation.

"After the dragon attack in Horvirstead I began digging into my books. What I found there set me on the road for Waterdon right away. I knew that the return of the dragons meant that a new Fireblood would soon arise, and I knew that I had to find whoever it was and guide them."

First the Old Ones, and now... an innkeeper? Giselle continued, "By the time I was able to speak with the eorl I learned that the new Fireblood had already appeared, and that you were off on your way to Eberburg. Getting there by myself was difficult, and I spoke with the Old Ones only to learn that you had already left on a quest to find and return the Staff of Zauber."

"That's right," Bernadette said, still waiting for an explanation of *why* the woman had gone to all this trouble. She went on, "I knew that if you were able to find the staff and reclaim it that meant you were truly the Fireblood foretold by the prophecy," she said. "So I pitched camp not far from Eberburg and waited for you to reappear. The Old Ones wouldn't let me stay in their hostel for another night. They make their living off pilgrims, I guess, but their rules are strict. And I wasn't anxious for them to learn who I truly was."

"Not actually an innkeeper from Forestville, then?" Bernadette asked, cocking an eyebrow.

"Oh, I am that," Giselle replied. "I have been for the past twenty years, since the end of the Elven Conflict." From a time before Bernadette had been born until around twenty years ago, the Reman empire had been involved in an escalating series of confrontations with the light elves of the Ljosalfar Union, a sovereign nation occupying a large peninsula east of the empire's province of Zahar and south of Remus itself. The settlement that ended it had proven to be a sore point for many imperial citizens – especially the Norse of Iscandia.

Platters of food and bottles of ale began arriving, and for a few minutes conversation ceased as hunger and thirst were slaked. Bernadette hadn't lost track of the subject at hand, though, and soon picked up the thread of the conversation again. "You were saying you've been an innkeeper for the past twenty years, Giselle. And before that, you were…"

"I am one of the last surviving members of the Guardians," the woman said flatly. The Guardians had been the subject of many a tale Bernadette had read, fuel for her girlish dreams of heroic combat and daring deeds. They were, or had been, sort of the Reman equivalent of the Brave Company. Perhaps a bit more formalized, though. In the days when the Reman empire's royal line had supposedly been Firebloods, they had operated as almost a holy order devoted to protecting the emperor and his heirs.

"Are you telling me the Guardians still existed in modern times?" Bernadette asked, scarcely believing it. She sopped up the last of the gravy from her plate with the last bite of bread, and popped it into her mouth.

"The ljosalfar did their best to wipe us out," the older woman said bitterly. "Since the death of the last Fireblood emperor we had been seeking to serve the empire in other ways, and we had done everything we could to oppose the ljosalfar during the Conflict. After the truce we scattered and went into hiding, but they've been hunting us down one by one."

"And what does this have to do with me?" Bernadette asked, sitting back in her chair and sighing. A hot bath was next on her list, and she hope this wasn't going to take too long. "Among the Guardians' other responsibilities, we have long preserved the lore that tells of the Fireblood, and of the Fireblood's role when the dragons return. It is you that must stop them, and we – I, perhaps – who must help and guide you."

Bernadette smiled. "Well, great… I guess. I hope you'll excuse me but I've had a long, trying time the last few days and I'm really in need of a bath. We can talk more after that, if you like – or get yourself a bed and join us, maybe." Giselle gave her an annoyed look, but got up from the chair and went over to talk with Lev. She carried her belongings over to a bed in the nearby sleeping area, then stripped down and put on a robe.

The rest of them had done the same, and the hot pool was a little crowded as they all squeezed in for a soak. "You didn't let me finish what I was trying to tell you," Giselle said. After days spent camping in the snow atop the Hochstein the hot water felt absolutely wonderful; but she really needed to get this off her chest. She completely ignored the naked Andrion sharing the pool with them.

"Here's the important thing you need to understand," Giselle said. "Dragons aren't just coming back, they're coming back to life. They weren't gone somewhere all these years. They were dead, killed off centuries ago by my predecessors. Now something's happening to bring them back to life. And we need to work together to stop it."

"How do you know this?" Bernadette asked, puzzled.

"I know they are," Giselle averred. "After finding what I was looking for in my books I visited some of their ancient burial mounds and found them empty. And I think I know where the next one will come back to life. We're going to go there, and see for ourselves. I'm convinced that the ljosalfar are the ones doing it."

"The ljosalfar?" Bernadette asked in amazement. "Why, let alone how, would they do such a thing?"

"Think about it," the older woman said persuasively, "Dragons prefer colder climates. It was here in Iscandia, and to the east in Darkreach, where they held their greatest sway. The Ljosalfar Union is a thousand miles south of here. By bringing back dragons, they can cause a world of trouble for the empire. As if they didn't already have enough trouble on their hands in Iscandia, with the rumblings of the Norse partisan movement. It only benefits the ljosalfar, can't you see?"

Bernadette hadn't ever paid all that much attention to politics. The Conflict had been over long before she was aware of such things, and in her rural part of Auverne the biggest public concerns were disputes by farmers over land or wandering livestock. Giselle's argument seemed as likely an explanation as any for the sudden reappearance of dragons. Maybe the end of the world would come about as the result of some battle spell gone wrong, in the midst of a continent-wide war triggered by the light elves' arcane political ploy?

And how would they be able to do it? Their mages were powerful, it was well-known. The dragons Bernadette had seen certainly looked like living creatures and not revenants, but perhaps there were other aspects of the necromantic arts, ones that could bring back the dead as they had been when they were alive. She had been feeling relaxed and happy, but suddenly she felt a sense of urgency. They needed to go investigate this, and now!

"You're right, Giselle," Bernadette told the older woman, and got a satisfied smile in response. "Where is it you think the next dragon will be brought back to life? Can we get there in time?"

"It's a little outside the mining village of Delvewood," Giselle told her. "If we move fast, we could probably get there before nightfall. I can't say exactly when it will happen, but we need to get over there and stake out the burial site so we can find out who's resurrecting the dragons, and how."

They all climbed out of the bathing pool and quickly toweled off, then went to get back into their armor. Bernadette sighed. At least she'd gotten a good meal and a bath, but she'd been hoping for a little special time with Andrion now that she'd finished with the Old Ones. After going through the contents of her pack and throwing a few items into it, she went over to where Lifa was bunking. "I think Andrion and I can handle this one by ourselves," she told the woman. "Can you stay here until we get back?" "As my warden wishes," she replied.

Gods, when is that woman's shell ever going to crack, Bernadette wondered? They had been battle companions, fighting at each other's side, sleeping rough together… and she acted as if they were scarcely acquaintances. Brushing her annoyance aside, she and Andrion went downstairs and met Giselle. "Delvewood is not that far from Coldstein," he told her. "We'll need to go back down the road we took a few days ago, but keep heading east."

Bernadette pulled out her map and considered. The village was now showing on it, some distance south of Coldstein beside a road that ran alongside a river. There really was no faster way to get there than to run. They shouldered their packs and set off at a trot, putting Bernadette in mind of her nighttime run to Waterdon not that long ago.

This time they went south to pick up a bridge over the Brightwater, then picked up the road that curved around, following the river, and continued on the north side of the Hochstein. The forlorn tower where Bernadette and Andrion had killed the bandits a few days ago remained empty, fortunately. Likely it wouldn't be long before it found new tenants, though.

Giselle, who seemed to have an astonishing turn of speed and endurance for a woman of her age, led the way as they came to a crossroads and took the left fork. The road ran along beside a river canyon, then came over a bridge across another river before turning south.

They stopped from time to time to catch their breath, have a drink of water, or use the bushes. But mostly they just ran, with little breath left over for conversation. Mercifully there were no bandits on the road – they even managed to avoid wolves, bears, and other hostile wildlife.

As they took a breather, slowing to a walk across the bridge before the turn to the south, Andrion gestured to a high-walled stone city off to their left. "That's Coldstein," he said. They seemed to have left summer behind them, as there was snow on the ground and a cold stiff breeze blowing. "We're at a higher elevation here," he explained, as they crossed the bridge and picked up the pace again. "I like Waterdon a lot better."

Jogging along the road beside the river, Bernadette's eyes were drawn to a lot of interesting vegetation. There were bushes covered in berries, exotic and unfamiliar flowers, and a host of other plants – despite the cold conditions – that looked as if they would probably be good ingredients for crafting potions. She wished they could move at a more leisurely pace, so she could collect some – but that would have to wait.

The sun was nearly on the western horizon as Giselle led them up a slope to the left and they discovered the village of Delvewood before them. What there was of it. It was really no more than a smallish inn and a mine, with an attached smelter and a few miners' shacks scattered around.

They didn't go into the inn, but hurried along a trail leading up a slope beyond it. Giselle seemed to know exactly where she was going. Finally they crested a rise among tall pine trees, drifts of snow here and there on the ground beneath them, and beheld a large circular mound of earth with a stone ring around it. It was slightly convex and had some grass sprouting on top, amid the drift of pine needles.

"Thank the gods, it's still intact!" Giselle said, drawing to a halt and heaving a sigh of relief.

"So that's a dragon burial mound?" Bernadette asked. She had seen things like this once or twice since coming to Iscandia, but had thought they were the ruined foundations of domed buildings, or something.

"The dragon worshipers buried the dragons that died in the Uprising," the older woman told her. "Supposedly there were special rituals involved. They knew from the prophecy that they were to rise again, you see."

Andrion looked interested. "Well," he said, "it's about to get dark. Can we assume if there's a ljosalfar necromancer around he'll wait until daylight to begin his spell?"

Giselle seemed uncertain. But it was cold out here, and she wasn't eager to camp in the snow all night when there was a nice warm inn less than a quarter of a mile away. "Let's go down to the inn," she said. "If there are any ljosalfar around there will probably be a whole party of them, and that's as likely a place as any to find them. It's the only public building in town."

Peering into the woods around them with an eye out for lurking spellcasters, the three made their way back down and into The Delvers' Rest. There were no ljosalfar to be seen. Indeed, there seemed to be only the grizzled old innkeeper and a younger woman who was probably his daughter, and a couple of grimy-looking Norsemen who were probably miners – lifting a bottle of mead together at the end of their long day in the mine.

Giselle went up to the bar, and her posse followed her. "Evening, Bjorn," she said to the old innkeeper. He smiled at her, a grin that was missing a few teeth.

"Good to see you back again, Giselle. What can I get you?"

"I think we're going to need beds for the night," she said, "and some of whatever's on the fire."

He looked the party over, maybe sensing from Bernadette and Andrion's body language that they were a couple. "Three singles all right, I hope?" he asked. "It's all I've got." They were shown to three tiny rooms, each scarcely wider than the narrow bed that took up most of its space. At least there was also a chest of drawers.

Bernadette went into hers and tossed the pack on the bed, rummaging through it. She wriggled out of her armor with some difficulty and put on the dress she'd brought along. It was made of a soft woolen knit fabric, long-sleeved but low-cut, and looked pretty good on her – or so she thought.

After changing she went next door to Andrion's room and helped him with his armor. He'd been looking forward for days to a little fun, and as soon as he was down to his underclothes he reached for her to give her a full-body hug and a lingering kiss, his hands stroking down her back to cup her buttocks beneath the flowing skirt of the dress. "Mmm!" he murmured. "You look good enough to eat!"

"And eat me you shall," she replied archly. "But later. I'm starving, after that run."

Andrion had a suit of casual clothing with him as well, and he looked quite fetching in it. "*Damn*, man, you clean up well!" she exclaimed, running her hands over his torso and gazing up into his eyes. "Definitely, *definitely* later." The pair returned to the common room and found Giselle at a table, so joined her there. She had opted to leave her armor on, prepared to run out at any time and apprehend any ljosalfar agents that might be trying to dig up dragons.

Bernadette let the older woman pick up the check. After all, they were here at her behest. They ate cabbage potato soup with bacon, fresh bread, and cherry pie for dessert, all washed down with several rounds of ale. The ale had little alcohol in it, and she had no trouble keeping a clear head.

Bernadette and Andrion conversed through the meal and for an hour or more afterward, then bade Giselle a good night. They discretely strolled off together to his room, closing and latching the door. "Now, where were we?" he said. Resting his hands on her shoulders, he kissed her gently but with concentration. "How does this thing come off?" he asked.

"There are hooks down the front, see?" she gestured, showing him how the steel hooks were cunningly hidden under a flap of cloth.

"How convenient!" He began deftly unhooking them, one by one, stooping to plant a kiss on each patch of skin as it was exposed.

When Andrion had the dress unhooked to Bernadette's waist, her full breasts popped out as the top of it fell away. Her underwear wouldn't work with this outfit. He grasped them in his hands, squeezing them gently and then bending to tongue the nipples. "Ooooo!" she exclaimed involuntarily, as a thrill shot through her body and she felt her loins grow warm and moist. "Yes, I like that…"

Andrion continued these ministrations for another few moments, then finished with the hooks and the entire dress spilled to the floor. Bernadette had not been wearing any underwear below either, and now stood looking like a forest nymph amid a pool of green fabric. He stepped back and just stood there admiring her. "Berni, has anybody mentioned to you that you are absolutely beautiful?"

"Why thank you, kind sir." She replied in a ladylike fashion. "The subject has come up once or twice. And might I say that you look ravishing? …How'd you like to ravish me?"

"I thought you'd never ask," he leered.

Bernadette stooped to pick the dress up and gave it a shake, then threw it onto the top of the room's chest of drawers. It might not be much, but it was her only presentable outfit and she'd like to keep it reasonably clean. Then she approached him and began stripping him of his shirt and trousers. He *was* wearing underwear, and a prominent bulge in the bottoms indicated he had risen to his task. Bernadette got Andrion completely naked, taking his rock-hard cock in her right hand and stroking it as she stepped into his arms for another deep kiss. Then she sat down on the edge of the bed and said, "All right, kneel."

Andrion grinned at her and knelt on the small rag rug beside the bed, stroking her belly and thighs and spreading her legs as he bent his head between them. Then he applied his mouth to her quivering sex, licking deep within her folds with his tongue and using his lips to suck and squeeze as he drew out her juices. "Ooh, yes!" Bernadette cried in ecstasy, leaning over him to grasp his head and stroke his hair as he bent to his work. Then she let herself fall back on the bed, her mound humping up into his face, as she screamed and spasmed in orgasm.

Berni's excitement had Andrion so hard he felt like he could use his cock for a mace, and he wanted her very badly at that moment. But patience! He didn't want to come just yet. He climbed up onto the bed beside her and they lay facing each other, his hot, rigid member rubbing into the groove of her dripping slit without penetrating it. She was almost ready to come again immediately from the stimulation as he pushed it against her clit.

"I want you inside me, now!" Bernadette moaned. Then taking matters into her own hands, she threw Andrion over onto his back and climbed onto his stiff prick in one smooth motion. What a woman! he thought, as she engulfed him. She began riding him like a horse, bouncing up and down on his pelvis. The sight of her impaled on him like that was thrilling, her breasts jiggling up and down in a motion he found fascinating; but this wasn't the best position for friction. He grasped her around the waist and rolled her over in the bed, so he was now on top, and began fucking her harder and faster, as she wrapped her legs around his hips and thrust up at him as he was thrusting down into her.

As Andrion seemed about ready to explode, Bernadette stopped him. "Wait, I want you to take me from behind." She was definitely not shy about making her desires known, and it seemed to Andrion as though those desires usually coincided remarkably well with his own. He pulled out of her for a moment, his cock glistening and reddened, almost glowing in the room's dim light. She turned over and crouched, her perfectly rounded, firm buttocks like a beacon calling him home, on either side of her slickly swollen cunt.

Andrion grasped her left buttock firmly, then used his right hand to guide his throbbing cock into Berni's gateway. Both hands squeezing her now, he began moving in and out slowly but fully, encasing his entire length inside her. Shortly his movements grew faster and faster, as her cries became more frantic and his moans more urgent. They were both riding an avalanche, and it came crashing down the mountain in a cascade of searing sexual power that left them moments later, gasping and exhausted, lying flat on the bed.

"Andrion, by the gods!" Bernadette murmured. "That was incredible." He didn't quite manage anything coherent in reply. They rested entwined for a long moment, finding little to say. But they were seemingly more compatible in the throes of passion than in post-coital bliss. At about the point where Andrion felt ready to fall asleep, his darling hellcat wrapped in his arms, her brain had gone back on the alert. Sex often seemed to energize Bernadette, somehow, rather than putting her to sleep. Even though her body was tired, her mind was racing with thoughts and schemes.

"I need to go back to my room, love," Bernadette told him. "I'd like to catch some sleep before this dragon resurrection takes place, and this bed is just a bit narrow." She kissed him tenderly and with feeling, then gathered up her things. She was sorry to have to fasten all those hooks again just for the trip from this room to her own; but it would hardly do to be darting around the common room naked and looking very much like she'd just been laid. "Keep an ear out and come over if you hear anything," she requested as she left.

Back in her room, Bernadette took the dress off again. After giving it a bit of thought, she decided to don her underwear before lying down in bed. She might find herself needing to get dressed in a big hurry. As she lay down in the narrow bed and began drifting off to sleep, Bernadette thought back on her recent encounter with Andrion.

Sex with him just seemed to be getting hotter and hotter every time, rather than going stale as had been the case with most of her other lovers. Not that she had a lot of experience with real men. Back home in Pied-de-Puce, most single guys were adolescents for whom, like as not, she had been their first and only sexual contact.

112

She'd figured out a few things on her own over the years, but none of her partners had had anything to teach her about love.

Bernadette was usually a sound sleeper. Her youth and active lifestyle tended to send her into a deep sleep that little could disturb. But anxiety over the possibility that they might have to go deal with a dragon at any moment had her restless. Finally, though, she dropped off into dreamless sleep.

Chapter 17: Resurrection

A pounding on the door roused Bernadette some unknown amount of time later. "A dragon, there's a dragon!" It was not Giselle calling, but the woman innkeeper. Had they slept through, and missed their chance to see who or what had brought that dragon forth from its tomb?

Bernadette jumped into her armor, pulled on her boots, and grabbed her bow and quiver of arrows – leaving the rest of her gear in the room. As she came stumbling out of into the common room, she found Andrion and Giselle doing the same. "What's going on?" Giselle asked anxiously, addressing the woman who had roused them.

"A great big dragon is flying around outside, roaring!" the innkeeper cried. "Do something! I'm afraid it's going to burn down the inn!" A real enough threat, Bernadette realized, as the three of them dashed out the door and hurried toward the trail up which they'd climbed the evening before.

It was light out, barely, though the sun had not yet come up above the forest to their east. A couple of hundred feet above them an enormous dark gray dragon was lit by the dawn's rays, looking dull pink in the early sunlight. "That…" gasped Bernadette, as she charged up the hill behind Giselle, "that looks like the same dragon that attacked Plainview!"

As they approached the burial mound, they saw that it was unchanged – the dragon circling above them had *not* emerged from this burial site! Crouching, Giselle hissed "Stay under cover. This is what we came for. We need to see what happens." Wrestling with disbelief, Bernadette watched in stunned silence as the enormous dragon called out in its deep, chilling voice. She could not understand many of the words, but one seemed to be a name: "Fanhimjaag." And it sounded like he was bidding this Fanhimjaag to rise.

As the elder dragon peeled off again, keeping to the air, Bernadette's eyes widened still more as a skeletal dragon form burst from within the confines of the mound, moving as if it were a new-hatched chick emerging from an egg. As it struggled to crawl forth from the disturbed soil, a nimbus of translucent flesh surrounded the bones. Then that nimbus began to coalesce into solid muscle and hide as the form of a green-scaled dragon appeared before them. "I am Fanhimjaag!" it bellowed.

Bernadette had an arrow flying from her bow even as Giselle cried out "Kill the dragon!" The three of them were soon attacking it from all sides, and its recent resurrector flew away – offering no aid. It put up a fierce fight, but never managed to get off the ground before they had returned it to the death it had so recently escaped. Bernadette approached it, knowing what she could expect.

The dragon's flesh vanished in an instant as soon as she drew near, and she felt a sense of exaltation. Aethelred had told her that she was actually absorbing the creature's soul along with its mana, its life force, which explained how overwhelming the sensation was.

She bent to rummage through the collection of items left behind, and plucked up a glittering gem that glowed a deep forest green. It melted into her palm within moments, but again there was no text, no way to learn what spell it could power. There was a slight gasp from Giselle. "It's true, isn't it? You really are fireblood." Bernadette just gave Giselle a look, as the powerful surge faded and she could once again focus on other things.

"So, the dragons are being resurrected by a dragon," Bernadette said. "Of course, I suppose that doesn't necessarily mean the ljosalfar aren't involved. Maybe they could have resurrected one like a zombie slave and then sent him to continue the work, eh?"

The woman replied, "We need to find out for sure, but the ljosalfar are the only people I can think of with a likely motive. And if they aren't involved, they'll know who is."

"So, we need to find out what the ljosalfar know about the dragons. Where would they keep secret information, if they have any?" Bernadette prompted.

The ljosalfar, the "light elves," were widespread in all walks of life throughout Agena, and they certainly could be arrogant enough to rub others the wrong way. But that didn't necessarily mean they were plotting the destruction of Terris. On the other hand, she had only the vague mention of an "old prophecy" to tell her that the dragons' return and the end of the world were related. What if they *were* just a political ploy, as Giselle seemed to believe?

"If we could get into the ljosalfar consulate... it's the center of their operations in Iscandia... Problem is, they've got more guards than anyplace else in the province," Giselle replied thoughtfully.

"How do we get in there, then?" Bernadette asked.

The older woman looked pensive as she replied, "I'm not sure yet. I have a few ideas, but I'll need some time to pull things together... Why don't you meet me at my inn in Forestville? If I'm not back when you get there, wait for me. I shouldn't be long." She handed Bernadette a key. "My room at the Laughing Herdsman has a secret door in it. This will get you into the room where I keep my Guardians materials," she said.

"I have a few things to do myself, so take your time. It might be awhile," Bernadette told her. Then they parted ways. Bernadette walked a few feet away from the skeleton of the dragon, then pulled out her map. "Andrion, before we go home I'd like to add Coldstein to my map as a fast-travel point in case we need to return this way again," she said.

The two of them filed back through Delvewood and took the road to the north. Within a few minutes they found themselves looking through falling snow at Coldstein in the near distance. They hadn't gotten close enough on their fast trip past here yesterday. Where they were standing, at the crossroads of the road they had taken and another that ran along the riverside, were Coldstein Stables. Bernadette saw that the name had now appeared on her map, and that seemed to be good enough for the time being.

She touched the map again, and took them to the Bathing Maiden. Now that their business with Giselle was concluded for the moment, it was time at last to go home.

Chapter 18: Rest and Revelation

In moments Bernadette and Andrion found themselves standing outside the inn again. As they made their way in the front doors, Bernadette's curiosity was beginning to get the better of her. She asked Andrion, "What *is* the story with this place? Do you live here permanently? Except for when I bought supplies from Lev, nobody has ever asked me for money." He assumed a look of great seriousness, which she did not believe for a moment. There was glee peeking out from the depths of his warm eyes.

"It's time you visited the Well of Truth, I think," he said.

"The what?" she asked, confused.

"In the basement, my dear," he responded. They trooped over to the trap door behind the bar and as they entered the long basement room Bernadette realized that there was a wooden door in the far end of the wall on her left. In her dazzlement at the wonderful (and apparently complimentary) crafting facilities, she had completely overlooked it. "Through there," Andrion gestured, smiling now.

The first door led to a stone passage and a second door. Behind that, a large black stone brazier was glowing with a radiant blue light. As Bernadette approached a quiet female voice spoke out of the air. "I can sense your essence. I am the Well of Truth, and you are the new owner of this place." Seriously? Bernadette thought. Wow!

Aloud she asked, "How do you know that?"

"I know," came the brief reply.

"Why are you here?" Bernadette demanded.

The ethereal presence replied, "The builder put me here. The first owner." "Who was that?" she asked. "He was *fjurblut*, like you," the voice responded.

"Like me?"

"Yes," came the answer. "Mirdokh was *fjurblut*." *Fjurblut*, Bernadette thought. That's dragon tongue for Fireblood.

"Mirdokh built this place?" she asked.

The voice replied, "Before he passed on to other planes, Mirdokh built this sanctuary to meditate beneath the High Stone.

He placed me here, that I might welcome each new fireblood, and preserve the knowledge of the fireblood heritage."

Bernadette spun to find Andrion standing in the doorway, watching her with a pleased expression. She threw herself into his arms. "Andrion, this is wonderful! I *love* this place, and it's all mine?!" Then she peered into his face at close range. "How long have *you* known about this? Why didn't you tell me?"

He looked a little sheepish, but still pleased. "As soon as you said you were The Fireblood I suspected. I've talked to Fenris and I know the history. But it wasn't until after we visited the Old Ones and they went through their ceremony that I knew it was really true. And then, we were running all over the place and I was... distracted. Do I need to start calling you 'Boss' now?" He hugged her and planted a kiss on one cheek.

"Boss?" Bernadette asked, giving him a questioning look. "Yeah," he replied, "I'm actually an employee of the Maiden. Lev, Erik, Fenris and all the rest, we were hired by the Trust. We get to live here and we assist the customers with whatever they need, pick up work as questing companions, and so forth."

A horrible suspicion forming in her mind, she frowned at him. "You mean you're a *gigolo*?!" she asked frostily.

"Oh! No baby, it's not like *that*. You and me, that's entirely on my own time. Well, not the part about following you around, taking orders, and helping you kill your foes. That's part of my job description. But making love with you has nothing to do with any of that. I love you." He gave her his best look, which damn near melted Bernadette into a puddle on the spot. But she was irked to discover he had not been entirely forthcoming with her. How much intimacy did they really have, if he was hiding secrets like that?

"Since I'm the boss around here," Bernadette said with an edge in her voice, "I guess I can give the orders. You look like you could use a bath. We both could, for that matter."

"How can I argue with that?" he grinned. It was hard to stay mad at him, and she still felt powerfully drawn to him despite the betrayal. But he had dented if not broken the trust between them, and she felt as if she wanted to get a little distance.

Bernadette stopped for a chat with Lev after they emerged from the basement. "Are there any profits?" she asked. He handed her a few coins. "Oh, and could you please ask everyone not to sleep in the Maiden's master bed? That's going to be my bed while I'm here. For me and *whomever* I ask to join me in it," she added. She glanced meaningfully at Andrion. He looked a bit pained.

She was pretty sure his feelings for her were sincere. But let him suffer for a while. He deserved some payback for keeping her in the dark. Though she felt far older than her 22 years, there were times when it seemed to Bernadette as if those who were older and wiser were playing her, taking advantage of her youth and naiveté.

They clumped up the stairs, and Bernadette dropped her pack in the trunk beside the master bed. Then she stepped forward to Andrion, and helped him get his armor unstrapped. He reached for her as her clothes came off, but she sidestepped him. "Later for that, sweetheart," she said. She was still mad at him. They put on robes and went down to the hot pool in the middle of the Maiden's main floor area.

Bernadette slumped down so that the water came up to her chin, and gave a long, peaceful sigh. Closing her eyes, she sat there trying to sort out her emotions. This place was all hers! That was the most wonderful news she had heard since coming to Iscandia, even better than being made Warden of the March; and it seemed like a *huge* compensation for the responsibilities that had been heaped on her since she'd been revealed as The Fireblood. That was all for the good.

As for Andrion? She still felt a powerful connection to him, and one of the reasons she had her eyes closed was so she wouldn't see him sitting there in all his butterscotch-skinned glory and be tempted to jump his bones on the spot. She needed time to heal, to get over the wound he had caused her when he admitted that their relationship had not begun quite as she had believed. She'd thought she had found a handsome chance-met stranger, and all the while meeting her had been part of his *job description*.

In any case, there were plenty of *other* good-looking guys around. Aside from the employees, the Maiden seemed to be a big

119

draw. Men from all over the province could be found here relaxing *au naturel* in the bathing pools or dancing to the house music. A girl who was not tied down to one guy could have some *serious* fun here. Bernadette opened her eyes and looked around. There weren't that many people in the Maiden just at the moment, but the day was young. She made a mental note to have a chat with that blond hunk she'd spotted a few times before. He was probably one of Andrion's coworkers, since he always seemed to be around.

Bernadette caught Andrion gazing at her, and asked him, "So I suppose you just stay around here when you're not on a companion assignment?"

"Uh huh."

"Good. I'd like you to stay here while I go into Waterdon. I'll be back later today." She darted up out of the pool and grabbed a towel, gave him a fleeting smile as she headed upstairs to get dressed. He sat there looking uncertain and a bit forlorn. *Good*, she thought.

Bernadette did have some decent garb that wasn't made out of steel in her trunk, and she put on a pair of close-fitting soft breeches with tall leather boots, a linen shirt with full sleeves gathered at the wrists, and a snugly-laced brocade short vest. Just for fun she added a rakish velvet cap. She checked herself out in the master bedroom's mirror as she shouldered her pack and headed out. Not bad, *Fjurblut*, she thought. During her travels she'd had little opportunity to explore this very feminine side of her nature, and for weeks recently her deepest concern in choosing an outfit had been how good it would be at stopping arrows, swords, and maces.

Bernadette stopped at the bar downstairs and tanked up on a meal she concluded was probably brunch, before leaving. She had a pack full of weapons but only a steel dagger at her waist, and though the road between here and Waterdon was fairly civilized you never could tell where or by what you might be attacked, in Iscandia. And she certainly was not armored. So she used the magic map to make the short hop into town, and found herself seconds later standing just inside the city's main gates.

On her previous visits Bernadette had barely had time to do any daylight exploration, and she now eagerly set out to make up for that omission. She started with Valkyrie, the armorer's shop with a smelter, forge, and crafting stations immediately to the right of the main gates. There was also a good-sized store. Bernadette spent some time chatting with the "Valkyrie" herself, a youngish Reman woman by the name of Alessia Adelini.

Bernadette was eager to build up some good relationships with the local merchants. If the Maiden were to be her new home, this would likely be her local trading area for anything Lev could not supply. And since selling her weapons and armor to Lev would be like selling them to herself, she decided that from now on she would bring them here. After using Alessia's smithing facilities to improve some of the items in her pack, Bernadette headed inside the store. "Ooh, there's a fine specimen," she thought as she stepped in and saw an enormous, red-bearded man in full armor standing behind the counter.

He was Wolaf Redknife, Bernadette learned, and she was definitely adding him to her list of local good-looking guys she wouldn't mind getting into bed with. In addition to pretty bards, she had a thing for oversized hunks as well. Come to think of it, any number of different types of men could get her blood racing, and it had been that way since she hit puberty. Might there be something to this fireblood business besides being able to use dragon spells?

Alas, in the course of their bartering session it came out that he was married to Alessia. Bernadette might be loose with her affections, but she had a personal rule against poaching on another woman's preserve. This did not include "interest" or "courting"; but marriage was the kicker. For one thing, this policy kept enmities down to a minimum – and she would prefer to make a friend of Alessia Adelini.

After finishing at Valkyrie Bernadette continued on up the main street, in the direction of the city's market square, and stopped off at a general store called Bernard's. Bernard proved to be a Galise in early middle age, tall and good-looking; but his personality was so abrasive that she quickly dismissed any thoughts of romance. "Everything's for sale!" he declared bombastically. "I'd even sell you my sister, if I had one."

"No thanks," Bernadette replied. "What else have you got?" This was a lead-in to her offering items of her own for him to purchase. It annoyed her that her bartering skills were still so inadequate that she could have sold an item for 20 guilders that would cost her 45 to buy back. But she'd picked up an Amulet of Iouna, the goddess of love and beauty, and it magically improved her abilities in speechcraft. This included bargaining as well as persuading people to her way of thinking or, perhaps, getting them into bed. Not that she'd had a lot of difficulty with that last thing so far in her life.

Nothing for it but to practice, Bernadette thought. So she continued her bartering session until she had sold off her entire supply of extra trinkets, jewelry, clothing, etc. Feeling some remorse for having been so harsh with Andrion, she succumbed to temptation and bought him a fine suit of clothing. "Come back anytime!" Bernard called in his grating voice, as she swept out the door and headed for the chemia shop to the right of it. Clearly he was pleased enough with their session, which left her convinced she'd been had.

This next shop, called The Potent Potion, appeared smaller than Agna's Perfumery in Sylvanian but still reasonably spacious and well-stocked. The proprietress, Adele, was a rather scrawny middle-aged woman, plain of face. She peered at Bernadette as she entered the shop and said, "You look rather pale. Could be Aphasia. It's quite a problem back in Remus." So, the woman was a Reman. Bernadette had downed a potion claimed to be able to cure any disease on her way up here from Valkyrie, in fact, as she had been feeling a little off-color. So she was quite sure Adele either didn't know what she was talking about – or was intentionally misleading her into buying a cure.

Nonetheless, this was another of the people in town Bernadette needed to develop a good working relationship with. She asked Adele friendly questions about her shop and the area, and even paid her for some lessons. With her newly improved skills, Bernadette then used the shop's chemia station to craft some more potions – including a couple of spare ones to cure disease. Not only would it cure whatever infection you might be harboring, it would also cleanse the body of poison.

Bernadette made a few potions she didn't need again, whatever was easy to make with the ingredients on hand. Every trip she took seemed to yield new ingredients for her to experiment with. Selling these off, she then took her leave of Adele. "I'll be back to visit again soon," she promised. She walked out the front door of the shop and into the market square, where 3 or 4 booths were set up. Bernadette stopped and talked with the vendors, making idle conversation while taking note of what was for sale.

Climbing the steps to the plaza above, Bernadette cast a glance up to her right. The Brave Company's handsome mead hall, Ynglingar, overlooked the plaza from another long flight of steps. She was tempted to go up there, but decided she did not need to get involved with more people wanting her to do things for them right now. With Giselle's plots against the ljosalfar and the quest to find more dragon spells, she felt she had more than enough to do. Well, *almost* more. The ongoing efforts to stop the resurrection of the dragons were crucial, but spending all her time on those quests left Bernadette without much of an income stream.

Bernadette headed straight and mounted the series of staircases leading to Wyrmshalla. Once there, she collared Paolo Adelini, the eorl's steward. "I'm looking for work," she told him. She thought it might be nice to have a few relatively small, easy tasks to perform, preferably ones not that far from home.

"Let me see your map," he replied smiling. "Here, I've marked down the location. We would greatly appreciate it if you could do away with the bandits that are infesting this ruined fortress and killing travelers."

"Sure thing," she replied breezily, and left him with a smile.

After exiting the hall Bernadette paused at the top of the steps outside Wyrmshalla. The location commanded a marvelous view of the city below and the countryside around it. You could even see the Maiden from here. Her mood was improving by the minute, and her annoyance at Andrion was starting to recede. She fast-traveled down to the Maiden, imagining she was an eagle soaring down there in one long glide.

Evening was coming on, and when Bernadette walked in she found Andrion sitting at one of the mezzanine tables with that very same blond hunk she'd noticed earlier. She came over and joined them, pulling over a chair from a neighboring table. "Introduce me to your friend, Andrion" she said with a winning smile.

He smiled back at her. "Bernadette, this is Erik."

On closer inspection, Erik was not just a hunk. He was gorgeous beyond belief. Taller and broader than Andrion, with a classic Norse complexion and blond hair hanging to shoulder length, he had blue eyes that looked at her with a twinkling warmth as he said, "Erik Johannessohn. Glad to meet you, Bernadette." He had a short-cropped blond beard and chiseled features that still managed to look friendly, and he appeared to be closer to her own age than to Andrion's.

Turning to Andrion, Erik said, "You dog! Where have you been hiding this one?"

"Bernadette is The Fireblood, Erik…"

"The…! By Mirdokh, why didn't you tell me?" he said, giving her a more thorough inspection.

"We only just found out before we got back from our last trip," Andrion replied.

Erik thought that over before saying, "I'm at your service, Fireblood."

Bernadette could think of a service or two he might perform. But for now, they were just comrades enjoying an evening in a pleasant inn. "Lev!" she called to the innkeeper as she spotted him passing on the floor below. He hurried over.

"Yes, Fireblood. How may I serve you?"

"Please, call me Bernadette," she said. Damned if she was going to have every guy in the place treating her like she was royalty. "We'd like wine here, please bring a couple of bottles to start. And whatever's good in the kitchen. Thanks."

He said "Coming right up," and scurried off to fulfill her order.

Bernadette was unused to drinking anything stronger than ale, and by the time they had finished their meal and the second bottle of wine she was feeling *quite* celebratory. After all, she had now achieved some of the fame and fortune she'd been looking for. And here she was in *her* wonderful inn, seated between two of the finest-looking men in Agena.

They ate and drank and bantered the evening away. Bernadette shared simmering glances with Andrion, letting him know he was mostly forgiven. And cast many an admiring glance at Erik, as well. He seemed made in the mold of some god, or a hero from legends. And he was great company, too. When Lev surprised her by producing a lute and bursting into song, Erik got up and, raising his tankard, moved to the music. Andrion just sat there, but Bernadette got up and she, along with Erik and several others of the Maiden's inhabitants, danced and sang along.

What fun! Bernadette felt as if she hadn't a care in the world. Or at least as if all of her cares had taken a short vacation and had no power to bother her for this one night. Ribald laughter filled the air and there was an atmosphere of merriment throughout the Maiden – helped along by Bernadette's insistence that tonight, all patrons drank free.

But the evening grew late, and finally Erik got up and stretched. "I think I'd better turn in now," he yawned.

Andrion said "Goodnight, friend!" with regret in his voice, though deep inside he was thinking *finally* I have her alone. As Erik made his way toward the stairs Bernadette bobbed up out of her seat and trotted over to catch him. Standing on tiptoe and urging him to bend to hear her, she spoke a few words to him, too quietly to be heard.

He stood and nodded, saying "All right, see you then," and continuing his passage toward the sleeping loft while Bernadette returned to Andrion's side.

Andrion eyed her thoughtfully but, mindful that he was still in the doghouse, he did not query her about her actions. "It's just you and me now, love," Bernadette said coquettishly, smiling and perhaps the tiniest bit bleary-eyed. "You never said – do you like my outfit?" She whirled before him, showing off the snug fit of the breeches and the glistening knee-length boots. He grinned, feeling pretty mellow himself.

"It's very appealing, love," he replied. "And so are you."

"Oh! Do you think so?" She plopped herself down in his lap, throwing her arms around his neck and kissing him in the general vicinity of his ear. "Feel how soft the fabric is!" He obligingly ran his hands down her hips, stroking the velvety material of the breeches and her firm buttocks beneath. Then he squeezed them, and claimed her mouth for a deep kiss.

"Berni…" he said, coming up for air. "I'm sorry about… you know…"

"Don't worry about it love," she replied. "It just threw me for a loop is all. But I still love you." She found herself able to say the words blithely, as long as she didn't really, completely mean them.

They sat there necking openly at the table in the midst of the Maiden, which was emptying out as the hour grew later. Lev was still at the bar, though, and through her haze of wine and sexual arousal Bernadette concluded that, fun as it might be to have Andrion fuck her right here on the table, it would be more appropriate for them to go to bed.

Bernadette hopped down from Andrion's lap and stood. "Oh, I'm tipsy!" she declared. "Carry me upstairs!" She was perfectly capable of walking up there on her own two feet, but found it enjoyable, instead, to be scooped up in Andrion's arms like a small child (oh, those *strong* arms) and carried aloft. After negotiating the stairs he demonstrated that he wasn't all that drunk, as he managed to carry her down the length of the gallery to the master bedroom at the back, all the while covering her mouth with hungry kisses.

Furthermore, Bernadette could feel that his cock was as big and hard as ever. The alcohol they'd drunk might have loosened their mood, but it was not interfering with his sexual prowess. Rather than laying her down on the bed Andrion stood her on her feet at the bedside, then began gently removing her vest and shirt. Next, he beckoned her to sit on the bed so he could pull her boots off, followed by her pants. As he'd suspected, she was not wearing any underwear. Andrion assisted her back to her feet and she stood there naked as the day she was born, pink of skin and sparkling of eye, grinning wickedly at him.

"Now you," Bernadette said, reaching up. "Hold still." After their bath earlier today Andrion had put on a simple tunic and trousers, and like her he was not wearing any underwear. It didn't take her long to strip him completely. She stepped back, taking him in. By the gods, he was so beautiful! From his blond-streaked hair and warm brown eyes, to the rippling musculature of his torso, arms and legs beneath that smooth butterscotch skin, his buttocks rock-hard and powerful, his cock ditto.

"And untrustworthy," a tiny voice niggled in the back of Bernadette's mind. "Shut the fuck up," she replied to it. "He's sure as *hell* mine right this minute." Aloud she said, "I'll be in charge here. Just stand back and enjoy yourself." She knelt before him and took his cock in her mouth, unable to engulf very much of it but at least able to wrap her lips around the head and a little of the shaft as she sucked and licked him into slippery, quivering readiness.

Bernadette was soaking wet herself, excited by the wine and the stimulation of having spent the evening carousing with two such exceptionally fine specimens of the male sex. Now, in a move that caused Andrion to gasp with surprise, she stood and threw her left leg up to rest on his left shoulder, impaling her cunt, thus opened wide, on his rigid member. By flexing her right knee, she was able to slide herself up and down his shaft, at the same time twisting her torso around so that she could look him in the eyes.

Andrion moaned, excited beyond belief by her unexpectedly athletic move and the sensations it was causing as his stiff cock was swallowed to its full length within her, then slowly released. Holy gods! he thought. This woman is incredible! Bernadette was enjoying this a lot, and it felt marvelous. But it was also a lot of work, and she was beginning to feel a bit lazy. As her scrutiny of his face told her he was approaching the edge, she unhooked her ankle from his shoulder and then slipped off of him.

"Now," Bernadette said softly, pulling him toward the bed. "Make love to me, Andrion." Her wish was his command. They reclined together on the bed, face to face, and he looked deep into her eyes while sliding his reddened and glistening cock back home. Then kissing her face, lips, eyelids, neck, shoulders, and breasts, he used that cock like a maestro's baton, conducting a symphony of sensations within her until they reached a crescendo of frenzied pumping that left them both pooled on the bed as if their bones had turned to jelly.

After that powerful orgasm, Bernadette for once did not find herself full of thoughts and plans. The wine had begun to make her drowsy, and she drifted, safe in her lover's arms, into a deep and peaceful sleep.

Chapter 19: Erik

Bernadette awoke feeling a slight headache and a terrific thirst. There was a pitcher of water on the bedside table, and she sat up to drink a few swallows and rinse out her mouth, which tasted as though a very small dragon had crawled inside there and died. Andrion was oblivious to this, but as she lay back down and snuggled her naked body against his he awoke.

Andrion snaked an arm around her neck and drew him to her for a kiss, making her realize that he could use some water too. Bernadette pulled away from him a little, and looked into his eyes as he became more alert. "Good morning, sweetheart," she murmured. "Did you sleep well?"

"Great," he replied sleepily. "Could do it some more, though."

"You can go back to sleep if you want, love," Bernadette told him. "I need to get dressed and go kill some bandits."

"Alone?" he asked, looking concerned.

"No of course not, dear. My battle skills are improving, but I still need help. I'm taking Erik along to see how he'll work out as an adventuring companion."

"Erik?" Andrion's voice sounded a little disappointed and uneasy.

"Don't worry, we'll be fine. He's pretty good with edged weapons and I bought some spellbooks yesterday. We'll be back in a day or two. I'm The Fireblood – what could go wrong?"

"It's not the bandits I'm worried about, love," he replied. "It's, uh…" he trailed off.

"Andrion Lamonte," Bernadette replied with an edge of steel in her voice, "there's something we need to get straight between us. And no, it's not that," she snorted, nudging his turgid cock as it rose to graze her belly. "I love you. But I don't belong to you, or to anybody but myself. If you want to be with me, you're going to have to take me as I am."

Andrion frowned at this, but he was a big boy. "Berni, I love you," he said. "I'll take you however you will let me have you." He kissed her deeply, then propped himself up on one elbow to watch as she got out of bed and donned her underclothes.

Andrion climbed out, then, to lend Bernadette a hand getting into her armor. Before she picked up her pack, he enfolded her in a tender embrace. Not a very tight one, considering he was still naked and she was wearing armor. "Take care, love. I'll be waiting for you," he said softly. Her heart quivered a little as she bid him farewell, and she felt a deep surge of love for him warring with her slight hangover.

Downstairs, Bernadette found Erik sitting fully armored, having some breakfast as he waited for them to leave. That seemed like a good idea, so she joined him in consuming some bread rolls and apples, washed down with hot herbal tea. By the time they finished, her headache was almost completely gone, and she was ready to get businesslike.

"Show me what you've got, Erik," Bernadette commanded. He grinned at her and made as if to unfasten the bottom half of his armor. "Not *that*," she said grinning back. "I've *seen* that." She had, sort of, spotting him in the bathing pool two or three times since coming to the Maiden. She had an idea from its flaccid size it must be something to behold when rampant. But that was not the topic of discussion.

Erik displayed his weapons and armor. He was carrying an indifferent steel sword and a simple longbow but no arrows, and was dressed in hide. This would not do. Bernadette led him down to the basement crafting area and worked over his gear, providing him with better armor, steel-tipped arrows, and a gleaming, wicked-looking steel battleaxe. If anybody could handle such a weapon with ease, it was Erik Johannessohn. His shoulders were wider than most of the trees in Iscandia's forests, and his arms looked almost like tree trunks themselves.

Bernadette and Erik arrived at the bandit stronghold some hours later. It had taken a long while to reach it on foot. She'd been maintaining a professional attitude on the trip, so far. Her motivations for taking it included the need for some cash, the desire for a bit of exercise, a wish to make Andrion realize that she was not his property – and a sharp attraction to the blond giant walking beside her. Looking at Erik standing there with his golden

good looks, chiseled features, and warm blue eyes sent a tingle
through her that started in her crotch and radiated up through her
midsection to her fingertips.

As the pair sneaked up to the gates of the partially ruined
fortress where the bandits made their lair, they soon found
themselves being fired upon by half a dozen archers. Bernadette
was pleased to see that Erik knew what to do with the improved
bow she'd given him, as they dropped around half the enemy force
while moving closer. When they were nearer to the main gates he
bellowed, "Stand before me, and die!" in his deep voice, and
charged toward the fortification.

Bernadette was moving quickly too, still using her bow. With
the enchantment she'd placed on it, it packed quite a punch. She
and Erik quickly climbed steps onto the walls and tracked their
enemies, killing them as they found them. After searching the
bodies and gathering quite a few coins as well as other loot,
Bernadette led the way to an inconspicuous wooden door that
appeared to be the entry to the interior of the fortress.

Erik stayed behind Bernadette, wielding the battle-axe she had
crafted for him. From time to time as they crept through the
ruinous stone passageways they would encounter a bandit or two,
chewing the fat by a fireplace or working a forge. For bandits, they
led quiet lives little different from ordinary citizens, when they
were not out killing travelers for their gold. The pair quickly killed
each one, searching the corpses and then moving on, deeper into
the labyrinth.

Eventually they emerged at a large dining hall, where an uruk,
an Afran woman, and a Norseman sat at table along with their
heavily armored chief. The men rushed toward them with swords
drawn while the woman pulled out a bow and began firing arrows
at them. Bernadette and Erik's armor was superior by far to the
hide worn by the bandits, but the chief's steel was a match for
theirs.

Bernadette sent the woman archer to oblivion with a well-
placed shot, then switched to her heavy dypalfar shield and steel
short sword for close combat. Meanwhile Erik was slashing right

131

and left and cursing them in his deep voice as he moved like a golden whirlwind among their foes.

Within moments only the bandit chief remained standing, and with both Bernadette and Erik attacking him he soon fell to his knees. "Yield! I yield!" he cried, but they knew better than to accept surrender from an opponent who was still holding a greatsword. Sure enough, in a heartbeat or two, the bandit was on his feet again. And they cut him down for good.

Bernadette let her sword fall to her side, blood running down the blade, quivering slightly inside from the adrenaline surge. She had taken a few cuts despite her armor, and was feeling a bit weak; so she downed a healing potion that restored her in moments. The surge of wellbeing from the potion accentuated the other side effect of a hard-fought battle for her: her blood was up, and she felt ravenous for both food and sex. It was in moments like this that she felt most alive!

Erik stood there breathing deeply, his face returned to its usual expression of calm happiness from the ferocity it had assumed in the midst of battle. He, too, had a few scrapes and cuts. "Oh! You're bleeding!" Bernadette said, and stepped closer to him. He was glistening with perspiration and the scent of blood and testosterone permeated the air. She put a finger to his brow and wiped away a splash of blood, tasted it. Uruk. She knew the coppery taste well. So, Erik was in no immediate danger.

"Let's go find someplace warmer," Bernadette said, and led Erik around another couple of bends and up a flight of stairs. As she had expected from previous visits to places like this one, the bandit chief had resided in a comfortable apartment near the tower top. It had a spacious bed and a private fireplace, chairs and a small table laden with bread, cheese, and ale. There was also a basin and a ewer of fresh water, with some small linen towels.

Bernadette removed her gauntlets. "OK, let me have a look." She reached up – *way* up, to unbuckle the top half of Erik's armor and set it on the floor in a corner. Pouring some water into the basin and dipping a towel in it, she began to inspect his massively muscled torso, arms, and shoulders for injuries, dabbing away blood and grime gently with the towel.

His chest and rippled midsection were lightly dusted with pale golden hairs, glinting in the firelight. As Bernadette worked on his chest his nipples stiffened, and he tensed with a barely audible, sharp intake of breath. She looked up into his face with concern, afraid she might have hurt him; but he was smiling slightly. "Berni," he said quietly and gruffly, "I want you."

The pupils of Bernadette's dark sea-gray eyes dilated as she gazed into his. He stood there nude to the waist, a healthy young male animal in his prime, radiating desire. And she responded to that desire. He bent to kiss her gently, then removed the top section of her armor for her. She reached down and pulled her undershirt up over her head, her breasts falling free. He clasped her to him, his tongue finding its way inside her mouth.

They stepped apart for the moments it took to shed the rest of their armor and underclothes. Erik gazed at her with excitement, taking her in. Her slim and muscular midsection and flat belly flowed into curving hips and smooth but muscular legs, flanking a pubic bush as ruddy as the long silken hair on her head. He had seen her, too, in the bathing pool at the Maiden; but this was his first close-up look and the excitement was like a blazing fire within him.

Bernadette was doing some avid gazing of her own. By the gods, he was so *big*! His monster cock stood erect amid a nest of tightly curled pale gold hair, quivering with eagerness. She reached out and squeezed it, and it pulsed in her hand like a python. There was an enchanting table in a corner of the room, and Erik picked her up by the buttocks, clasping her to his chest, and carried her over to perch on it. Then, without any further discussion, he pushed that enormous ramrod into her tight, slippery folds. Their coupling was brief and savage, both of them in the grip of a frenzy that brushed aside all concerns but the desire for each other, right *now*. When both of them were spent, they clung together for a few moments, panting and grinning. Wow!

The initial overwhelming hunger satiated, their thoughts turned to other needs. Bernadette threw on a robe from her pack and Erik donned an embroidered tunic he found in one of the bandit chief's chests. It was a bit tight on him and only came down to a few inches below the crotch; but it would do for now. They sat at the table in front of the fire and demolished the bandit chief's repast. There was a cookpot beside the fire, and Bernadette got up and prepared some more substantial fare for them out of her pack. Then they sat, just enjoying the fire's warmth for a while.

Instead of traveling straight back to the Bathing Maiden, Bernadette and Erik decided to enjoy the dead bandits' hospitality for the night. They stripped off and climbed into the big bed, where they soon began stroking and kissing. Before sleeping they made love for an hour or more. His enormous strength and stamina were astonishing, especially considering how many bandits he'd killed this afternoon.

Hours later, Bernadette stirred. She'd been sleeping with her head on Erik's shoulder, curled into the warmth of his body. Faintly, she could hear the sounds of birdsong coming through from outside, telling her that morning had arrived. As she made to sit up he reached out with his massive arms and clasped her to his chest, his cock beginning to harden. Erik's first conscious thought had been memories of their passion of the night before, and he was hungry for more.

Mmmm, Bernadette thought. Tempting. But she was feeling a bit sore after last night, and besides she needed to find a chamber pot. "Noooo!" he moaned piteously as she slipped from his grasp. "Come back! I have something for you!" She smiled winningly but continued her nude dart to the privy. Returning, she threw on her robe. Breakfast, she thought, then time to get going. But Erik was lying there on the bed, his throbbing cock standing to attention. "Pleeeaase, Berni! I need you!"

Well… "Sit up," she commanded. He sat and put his feet on the floor. Bernadette knelt at the side of the bed, her bare knees protected by a small but elegant carpet, and took him in her mouth. Or tried to. His member was so massive that, try as she might, she could not wrap her mouth around much of it. She applied her tongue and lips mostly to the swollen head and gripped the shaft in both hands, squeezing firmly up and down it. Erik shuddered in ecstasy, toes curling and powerful legs flexing, a hand cupping Berni's head as she bent to her work. Before long she was licking off her chin. Breakfast? Of a sort, perhaps.

Shortly thereafter the two had donned their armor again and were on their way. It had been Bernadette's intention to take Erik out for a couple of days, to see how they worked together as battle companions (and yes, she admitted, to see whether their clear mutual attraction would lead to something interesting). She'd completed the quest Paolo had assigned her, and didn't have another one lined up. But they were in unfamiliar territory, and the weather was fine. Bernadette figured if they just started walking down the road, she could add some points of interest to her map and probably rustle up a little exercise for them to while away the remainder of the day. Plus, of course, get some loot.

Bernadette's recent acquisition of the Bathing Maiden meant she never had to worry about having a roof over her head and food in her belly again; but the lure of more and better enchanted weapons, exotic armors, gold, and gems kept her coming back to these dungeons and bandit dens. Given her choice, though, Bernadette thought she'd rather go after bandits than raiding tombs any day. Aptrgangr were just so… creepy.

They set off down the road in the general direction of Waterdon, Erik staying a little behind her to guard her back as a companion should. For not even the most idyllic of days in Iscandia's wildlands was free from peril. They were soon forced to scramble to kill an attacking bear, then again for a pair of smilodons. In between emergencies, Bernadette strode along admiring the scenery and musing about her love life. She missed Andrion's company, but she was also beginning to fall in love with Erik. His sexuality was so strong, so magnetic that she could almost feel it pulsing at her from several feet away as he walked behind her.

Bernadette's preference was for a simple life: plenty of action, clear-cut causes, good food, hard beds, cheap wine, and the sweetness of being swept away by overwhelming desire. No long philosophical discussions, moral conundrums, or complex problems to solve (if you didn't count the occasional puzzles to be found deep in some of the dungeons she'd quested in). Even the recent revelation of her Fireblood status was unambiguous. So a complication in her relationships was not something she'd thought to encounter.

Andrion was smart, stalwart, ever-reliable, valiant and skilled with spell and sword. As a lover he was increasingly familiar yet exciting and skillful, and warmed her to the core. Erik on the other hand was a force of nature: so physical, a golden giant who could lie sleeping like a huge, lazy cat or erupt into action – or passion – like a volcano at a moment's notice. As the warm sunshine beat down on her armor, Bernadette concluded that there was no need to choose between them. At least, not anytime soon.

Unknown to Bernadette, as he walked behind her Erik was thinking about much the same subject – but from his own perspective. He'd wanted this woman from the moment he first set eyes on her, but she was with his friend and he hadn't wanted to intrude. Now, it seemed, she had declared herself free to choose whom she took to her bed – and Andrion wasn't raising any objections. And once Erik had had her in his arms, he was finding it hard to concentrate on anything else. It was if she possessed some magical hold over him, though they'd barely spent more than a few hours together. He simply didn't know what to make of it, but he hoped she'd be back in his bed again before too long.

They stopped briefly at midday, tossing some fur sleeping mats down at the side of the road near a small meandering stream, and lunched on bread, cheese, and ale from their packs. Erik was looking at her with hunger again, and Bernadette was feeling a little regretful that she'd turned him down when they got up this morning. But as appealing as the idea of making love in the grass at the roadside might be, she felt it was too hazardous. So they kept their armor on, and were soon on their way once more.

Eventually they followed a small side trail that led up off the road into a lightly wooded area, and discovered an ominous-looking ruined keep. This place had a less healthy feel than the bandit lair where they'd started their day. Erik, like Andrion, proved to have far more knowledge of Iscandia and its hazards than Bernadette did as yet. The two friends had been working as sellswords for years. "Looks like vampires," he remarked quietly. "Are you up for it?"

"Blood-sucking fiends?" Bernadette responded lightly. "No problem."

She and Erik crept into the keep through the front entrance, having arrived in daylight when no vampires were to be found in the outer bailey. Erik held his deadly axe while Bernadette had her fire damage bow at the ready. Vampires, like certain other creatures, are particularly susceptible to fire. Inside they found the place gruesome, awash with bloodstains – dismembered corpses lying here and there. The vampires did not seem to enjoy each other's company, and they found several alone – easy meat for the deadly pair of adventurers.

Deep within the labyrinthine keep they came upon a throne room where the Master Vampire sat a wooden throne, and they dispatched him with blade and bow. Bernadette and Erik were exultant as he fell at their feet, the last of the blood-sucking crew. But the somber setting made them both anxious to leave. The corpses of the vampires they'd slain had yielded relatively little treasure. A few knives, some vampire dust, and a couple of gems were all they had to show for their foray – other than the satisfaction of having rid Iscandia of these once-human predators.

Finding a secret door that led back to the anteroom near the entrance, Bernadette and Erik were soon once again in the clean air of Iscandia; though during their time spent hunting vampires night had fallen. A good thing all of them were now dead twice over. "Honey," Bernadette said, "What do you say we head back to the Maiden?" She was feeling tired and oppressed after wading through blood the past few hours.

"Sure, why not?" he replied. He was hoping that in the clean, safe environs of the Maiden, he might soon get her back in the mood for love.

Chapter 20: Choices

Bernadette used her magic map, and in a few moments she and Erik were standing outside the Bathing Maiden once again. Home sweet home! Right now she felt deeply in need of a soak, and shortly after getting in the front door she stripped down and went into the hot central bathing pool for a dip. Erik stripped and joined her, but he was not the only gorgeous naked stud sharing the water with her. There were a couple of hunky elves, as well as several beautiful, voluptuous young women.

While relaxing in the pool, Bernadette got Erik to give her a shoulder rub. Pulling that bow dozens of times had left her feeling a little sore. Erik found it hard to maintain his composure, touching her as they sat naked in the water; but tiredness from their recent quests and the presence of the others in the pool helped to keep that one-eyed snake under control.

After the hot water had unknotted her muscles and soaked away some of the emotional miasma of the vampire den Bernadette emerged from the tub and, followed by Erik, headed up the stairs to the mezzanine level and the master bedroom. She felt in need of a nap. Erik lay down with her, showing a remarkable degree of restraint. He'd been wanting her all day, but he could see that what she really needed now was sleep.

After a couple of hours Bernadette awoke feeling refreshed – and hungry. There was always plenty of food around the place, and after donning a robe she had shortly satisfied that appetite with some hard crackers and soft cheese, washed down with a bottle of mead that left her feeling both energized and slightly buzzed. Erik had arisen when she did, dressing in casual clothes, and as they sat eating at the table in the master bedroom Andrion came in. Bernadette flew into his arms and gave him an affectionate kiss, then bade him join them at the table so she could relate their adventures.

He knew as soon as he looked at her, somehow, that his fears had been realized: she and Erik had become lovers. Could he get her back? Andrion didn't lack confidence in himself – but Erik was years younger, much closer to Berni's age. And he had the kind of personality that made everyone love him.

Erik had so far not had the opportunity to get Berni into his arms again, and now it was looking as though she might slip completely out of his grasp. He took her aside, standing a few paces from the table. "What now? Are you going back with him?" he asked *sotto voce*.

Bernadette stepped back and looked him in the eyes. "You and Andrion are friends, right?" He nodded. "You've been buddies since before I ever set foot in the Maiden?"

"Uh huh."

"Then what are you worried about? We're *all* friends, and I don't intend to choose between you." Erik was a bit puzzled by this concept, but he was willing to go along with Bernadette's take on the situation.

They poured wine, nibbled on cheese and nuts and discussed everything from the general stupidity and craven nature of bandits to the best techniques for killing dragons. As the evening wore on the three chattered away happily, but there was an undercurrent of tension. Andrion kept capturing Bernadette's eyes for meaningful glances as the hours passed by and other Maiden residents drifted away, off to their beds.

Bernadette sensed his desire, and it echoed her own. They had been apart for a couple of days, and she longed for his embrace. But how to handle this? She didn't want to precipitate a conflict between the two friends. She turned to Erik and looked deep into his summer blue eyes. Then stood and beckoned to Andrion. Taking Erik by the hand, Bernadette pulled him up and then threw an arm around his waist. Andrion stood and she wrapped him in her other arm, so that she was flanked by the two powerful young men.

Bernadette stretched up to plant a deep kiss on Andrion's mouth, then Erik's. Both men were aroused, the more so as they grasped what Berni had in mind. As she turned toward Erik and set about unfastening his clothing, Andrion behind her was untying her robe and sliding it off her shoulders. Then she rotated toward

140

Andrion to begin removing his tunic, while Erik shed his trousers and rubbed up against her from behind.

Erik kissed her firmly yet tenderly on her neck where it joined her shoulder, while his stiffening cock nestled between her buttocks. Bernadette finished stripping Andrion and ran her hands down his chest, grasped his own rising member and stroked it. The three then moved to the bed, where Bernadette knelt in the center with Erik standing on the floor in front of her and Andrion behind.

Bernadette seized Erik's fully erect cock in mouth and one hand, supporting her weight with the other, and began to work him over while Andrion, after assuring himself with a couple of fingers that her cunt was wet and ready, applied the tip of his throbbing rod to her vulva and began working it inside – slowly at first, then faster and deeper until he was plunging inside her to his full, powerful length.

Bernadette gasped and moaned, then used her lips, tongue, and free hand on Erik with even more enthusiasm as Andrion's rock-hard cock sent her into paroxysms of ecstasy. The two friends' eyes met across the back of this woman they were both in thrall to, and a moment of understanding passed between them. However they had to do it, they were both going to have her – and that was all that really mattered.

Bernadette was overwhelmed by sensation, sandwiched between her two lovers. For them, the unusual situation was both exciting and a little off-putting… just enough to keep them on the edge for a while, so that it took longer than it might otherwise have for them to come. Then as Bernadette rocked and spasmed in the throes of a massive orgasm Erik spurted all over her face, and the combined sights and feelings sent Andrion over the edge as well.

Bernadette collapsed face-down across the bed for a moment, panting. Then Erik handed her a towel, and she sat to get cleaned up a bit. The two men joined her on the bed, and they lay there flanking her as the three of them drifted off into exhausted sleep.

In the morning, Bernadette awoke before Erik and Andrion did and admired them, sleeping on either side of her. Her two titans. They shared a basic sweetness of nature at odds with their deadly combat capabilities and fierceness in battle. Should she take both of them questing? It was a thought. But on further consideration she concluded that the three of them would be tripping over one another in tight dungeon corridors, and she'd be unable to loose arrows for fear of hitting them as they rushed into the fray. Better bring only one along at a time.

Bernadette turned to Andrion and nuzzled him in the neck. His warm tan skin smelled of sex and perspiration, not unpleasant but... she murmured in his ear, "You could use a bath."

He woke with a slight smile and said sleepily, "How can I argue with that?" Rolling out of bed he padded sleepily downstairs to use the Maiden's bathing pool, grabbing a robe on the way.

Now she turned to Erik. "Good morning, sweetie." She kissed him gently but firmly. First thing in the morning wasn't her best time for passion. He, of course, was stiffening already but a lot of that was just the need to get up and take a piss. She stroked his face. "Erik, I want you to stay here at the Maiden for a while. I have some things to do." He looked disappointed, but his usual sunny disposition soon reasserted itself.

When they were both out of bed, Bernadette threw on a robe and then took Erik down the hall and introduced him to Lifa. If anybody could crack that woman's stern façade, it was this godlike young warrior with his angelic face and sweet disposition. Lifa was a bit humorless, but she was also stunningly beautiful and built like a goddess. Bernadette could see Erik appreciating those enormous breasts and rounded backside, and felt sure that he would not be suffering in loneliness while she was gone.

Bernadette headed downstairs to join Andrion in the pool. "I told Erik to stay here for a while," she told him. "I think you and I should go investigate the possible dragon spell that Aethelred told us about." He smiled warmly. "I wish I had some better armor for us, honey," she mused. "All three of us. But if you want the good stuff, you've got to go steal it from the bad guys." Bernadette frowned, then shrugged. "Maybe we'll run across a few bandits along the way." Bandits, she was coming to learn, always offered the best loot for the least amount of effort.

Chapter 21: The Westmarch Road

After she and Andrion were dressed and equipped, and had had some breakfast, Bernadette studied her map. The spot Aethelred had marked was far to the west, and there were few other landmarks. Almost all the way to the map's western border a city was shown, Alfenstein – where she needed to go to collect the bounty for ridding that mine near Underhill of bandits.

But they couldn't fast-travel there until they'd gotten there the hard way first. Seemingly, the closest fast-travel point for them was Floradel, the village where she and her fellow wagon riders had stayed the first night out of Underhill. Then they would have to backtrack to the east quite a few miles. A pity the map wouldn't take you to anywhere you'd passed through before, whether there'd been any landmarks or not.

"Looks like we've got bit of a walk ahead of us, love," Bernadette remarked as she wished them to their jumping-off point. Instead of entering the village from the point along the road where its one street led off, they immediately turned to their right and began heading east.

The weather was fine, and Bernadette was enjoying herself as she and Andrion went along the road at a slow jog. Within an hour they spied stone battlements rising above the road to their left. Another bandit lair? Bernadette crept forward carefully, staying close to a dirt and stone embankment on the opposite side of the road, trying to avoid notice.

As the two companions crept closer they could see no sign of enemies on the battlements to their north. "What do you think, love?" Bernadette asked, gesturing at the stone fortifications. "Shall we see who's there?" She was thinking of her resolve to score some useful loot while they were on this trip.

"Could be bandits," he replied, gazing up at the seemingly deserted walls. "Let's go investigate."

There did not seem to be any gates on this side, not that they wanted to stroll in through the main entrance in any case. While looking for a way up the hillside that might lead to an opening of some kind, Bernadette and Andrion found a cave entrance hidden in the rocks. Weapons and battle spells at the ready, the pair crept inside. But the opening led only to a medium-sized cave, floored by natural stone, with a hole in the ceiling.

The body of an armored uruk lay on the floor in a pool of drying blood. He'd been there for a while, it seemed. Tossed down here through that hole? There was little else to be found here, and they soon returned the way they had come. Bernadette spotted a trail of sorts winding up between the main fortress and an isolated tower at its east end.

The companions first searched the tower from bottom to top, finding much evidence of habitation but no people at all – hostile or otherwise. After leaving the tower again and continuing uphill, they rounded another tower and found themselves approaching a pair of wooden gates, standing open. Bernadette and Andrion tiptoed inside to find a courtyard, with buildings on either hand and stairs leading down to their right toward the main body of the fortress.

Andrion touched Bernadette on the arm, and wordlessly pointed to a male figure that could just be seen up a flight of stairs ahead of them, evidently on watch. He certainly wasn't much of a sentry, if he'd failed to take note of them coming up the road right in front of him.

Bernadette nocked an arrow, one of the ancient Norse ones she'd collected in Grabentief, and took him down with a single shot right between the shoulder blades. No alarm was raised. Now… she moved stealthily forward and peered around a stone corner. At the bottom of the steps leading down on their right, stood something man-shaped. But it definitely was *not* human.

As she'd feared, a single shot from hiding wasn't enough to bring this one down. It immediately swarmed up the stairs and began rushing toward them, croaking in some strange language. Bernadette put two more arrows into it, backpedaling frantically, after which Andrion sent it flying with a sizzling bolt of lightning shot from his hands. Just as the creature fell, Bernadette came under attack from a ferocious young woman dressed in skimpy furs, wearing war paint, and wielding a "sword" that appeared to be made out of wood, feathers, and animal teeth.

Bernadette flung her assailant back down the stairs with her Gale dragon spell, a weapon in her arsenal she was really beginning to appreciate. Too bad it required the better part of a full minute's rest before the stone would recharge. Meanwhile, all hell had broken loose around them and Andrion was busy fighting two foes at once, human men dressed and armed similarly to the woman she had just hurled across the courtyard. Bernadette wanted to come to her lover's aid, but first she put two or three more arrows into the female savage, eliminating her as a threat.

Andrion scarcely needed her help, Bernadette realized as she turned around and found the fortress silent once more. Three or four additional bodies were now scattered around. All of them were dressed in furs and feathers, their weapons looking homemade. Studying one of them as she ransacked his corpse for valuables (of which there were few), Bernadette remarked "I don't think these are bandits."

"No," he replied. "They're Insurgents. Rebels." Bernadette pondered that.

"You mean like the Norse partisans?" she asked.

Andrion responded, "No, these fight *everybody* in Westmarch – Norse partisans, Remans, you name it. I should have suspected we'd be running into them, this far west. Some call them 'The Lunatics of Westmarch,' because they seem crazy to the rest of us. They practice some kind of hedge magic. Nasty stuff."

"Oh," Bernadette responded, thoughtful. One more thing to watch out for, in this perilous land. She looked about her, and realized that dusk was falling. "Let's check the rest of these buildings, love. Then I think we'd better camp here for the night." She studied her map, and found that the place they were standing in was called Fort Weston.

Not for the first time, Bernadette wondered what the Remans were playing at. With a little effort and the mighty resources of the empire, this place could be turned into a real stronghold and manned by Reman troops to keep order in the region. Instead, like most such places she had visited in Iscandia, it was left to fall into ruin and become a refuge for human predators.

Bernadette and Andrion combed the stronghold from one end to the other, finding a dining hall, dormitories, and some food stores but little of any monetary value. Down in the dungeons, there were empty jail cells. They took a meal in the dining hall, mixing up a sort of soup from their trail rations and some potatoes and carrots that they found in one of the storerooms.

After their supper Bernadette and Andrion pulled up a bench and sat pressed against each other, talking quietly in front of the fire. "I'm so glad to have you along, love" she said softly. "If you hadn't stopped four of those Insurgents while I was busy, I'd have been toast."

"You're becoming pretty dangerous yourself, Berni," he replied. "Remind me not to make you angry." (Again, was the unspoken thought.) Their rift mostly put behind them, they felt their bond growing stronger again – if perhaps there had been a shift in their relationship.

The two sipped bottles of mead plundered from the Insurgents' pantries, and after a while they began kissing. As powerful and exciting as their lovemaking could be, they found they also enjoyed just kissing and stroking each other. This went on for a long time, with occasional breaks for quiet talk. But Bernadette's hunger had become aroused, and she finally said "Want to see if there's a captain's quarters?"

They did a little more exploring, and sure enough the complex held more than narrow bunks for soldiers. There was a broad bed in a decent bedchamber, with nightstands and a wardrobe nearby. Stripping down, Bernadette and Andrion engaged in a long full-body hug, pressing their flesh together. The room had its own fireplace, and was comfortable enough even without clothing.

Next Bernadette sat on the edge of the bed and Andrion knelt before her, at a height with her in this juxtaposition. They resumed their necking for a while, but with more stroking and fondling now they were both naked. He massaged and kissed her breasts, licking and suckling her nipples, and put two fingers of his right hand into his mouth before moving them to her soft slit and working them inside. She gasped and grabbed his stiff member, squeezing it firmly as his fingers moved within her.

"Oh, hell" Bernadette murmured, gently pulling his fingers away from her and guiding his cock into their place. He teased at the opening, letting it slide in just enough for the knob to clear the entrance, then rubbing it back and forth in small movements before pulling *almost* all the way out again. Next time, he went a little deeper as she moaned in delight and her breathing came faster and faster.

Finally he pushed all the way in, and began giving her full strokes with his hot, steely member dipping its full length in and out each time. Bernadette cried out, pulling him to her, and put her ankles up on his shoulders so that her cunt was fully open to him and he could push in even deeper. With an animal growl, he began pumping faster and faster, pushing in so hard on the down-stroke it almost seemed like he was trying to crawl all the way inside. His cock was bouncing off her cervix with every plunge, and she was screaming in one long high-pitched ululation as he spasmed and shot his seed deep, deep inside her.

As she clutched him to her and tried to get her breath back, Bernadette thought, Thank the gods for that amulet! Aloud she said, in a voice that was quavering from exhaustion, "I'm surprised I don't have your cum dribbling out of my mouth. That felt like you shot straight through me." Andrion just grinned, panting, and kissed her. She dropped her ankles down and still lay beneath him, recovering her strength, until he softened and slipped out. Then they crawled higher up the bed and curled up, ready to sleep.

Chapter 22: Siegfell

In the morning almost as soon as they awoke, Bernadette was in Quest Mode. It appeared she was out of synch with much of the male population in this, as Andrion was arisen in more ways than one and would have been quite happy to dally for another hour or more before getting on the road. Shortly, though, she had them out of bed, dressed, fed, and moving.

Before they had traveled very much further beyond Fort Weston, the pair came on a pretty little river cutting its way through a fairly steep gorge. The area of the river canyon was rife with scrubby little trees, which Bernadette identified as manzanita. She hadn't seen them anywhere else in Iscandia, and took a few moments as they came upon each one to harvest some of their berries. These were a valuable ingredient in chemia, and she wasn't sure when she would have this opportunity again.

According to the map they needed to cross the river here. There was a clearly defined trail climbing the hill on the far side of the stream, and Bernadette was somewhat surprised there was not a bridge to cross on. But one must make do. As the stone-paved road continued to the west, they picked their way over moss-covered stones and then forded a stretch of clear running water no more than two paces across, heading south.

Climbing the hill on the far side, Bernadette soon spotted a white blob that resolved itself into an attacking snow cat. This close relative of the familiar smilodon was as large and as fierce, and she was glad of Andrion's assistance in stopping it before it got its claws into her – after two of her arrows had failed to halt its charge. She skinned it and took its eyes, yet another ingredient for chemia. If I were going to go in fur like those Insurgent women, Bernadette thought, this is the fur to use. It was beautiful, almost pure white with a few small spots, thick and silky.

They mounted the hillside and proceeded up the trail, which wound among rocks and more of the small juniper trees. In order to make any speed Bernadette needed to walk at a normal pace, bow at the ready but not creeping along. Yet she found herself dropping to a crouch over and over again as one peril after another presented itself. A few minutes along she heard the unmistakable sounds of a bear growling – and ahead, she saw four men in unfamiliar armor confronting the beast.

Bernadette didn't think they were bandits or Insurgents, so she took a chance that they were friendlies (as unlikely as *that* seemed, given how it appeared that every hand was turned against them in Iscandia's hinterlands). Once the bear had been dispatched, Bernadette slung her bow behind her back to show her benign intentions and approached the man who seemed to be the leader of the party.

He was a youngish fellow who might have been handsome, with dark hair and curiously light blue eyes, if his face had not been so smudged with dirt. His name was Stavos, he said, and after observing her prowess in helping them to kill the bear he urged her to come to Ynglingar and join the Brave Company. Oh, *those* guys. Joining that band had been her dearest ambition for years, before she came to Iscandia. But if she were ever to join them now, that day was still far in the future.

Bernadette and Andrion continued up the hillside while the party of Companions continued searching the area where the bear had attacked. They were evidently looking for something, but she didn't try to pry into their business. The trail they climbed took another couple of bends, and they found themselves standing before an ominous-looking cave opening. Bernadette checked the map, and discovered that they were looking at the entrance to Grimbore.

It lost her at the name, not that Bernadette was planning on taking a major detour at this point in any case. Some oddly-ornamented stakes driven into the soft earth on either side of the yawning cave mouth suggested occupation by the sort of people (or *things*) that would not welcome their visit; and the two pushed on up the trail. A few more bends, and they came upon a substantial wooden stockade.

As they approached this, following the broad and well-beaten trail, a figure atop a platform behind the vertical wall of sharpened stakes warned her away. He addressed Bernadette: "Hail, outlander. By the Code of the Verdalfar, this stronghold belongs to the uruks. Your kind are not permitted to enter here." Ah, she thought. The Verdalfar or green elves, less human-looking than any of the other elven races she'd seen so far, evidently kept to themselves in this province so far from their homeland. Yet she'd encountered many of them out and about in the world – merchants, adventurers, bandits. What would it take to get them to welcome her as a visitor?

Finally, an opportunity to learn more about this fierce, clannish people! "I'm just a traveler and intend no harm," Bernadette replied. "Do you not allow others to come in and trade?" The uruk atop the walls answered back "You're not an uruk, or an uruk-friend, so stay out. We only welcome our own." Despite the unfriendly tone, Bernadette sensed that there was no finality in the uruk sentry's words. "How could I become an uruk-friend?" she asked. "You would need to perform a service for the uruks," came the reply.

Bernadette was always anxious to make friends, especially as she was just starting out her career in a new land full of many different sorts of people. But she could scarcely drop what she was doing (including, trying to learn how to stop the end of the world) right this moment. "Thanks for the information," she called back, as she and Andrion continued on their way. "Another time, perhaps."

They filed between steep rocky hillsides, then the trail opened out and Bernadette spotted some ruins that had an architectural style she did not recall seeing before. "What do you suppose that is?" she asked Andrion. "It looks like a dypalfar ruin," he replied. After observing her blank look he continued: "The dypalfar were a race of elves, supposedly. They were big on underground cities filled with machines, and some of those machines are still running deep in the bowels of those cities. Nobody's seen a living member of the tribe for thousands of years, but you'll find their ruins all over Iscandia. There's nothing alive down there but leukalfar and mandimants, for the most part."

Bernadette stepped close to him and gently took his arm. "Leukalfar?" He rolled his eyes. "I keep forgetting you just came in on the turnip wagon," he said with a sly grin, then executed a surprisingly agile move that took him out of the range of her swift strike. While Bernadette glared at him, he went on: "Leukalfar means 'white elves.' But today's look little like the other elven races. They're ugly as sin and don't have any eyes, and they like to live down in the dark places. They use a lot of poisons, so you really have to watch out for them. Mandimants are black or sometimes red eight-legged critters, maybe the size of a mastiff, and they can shoot poison at you from a distance. The leukalfar tend them like livestock, and they use the mandimants' chitin in their weapons and armor."

Bernadette had ceased her attempts at mayhem and apparently abandoned her ire completely, in favor of gaping at Andrion open-mouthed. She stood there staring at him for a heartbeat after he finished talking. Then she blinked, and took a breath. "Whoa," she breathed. "Andrion," she said after another moment, "you never cease to amaze me. On due consideration, I think that now would *not* be the time to explore this oh-so-tempting ruin." And with a sigh and a shrug of her shoulders, she walked on. She did, however, pull out her map for a peek and found that "Gradnezh" had now appeared upon it. Argh, she thought. Never mind going in there to fight automatons, leukalfar, and mandimants – how in all the hells do you even *pronounce* it?

Bernadette's glance at the map had told her that their destination was at hand; and after following the trail for another couple of bends, they found themselves looking upon the ancient Norse barrow of Siegfell. At last! It had been a long journey, and more fraught with peril than with promise; but she hoped that here, at last, they would find something that made the whole trip worthwhile.

Once inside the barrow, they entered a broad room laid out a bit like a crypt. "Looks like it's aptrgangr again," Andrion said. Pushing through the door, the two moved quietly through a maze of corridors – speaking seldom. Their weapons were at the ready and their senses were alert. Bernadette put arrows into several aptrgangr that were motionless, but had enough flesh and armor on them that going on the attack seemed a possibility. Some just lay there and she was able to retrieve her arrows along with oddments of weaponry, armor, or gold from them. Others exploded into flame and collapsed, making her sure that had she tried to sneak past them she and Andrion would have had a fight on their hands.

Not that fights did not come. This tomb was as labyrinthine as any Bernadette had yet visited, sprawling in all directions and with many corridors that split apart then joined again; and some aptrgangr were already on the prowl before they even came close to them. Bernadette found herself growing to hate the sound of shattering stone that announced another of these undead monstrosities had burst from its sarcophagus.

Deep within the tomb's bowels, and beginning to lose track of all the turnings they had taken, Bernadette and Andrion suddenly found themselves confronted by one of the more powerful aptrgangr, shuffling toward them. There seemed to be different ranks, each harder to kill than the last, and identified to some extent by their dress and armament. This ancient undead warrior had not yet spotted them, and Bernadette hit it squarely from hiding with an ancient Norse arrow, the most effective arrows she had in any abundance.

Not good enough! It was staggered, but soon came on again. And behind it came two more! The one at the rear, towering a head higher than the others, appeared even taller still because of the black helmet it wore, surmounted by what appeared to be bull horns forming a circle with a medallion of some kind slung between them. Quite a party hat! "Oh, shit!" Andrion shouted. "It's an Overlord!" Bernadette didn't need another of his scholarly explanations to know this creature was bad news.

Bernadette tucked some health potions into the top of her armor, where she could grab one in a hurry, then began riddling the oncoming undead hostiles with arrows. The enemies had all spotted them by now, and were moving slowly but inexorably toward them with their slightly shuffling gait. Andrion's battle spells worked just fine, and between them they had soon stopped the aptrgangr Bernadette had initially shot. But the other two, including the Overlord, kept coming on.

As it approached it gave an ear-piercing, echoing shriek – which Bernadette now realized was a *furml,* a dragon spell. She had heard this before, from the aptrgangr she and Staeven had defeated in Deadfall Barrow; but at that time she'd known nothing of dragon spells. Studying the dragon magic and their arcane spoken spells must have been more common in the days when these warriors walked the earth as living men and women. Or perhaps, if they were as reported the servants of the dragons, their knowledge had been passed to them directly from the dragons themselves. The revenants were getting closer and closer, and Bernadette used Gale to hurl them back. It scarcely stopped the Overlord for a heartbeat, though the other aptrgangr took longer to get back on its feet.

Bernadette hit the Overlord with several more arrows, but it kept coming on. When it was a few feet away it shouted a spell again, one she didn't know, and her bow flew from her hand, just as Andrion's axe flew from his. This is an advantage of battle magic, the fleeting thought crossed Bernadette's mind even as she grabbed for her mace. You can't be disarmed unless you run out of magical power. Andrion was staggered, and Bernadette was almost driven to her knees by the Overlord's relentless attacks. Her armor was preventing her from being sliced into dog-meat, but it felt as she were being beaten with a hammer.

Bernadette had recouped enough of the stone force needed to use the dragon spell one more time, and as their enemies flew back again Bernadette grabbed Andrion's hand and hauled him to his feet. "Run!" she screamed, and scooped their weapons up off the floor even as they bolted back down the corridor, taking several turnings in hopes of losing the Overlord in the maze. This tactic only bought them enough time to drink a few potions, somewhat restoring their health, stamina, and magical power. Then their implacable enemies were upon them again.

Fortunately, while the Overlord was moving in the right direction, he had not yet spotted them where they hid. Applying some poison to an arrow tip, Bernadette hit him with a shot that staggered him. Before he could get moving again, she hit him three more times; and Andrion's lightning bolts ripped the last of the animating force from his preserved corpse and sent him tumbling along the corridor. His cohort, an aptrgangr of more ordinary type, soon fell beside him.

Andrion's face was contorted in an expression of ferocity, and the whites of his eyes were showing all around the irises as he stood there panting. Bernadette wondered fleetingly if her own face resembled his. She felt slightly weak in the knees, both from recent battle damage and the reaction to the adrenaline surge that had helped to save their lives. Breathing hard, she pulled some more potions out of her pack and shared them with him. Not much point in having them, unless you're going to use them when needed.

They had found many such potions, along with small quantities of gold and other items of value, as they were searching through the rooms and corridors of the barrow for the promised Spell Wall. On the now firmly immobile corpse of the Overlord, they also found some items of sablium armor. This was just the sort of thing Bernadette had been hoping to acquire on this trip, but not at the cost of their lives!

They met still more aptrgangr as they pursued their goal deeper into the labyrinth, but fortunately no more Overlords. They'd also found handfuls of gold, small gems (but not dragon spell stones), even a few minor vials of the magical essence needed for enchanting. All grave goods, for the honored Norse dead.

Finally Bernadette and Andrion spotted the Spell Wall, buried deep within a good-sized cavern. A large and ornately carved chest stood before it, but they first approached the wall. There, an entire line in ancient runes glowed with blue fire. Bernadette heard that unearthly chorus ringing in her ears and she realized that the entire Finder spell – all four words of it – had embedded itself in her brain along with the understanding of its power. Spoken quietly,

Finder would fly gently out to reveal any life sources in the area by causing them to glow in the spell caster's vision. Very useful if you're sneaking into a dark cave that may or may not be full of enemies, she thought. Though it didn't seem likely to be all that much help against dragons. The creatures, in her experience so far, did *not* sneak up on you.

Andrion was eyeing her curiously. "Did you hear the singing?" she asked him. The sense of exaltation that accompanied the acquisition of a spell word, or the absorption of a dragon's soul and life energy, seemed to suggest it might be something only a Fireblood would be aware of.

Her theory was confirmed when he looked at her blankly and said "Singing? Nope. Did you get a spell?"

"Yes, one that lets you detect living creatures in your environment," Bernadette replied. "From what Aethelred told me the fact that it lit up for me must mean we'll find the gem for that spell somewhere close by."

"Oh," Andrion replied matter-of-factly. "There's a regular spell that will do that. I don't know it, since I mostly studied battle magic. But we could probably buy a spell book to learn it."

Bernadette thrust her lower lip out sulkily and glared at him. "That's right," she pouted. "spoil my fun after we nearly got killed coming down here."

"Sorry," he said with that half-smile that made her heart race every time she saw it. "The Gale spell and the Stasis one are like nothing I've ever heard about. I'm just surprised to find out that not all the dragon spells are unique."

She smiled back at him, and set to rummaging in the chest – so large she could have curled up inside it for a nap. Ooh, there was some nice armor and some pretty good ancient weapons in here. The cool, dry underground environment seemed to preserve things as if they were new. Even the aptrgangr, who'd presumably died millennia ago, still mostly had flesh and the remains of armor and clothing on them.

They had to take everything out of the chest to get to the bottom of it. Gems, being small, always ended up beneath anything else. Wow, there were a lot of them! One Bernadette realized was a flawless garnet, deep red and quite pretty but hardly valuable. Another was an emerald. But there were three that looked like dragon spell stones, and she gingerly picked them up one by one starting with the one that looked least familiar.

It was a very pale yellow like a citrine, but seemed to be glowing faintly with its own internal light. And when she held it in her palm it seemed to melt into the skin, becoming one with her body. Bernadette felt a surge as its power came on line. "Leb-Such-Jag-Fun," she murmured quietly, and a tiny glowing comet trail wound its way out from her fingers and looped its way to Andrion. He took on an unearthly glow.

"That one was Finder," she told him with a gentle smile. "But what are these others? Shouldn't the wall have lit up for whatever gems were here?"

"Go ahead and pick one up," Andrion told her. "I have an idea about that." She selected the orange one, the one that looked just like the stone for Stasis. It remained in her palm, curiously warm. But it stayed a hard gem, not melting into her flesh.

Their eyes met, and they said in unison, "One's the limit!"

"Of course," Bernadette went on, her mind racing to form a clear picture. "Every dragon that learned the spell would form its own gem to power the spell. So when there were lots of dragons, there were lots of multiple copies of the gems for each spell. But the gems last forever, so there's no point in you having more than one copy for a particular spell inside your own body."

Andrion gave her a look of fond appreciation. As sexy and beguiling as his lady-love was, he was truly coming to love her for her mind. "I'll bet these are valuable!" Bernadette went on, still working out all the implications. "Even if there aren't any other Firebloods to absorb them, people who were taught to use the spells by the Old Ones' founder could still use them to fuel the spells. I suppose that would be the equivalent of adding vials of magical essence to recharge enchanted weapons. Cool!"

She scooped up the last one, blue like a sapphire, and it too remained solid. "This one has to be another stone for Gale,"

Bernadette said confidently. "Next time we're up at Eberburg I'll have to ask Aethelred if he has something like an illustrated chart. It would sure save a lot of time and trouble while I'm looking for spells that can help us defeat the dragons."

"Considering how widely respected the Old Ones are in Iscandia," Andrion remarked as they began looking for the exit, "they didn't seem all that eager to help you fulfill your supposed destiny. I hope they know what they're doing."

"Me too," she remarked as they wound their way back to where they'd come in. These ancient Norse barrows, she was coming to find, usually had a shortcut to let you back out once you'd reached the center. "And why didn't that Spell Wall in Deadfall Barrow give me the whole spell instead of just the first word?"

Andrion gave her an amused glance. "Maybe it was being gentle with you because it was your first time," he suggested. Absorbing all four words just now *had* been a little intense.

The pair stepped into a rainy evening outside Siegfell's main gates, but they were only there for moments before Bernadette had them materializing outside the Bathing Maiden. Despite their ordeal, the potions she had ingested had left her feeling pretty good. They had gotten what they'd come for and a lot of loot as well, and they were alive. With that and the resilience of youth Bernadette felt amazingly energized. But grubby.

"A bath sounds good to me," Andrion replied to her suggestion, and they both dropped their things on a nearby table and were soon naked and soaking in the wonderfully hot water of the main floor's central bathing pool – the very spot where they'd met, not so long ago. The potions had done their work on him as well, and his smooth skin was unmarked though there were traces of dried blood. But he had a decade on her, and it appeared the hot soak was putting him to sleep.

Andrion shook himself awake after almost nodding off in the water, and told Bernadette "I'm going upstairs for a nap. I'll see you later." He gave her a squeeze and a quick kiss, then grabbed a towel and padded off. She sighed, watching him out of sight. The hot water was having the opposite effect on her. After sitting and soaking for a while, and playing with herself a little, she got out and toweled off at poolside, then got her robe out of her pack.

Bernadette carried it upstairs and spotted Andrion dead to the world, sacked out on one of the single beds in the sleeping loft. Then she went looking for Erik. She found him sitting at the table in the master bed area, dressed in casual clothing and having a light snack. He looked up with surprise and pleasure and stood. "Berni! It's good to see you."

"Hi, sweetie. Did you and Lifa have a nice time while I was gone?" she teased.

Erik's perfect golden features suffused with pink. "Um, yeah, it was OK," he stammered. "But she's no you," he added.

"You've got *that* right," Bernadette said grinning. Then she leapt at him like a cat, throwing her arms around his neck and her legs around his hips and planting a deep soul kiss on his lips. "Did you miss me? Huh? Oooh, I think you missed me!" she crowed as she felt his manhood stirring to rigidity beneath his trousers.

Bernadette dropped to the floor and helped him pull his tunic off over his head. Then she planted both hands on his hard-muscled chest and shoved, walking into him, until the backs of his knees connected with the edge of the nearby bed and he fell over onto his back. He was not putting up much resistance. She climbed onto the bed herself and straddled him momentarily, grinding her crotch into his, as she kissed him again. Then she sat up and pulled her robe off. She was naked underneath, glowing pink from the recent bath.

Bernadette climbed off of Erik again and stood at the bedside while he lay there drinking her in, as she unfastened his trousers and pulled them down past his buttocks and halfway down his thighs. His cock sprang free, and she paused to give it a few strokes and a lick or two until the head was swollen, pink, and glistening. Then she pulled his trousers the rest of the way off before straddling him once again, reaching down to apply a little spit to her vaginal opening before spearing herself on his massive cock and slooowwwly working herself down over it. He was watching all this, flushed, his warm blue eyes dilated with desire, and when she had completely engulfed him he gave a low, gruff moan. "Oh, Berni! I *did* miss you…"

Bernadette leered down at him, savoring the fullness of his stiff cock filling up her cunt, along with his expression of being transported beyond the power of thought or conscious action. "Now I have you just where I want you!" she purred. But a moment later he surprised her. Reaching up and clutching her to his chest, he writhed in the bed and flipped them both over in one smooth movement that found her lying supine while he rode above her, his powerful cock thrusting into her as she lay there helpless beneath him.

Not that Bernadette minded! Perhaps her assessment of this blond godling as all primal energy and no finesse was mistaken. He challenged her assumptions further by slowing his powerful thrusts, changing from a rhythm that was likely to send them both over the edge in moments to one that tantalized, bringing her ever so slowly toward a mind-blowing climax. She had been playing with him, passing him off to her voluptuous but chilly and inflexible body servant; and now he was playing with her – withholding the surge of sexual energy she knew was coming, letting the sensations build.

Erik pressed his body against hers and kissed her deeply, tenderly yet passionately. The sensation of his mouth on hers and his tongue within her combined with the overwhelming heat of the pulsations as his enormous cock slid slowly, teasingly in and then out of her yearning cunt. Bernadette was transported, feeling as if she had gone to some other plane of existence where time was meaningless and the only thing that mattered was the feelings in her fingertips, her mouth, her inner core.

Then Erik changed it up again, using the immense strength of his powerful young body to bend Bernadette to his will. Without removing his cock from her cunt, he gently pulled her right leg up, toward her shoulder, and over so that he could rotate her beneath him. Now he was fucking her from behind, and he pulled her up onto her knees so that he could kneel behind her and thrust into her like a dog. And she felt like a bitch in heat!

Yes! Yes! His thrusts came faster and her mind went white and red. His cock was glistening in the dim light, pounding repeatedly into the incredibly warm and slippery depths of her pulsating sex. They both reached a blinding climax and continued thrusting together and quivering, with decreasing pace, for a few moments afterward. Holy gods! Bernadette thought she would drop on the spot, poleaxed by the power of Erik's raw sexuality and the force of her response to it.

They remained locked together for a while, then gradually came to their senses. Bernadette felt shaken. For the moment, Erik eclipsed her universe. But as she lay there panting, nestled in his arms, it came to her that she had other considerations. Which could reasonably be put off until after they had both had some sleep. *Now* she was tired.

They dozed, snuggled together in a heap, for a couple of hours. Then Bernadette awoke and kissed Erik on the ear. He stirred, but seemed disinclined to wake fully. She slipped out of bed, still naked, and tiptoed down the hall to where she'd seen Andrion sleeping. He was still there, seemingly out like a light, and by now it was late enough that most of the Maiden residents and guests were sleeping too. Bernadette slipped into the narrow bed beside him, pressing her warm naked flesh up against his. He took a deep, sighing breath and, without opening his eyes, rolled over and reached to enfold her in a hug. Andrion sleepily kissed her hair, squeezing her close. Then he dropped back off to sleep and she soon fell asleep in his arms.

Chapter 23: The Ljosalfar

Bernadette awoke in the early morning, still happily wrapped in Andrion's warm embrace. As her conscious mind asserted itself she first thought, "This is bliss." Followed a moment or two later, as her list of worldly concerns began to clamor for attention, with "I've got to stay strong." Andrion was nearly half again her age, superb in every way, and the urge to just melt into his arms and give up all that was herself in exchange for the comfort and security of his love was a definite temptation. But would he want her, stripped of the indomitable will that made her uniquely herself? Bernadette doubted it. Nor would she want to become that person, the pampered and helpless pet of a commanding and powerful man.

No denying, Bernadette loved him. And no denying, she also felt a nearly irresistible attraction, and growing love, toward Erik. In addition to which she was, still, quite likely to get distracted by any other sufficiently attractive man that crossed her field of vision. Emotional connections were one thing, and they were important. But her libido seemed to have a mind of its own, and it wanted them *all.* What was she to do? At the moment, Bernadette thought lazily, "go with the flow" seemed like a good motto. In any case, she was pretty sure she wanted to take Erik along on the expedition she planned next.

"Good morning, love" Bernadette murmured softly to Andrion as he stirred and opened those melting brown eyes. He seemed a little confused, still too sleepy to recall all that had gone on in the last few hours.

"You're here," he breathed. "I thought… never mind." He squeezed her tighter and kissed the side of her face, radiating a deep affection, a wave of warmth that flooded her heart.

Bernadette reasserted herself, pulling away from a little. "But I'm about to run off again," she said.

His eyebrows knitted briefly. "Oh?"

"I'm going to take Erik down to Forestville," she said, "and see if Giselle has figured out a way to find out if the ljosalfar are behind the dragon resurrections. I should be back in a few days, and I'll take *you* with me then." He was blissfully unaware of her soul-shaking liaison with his friend the night before, and she thought it best if it stayed that way. Juggling these two was more work than she'd hoped, but it certainly seemed worth the effort.

They both arose and Bernadette gave Andrion a hug and a deep kiss. "See you soon," she said a bit wistfully. Then she headed for the far end of the mezzanine and the master bedroom. She found Erik up and getting dressed.

"Where'd you go?" he asked, giving her a bear hug with an undercurrent of lust in it. He might feel affection for her, but Bernadette suspected that Erik's desire for her was the driving factor in their relationship to date. And hers for him. Gods, he was so unbelievably sexy!

"I want you to come with me to Forestville," Bernadette told him. "There's a woman there Andrion and I met a while ago, who thinks that the ljosalfar are behind the reappearance of the dragons. While we were down near Delvewood we actually saw what looked like an elder dragon calling a dead one out of its tomb."

"Like aptrgangr?" Erik asked. "Not the same…" she mused. "Aptrgangr are obviously animated corpses. After this dragon came out of its burial site as a skeleton, it grew flesh and looked just like a regular living dragon. Then we killed it again and I captured its soul."

"You captured… its soul?" he asked, disbelieving. While Andrion had told him that their lady-love was The Fireblood, Erik had not witnessed this for himself as yet. Bernadette was thinking to herself, "Why haven't I brought Erik up to speed?" She felt as if she might be unfairly discounting him again. With his amazingly graceful, muscular bulk and dominating abilities in battle, it was easy to assume that his intellect wasn't up to the challenges of problem-solving, or that it wasn't necessary to give him details.

Making up for past omissions, Bernadette did a short-form recap in which she explained the nature of her relationship with dragons, recounted her dealings with Giselle, told Erik of the history of the Guardians, and explained the likelihood that she would be called on to infiltrate the ljosalfar consulate, up north

162

near Sylvanian. "You might not have much to do, but I'd really appreciate having you along," she said.

"Any time you want me, Berni" he proclaimed in his deep voice, "I'm your man." One of them anyhow, she thought, as she gave him a smile and squeezed his bicep.

"C'mon," she told him, "let's see what I can do for you in the smithy." They headed down the stairs, waving to Andrion as he was getting dressed, and down the back-bar trap door to the basement. Bernadette was beginning to feel as though her abilities in smithing were really taking off, and she was anxious for more practice and improvement. She and Andrion had liberated some fine pieces of weaponry and armor on their most recent quest, and she now set about improving them.

Bernadette had found a complete suit of elven armor, made of a lightweight metal with a silvery glimmer, down in the depths of that most recent Norse barrow. It had been made for someone bigger than she, but she was able to refit it for herself and reinforce it to give it a little more stopping power. This stuff was great! It was good-looking, lightweight, and protective – as strong as the steel armor she'd gotten from the eorl, but half the weight.

Wishing she had more of these spells in her repertoire, Bernadette put enchantments for health, stealth, magical power, and stamina on her newly acquired set of armor. She also improved and refitted a set of dypalfar armor she'd found on her travels, and enchanted it with enhanced health before giving it to Erik to protect him. He looked as she imagined one of those dypalfar automatons Andrion had told her of might appear: a gleaming, golden-metal embodiment of masculine power. Bernadette added an enchanted sablium warhammer to his arsenal before they departed via a second trap door leading directly to the Maiden's handsome rear deck.

Armed and armored to the teeth, the two soon had a walk of a little over two hours to Forestville. Bernadette led Erik down the dirt main street to the Laughing Herdsman Inn, and they entered. She found Giselle, still dressed as she had last seen her, seated at a table in the inn's common room.

"You're here," Giselle remarked. "Come with me." She led them down to her secret room in the inn's basement. "I've worked out a plan. The ljosalfar consul likes to throw parties, intended for public relations. He, the consul Dularion, thinks that if they lay on the food and drink for the prominent Iscandians they'll look more favorably on the Ljosalfar Union."

Bernadette attempted not to look impatient while waiting for the point to arrive. She was a young Galise who'd been in the province for less than three weeks, not a prominent Iscandian likely to be invited to such an affair. "I have an agent, a sylvalfar man named Lorien, who knows the place inside out. He tells me that during their bashes most of the security is concentrated around the front side, and the areas where party guests are allowed. They don't trust their invitees, and I can't say I blame them. There's still a lot of resentment against the ljosalfar throughout the empire, but especially here in Iscandia."

"So," Bernadette said, abandoning her silent wait for information. "How am I to get in there? I imagine I'd need to get into the offices, the places where the consul and his staff are actually working their little plots. Am I right?"

Giselle look a little annoyed, but pushed on. "Lorien knows an unguarded way in through the consulate's basement," she said. "You need to get up to Sylvanian as soon as possible, because there's a party tomorrow night. He'll take you around the back and show you the way in, but it'll be up to you to sneak in there and find the proof we're looking for. And it needs to be done quietly! If you get caught, or kill anyone, we're screwed. Understand?"

The woman's tone and attitude irritated Bernadette. Weren't the Guardians (who, as much as she could tell so far, consisted of this one woman with an obsessive suspicion of the ljosalfar) supposed to "serve The Fireblood"? But the ljosalfar had probably wiped out a lot of Giselle's friends and companions, and she was at least twice The Fireblood's age. Maybe she figured it was on her to give orders and the talent to obey them.

Giselle replied, "You'll meet with Lorien at the Dancing Rabbit in Sylvanian. He'll help you any way he can. The ljosalfar killed his family back in Alvenwald, so he's got plenty of reasons to work against them." Bernadette remembered the Dancing Rabbit. It was the only inn she'd seen in Sylvanian, the first building after you stepped inside the main gates. What an odd name. She suspected that the story of the place's origins was probably going to involve alcohol.

Acting the good little subordinate Bernadette replied, "I'll be there shortly." It was fortunate that she, Andrion, and Lifa had taken the time to go to Sylvanian earlier. Now returning was as simple as a touch of the map and a firm desire. They had until tomorrow evening, but it might be a good idea to be there a few hours ahead of schedule. There could be preparations she needed to make.

On leaving the inn, Bernadette pulled out her map. Moments later she and Erik found themselves standing just inside the gates of Sylvanian in what appeared to be the middle of the night. She was starting to notice that traveling by map seemed to take longer than the few seconds it appeared to – but was it random, or was there some correlation? She had still not had much of an opportunity to take in the sights here, but it appeared that now was not the time to begin.

Bernadette led the way into the inn, which she had not so much as poked her nose into on her previous visit. She strolled up to the bar, Erik trailing, and asked the barkeep "Do you have the time?" Inns were among the few places in Iscandia where one might find a clock. "It's two in the morning," he told her. "You want a room?" Her eyes darted around the place, looking for anybody that might be their contact. There was almost no one in the common room at this late hour, and certainly no elves. "Yes please," she told him, and handed over the five guilders he requested.

They were shown to the room, a fairly spacious one on the upper floor, and after the innkeeper had returned to his station Bernadette and Erik dropped their packs on the floor. They'd brought along a fair amount of equipment and clothing, not knowing what they might be expected to do after talking with

Giselle. "Looks like we might as well catch a little sleep, honey," she told him with a smile.

"Sleep?" he rumbled, stepping close to take her in his arms. "Can't you think of any other way to pass the time?"

They slept in a little the next morning, figuring they would have hours to fill before the mission tonight. But Bernadette drew the line at making love again before getting out of bed. She'd been well-sated before sleeping, and she was eager for a chance to spend a few hours exploring Sylvanian. Erik took her refusal of his advances with good grace. They'd have at least another night here together – plenty of time.

Emerging dressed in town clothing, the two went downstairs and got some hot tea and a plate of pastries to eat. As they sat finishing their breakfast, a wood elf came in the door and took a seat nearby. Bernadette was up like a shot and walked over to his table, after checking to make sure that no one was watching them.

"Lorien?" she asked.

He eyed her questioningly, then said quietly, "You must be Bernadette." She took the other seat at his table, as Erik came over to stand beside her. He favored the elf with a neutral gaze. Lorien glanced surreptitiously around, also making sure they were not observed, then spoke in an undertone. "Glad you're here early," he said. "If you hadn't made it by today we'd have had to wait weeks for another opportunity. Did Giselle tell you the plan?"

Bernadette nodded, and answered him as quietly. "I'm to sneak in through the consulate's basement area, and look for evidence about a connection between the ljosalfar and the dragons without setting off any alarms."

"That's right," he said. "Your buddy here looks like a mauler, but I think he'd better stay behind. He's too big, too conspicuous." Erik looked disappointed. But he'd had an idea, as soon as Giselle had said this was a stealth mission, that he was not going to be ideally suited for the job.

"I've got street clothes and armor," Bernadette mused, "but this sounds like a job for burglar gear. Do you know where I can get some?" Lorien's face brightened. "Good idea," he said. "I know somebody who can probably come up with something. Probably even enchanted to make you silent and harder to see. You have some coin?" So now she wasn't just putting her life on the line for the cause, she was supposed to contribute her gold as well? Giselle owned an inn, though. Maybe she could get reimbursed for expenses.

"How much do you need?" she asked, and the elf waved her away.

"I'll get the stuff, and you can pay me later," he said. "I've got lots of connections in this town." After a moment he added. "You any good at picking locks?" Bernadette smirked. She pulled a handful of picks out of a pocket of her tunic and showed them to Lorien.

"A hobby I picked up in my misspent youth," she confessed. Teenaged Bernadette had taught herself to pick locks, mainly because it was a skill she figured she would need when she was questing in ancient tombs for treasure looked up in massive wooden chests. In Pied de Puce, nobody even locked their doors.

The elf smiled at that, then looked serious again. "You are going to need some weapons, though. It'd be a lot better if you can get in and out of the consulate without anyone knowing you were even there, but you'll need to protect yourself. Getting caught would be bad, but getting killed would be worse."

"I have a pretty decent elven-forged dagger," she said. It was upstairs with the rest of their gear.

"Something more than a dagger might be needed, too," Lorien went on. "This secret entrance I'm taking you to leads in through an ice cave that's frequented by snow trolls." Snow trolls! That one they'd met on the walk up to Eberburg from Bohrsstead had taken her, Andrion, and Lifa working together to defeat!

Erik spoke up. "I'm going along," he said firmly. "I'll come heavily armed and armored and take care of trolls or anything else that comes along while I wait for Berni to come back out. And if she *doesn't* come out, I'm going in. I don't care what Giselle wants."

Lorien eyed him with a trace of alarm. The gigantic Norse warrior overtopped him by at least an inch, thought sylvalfar were a tall race – and he was twice as wide. "All right," he said after considering the chances that Erik would let himself be ordered otherwise. "We'll all go there after dark. Meet me right here this evening. Bernadette, I'm going to go see about your 'burglar gear.'"

With that he got up and left, and The Fireblood and her companion soon walked out behind him. A nice summer day was well underway in Sylvanian, puffy clouds being scattered by a slight cool breeze in a deep blue sky the color of Erik's eyes – Bernadette noticed. His sunny disposition coupled with his almost irresistible animal magnetism was making her like him – and love him – more each day. But her heart beat faster at the thought of Andrion, as well.

Shaking off her confusion, Bernadette spun around in a circle with her arms held high, whooping with glee at the sights all around. "Come on, let's explore!" she declared, and he smiled down at her. She was such a bright spark, his little fire-hair.

"Why don't we stroll up to the palace," he suggested, "And pay a courtesy visit to the eorl? Then we can work our way back again."

And so they did. The eorl's palace here was an order of magnitude fancier than Wyrmshalla in Waterdon. Built all of stone, it had its throne room on the second floor. The eorl, a rather ordinary-looking middle-aged Norseman with thinning sandy hair, greeted them politely and welcomed them to his city. And his steward, a younger man, said he'd be happy to offer them paying work if they felt like doing service to the march.

They paid a visit to the famous Bards' Academy Donatien had told her about. The Academy had a very nice physical plant, but neither of the adventurers had any bardic ambitions. Houses in that part of town were enormous and elegant. Up above the city's market district was a sprawling stone fort, where the empire had its most substantial presence in Iscandia. Yet they were happy to recruit non-Remans to the imperial ranks, and the visitors were

168

invited to sign up if the life of a soldier appealed to them. It didn't. Neither she nor he was the sort to enjoy taking orders.

They even walked down to the nearby river docks, admiring the ships, and visited the offices of Imperial Trading. Instead of returning to the Rabbit for lunch, they bought apples, bread, and cheese from stands in the marketplace and washed them down with some bottles of mead. Then they visited the smithy, the perfumery, a general store, and – something Bernadette had never seen before – a tailor shop where a pair of ljosalfar sisters made fine clothing for the elite.

Suppertime found them back in the Dancing Rabbit's common room, dining lightly on venison steaks with roasted potatoes and wilted greens. Bernadette ate sparingly (for her) and washed it down with a single mug of the mildly alcoholic ale, wanting to keep a clear head. They had just finished their meal when they saw Lorien coming in through the door.

He spotted them immediately and handed Bernadette a cloth bundle. "As soon as you're ready, we can go," he said. Dusk was falling outside, and from what Bernadette gathered it was a bit of a walk out in the country to the consul compound. She got out her purse.

"How much do I owe you?" she asked, but he waved her off.

"I picked those up at a deep discount," he said. "Don't worry about it."

Hmm, I wonder if he stole them, she mused as she and Erik climbed the stairs to their room. She helped him get into his armor, and he slung himself about with bow, blade, and the new warhammer. Then he watched with an appreciative leer as Bernadette stripped down to her underwear to put on the garments Lorien had brought.

Oh my, they were like nothing she had ever worn before! There did seem to be some minimal armor value in the form of stiff leather girding the torso from shoulders to hips; but other than that it was made entirely from soft, supple cloth. The overall color was a dark, slightly mottled gray and it fit loosely enough to allow easy movement while being gathered at wrists and ankles to keep the material from getting in your way. The outfit came with snug-fitting gloves and a hood that could be fastened to hide your face, showing only the eyes.

Erik was impressed. "Wow, Berni," he said softly. "You look like a member of the Guild of Thieves!" Rumors of such an organization were widespread throughout the empire, with some claiming that it had been organized centuries ago – and that it had been headed, throughout those centuries, by the same man. Bernadette doubted the tales were anything more than stories. But considering that elves lived for many lifetimes of men, it was theoretically possible they could be true.

Bernadette pulled the face covering away, exposing her grin. She didn't want to stroll through the common room below looking too mysterious. There was also a fairly ordinary-looking cloak, dark gray in color, and she threw that on over the top of the burglar suit. Her own soft boots would do well enough to complete the outfit. She strapped on her dagger, and took along a few small vials of poisons and potions plus her lockpicks. Everything else could stay here for now.

They came downstairs, feigning nonchalance, and slipped out the front door. Lorien was sitting at a small table finishing an ale, and they waited for him outside until he appeared. He grinned at Bernadette in the near darkness. "Perfect, you're practically invisible," he told her. Then, "Come on. We've got around a ten-minute walk to get to the consulate."

There could be wolves or other predatory animals out and about in the darkness, and Erik was on the alert with his sword drawn as they followed the elf along a barely-visible path running west from the city gates. "Why don't the ljosalfar have their consulate inside the walls, Lorien?" Bernadette asked quietly as they walked along.

"Too built up," he replied – concentrating on finding the trail in the dim light from the smallest of the three moons, which was setting ahead of them. "There's very few buildings inside Sylvanian that would offer the space they have out here, and with a safe perimeter around it. The ljosalfar see themselves as superior to all other races of elves and men, and they automatically assume the worst of us. Their security precautions are extreme."

Huh, Bernadette thought, concentrating on her feet. She was walking between the two men, with Erik bringing up the rear, and being armed with only a couple of dragon spells and a dagger she was glad of her position. After several minutes of walking they turned up a hillside, leaving the trail behind, and then picked their way down a rock-strewn, snowy slope.

Ahead of them, silhouetted against the darkness, stood the massive edifice of the consulate building. Lorien was right, Bernadette realized. Nothing they'd seen in Sylvanian today except maybe the eorl's palace came close to this in size. They were looking at the rear of the building, dimly illuminated here and there. But around to the front the approach was lit up with torches, and light spilled from windows across much of the bottom floor at the end furthest from them.

"Over there's where the party is going on," Lorien murmured unnecessarily. "We go this way." He turned toward the darker end of the building, and led them down into a narrow, snow-filled ravine. Ahead was a deeper blackness, the irregular mouth of a natural cave. And issuing from that cave opening was a charnel reek mixed with a sort of musk: the smell of troll.

They halted outside the opening and Erik came up, hefting his warhammer. "The ljosalfar have a sort of dungeon in the basement, where they keep and interrogate prisoners," Lorien told them quietly. "They throw the bodies out into the cave, and the trolls take care of them."

"Trolls, plural?" Bernadette asked, alarmed.

"Only one at a time," the elf assured her. "They don't much like each other's company. But if we kill the one that's in there now, it's unlikely another will move in before you're finished with your mission."

She'd have been happier if the word "unlikely" had instead been substituted with something more like "impossible" or "unthinkable." But it looked like she'd have to take what she could get. "Wait here, Berni," Erik rumbled softly. Then catlike, incredibly lithe and quiet for a heavily-armed giant, he slipped through the cave opening. It was more than tall enough.

Inside the smell was so pungent Erik almost regretted the supper they'd eaten an hour or so before. Partial skeletons, with bits of rotting flesh clinging to the bones, littered the uneven floor inside. A ledge ran across the far wall, too high for a troll to climb; and in a sconce beside an iron ladder leading up into the ceiling, a torch was burning. It cast flickering shadows and made it hard to see what else was in the cavern.

"Here, trolli trolli trolli," Erik said softly. Suddenly there was a savage roar, and his view of the ledge was blocked by an enormous white-furred shape nearly seven feet tall – a few inches taller than he was, and with arms that must have been a foot longer than his. It was unarmed, though – thank the gods! As it swung at him, no doubt intending to rip him limb from limb, he ducked nimbly out of range and then swung his hammer hard, breaking the troll's left forearm and setting its fur ablaze.

It roared in agonized fury, and came at him again. Just then an elven arrow sprouted from the troll's chest a little below the right shoulder, causing it to falter. Erik turned again and swung the warhammer with all his might, smashing the snow troll's skull. It collapsed to the rock-strewn floor of the cavern with barely a moan.

Erik grinned at Lorien as he came inside, bow in hand. "Thanks, pal," he said.

"I was just softening him up a little for you," the elf replied. Bernadette had been watching from the cavern entrance, and she now joined them. She looked down with a touch of horror and pity at the enormous brute lying smashed at their feet. It didn't seem fair, somehow, to be going up against unarmed creatures one didn't intend to eat, unless they attacked you first.

Lorien gestured at the ladder, rising from atop the nearby ledge. "You'll need to pick the lock to get through the trap door at the top," he told her. "And from then on, stay low and quiet. I don't know what if anything they've got going on in the cells now, but you'll probably find the information you're looking for on the floors above. There are two stories, with offices and living quarters."

Bernadette gave him a grin and a cheery salute, then fastened the face flap over her hood and dropped her cloak. "Erik, give me a boost up?" she requested. He seized her by the waist and swung her up to the ledge as lightly as if she were a small child. She weighed less than half what he did, after all.

"I'll wait here for you, Berni," he told her.

"I'm going back to Sylvanian," the elf said. "Giselle said you have a magic map?" Erik nodded. "Just use your map to get back to town after you come back out of the cave," Lorien suggested.

"Thanks, we'll do that," Bernadette told him. She had the map folded up and tucked into the tunic of her burglar suit.

Bernadette scaled the ladder and listened at the iron-bound, wooden trap door. There were no sounds from above, and she set to work with her picks. Doing it one-handed was kind of a pain, but she had plenty of light from the torch. The lock was well oiled, evidently in frequent use. And it was an old-fashioned type, the kind usually opened with a skeleton key. She soon had it open.

Her heart was racing with excitement as she pushed the trap door up and slipped inside the room above. The floors were wood though the walls were stone, and she found herself in a relatively small alcove tucked in beside a stairway leading to an upper floor. She silently closed the trap door but didn't re-lock it, then peeked out into the room.

There was a central block with perhaps half a dozen cells, each with three walls of stone while the ceiling and front were iron-barred. There was an occupant in one of them, a man shackled to the stone rear wall of the cell across from the trap door and one down. He appeared to be unconscious.

There were no sounds of guards or other personnel in this basement room, so Bernadette crept out of her alcove and moved silently up the wooden steps – glad that Erik was not along. As catlike a warrior as he was, it would have been hard to move up these with his 250 pounds and not make any noise.

At the top of the stairs was another door – locked. This one too was well-maintained, and she had it open in under a minute. All the while, she was listening for the sound of footsteps but heard nothing. Perhaps Lorien was right, and all the guards were keeping an eye on the party guests.

Bernadette found herself in a small ante-room, beyond which was a hallway. She approached cautiously as she heard voices, and was able to listen in on a conversation between two guards. It suggested that Giselle's idea of ljosalfar involvement in the return of dragons to Iscandia might not be accurate. "Did you see those mages arrive this morning? Who're they with? More enforcers?" one asked.

The other replied, "No. Rumor has it the consul is finally getting worried about all the dragon attacks."

The first guard said "About time. I've been wondering how we were supposed to defend this place if a dragon attacked."

His fellow responded, "If a dragon does show up, maybe we'll get lucky and it will eat the mages first. Might give us enough time to kill it."

"Ha. I'd like to see those arrogant bastards taken down a notch. Always looking down their noses at us lowly grunts," said the first.

Hmmm, Bernadette mused silently. At least the "grunts" don't know anything about why the dragons have returned. That didn't necessarily mean their superiors weren't involved, though. And it was interesting to note that even members of the ljosalfar themselves thought others of their race were arrogant. But she was going to need more than an overheard conversation. The two guards laughed nastily, then one said "Well, we'd better get back to our station." They walked off, into a room leading off the same hallway.

Bernadette didn't hesitate. As soon as they had exited the hallway she stole past the door to the room they'd gone into. A quick glance in passing showed her that it led to a broad staircase. On the far side she stood, back pressed to the wall, and listened. Their footsteps had stopped, so were probably tasked with guarding the stairs. She hoped there was another way to the second floor!

Carefully, she began exploring the rooms on either side of the hall. Some appeared to be living or dining areas, others storage. She didn't see or hear any more guards. At the very end of the corridor a locked (briefly) door opened onto a sumptuously appointed bedroom. This part of the building, Bernadette realized, was closest to the part of the consulate where the public was admitted, where most likely the consul conducted his daily business. So perhaps this was his personal sleeping quarters.

In addition to the bed, wardrobe, and chest of drawers there was a small desk over on one side of the room near the door. For conducting private correspondence, perhaps? Unlike what usually passed for a desk in Iscandia, this one had drawers – one on the left and three more in a stack down the right side. And they had locks!

Moments later, after first re-locking the door to the sleeping quarters, Bernadette was seated at the consul's desk and going over a stack of papers she'd found inside those locked drawers. As she'd gathered from the conversation she'd overheard between the two "grunts," the ljosalfar were as mystified as anyone as to the cause of the sudden dragon reappearance. They actually knew less about it than she and her friends and cohorts did, not realizing that the dragons were being brought back to life.

Letters from the Ljosalfar Union government, south of the empire, demanded that Dulerion investigate the phenomenon. While so far dragons had been seen only in Iscandia, there was no reason to assume they would stay there. It was true the hot creatures preferred cold climates, but there were mountainous regions throughout the empire, and even within the Union, where a dragon might find a comfortable home – with plenty of nearby people and livestock to eat. The Union, who regarded themselves as the real power in this part of Terris, wanted to know exactly what was going on and who was responsible.

Bernadette would very much have liked to carry off that one letter from a High Minister Bendilien, as it was clear documentary evidence that the official ljosalfar government had no part in what was happening. But suppose Dulerion wanted to refer to this letter again? She was supposed to be passing through here like a breeze, unseen and leaving no trace. So instead of stealing the letter she took a roll of paper from the desktop and borrowed the consul's quill and ink to jot down some notes – including all names mentioned and the gist of what had been written. She tucked that into her tunic with the magic map, and put everything back where she'd gotten it before re-locking the desk drawers.

There was a second door in the room, near the back beside the bed, and Bernadette investigated it. Aha, a narrow wooden staircase leading up! This must be the consul's private, more convenient passageway to the upper floor. In moments she had crept up it and found herself, after passing through another door, in a room that looked like a cross between a lounge and an office. There were two desks here, but neither contained anything useful.

A door on the far side of the room led out into a large central space. It had a broad staircase heading down at the far end, and several rooms leading off it. Bernadette heard voices, and she crept along to take cover behind a potted plant, a few paces from the open door of a room from which the sound was coming.

"I earned that money, and I want it now," a whining voice complained.

It was answered by one that spoke with authority and disdain: "Don't press your luck, Emond. You're not our only informant."

The subordinate replied, "But I got you the real goods. Ricard will tell you. He knows where the old man is hiding, I'm sure of it!"

The voice Bernadette was assuming to be that of the paymaster replied, "You'll be paid in full when the story has been checked out, and not before."

The informant cried, "So he *has* talked! I knew it!" The paymaster's voice was harsh, and final.

"Everyone talks, in the end. Now, I have work to do. Leave me to it, if you ever want to see the rest of your payment."

"You should let *me* question him!" Emond urged. "He trusts me! I'll bet I could get the full story out of him."

"Your services are not required," the other man replied coldly. "Get out. I'll contact you when the information we get from the prisoner has been confirmed."

Bernadette froze as she heard footsteps coming. A ratlike Norseman, little taller than she was, came skulking out of the doorway with his shoulders hunched and an expression of repressed fury on his face. Without so much as a glance in her direction, he turned to the left and shortly disappeared down the staircase at the end of the room.

That prisoner she'd seen in the cell must be this Ricard they were talking about! Could *she* get him to reveal whatever it was he'd told his ljosalfar interrogators? Turning silently, Bernadette quickly made her way back to the room she'd come out of and down the narrow staircase to the consul's quarters.

She needed to get back down to the basement, quickly! Who knew how long it would be before they began torturing the prisoner again? Aside from the loss of some useful information, having the area around the cells occupied by ljosalfar guards might make getting back out the trap door without being seen impossible.

But how could she get back to the staircase up which she'd come? Suppose those two guards were staring out at the door of the room they were stationed in? Bernadette looked around the bedroom for something that might help her distract the guards. There was a small handful of coins on a nightstand beside the bed, and she pocketed one of them.

As she crept silently down the corridor, she heard voices coming from the room in which she'd last seen the guards. Stopping just short of the door to that room, she risked a glance around the edge of the doorway. This room's double doors stood open, inward toward the stairs.

The informant, Emond, whom Bernadette had seen leaving the office upstairs after his failed attempt to pry money out of a ljosalfar paymaster, was standing at the foot of the stairs. Flanking him, the two elf guardsmen towered over him by half a foot – and by their body language, their interaction was not a friendly one.

177

Bernadette didn't hesitate. In half a second she had ghosted past the opening, unnoticed by the three who stood twenty feet away. Then she pressed herself against the wall on the far side and listened in. "You're seriously trying to tell us Derynath agreed to let you question the prisoner by yourself?" one of the guards asked scornfully. Clearly, the little informer was known around here – and not well regarded.

"I convinced him Ricard would open up to me more than he would to your interrogators," Emond said. The lying little shit! What was he planning?

It seemed that the guards were willing to believe the story though, and after another minute of discussion the senior one said, "Watch yourself, Emond. If anything happens to our prisoner, we'll know who to go looking for."

At that Bernadette took flight. In moments she had the door to the basement unlocked and was hurrying down the stairs silently. Less than a minute after she'd taken refuge in the alcove with the trapdoor in it, she heard the light pattering of Emond's feet as he came down the stairs.

She peered around the corner and saw him go, not to the cell where the prisoner hung unconscious, but around beyond the end of the cell block. She could just see a table there, but Emond was invisible for a moment. He soon returned jingling a set of keys, and opened up the cell door. Then he dipped a cup into a bucket of water that sat on the floor of the cell and held it to the prisoner's lips. He patted him on the cheek, saying softly "Ricard! Wake up!"

The unshaven and miserable-looking fellow, who must from his name be a fellow Galise, lifted his head and looked bleary-eyed at his visitor. His face was marked by numerous bruises and small cuts, as if his captors had been using him for a punching bag.

"Emond?" the man asked, in tones of disbelief. "What're *you* doin' here?" His speech seemed a little slurred, either from grogginess after days of abuse or perhaps from broken teeth.

"I heard the Snarks had somebody down here in their cells, and I was afraid it was you," Emond lied. "So I sneaked in!"

The informer held the cup of water to Ricard's lips and the man eagerly drained it. Revived, he said "Emond! We've got to get out of here before they come back! That Derynath guy is a mean bastard, he'll have you strung up next to me if you're caught!"

"Don't worry about it," Emond said. "The Snarks are all having a fancy party this evening, and likely ain't no one going to be down here for hours yet. Maybe the rest of the night. So what were they askin' you?" The Norse informer had his back to Bernadette, but she could see Ricard's face. He looked confused. If his friend was here to rescue him, why wasn't he doing so?

"It was like I told you, last time we met," the prisoner said. "I was down in the Depths below Lakedon, where the Guild of Thieves has its hangout, and this old guy came through that tavern they've got down there. He paid Hamish, their lieutenant, to keep his mouth shut and then vanished into the maze of tunnels beyond the back door. Didn't get his name, and I didn't have no coin to pay Hamish for telling me. Wasn't my business anyway. But the Snarks are convinced the old guy was involved with the dragons, somehow. I told 'em the one they were looking for was probably hiding below Lakedon, but I didn't mention Hamish. The Guild of Thieves has ways of dealing with snitches."

"I'm impressed that you were able to hold out that information," Emond said thoughtfully. "It looks like they've been working you over pretty good."

"I ain't no snitch!" Ricard declared. "Now get me out of these shackles and let's get out of here before somebody comes!"

Emond took a step back. "Oh sorry, Ricard," he said. "I don't think I can do that. I've got to be going now…" The prisoner's eyes widened. In furious recognition that he'd been betrayed by a man he had thought a friend, Emond assumed. Actually, he was reacting in shock to the sudden appearance, just behind his betrayer, of a small figure clad head to foot in dark gray clothing. It had appeared out of the shadows beyond the cell like a wraith.

While the little informer had been weaseling information out of the prisoner an idea had come to Bernadette, and she had quickly decided to act on it. Before Emond could turn and leave,

her elven dagger came down point first on the back of his neck –
cutting through skin and the cartilage between the cervical
vertebrae and severing his spine. With scarcely a drop of blood
spilled, the Norseman collapsed to the stone floor – alive but
paralyzed.

Ricard's face writhed in a grimace of fear. "Wh-who are
you?" he asked in awed tones. He'd been through a lot in the past
couple of days, and this latest apparition had him wondering if the
ordeal had begun to affect his mind. Bernadette removed the cloth
cloaking her face and grinned at him.

"Let's just say I'm your rescuer," she said. She nudged her
victim with the toe of her boot. "Emond here was in the pay of the
ljosalfar, you should know."

The prisoner shook his head. "I was just beginning to get that
idea," he groaned.

"Is there a key to these shackles?" Bernadette asked him,
anxious to get moving.

"Check Emond," Ricard suggested. "The key to the cell and
the key to the shackles are on the same ring."

Soon the prisoner was free, and Bernadette had him drink one
of the health potions she'd brought. He gave her a dazzling,
crooked smile. "Thanks, lady! You really saved my ass."

"We're going out by the trap door over there," she told him.
"Could you drag your 'friend' over there while I check on
something?"

Ricard was a middle-sized man in his late thirties, and now
cured of his bruises and other injuries (including a couple of
cracked ribs) he easily managed dragging Emond over to the trap
door while Bernadette went around to the far side of the cell block
to see what she could find.

There was a locked trunk beside the table, on which sat paper
and writing implements, and a set of hooks on which keys were
hung. The key to the trunk was not among them, though. She got it
open with her lockpicks and rummaged through it. Not much in the
way of treasure, but she found a couple of what looked like bound

notebooks. One read "Dossier: Giselle" and the other "Dossier: Adalbert."

Anxiety to be moving before anyone should come down here warred with Bernadette's desire to read what these notebooks had to say. She just flipped through a couple of pages of the first one. Giselle, as she'd told her, was one of the last living members of the now-disbanded Guardians. And perhaps, the woman's belief that she was being targeted by the ljosalfar was not so groundless after all.

Bernadette took a full minute to study the other one. A pity she could not just take it with her! But she didn't want to blot what so far had been a perfectly-executed mission by leaving evidence of intrusion... But wait! She had reasoned that the escape of the prisoner Ricard would be blamed on Emond – why might he not also have stolen anything that wasn't nailed down? She had the suspicion that both Emond and Ricard were members, or at least associates, of this Guild of Thieves she'd thought to be nothing but a story until very recently.

"Hurry up!" Ricard called, and Bernadette slipped the two slim notebooks into her tunic – then scooped up the rest of the trunk's contents. With a smile on her lips, she hurried over and opened the trap door, kneeling on the floor.

"Erik?" she called, and got an immediate "Berni! Are you all right?"

"Fine," she replied. "I've got some things I'm going to throw down." She hadn't brought a pack with her, wanting to be able to slip through narrow spaces with ease. To her astonishment, Erik's handsome face suddenly appeared in the opening. That ledge must be ten feet off the ground! How had he managed to climb up onto it wearing dypalfar armor?

He took the rest of the trunk contents from her and stuffed them into his own pack. Then Bernadette and Ricard lowered the motionless body of Emond down through the trap. "This guy's dead," Erik reported as they were climbing down themselves and locking the door behind them.

It was probably just as well, Bernadette thought. If the severing of his spine had not killed him, he would have been paralyzed for the rest of his life – which wouldn't have been long, as they would probably have needed to kill him anyway. Emond and Ricard both needed to vanish, lest the ljosalfar find out who really made off with their prisoner.

Erik slung the body over his shoulder and hopped down, then helped Bernadette and Ricard climb down before the three of them made their way out of the cave. They needed to leave the area, fast. Good trackers might be able to tell that three people had come in this way; but it was the sylvalfar, not the ljosalfar, who were good at woodcraft.

Bernadette took them all by map to the docks where Imperial Trading had its offices. All was shut and dark, now. "We need to get rid of that body where nobody's going to find it," she told Erik quietly.

"I've just the thing," he replied casually. He hastily stripped off Emond's clothing, lest there be anything identifiable on the body. Then, taking the limp, nude form by an arm and a leg he swung it around in a circle once and flung it off the pier – out into the center of the current.

The body was only a faintly visible dark shape as the river took it and began carrying it out to sea. "By the time the razormouths get finished with him, I doubt he'll be recognizable," Erik said confidently. "Was he somebody who'll be missed?"

"Very much so, I think," Bernadette replied. "He was working for the ljosalfar as an informer. He put them onto Ricard here and they were trying to find out about another surviving member of the Guardians, a guy named Adalbert. The ljosalfar are going to assume that it was our unlamented friend there (a gesture toward the estuary) who broke Ricard loose. But I doubt they'll realize anyone else was there tonight."

Erik clapped her on the shoulder, gently enough not to knock her off her feet. "Good job, Berni!" he said enthusiastically. "What about Ricard here?"

The man eyed them both. "I… think I might just head back to Auverne for a spell," he remarked. "Good idea!" she said. "Do you want a lift?"

Chapter 24: The Next Move

Using her map, Bernadette was able to take herself and the two men to Milburn – the very first point her map had acquired after she'd bought it. They bid farewell to Ricard, then turned right around and fast-traveled back to Sylvanian, to find it was still night. But the night of which day, she wondered?

The innkeeper looked up as they came in, frowning. "You paid for one night and then disappeared," he pointed out. "You owe me two more nights' lodging." So, they'd lost an entire day delivering Ricard on the way to the land of his birth. Bernadette apologized and handed over the requested gold, along with a tip. There'd been almost enough in that basement chest to cover it, in any case.

Bernadette didn't remotely feel as if it had been 24 hours since their last meal, but she was feeling a little peckish – and a little tired. They got some bread rolls, cheese, and a bottle of wine and took it to their room. Once they were inside the door, Erik enfolded her in his arms, lifting her off the floor, and kissed her enthusiastically.

"Ow, armor!" she protested, and he put her down again.

"Sorry," he murmured. "There's something about you in that outfit…"

"I'll get out of it then," Bernadette promised; and a big grin spread across his angelic features. "First, though," she went on, "Let's have some food and drink and I'll tell you about my visit to the consulate."

Erik got out of his armor, wearing trousers and a tunic underneath it, and Bernadette left the fairly comfortable burglar suit on as she seated herself at the room's small table. They were soon munching on bread and cheese, and washing it down the wine. "It went really well!" she said enthusiastically. "I found out the ljosalfar are *not* behind the dragons coming back. They're as mystified as anybody else. That's going to set Giselle back, I'll bet. But they're into a lot of other stuff. A pretty nasty bunch."

"So," he said, connecting the dots. "I guess that means we need to go back to Forestville and report?"

"Not before tomorrow morning, I think" she said with irritation. "That woman has been acting like she owns me. She can bloody well wait for her report." Bernadette sighed, stood up, and began taking off her burglar suit. "I can think of one or two things I'd rather be doing, the rest of tonight," she said with a grin.

Bernadette was soon in her underclothes. "*Man*," she said ruefully, "I sure wish the rest of this benighted province would wake up to the benefits of hot bathing pools." To date, her beloved Maiden was the only place she had found with hot water for bathing. Most places, you were lucky to get a basin, a pitcher of cold water, and maybe some towels.

Erik gave her a small grin. "Lie back, dear. I'll bathe you." He reached down to pull her undershirt over her head, then knelt to pull her underdrawers down to the floor until Bernadette could step out of them. Then he led her to the bed, and directed her to lie flat on her back. He now peeled off his shirt and trousers to reveal he was naked underneath. She peeped at him admiringly, while maintaining the pretense of lying limp on the coverlet.

Erik was not erect as yet, but his big cock was beginning to swell as it dangled between his massively muscled legs. As Bernadette lay there, trying not to move, he commenced giving her a tongue bath. He began by bathing her feet with his tongue, sucking her toes. Then he worked his way up her legs, licking the tender places around her knees after a quick stroke up the shins.

Erik applied his tongue in long strokes up her outer then inner thighs, a burning wetness along the tender skin of her groin, then continued upward. Bernadette lay there bemused, enjoying the sensations though for the most part they tickled. Nor did they leave her feeling particularly cleansed, but still… This was a new, tender side of her enormous blond lover. Before he had been a thunderbolt, yet now he teased and tantalized her. He continued upward in his progress, diving from her hips to her fingers, first on one side and then the other.

Erik sucked each finger gently, licking the palms, then the wrists and quickly up the forearm to the bend of the elbow. He took a little extra time there, licking and sucking, then on up and licked salt sweat from her armpits before working his way over her shoulders to her collarbones. Bernadette was particularly sensitive in that spot where her neck met the shoulders, and Erik's ministrations began to stir a warm, wet sensation that spread from between her legs up the center of her torso, as he moved from the shoulders and neck to apply tender kisses to her face, her ears, her mouth. As he was lying across her at this point and naked, she could feel that he was now fully erect and as aroused as she was.

He was not finished yet. Moving back down from her mouth to below her chin, Erik licked down her midline to between the breasts, and circled first one breast, then the other with his tongue before gently taking the nipple in his mouth and sucking, running his tongue around and around as the nipple rose to his touch.

Leaving her glowing and aroused breasts behind, Erik next ran his tongue down the center line of her body, stopping to tickle her navel and fill her with curious sensations as he applied suction to it. Then, as Bernadette's anticipation grew and her body tensed involuntarily, he continued his progress down past the navel, working his tongue into her light bush of silken, curly auburn hair and finding the clit beneath, hiding within its hood and already stiffening.

Bernadette gasped as Erik finally, after all that teasing, lowered his golden head to her slit and began working his tongue inside it, sucking at her labia. He added a couple of fingers and pushed them in and out, slowly, while continuing to worship at her gateway with lips and tongue. She couldn't stand it anymore! Both hands pressing on his head, she arched her back and spasmed with a cry as her orgasm swept over her. When she had stopped grinding her pelvis into his face, he looked up at her smiling. "All clean, now?" he asked.

"Clean enough!" Bernadette gasped. "C'mere!" She hauled him bodily up her, until his face was even with hers, and kissed him. Very sloppily, considering that his short beard was soaked with saliva and her juices. She didn't care. She tilted her pelvis to receive him, and his throbbing and ready cock pushed eagerly into her wet, slippery hole. In moments, as he began thrusting into her faster and faster, she was coming again. He would have liked to hold on and take her there three or four more times, but their long session of foreplay had left him with an aching in his loins that demanded release and as she cried out in ecstasy he joined her with a deep, drawn-out groan – his cock quivering within her, pumping out his seed.

With Erik sunk within her as far as it was possible to go, her cunt still clutching at him spasmodically as the waves of amazing pleasure receded, Bernadette clasped him to her – her fingers digging deep into the muscles of his back. Aaah! She relaxed and lay there motionless for a few moments, as did he. Then she wiggled slightly beneath him. "Love?" she mumbled, her mouth partly obscured. "Could you let me breathe, please?"

"Oh, sorry" Erik said softly, rolling over. He weighed about twice what she did, and it was all muscle. She rolled onto her side and locked her lips on his.

"Fantastic, baby," she sighed. Then, tucking her head into his shoulder and resting her hand on his chest, she drifted down, like a leaf fluttering gently to the autumn forest floor, into sleep.

Came the morning, and as usual Bernadette found herself alert early and eager to seize whatever the day had to offer. What it had to offer right off the bat was a superb young blond giant, lying sleepily beside her and enfolding her in his massive arms. He already had an enormous erection, so she seized that. She knelt beside him as he lay there on his back, squeezing with one hand while she ran her tongue from the base of his scrotum, right up the shaft, to flick over the head. It expanded under her touch, and a drop of clear, slightly salty fluid appeared. She licked it off.

Erik's powerful muscles tensed, which was very interesting to watch. By the gods, he had the smoothest skin. You could see every muscle moving beneath it, too. As much as he appeared to be enjoying this he also seemed to be a bit less energetic than usual, still drowsy. Bernadette rotated in the bed so that her rear was pointed toward the head of it, then straddled him with her knees resting on either side of his head, and thrust her glistening cunt into his face as she bent to suck and stroke his cock.

187

"Mmmlgl!" Erik said with what sounded like enthusiasm. He began licking and sucking her as well, and using his fingers in interesting ways up there while she gobbled him (or as much of him as she could get into her mouth) down below. This position was wonderfully exciting, and her vulva felt as if it were swollen to twice its normal size and possibly glowing as well; but Bernadette found it hard to let herself tumble all the way into orgasm like this. So she executed an athletic maneuver, spinning back around, and impaled herself on that throbbing, rock-hard member instead – locking mouths with Erik and thrusting her tongue eagerly between his lips.

In a minute or two of vigorous bouncing they both reached climax, and Bernadette collapsed on top of him, panting, for a little while. Then she kissed him more gently and, with a smile on her lips and a song in her heart, leaped from the bed to go clean up with the basin and towels provided by the Dancing Rabbit's management. What a great start to the morning! I've really got to take time for this more often, she thought to herself. Usually, her restless mind became so focused on her next quest or challenge that she tended to be all business in the morning – saving play for later on in the day.

Erik lay there flat on his back, his member lying limp, a beatific smile on his lips as he watched Bernadette about her ablutions through half-closed eyes. What a woman, he thought. I think I'm in love. But it's like trying to catch moonbeams... Sighing not unhappily, he lifted himself up on his elbows and then sat up, padding naked over to use the basin himself before putting on his underclothes and armor.

When Bernadette and Erik had finished kitting up and were ready to leave, they stopped in the Rabbit's taproom long enough to have a little breakfast. Anxious to get moving, she ate a small bread roll washed down with ale, then exited the place munching on an apple. That ought to hold her at least until they'd had a chance to confer with Giselle back in Forestville.

Bernadette pulled her magic map from its hiding place and the pair of them were soon standing on the road a little bit to the south and west of Forestville's gate, near the smithy. It appeared to be early afternoon. Bernadette had yet to figure out exactly how the map's translocation abilities affected time. Evidence was beginning to pile up, though.

The pair strode into the Laughing Herdsman, blinking in the dimly lit common room after coming in from bright daylight outside. Bernadette peered around, but there was no sign of Giselle. She approached the bar where Giselle's employee, Sorgi, was studiously polishing its surface with a rag. "Hi," she said. "Uh, is Giselle here?"

The man gestured toward the door to the right of the bar that led to Giselle's room – and the secret entrance to the basement hideaway. Bernadette pushed the door open hesitantly, but saw no one inside. Beckoning Erik to follow her, she approached the "wardrobe" and used the key Giselle had given her to let them into the basement.

Ah, there she was, seeming as if she'd been waiting for them. On seeing them Giselle's face lit up with the closest thing Bernadette had yet seen to a smile, as she said "You're here!" she cried. "I was beginning to get worried you'd been captured by the ljosalfar."

"We had to run a couple of errands after getting back out of the consulate," Bernadette explained, "The ljosalfar know even less about the dragon attacks than we do, I'm afraid." Giselle eyed her blankly, and Bernadette went on. "I didn't take anything with me except some stuff out of their basement prison, so they wouldn't realize they'd been infiltrated," she said. "Take a look at this transcript of a letter I found locked inside Dulerion's desk."

She handed the notes over, and the older woman studied it. "You're sure this is what it said?" she asked, seemingly unwilling to give up on her idea that her favorite set of suspects were at the root of their troubles.

"Oh, they're up to some stuff, all right," Bernadette assured her. "Here's a dossier I found on you down near where they were torturing a prisoner. It appears they suspect the Guardians just as you suspected the ljosalfar, and they're trying to track down all the former Guardians who are still alive."

Giselle read the slim notebook with her name on it, and her eyes hardened. "I knew it!" she said bitterly, but Bernadette thought she detected a hint of anxiety in those eyes. When you're one middle-aged woman, alone, and the might of a powerful political entity is focused on your extinction, it could cause you to lose some sleep.

"You said they are looking for other members of the Guardians?" Giselle asked, and Bernadette handed her the second notebook. She and Erik had both read it while they were eating their bread and cheese last night. There wasn't all that much to it.

"They were trying to get the prisoner they were torturing to tell them about a man he saw in the Depths under Lakedon," she told Giselle. "Do you know this Adalbert?"

"That crazy old man," the blonde woman murmured softly, as she turned the pages of the dossier. "I can't believe he's still alive. I thought the ljosalfar would have gotten him years ago. Haven't seen him in nearly twenty years…" Either Giselle had been scarcely more than a girl during the Conflict, or she was remarkably well-preserved. This Adalbert must have been something of a father-figure to her.

"The dossier said he was an important figure in the Guardians back during the war. Some kind of super fighter?" Bernadette asked.

Giselle replied "He's a fairly competent battle mage, or he was back then. But most importantly, Adalbert was one of the Guardians archivists. He knew everything about the ancient dragon lore of the Guardians, was convinced that it was more than interesting old stories. Nobody thought those stories had any relevance. I guess he wasn't as crazy as we all thought."

Bernadette considered that bit of information, recalling something she'd heard on her recent mission. "I think the ljosalfar believe the Guardians know about the dragons," she said.

"And they may be right," Giselle replied. "We've got to find Adalbert before they do. He'll know how to stop the dragons if anybody does. So they think he's gone to ground in the Lakedon Depths?"

"The guy the ljosalfar were holding was from there, and he'd seen an old man who matches Adalbert's description buying silence from members of the Guild of Thieves and vanishing into the tunnels down there," Bernadette responded.

"You'd better get to Lakedon," Giselle told her. "Talk to Hamish. He's... well-connected. A good starting point at least."

"He's the one the prisoner said took money from the old man," Bernadette pointed out. "I guess we'd better go talk with him." She wasn't happy to be dispatched once more by this woman who seemed to think The Fireblood should be jumping at her every command. But she also felt convinced that this woman, and these Guardians, had something important to do with her destiny here in Iscandia.

As Bernadette and Erik shouldered their burdens and prepared to leave, Giselle had one last word for them: "Oh, and when you find Adalbert... You may have some trouble getting him to trust you. Just ask him where he was on the first of Pluvia. He'll know what it means."

Chapter 25: A Night in Bohrsstead

As soon as they were out in the daylight again, Bernadette pulled out her map. Erik put an arm around her back and leaned over her shoulder, showing her with a massive forefinger where Lakedon was, way over beyond Hochstein and many leagues to the east of Bohrsstead.

She said, "That's a really long walk, sweetie. Are you up for it?"

"With you my love, no road is too long," he replied gallantly and uncharacteristically. She peered at him dubiously, but he only gave her his most cherubic smile. He was too damn cute for his own good, if anything that size could be said to be cute.

"We'd better lay in some supplies then," she said, and led the way down the street to the village's general store.

Bernadette bought an assortment of likely trail food, filled some water skins, and even picked up a couple of bottles of wine just in case the opportunity for some relaxation came up along the journey. Their nearest fast-travel point was Bohrsstead. When she and Erik arrived there, it was getting on toward late afternoon.

Bernadette had a thought. "Erik, when I was here with Andrion and Lifa on the way up to Eberburg to see the Old Ones, I noticed there's an ancient Norse barrow here. Want to explore it? I think it's probably already too late to leave for Lakedon."

He gave her his friendliest grin. "Spiders, spooks, and walking dead? Sure!"

She grinned back, and they headed up to the north end of town. The barrow was easily visible from the road, on a slight rise behind the farmstead Bernadette had passed on her first trip into the village. This one was a type Bernadette had not seen before, though Erik assured her they were a standard ancient Norse design and could be found all over the province. Entering through a doorway, they found themselves looking at a circular stone wall contained within an outer one. They encountered open sarcophagi with scattered bones in them as they circled the gallery. On the side of the circle opposite the one they'd entered on, ornately carved double doors sat in the inner wall.

Bernadette pushed it open, somewhat hesitantly. Ahead of her, a rickety-looking wooden staircase spiraled down to a lower level. She gripped her bow and crept down it carefully, as afraid of falling through and breaking a leg as of encountering malign spirits. Erik stayed close behind her. The stairs proved sturdier than they looked, and they shortly walked out into a ruinous stone gallery. Ahead of them an open doorway led into a tomb area, and a tall and imposing-looking mummified corpse stood guard in a recess.

That doesn't look good, Bernadette thought, and after sneaking a little closer she put an arrow into it. There was a little dry "splat" as the arrow pierced the corpse; but no flame, no collapse. The thing was dead-dead, not walking-dead. Good. As she and Erik crept all the way into the room, they saw a barred iron gate to the right.

The place was much less extensive than many such places they had visited, and no aptrgangr walked the halls. Odd. To the left they found a small stone room with a collection of levers in it, and had to figure out which levers to pull in what order to raise the barred gates that blocked doorways on three sides of the room they had entered from, while keeping the gate to this room open. Guessing wrong sent them ducking a stream of arrows that came shooting out of holes in the walls.

Bernadette got the gates opened, and headed down the hall through the gate they'd noticed earlier. They came to another room with two doors in it, one of which led to a short corridor with a chest in it, and a pressure plate trap in the floor. The other led to another room, with more doors. Through one of those the corridor bent around to the left and then entered another room with an open door.

Inside the room they found a little of the kinds of loot you could usually find in Norse barrows: small gems, weapons, and old books. Bernadette pocketed one she thought Andrion would be interested in, but didn't want to burden herself too much with a long walk ahead. A few more minutes' search failed to turn up anywhere else to go, and they made their way back out.

By the time they emerged into the open air once more, full
night had fallen. Erik's arm around her shoulders, Bernadette and
her gigantic blond companion strolled down the village's main
street in the dark, heading for the inn. "I can't believe that was all
of it," she remarked quietly, "We must have missed something.
We'll have to come back and explore sometime when I'm not so
busy trying to stop dragons from returning and destroying the
world."

He gave her a little squeeze (such as he could, with both of
them in full armor and draped with weapons) and said only, "Uh
huh."

At the inn, Bernadette headed right for the bar and greeted
Holmund. "Hi, remember me?"

"Weren't you heading up to Eberburg a few days ago?" he
asked.

"That's right," she replied. "Might we have a room for the
night?"

"Certainly, certainly," he replied. "You don't want to be out
on the road at this hour." He showed them to a room that,
thankfully, had a double bed.

Bernadette remarked, "It's too bad it got dark so soon. I don't
think it's been six hours of real time since we got up this morning,
at least it doesn't seem like it. Did we even eat lunch?"

"Now that you mention it," he replied, "I wouldn't mind a
bite. Or maybe a whole roast ox." A man that size doesn't keep his
strength up on a diet of bread and apples.

"Let's get changed and see what old Holmund can whip up for
us, then," Bernadette suggested. He helped her unstrap her armor
and she returned the favor. They stood there in their underclothes
eyeing each other somewhat hungrily; but other hungers were
more pressing for the moment.

Bernadette dug what passed for her "nice dress" out of her
pack and shook it out. It wasn't torn or bloodstained, and it *was* a
dress, after all. She even had a pair of soft slippers to put on her
bare feet. She peeled off her underwear before putting it on,
managing to do so while Erik was occupied with his own wardrobe

change. He had an enormous, theoretically white shirt, loose even on his massive frame, with full gathered sleeves and lacing at the neck. Below he wore an ordinary pair of trousers, a little snug (which Bernadette thought showed off his muscular buttocks to good effect), and some soft shoes.

The pair emerged from the room and took seats at one of the long tables that lined the room on either side. Holmund, who had become their good buddy, came right over and offered them what he had on the fire. They feasted on a roasted haunch of venison, with some green beans on the side, vegetable soup rich with carrots, peas, and potatoes, and more of the ubiquitous bread rolls (eaten at every meal of the day by most people in Iscandia), washed down with a nearly drinkable red wine and topped off with some apple pie for dessert.

By the time they had finished this excellent repast Bernadette, who had not eaten so well almost since she arrived in Iscandia, had come up with another idea. She called Holmund over and asked him, "Do you happen to have a washtub?"

"Oh aye," he replied. "The wife keeps one in the kitchen for laundry."

She smiled up at him. "Could you possibly have that brought to our room, along with a few pots of hot water and a few buckets of cold? And some soap?"

He smiled at her. "Most certainly, lovely lady!" Funny how putting on a dress seemed to bring out the gallantry in men, she mused.

Bernadette and Erik went back to their room to await the delivery of the washtub. It would take a while for the water to be heated. "I'm going to have a hot bath, I'm going to have a hot bath!" she crowed gleefully.

"Thank the gods," Erik replied fervently, his eyes twinkling.

"Are you implying I'm dirty?" she huffed archly, her eyes twinkling as well. "If I'm at all besmirched it's entirely *your* fault. Your tongue bath wasn't all that effective, and then you got me all sticky again this morning." She gave him a mock frown.

They had seated themselves on the bed, pretty much the only comfortable spot in the room. Erik sent her a shamefaced and repentant look, then took her in his arms and looked into her eyes. "Can I get you sticky again before the bath gets here?" he suggested wistfully.

Bernadette snorted in laughter, then pushed him away. "No! Holmund might be here any minute." He looked abashed, so she kissed him. Then he kissed her back, a little harder, stroking her hair and running his fingers gently down her back in the soft, snug fitting dress.

"Hey, this is nice," Erik said appreciatively. "I don't get to see you in anything but armor or your skin very often. Not that your skin isn't also very nice..." he leered. He pulled Bernadette into a closer embrace, squeezing her breasts against his chest through the thin fabric. They sat on the bed necking, enjoying the activity without getting too excited. As their relationship deepened, a little of the raw animal passion was seeping away to be replaced by genuine affection.

A knock came at the door, the two pulled apart, and Holmund bustled in carrying the washtub. He set it on the floor in front of the hearth, then he and his missus trooped in several times to deliver steaming pots of hot water along with several bucketsful at room temperature. "Will that be all, Fireblood?" he asked. I didn't think he knew who I was, Bernadette mused. It looks like my fame is spreading.

"That's wonderful, Holmund," she replied. "Thanks and good night. Somebody can come get the tub in the morning."

When the door closed again Erik pounced on her. "Alone at last!" he boomed, smiling.

She looked at him demurely from under her lashes, and then asked "Help me with my dress?" He eagerly leapt to do her bidding, unhooking the clasps at the front of the dress until the tight bodice had loosened to the point where it could be slipped down over her shoulders. Her ripe breasts spilled out as he pushed it down around her waist.

His eyes lit and he reached for them, squeezing gently and kissing each nipple. "Hey," Bernadette said, not about to be distracted. "Hot water. Now." Erik looked disappointed, but set about mixing hot and cold water in the tub until it was about halfway full of water that was just a little bit too warm for comfort. Bernadette stood there admiring the steaming tub, transfixed with joy. Holmund had even outdone himself and brought a small bath sponge. It had somehow found its way to this tiny village at the mountain's foot, from whatever ocean had given it birth.

Wriggling in a way that Erik found very interesting, Bernadette shrugged the dress down over her hips and it fell to floor. She stepped delicately from the puddled fabric and put a toe tentatively into the tub. Ooh! She took it out again. But she knew it would only be getting cooler, so it was time to face the challenge. This time she put one foot all the way in, then the other, standing flatfooted with the water up almost to her knees. Then, slowly, she crouched and carefully sat down. "Ahhhh…" she sighed.

Meanwhile, Erik had shucked out of his shirt and trousers, and was as naked as she. "I hope you don't think you're going to join me in here" Bernadette said, amused.

He laughed out loud "Hah! I don't think I could fit in there even if you weren't already filling it up. I just don't want to get my clothes all wet, when I wash your back."

"Mm?" She looked up at him questioningly.

"Lean back a little, and I can wash your hair," he said. Bernadette smiled and complied, but question marks were sparking in her mind. Who *is* this person? It seemed that the longer she knew Erik, the more facets of the man she discovered. So far, each of them had proven more endearing than the last. He used some of the soap to wash her hair, then mixed some of the hot and cold water in a bucket to pour over her head, rinsing it.

After Bernadette's hair was done, Erik took the sponge and rubbed some soap on it before working her over. He started with her neck, holding her hair up out of the way, then scrubbing her back down to her butt. Next, he came around to the front, grinning at her like a little boy who's proud of how helpful he's being to his

197

mommy. Weelll, not quite – now that he was facing her, Bernadette saw that his member was erect, and there was a gleam in his eye that was anything but childlike.

"I can wash this side by myself you know," she teased him.

"Oh no," he replied, looking concerned. "It's my fault you got besmirched. And I need to make up for the substandard bath I gave you last night. Arms up!" She obediently raised her firmly muscled arms over her head and he dipped the sponge in the water, washing from her fingertips down all the way past her armpits. The water sluiced down her sides as he did first one arm and then the other.

Bernadette was smiling at him now, and as she lowered her arms back into the water he bent close and kissed her tenderly on the lips. She put her hands on his shoulders and leaned into the kiss, slipping her tongue into his mouth. Then he rocked back onto his haunches, his member still jutting, and resumed his ministrations with the sponge. He soaped it and washed each of her breasts in turn, cupping water from the tub to rinse the soap away afterward. Then he bent lower with the sponge, washing her belly.

Erik's brows knit. "I'm doing this wrong," he said. "Give me a foot." She straightened out her right leg, extending the foot over the edge of the tub, and he scrubbed it with the sponge before gently handing it back in and reaching for the other one. Now that both feet and legs were clean, he took the sponge in hand and, leaning closer, ran it down between her legs. Spreading her labia with his fingers, he gently washed out her sex. It was slippery, as he'd hoped it would be.

"Okay," Erik said, regaining his feet. "All clean." Bernadette's eyes lit. An hour ago she had thought that nothing could be more delightful than to sit and soak in the hot water until she turned into a prune; but Erik's activities had begun to give her some other ideas. She got her feet under her and stood up, dripping.

"Towel?" she suggested.

Erik handed her one of the stack that Mrs. Holmund had brought in, and Bernadette bent to let the long wet strands of her hair hang down while she wrapped the towel around her head, then folded it back. She was glowing from the hot water, pink and wet.

Stepping out of the tub onto the hearth rug, she stood there and submitted to more of Erik's attentions as he gently blotted the moisture from her body with a second towel.

As Erik knelt to dry her legs and feet, he applied his mouth to her crotch, sucking water from the strands of her pubic hair and then putting his tongue into the opening. Bernadette nearly jumped. "Oooh, yes, Erik! But I can't do this standing up…" She led him over toward the bed and perched on the side of it, her legs spread to allow him full access to her inner folds.

Erik knelt at the side of the bed and began working her over with tongue, lips, and fingers, bringing a flood of juices to his mouth and setting Bernadette to panting, her hands clutching at his head. After she spasmed in release, he stood up. His cock was rigid, towering, and ready. She just lay back on the bed, feeling very relaxed now between the hot bath and the explosive orgasm, and invited him in.

Tonight, Erik felt more in control. Ah, he loved making love to this woman! He lay above her, plunging deep within her incredibly warm, incredibly wet folds, moving slower then faster. Then slower again, before turning her over so he could take her from behind. This position seemed to be one that was particularly good for Bernadette, and she was soon crying out loudly and repeatedly, the walls of her vagina pulsating and clutching at his cock like a squeezing fist as she came again. This time, he couldn't hold back the tide and his scrotum clenched tight as he exploded within her.

They fell to the bed together and lay there spooning, Erik kissing Bernadette's neck and shoulder from behind, arms wrapped tight around her, as their pulsations gradually subsided and he slipped out. She continued lying there with her back to him, holding his arms tight as they wrapped around her, for a while longer. Then she stretched and rolled over to put her hands on either side of his face and kiss him sweetly.

"See?" she murmured. "Sticky again." He hugged her, chuckling.

"I'm sorry," he rumbled, "I'm incorrigible. But I just can't help it. Every time I see you, I want to fuck your brains out." Bernadette sighed, snuggling closer.

"I hope you can restrain yourself while we're fighting aptrgangr," she said softly. After resting for a while, the sticky pair got up and used the water in the tub, with the rest of what was still in the pots and buckets, to clean themselves off.

Erik couldn't sit in the tub but he could stand in it, and Bernadette gave him a sponge bath. This activity had him on the rise again, but she quashed the idea. "If we keep doing that, we'll *never* get clean. Let's just get some sleep – it looks like a long walk tomorrow." She handed him a towel.

"Yes, Mistress," he replied with a wistful expression. Before long, they blew out the candles and slept.

Chapter 26: The Road to Lakedon

Erik felt completely comfortable: warm, sleepy, drifting up from a dream of rolling in Berni's arms that was starting to make his cock stiffen – trapped beneath his body as he slept face down. But something was niggling at the edge of his consciousness. Some... noise. There it was again. He opened his eyes and rolled over to find that selfsame light of his life, all business, clanking as she strapped on her armor and gathered her gear for travel. Oh.

Erik yawned and stretched, as Bernadette gave him a look that was half amused affection, half impatience. "Up and at 'em, Big Boy" she said. "We're burning daylight!" It didn't look as if he were going to be able to cozen her into any nude romps *this* morning at least, so he sat up. Then, he got to his feet and went off to find the privy. After that he splashed some water on his face, and began getting into his things. By this time Bernadette was fairly simmering with impatience, and she helped him get his armor strapped on to speed things up.

"What about breakfast?" Erik asked. Bernadette tossed him a bread roll, chewing on another. "We'll eat some more after we get down the road a ways," she said. "I really want to get to Lakedon today." They bid farewell to Holmund and his wife, tipping them for the extra effort, and were soon walking down the road that led south out of town before turning to the east.

The region they were walking through, the area known as Lakemarch (of which Lakedon was the seat), was pleasant to look at. Bernadette and Erik were traveling on stone-paved roads that seemed to meander a bit, splitting from time to time. Some smaller spur roads headed north toward the Woodrill River that, closer to the city, ran into the lake known as the Waldenmere. On either side of the road the pair were surrounded by a light hardwood forest, the leaves green and sparkling in the summer sunlight.

There were lots of wildflowers of all colors to be found growing here, but little else of interest to Bernadette for her growing collection of chemial ingredients. She had her mind on other things as well. Erik was so... *much* of a man. Words failed her. His humor and surprising tenderness were so at odds with his seeming stolidity, his competence as a killer, and his enormous sexual energy. When he stood there naked, looking at her with lust, it was as if all of her well-reasoned arguments were pushed right out of her mind by a flood of answering passion.

Bernadette felt almost as if she were getting addicted to Erik, against her better judgment. But at the same time, she missed Andrion terribly. His warmth, his blazing battle magic at her side in battle, his skill as a lover, even his occasional long-winded lectures on Iscandia lore, were things that she felt she needed. But much as she loved and wanted both of them, she didn't feel up to handling both of them at once. Her experience making love to the two of them together, while mind-blowing, had made her feel as if neither of them had gotten the attention he deserved. If Bernadette was to spend time with Andrion, therefore, she'd have to leave Erik behind for a while. And vice versa.

Her dilemma left her feeling frustrated, but she shrugged it off. Bernadette's emotional makeup didn't allow her to worry over problems for long. I'll deal with that when I come to it, she thought. Anyway, Erik and I have to find Adalbert before I can decide what to do next. Her reverie was interrupted at this point as a pair of snarling wolves attacked them from the left while a smilodon darted in from the right.

"Shit!" Bernadette yelled, drawing the bow she had held ready. She was getting faster with the weapon, able to draw and loose an arrow every few seconds. But it was lucky for her she was accompanied by a magnificently lethal young warrior. A couple of swings from the warhammer she'd given him cut the wolves down in a shower of blood. Then he turned to the wounded smilodon, which was now sporting three arrows shot at close range and was extremely pissed off. In a move that stunned Bernadette, Erik slung the handle of the warhammer across the spitting, snarling cat's neck and pushed down hard, while lifting its head with his knee. It fell dead, neck broken.

Panting, her heart racing, Bernadette gasped "*What* in all the hells is with the wildlife in this part of the world? Wolves *and* a smilodon?!" Slinging her bow over her back for the moment, she readied a new spell she had learned. As her coffers had swelled (especially since becoming owner of the Maiden, and being able to add its profits to her income stream), it had occurred to her that it would be nice to have some more magic at her disposal. Garimund, the court mage in Wyrmshalla, had sold her half a dozen spellbooks and she could now heal both herself and others, among other little tricks.

These abilities were limited, however, to the amount of magical energy she had. Bernadette had been told that her natural fund of this energy would increase, as would the speed at which it would recharge itself, as she practiced and developed her skills. But for now, she found that healing herself of the scratches and one serious bite mark the cat had inflicted used almost half her available supply. It was slower than taking a healing potion too, best used only when danger had passed.

Erik observed this quizzically. "Healing?" he asked. She nodded. "I've never done much with magic," he remarked. "I'm more of a sharp force trauma kind of guy."

"I noticed," she responded. "Thank you for your efforts!" She turned to him and stood on tiptoe to give him a brief kiss. Clearly, the wildlands of Lakemarch – even the wildlands of the official road running through it – were no place to let your guard down.

Bernadette took a moment to skin out the pelts and retrieve some arrows, also removing a tooth from the cat. With this and some luminescent fungi, often to be found in caves, she could make a potion that would improve her abilities at smithing by nearly a third, for a short time. Then, bow to hand and eyes scanning the brush on either side of the road, she led them on their way toward Lakedon once more.

The day was a bit overcast, high clouds casting a murky pall over the land as they travelled along the road. Bernadette and Erik remained on full alert, as they were attacked repeatedly by bears, wolves, and less familiar creatures. Each time, their antagonists swiftly regretted their aggression but failed to flee in time to escape death. Bernadette was beginning to wonder if all of the wild animals in Iscandia were rabid, or something. But she'd been bitten numerous times and wasn't foaming at the mouth yet, so probably not.

Rather than try to sit and have a picnic in this perilous place, the pair just dug into their packs for less perishable items like bread, hard cheese, smoked salmon, and apples, munching standing up while continuing to keep an eye on their surroundings. After several hours of walking, Bernadette realized that she was looking at the Waldenmere on their left, the clear waters lapping the shore only a few yards away from the road. Ahead in the distance, wooden structures were built out over the water. That must be the backside of Lakedon.

"I have an idea," Bernadette told Erik. "Are you up for a swim?" They bundled their clothes and gear and tied them to a log, then pushed it out into the water. Kicking across to the nearest of the buildings, which had a ramp going down into the lake, they got their things back and dressed. Bernadette was feeling quite pleased with herself. Not only did the cool dip feel good after walking and fighting maniacal wildlife for hours, but they had now sneaked into Lakedon without alerting the city watch. If they were shortly to be consorting with thieves and ruffians in Lakedon's infamous Depths, it would be a good idea to keep a low profile.

They made their way up a series of walkways looking for a way into the main part of the city, and discovered a small wooden door. It was not locked, and they slipped inside to find themselves in a narrow back alley behind a warehouse. There was a smell of fish here, as if some of those caught in the lakemen's nets had been discarded nearby. "So far, I can't say I'm impressed," Bernadette remarked. Erik just grinned.

"Let's hope the front side is better," he said.

Chapter 27: Among Thieves

Bernadette and Erik came out of a side street and found the city of Lakedon spread out before them. There was a canal running through the center of town, crossed here and there by wooden bridges and flanked by boardwalks. Ahead to the left was a row of substantial-looking buildings, where the city's rich resided no doubt; and on the other side of the canal from that was a stone-paved central square, bustling with commercial activity.

Talk to Hamish, Bernadette thought. Giselle had seemed to know the man, or at least know *of* him; but she'd provided no physical description. She spotted a well-set-up but shady-looking character leaning on a pillar just ahead of them to the right, and approached him. He gave her a suspicious look and asked, "What brings *you* to Lakedon?" "What business is it of yours?" she retorted.

He backed off a little. "The Meades pay me to keep an eye on things," he said with a hint of resentment. Bernadette herself, Fireblood or no, was certainly not an imposing figure. But with Erik at her side, any malefactor with a lick of sense would think twice about crossing her. "And who are the Meades?" she asked him. "Anything goes on in this town, the Meades know about it or have a hand in it," he replied.

"Including the Guild of Thieves, I suppose?" Bernadette asked, fixing him with a gimlet stare. The man looked her up and down. She sure didn't look like a member of any guard force he'd ever seen. "Might be," he admitted. "What of it?" She smiled at him, sorry to have gotten off on the wrong foot. "I might be looking for this Guild of Thieves," she said quietly. "I've got some business to transact with them." She rubbed thumb and forefinger together in the universal gesture that meant "money."

"You want to talk to the Guild, you need to speak with Hamish," the character said. "You'll find him over there in the market square, selling his potions." The second in command of the Guild of Thieves was a chemiast? That seemed odd. Thanking her informant, Bernadette slipped him a few coins and made her way across a bridge in the direction he'd pointed.

A tall, sparely-built man with dark red, shoulder-length hair was standing at one of the stalls in the marketplace, doing some kind of sales presentation for a potion that sounded too good to be true. He was rough-hewn rather than handsome, with a straggly short beard, and looked to be in his late 30s at least. But she found something compelling about him. Maybe it was just that she'd always had a soft spot for bad boys. This, she felt sure, must be Hamish.

As Bernadette approached, he had just finished his spiel. He fixed her with a cool blue-green stare and said, "Sell you some of my potion, lass? It'll put hair on your chest." She smirked internally at the idea.

"Pass," she said coolly. "I'm looking for a man called Adalbert."

Hamish raised an eyebrow. "Never heard of him," he said with a shrug. "If you'll excuse me, I'm busy here." At least he was giving Adalbert what the old man had paid for, Bernadette mused. It boded well for the former Guardian archivist escaping the teams of ljosalfar agents who were probably searching for him just as they were.

"We're friends of his," she explained, as the thief looked down at her with annoyance. "And we need to warn him – ljosalfar agents are on his trail." Hamish frowned. Guild members had caught a trio of elven battle mages in the Depths just a few days ago.

Hamish shrugged. "Just supposing I know where you might find this Adalbert person…" he said, a trace of a wheedling tone coming into his voice. Bernadette had her purse out and was counting coins.

"Naturally, I would make it worth your while," she said soothingly and began dropping guilders into his hand one at a time. The coins were small, and the thief's hands were large. By the time he said, "He's out in the tunnels beyond the Mended Mug, down in the Depths" she had put more than a hundred guilders into his palm.

They got directions to the Depths and were soon on their way. Suppertime was coming on and they were both hungry, but they didn't want to wait. Even as they spoke, ljosalfar agents might be hauling the old man off in chains – or killing him outright. As directed they crossed the nearest bridge and proceeded to a set of steps nearby, that led down to a lower level of wooden walkways near the canal.

Wooden walks lined the buildings just above water level on either side, and there was a bridge crossing to the other side right near the steps they had come down. Set into the wall of a building opposite, Bernadette spotted the iron grate Hamish had described, and they stepped inside.

Beyond the grate was a wooden door, then a corridor built of stone leading on into dimness. Here and there along the corridor, candles and lanterns provided an occasional circle of warm light. Bernadette and Erik were on the alert, so when two thugs suddenly burst out of the room ahead of them on the attack, they had their weapons ready. She took one of them in the throat with her dagger, good for close-in fighting, while Erik bashed the other one's skull in with his warhammer.

Bernadette bent to go through their pockets, finding a fair amount of gold and a few lockpicks on each. She did not think of this as stealing. This was just a tax for trying to kill her. She won, her assailant was dead, so she had a right to anything he (or she) had been carrying. It made as much sense to her as carrying off the pelts of the wolves that had attacked them on the road.

Around a couple of bends the two companions found their way blocked by a wooden panel that looked like it might form a sort of drawbridge; but if so, the lever for lowering it was on the far side. Lakedon above was all built of wood, but the Depths was almost like a second city of stone, lying below the other one. Bernadette wondered as she dropped from the walkway they were standing on and made her way to a doorway she'd spotted on the level below, if this might not be the original Lakedon – sunken somehow, or perhaps submerged after the lake's waters rose. If so, those ancient builders knew what they were doing. The stones were tightly fitted, and there was very little dampness down here considering the water level must be 10 feet or more above their heads.

Bernadette and Erik moved cautiously through the labyrinth, encountering only a shri or two and one old woman. Bernadette thought she looked motherly, standing there in an apron chopping vegetables for soup – until she spun on her heel at their approach and ran at them with the foot-long knife she was holding. Fortunately, Erik didn't have any compunctions about striking down hostile old ladies. Bernadette might have hesitated long enough to have gotten that knife in her ribs.

In the kitchen area where the old woman now lay still, Bernadette spotted a wooden door to their right. Ahead and to the left, a passageway looked familiar and she went over to investigate it. Sure enough, this was the other side of the walkway they'd been on after killing the two thugs. She pulled the lever she found on the wall, and there was now a bridge across to the area they'd come in from – just in case they needed to beat a hasty retreat.

That done, the two went back and opened the wooden door, finding themselves in a large, darkened space. At the far end, lit by lanterns, Bernadette could see a bar. "This must be the Mended Mug," she murmured to Erik.

"I wonder if they have any brandy?" he murmured back. She smiled at that, slinging her bow on her back and walking normally. It was probably not a good idea to be looking furtive, down here.

As they approached the bar, Bernadette saw several of what she assumed were Guild members having an acrimonious discussion. There seemed to be only a couple of women in the gang, a lithe Afrans woman sitting by herself over near the edge of the water and a stunningly beautiful but cold-seeming platinum blonde who was sitting at a table in the corner. The blonde looked like she was chewing nails.

Bernadette walked up to the bar. "Hamish sent me," she told the forbidding-looking bartender. "Said you could point me to where I can find Adalbert.

208

"That door there leads into the tunnels," he said with a gesture. "I don't know exactly where he's hiding in there. The place is a warren, and it's packed with the kind of people you probably don't want to meet."

Eyeing this fellow, Bernadette had to wonder just what kind of people *he* didn't want to meet. Thinking about wandering through a dark labyrinth on an empty stomach, she asked "You have any food here?" There was no sign of the usual stewpot you could expect to see at an inn.

"Bread and cheese, mostly," the barkeep said, gesturing at a collection of bottles and foodstuffs sitting on a counter behind the bar. They bought a few bread rolls and a small wheel of cheese, plus a couple of apples. Then they sat at the bar for a few minutes fortifying themselves, washing it all down with some surprisingly good mead.

Erik hadn't spent much time in this part of Iscandia, and asked, "Where'd you get this mead?" The barkeep looked at him questioningly.

"It's our local Honeylake mead," he said. "Have you been living under a rock?"

"Mostly in the area around Waterdon," Erik admitted. "They have a meadery there too, and that's usually all you can find in those parts. But this stuff is even better!" He downed his bottle, wiping his mouth on his arm, and looked down at his companion. "I suppose we'd better get going," he said, and she nodded.

The two got their weapons ready and went through the door into the tunnels beyond the tavern, now searching for Adalbert in earnest. They soon found themselves in a maze of stone corridors, occasionally passing galleries lined by iron grates. It almost looked as if it might have been a prison at one time.

Bernadette and Erik were expecting the area to be inhabited by the dregs of Lakedon – thieves, beggars, poppy addicts – but also found themselves running into a party of ljosalfar guards accompanied by a mage. They each got off a few arrow shots (Erik, too, now had a bow she'd enchanted with fire damage) but they were soon in a fierce toe-to-toe fight.

When the three ljosalfar lay dead on the stone walkway at their feet, Bernadette used her healing spells on herself and Erik. He's worth two of me in a fight, she thought. I've got to keep him healthy. Closer to the truth, she couldn't bear the thought of losing him. He'd gotten his hooks into her heart. To Erik, she said "These ljosalfar must have been down here looking for Adalbert. If there any more of them, let's hope we find him before *they* do."

Bernadette and Erik wandered the maze together, eyes and ears alert for danger; but most of the place's other denizens were more reclusive than hostile. Finally they came to a door that was three times as impressive and substantial as any other they'd yet encountered down here, and appeared to have a dozen locks on it. Bernadette had a feeling they'd found what they were looking for, and she knocked.

A spyhole a few inches tall and a foot or so wide was slid open, and she could see the face of a grizzled old man behind it, lit by candlelight. "Adalbert?" she asked. When he did not deny it she continued, "Giselle sent us to look for you."

"How do I know what you say is true?" he responded. He might look old, but he seemed to be pretty spry and fit. He must have been formidable forty years earlier.

Bernadette told him, "She said to remind you of the first of Pluvia."

The old man's expression changed, and he barked a short laugh. "Hah! I remember that! You must really have spoken with her. Glad to know she's still alive. There's not many of us left. Hang on while I get the door unlocked." Bernadette stood there in growing impatience as the spyhole was closed and a series of clicking sounds went on for what seemed like an hour. Finally she heard Adalbert's muffled voice say "That's it," and the door swung inward, admitting them.

Adalbert's room was fairly large and nicely appointed, for being down here in this dank labyrinth. "I'm truly glad to know that Giselle is still alive. But it's too late," he told them.

"What do you mean by that?" Bernadette asked him.

"Tarragin has returned!" he replied. "Just as the prophesies said he would: the Soul-Devourer. It means the end of the world is coming."

"Do you mean the dragon that's been bringing the other dragons back to life?" she queried. Bernadette recalled now, that when they had witnessed the resurrection near Delvewood, the dragon arising from its grave had said something that sounded like "Tarragin."

"Yes. If he's back, that means the world is doomed. Only a fireblood can stop him, but there hasn't been a fireblood in centuries," Adalbert explained. Bernadette felt both relieved and concerned. The good news is, there is one special person who can save the world. The bad news is, it's me.

"It's all right," she told him. "I'm fireblood."

Adalbert looked surprised and energized. "You are? That's wonderful! But we must go and talk with Giselle. We need to find the Wall of the Ancients."

Bernadette found herself wishing for Andrion again. She felt sure he would somehow just happen to have heard about this the Wall of the Ancients and where to find it. Perhaps it really was time to check back in at the Maiden. Adalbert gathered some things and announced he was ready to go, and they all headed out the door ready to thread their way back out of the maze once again.

Immediately, though, the three found themselves assaulted by another party of ljosalfar. Again a couple of soldiers were accompanied by a mage, and the mage was summoning some kind of extra-dimensional creatures to attack them. These looked very impressive but didn't seem to be very much harder to kill than, say, a troll. Bernadette was sure that the writhing figure covered head to foot in flames, whirling in the air and casting fireballs at them, could only be a fire demon.

After they'd fought their way through and the last foe had fallen, Adalbert told her that the towering creature that looked like a man carved out of ice blocks was a frost demon. Nasty beasts. Bernadette used her healing spells on all of them, saving on potions and getting in some practice. The more frequently one cast a particular spell, the more adept one became. She wondered if the same applied to the dragon spells, though they seemed to work so differently from ordinary magic.

The trio wended their way through the zigs and zags of the passageways and eventually exited the tunnels through the Mended Mug without speaking to anyone. Bernadette wanted to get on with her save-the-world mission, and return to Andrion. They trooped across the now-lowered wooden bridge and were very shortly out of the Depths, gathered on the wooden walkway beside the canal.

In a few more moments, Bernadette had them all standing in the road outside Forestville, on a glorious sunny afternoon. After their time in the dungeon-like environs of the Depths, she almost wanted to just stand there absorbing the sunshine and breathing in the fresh air. But, to business. They proceeded down the street and into the dimly lit Laughing Herdsman, and found Giselle prowling the common room.

"Adalbert!" she exclaimed, rushing to greet her old friend. The two had been boon companions many years in the past, or so they both said. Watching their reunion, though, Bernadette did not get the sense that they'd ever been lovers. Maybe the age gap was too great. Bernadette herself liked young guys for their vigor and enthusiasm, and older ones for their wisdom, skills, and greater grasp of the world. In her life so far, any reasonably good-looking male who kept himself in shape and had the energy for it, might find himself welcomed to her bed – and into her heart as well, if things worked out between them.

Giselle beckoned them all to follow her. "Come on, let's go where we can talk." She led them all down into her secret basement room, where Adalbert gave them details of what he was looking for.

"We need to find the prophecy that explains how The Fireblood can destroy Tarragin," he told them. "And for that, we need to go to the sanctuary of the ancient Guardians and find the Wall of the Ancients. But I don't know where it is."

His former comrade in arms looked at him in surprise. "Wasn't that where the precursors of the Guardians had their first temple in Iscandia?" she asked.

"That's right," he replied. "The Guardians as they were constituted in the modern era are said to be descended from them, and the place was described in some detail in the lore. But its actual location was never pinpointed."

Seeing that he was expected to say more, Adalbert went on. "It was said to be built into a mountainside, hidden beyond a labyrinth, where two streams came together somewhere in the area of Westmarch. Within, there were living quarters for the Guardians, a library, training facilities, and of course the Wall of the Ancients – carved with scenes from the histories."

Giselle mused on what he'd told them. "There's a place near Hag's Needle that fits your description," she said. To Bernadette she added, "Will you come with us to Hag's Needle? Or would you prefer to meet us there?"

"I'll meet you there," Bernadette replied, pleased to have been asked instead of commanded. She wanted to bring Andrion along on this mission, if ancient lore was involved. Besides, she just missed being with him.

Bernadette and Erik bade farewell to the two former Guardians. In the street outside the inn, without any further ado, Bernadette touched her map and they were transported to the road outside the Bathing Maiden, rain falling on them as evening drew near.

Chapter 28: Home Again

Inside the Bathing Maiden, Andrion stood on the upstairs balcony leaning against the rail. He was looking down at the main floor and the bathing pool, but his mind was elsewhere. Where was Berni? And when was she coming home? His memories painted pictures of her: fiercely charging into battle against aptrgangr and bandits; her face lit with excitement at the discovery of some great treasure; her sea-gray eyes luminous with love and desire as he held her in his arms.

Andrion had accepted her terms, and he knew it meant he could not obsess about her. She was her own woman, and he was one of the men in her life. But he couldn't stop thinking about her, wanting her, missing her. He noticed Lifa stepping into the pool below. They'd worked together, and he'd found her a warrior worthy of respect. And with that face and body!

He tried to picture himself burying his head between those enormous globular breasts, and there was a faint stirring between his legs. Erik had had her, he knew, so apparently she was neither unobtainable nor gay. But she was so stern! Andrion could not imagine her feeling joy in his embrace. Unbidden, other pictures came into his head: Berni in the arms of Erik, ecstasy painting her features as that blond giant pierced her with his oversized cock.

Andrion grimaced. Cut that out, he told himself. He turned away from the railing, fleeing from his thoughts, and went to sit at the table in the master bedroom, sipping some wine. Another evening ahead, with his friends and companions around him, at the best inn in Iscandia. And all of it gray and lifeless without the bright spark that was his lover, his Fireblood.

Downstairs, Bernadette and Erik came in the front doors. It had been a long trip indeed, from Forestville to Lakedon and back, and she had more trials ahead of her. She reached up to give Erik a kiss and a hug and sniffed his neck. "You could use a bath, love" she remarked mildly. He grinned.

"How can I argue with that?" he replied, shrugging. In a few moments he had dropped his things at one of the mezzanine tables, and was climbing into the central tub.

"I'll join you later," Bernadette promised, then after a quick glance around the room she headed up the stairs, eyes searching for one particular face. She didn't see him in the sleeping galleries on either side of the hall, but as she reached the master bedroom at the back, there he was at the table. She hurled her pack to the floor and rushed to him, crying "Andrion!"

Andrion looked up and his eyes lit, so glad to see her he thought he might forget how to breathe. Realizing she was coming at him like a rabid smilodon, he leaped to his feet and caught her as she barreled into him. "I've missed you so much!" she mumbled, her face pressed against his muscular chest.

"Whoa, easy there!" he said, grabbing her shoulders so he could step away slightly and look at her face, drinking her in. "You're all right! I was worried…" he trailed off. He didn't want to sound like a mother hen, least of all with this wild free spirit whom he loved to distraction.

Bernadette smiled at him so brightly it was as if the sun had just come out from behind a cloud. "About *me*?! Don't be silly! I've been really busy, but everything is fine. I've been thinking about you every day!" It was only a small lie, and now that she had him in her arms once more she felt as if she never wanted to let him go again. He bent to kiss her, deeply and hungrily. Then he reached to her shoulders and unbuckled her armor.

Clank! That much-mistreated collection of sheet metal and padding fell to the floor disregarded. As Bernadette stood there in her underclothes, Andrion reached down to cup her buttocks and pull her to him, up to where he could kiss her some more without bending over. She assisted by throwing her arms around his neck, and her legs around his hips. But he kept his grip on her buttocks as he drank her mouth like a draft of ambrosia. She might be travel-stained and a bit scuffed around the edges but she was here with him again, and all was right with the world.

Still held off the floor, Bernadette began showering Andrion's face with little kisses, murmuring between times "I want you. I want you. I want you." All *right*, he thought. Whatever she might have been doing with Erik while she was gone, clearly *he* still held a place in her heart.

"I want you too," he growled, capturing her mouth and slipping his tongue inside it. In a moment he added, with a gesture, "There's a bed right there."

"Yes!" she cried. Then, "Oh, but I'm filthy. And wait until you hear everything that's been going on! I..." Andrion was certainly interested in hearing about Bernadette's adventures, but right this moment there were other things that seemed more important. He got a grip on himself, recalling that this was a woman who put a surprisingly high value on cleanliness (not that he minded, much).

"Do you want to take a bath first, love?" he asked, showing more forbearance than he would have thought possible an hour before.

Still clutching him around the neck and practically glued to his body, Bernadette considered. Erik was down there, and the whole thing might devolve into a delicate dance of relationships. Fuck that shit. "No!" she responded. "I want you *right now*!" Right now is good, Andrion thought, joy leaping within him. He eased Bernadette down to stand on the floor and reached to the hem of his tunic, pulling it off over his head.

Bernadette watched him avidly. All of her soul-searching and careful rationalizations had been erased by the actual, physical, presence of Andrion. He was beautiful, and she wanted him so badly she could hardly contain herself as he continued disrobing in front of her. She still stood there in her sodden underwear, in which she had fought a dozen battles, but her entire attention was taken up watching him as he stripped.

Oh! That magnificent torso! Not as broad as Erik's, perhaps, but powerful and beautifully sculpted. Bernadette loved the caramel color of his smooth skin, the tiny reddish brown hairs dusted across its surface. Andrion pulled off his trousers, and she was delighted to see that he was wearing no underwear beneath them – and that his fine, powerful cock was fully aroused and eager for her. She stood there drinking him in with her eyes, her breath coming faster.

A couple of breaths later, Bernadette realized that it was time to stop using her eyes and start taking him in with some other parts of her body. Andrion brought this to her attention by stepping closer and beginning to pull her undershirt off, up over her head. Nude to the waist, she paused to press herself against him, feeling his warm skin against hers. Oh yes! Stepping back again, she stood there demurely while he peeled her underdrawers down over her rounded rump and thence to the floor. Then, glancing down, she stepped out of them before locking her eyes on his.

Andrion looked at her, and her look as she gazed into his eyes was exactly the same as in his mental vision of what *seemed* like days and *was* probably less than twenty minutes ago. His exultance was so overwhelming he could barely do anything but stare at her grinning, though his gaze did not stay fixed on her eyes. Berni was a total package, and if some of that package perhaps caused him problems, the rest of it was very fine indeed.

Andrion hardly knew where to begin, though by now they knew each other like an oft-read favorite book. Stepping close, he bent to claim her mouth as they pressed their nude bodies close together. His cock, stiff and throbbing, was trapped between them – a hot and hard presence that demanded attention from both of them.

Bernadette felt as if she'd been plunged into a sea of delicious warmth, infused everywhere with an urgency that drove her onward. There was no taking time, no conversation, no thought. Just the desire that flooded her as she approached the homing beacon that was Andrion. Rising above that sea for just an instant, a short breath, she thought "This is probably not going to take very long." She was right.

Moving to the bed, they fell down upon it together. Bernadette seized Andrion's rigid member in her hand, and guided him to her swollen, glistening cunt within moments. They were lying on their sides, face to face, and she threw a leg up over him as his cock slipped in. As he penetrated within her, all the way inside, they locked mouths and the feel of him there almost immediately sent her to the brink of orgasm. Her excitement was so great, it took no more than a few thrusts before she was screaming.

Andrion, as a mature man of 32, prided himself on his control. With Bernadette he had always been a skillful lover, able to draw out their lovemaking until she had come multiple times. Now, being back inside her after days of deprivation, he felt like a teenager on his first outing. As she came, her cunt spasming and gripping him from top to bottom in waves, his mind exploded along with his body as his cock erupted, filling her with his seed.

Bernadette enfolded his head in her arms, once again covering his face with kisses, as her breathing gradually returned to normal. "I love you, I love you," she said softly, so softly he could barely hear. So softly *she* could barely hear, though she knew it in the depths of her soul. Saying it out loud seemed hard, somehow. He just held her more tightly, also murmuring "I love you…"

After Andrion had slipped out of her and their heartbeats had returned to normal, Bernadette made an attempt to gather her wits again. "Oh love," she said in a voice that was still breathy from her recent passion. "I'm so glad to be here." Several possible answers crossed his mind, and Andrion rejected each of them in favor of just holding her close, applying soft kisses to her neck, her ears, and any other body part that was handy.

Awhile later he felt he had to speak, though. "Want to take that bath now?" he asked. Andrion knew this woman well enough by now to know the answer in advance. "Oh, that's a wonderful idea," Bernadette replied. Moving slowly, feeling as if her muscles had been melted and not quite yet congealed, she rose from the bed and located her pack where she'd dropped it earlier. She dug out her robe.

Andrion had his own robe that he kept while he was living in the Maiden, which had been most of the time for a couple of years before the arrival of The Fireblood had turned his life upside-down. His arm around her, they walked along the gallery and down the stairs to the floor below. They found Erik still relaxing in the pool, trying to engage Lifa in conversation, and joined him. Erik might be on the light side, intellectually, but he was no dummy. He knew where Berni had been and what she'd been doing, and seemed not to mind.

As she and Andrion entered the pool to sit beside him, Bernadette reached over to give him a squeeze and a kiss. Erik stifled the message that arrived from between his legs, suggesting that now might be a good time to sit up and beg. Meanwhile Bernadette sank back in the hot water, a delicious feeling of relaxation coming over her.

Shortly, she began to tell Andrion all about the Guardians, the ljosalfar consulate, Lakedon, the Guild of Thieves, Adalbert, and more. Erik cheerfully added many details as the three of them talked until all of them were beginning to wrinkle and had to climb out. They continued the discussion, robed and sitting at one of the inn's tables, over supper. And on into the evening, until bedtime.

Erik, seeing how the wind blew, went off to find a bed on the sleeping loft. Bernadette and Andrion sat quietly together for a few minutes more, while she filled him in on the latest mission she'd found herself caught up in. "I want you to come with me this time," she said, flooding his heart with joy as outwardly, he maintained his usual slight smile. "Hag's Needle's not that far from Fort Weston. And I'd really appreciate your input about the lore involved."

Andrion eyed her with mild surprise. So far, he'd gotten the sense that Bernadette bore his explanations of Iscandia phenomena with something approaching bare tolerance. Now she was actively seeking his help? It pleased him immensely, though he was loath to admit it. He'd spent years in Iscandia digging up information, and finally he had a protégé of sorts, ready to receive what he was eager to pass on. This wasn't in the same league with the passion he felt for her as a lover, but it might well get into second place.

Their plans for the morning solidified, Bernadette and Andrion went back up the stairs – his arm around her, holding her close, once again. They moved quietly through the eastern gallery, all the way to the master bedroom at the back. As they undressed for bed, Andrion moved close to her and folded her in his arms. "I'm not through with you yet, you know…" he growled softly. At a loss for once for a snappy comeback, Bernadette just looked up at him, her glowing eyes speaking what her words could not say. It was a long while yet before they slept.

Chapter 29: A Midnight Creep

Sated with love and still blissful at her reunion with Andrion, Bernadette slept well at first. But she woke in the night to use the chamber pot, and while she was up she had some second thoughts. I can't just ditch Erik without some kind of farewell, she thought. She didn't know *what* to think, really. While she was with Erik, he was everything she wanted in a lover. He was fantastic in bed, a valiant protector, and a jolly companion. But without Andrion by her side, she soon found herself missing him unbearably. And when she was with Andrion, he dominated her thoughts and feelings.

What in all the hells is wrong with me anyhow? Bernadette mused, frustrated. I can't pick either one of them, and I feel like shit whenever I leave one behind to be with the other. In her short life, her tendency to hop into bed with whatever guy caught her eye had not yet caused her such problems.

She'd been in love, yes. Half a dozen times at least, probably. Even those gormless farm boys had their charms initially – though the feeling seldom survived prolonged contact. But now she had found the "real men" she'd been dreaming of, and she was learning that real men came with real feelings that could not be ignored. What was she to do about it?

Bernadette decided to stick with what had worked so far for her, which was to ignore the problem for the time being and go with what her gut (or was it perhaps, a bit lower?) told her to do. Now she was wide awake, Andrion was snoring gently, and it seemed to be sometime in the hours of early morning. She padded off quietly down the western gallery, looking for Erik.

Bernadette found Erik sleeping, dead to the world, in one of the gallery's narrow beds. The inn's business was down a little at this time, and his was the only occupied bed on this side of the gallery. She crouched at his bedside, as naked as he was, and gently stroked his arm. "Erik!" she hissed. His eyelids fluttered. It was never really dark in the Maiden, with candles lit at all hours, and as his sky-blue eyes focused on her a sleepy smile curved his lips. Good, she thought. She'd been afraid he might be bent out of shape when she'd dropped him like a hot potato to be with Andrion, despite his relaxation earlier when they'd joined him in the bath.

"I'm going to Hag's Needle tomorrow with Andrion," she told him softly. "I'd like you to hang out at the Maiden until we get back." He didn't seem particularly upset. Bernadette had the feeling that Erik's attitude to life and love was pretty close to her own.

"I'll be here if you need me," he replied, reaching to hold her to him. "Did you come to give me a little goodbye kiss?" Well yeah, she supposed that she had.

As Erik pulled her close, Bernadette melted into his arms and her mouth met his in a deep kiss. She put her heart into it – all the love she bore him, along with her confusion about her similar feelings for his friend Andrion. And he injected an element of that implacable, irresistible animal passion that had marked her relationship with him almost from the beginning.

Though she had been well and truly loved by Andrion only hours before, coming multiple times, Bernadette now found herself responding to Erik as he beckoned her to passion once again. In moments his naked body was pressed against hers, his tongue in her mouth; his hands moving over her stroking, squeezing, his hard cock pressing against her belly.

Bernadette was momentarily reminded of the physical disparity between them. She stood almost a foot shorter and half his weight, and though she was becoming a formidable warrior her abilities were as nothing compared with the power of this golden godling. Yet, even while having all of the physical power in their joining, Erik treated her with tenderness and care.

Though in awe of Erik's power, Bernadette felt safe with him. He would never harm her. Though he might, she realized, fuck her until she couldn't string two thoughts together. This notion came into her mind as he mounted her and began thrusting powerfully, sending a searing burst of sensation rushing from the center of her being out in all directions, causing her fingers and toes to tingle even as her mind lit with white fire and she bit her lip, trying to stifle a scream of ecstasy.

Some considerable time later, Bernadette disentangled herself from Erik's arms as they were wrapped together in the confines of the narrow bed. Whispering "I'll see you later," she kissed him on the cheek and tiptoed downstairs. She didn't know what time it was, but the Maiden was quiet. Everyone seemed to have gone to bed.

She slipped down into the hot pool, letting the hot water soak away any remaining muscle aches along with the tensions that would not let her be. Her mind was a daze, not willing to come to terms with her conflict between Erik and Andrion, and not ready yet to start thinking about the mission to come. After a while, she got out and toweled off before returning to the master bedroom to slip in beside Andrion and fall, blissfully, into sleep once again.

Chapter 30: To the Sanctuary of the Ancient Guardians

A few short hours later Bernadette and Andrion were up and dressed, charged with excitement as they prepared for her next quest as The Fireblood. Would they, aided by Giselle and Adalbert, be able to find the ancient knowledge that would let her fulfill her destiny and prevent Tarragin from bringing about the end of the world? Despite Bernadette's usual enthusiasm for adventure, she felt a little subdued as she contemplated the consequences should she not prove up to the task.

But with Andrion at her side, what could go wrong? He was so strong, so confident, so… good in bed, well, that was kind of irrelevant in this case. But his presence lent her strength. They gathered all their gear before stepping outside. Erik was evidently still sleeping, and Bernadette felt she had already said her goodbyes to him in as thorough a way as possible.

Bernadette examined the map. The fort along the main east-west road, where they'd battled a group of Insurgents, seemed like the closest fast-travel point to Hag's Needle. No more than an hour or two away on foot, she judged. Though she could only *hope* they would arrive in daylight.

In fact they did, and creeping carefully away from the stone walls Bernadette and Andrion headed down to the main road. They had not gone far when they were suddenly jumped by a humanoid monstrosity somewhat bigger than a troll, with red, leathery skin and a single eye glaring at them as it rushed to the attack.

Bernadette went into a defensive crouch and as she raised her bow she yelled "Kraf-Luft-Struung-Wund!" The dragon spell sent the creature flying through the air to tumble in some brush thirty feet away. It lay there stunned for a moment, time enough for her to put three or four flaming arrows into its hide. "What…?" she gasped, scrambling to a better vantage point and preparing to fire again.

"Cyclops!" Andrion panted back, as he fired blazing bolts of lightning from his palms before reaching back to unlimber his axe. One last arrow from Bernadette's bow proved the final straw, and the hideous thing collapsed with a grunt of pain.

Bernadette approached it leerily. Yes, it was really dead. A pool of dark blood was spreading around it and soaking into the earth of the hillside. "Any idea what these things are good for?" she asked Andrion. She was coming to rely on him for local lore, and could usually count on him not to be a snot about it. In this instance he replied thoughtfully, "I believe their eye is a chemial ingredient. And I suppose you could cook one up in a savory stew – but you might need a lot of salt."

Bernadette wrinkled her nose, then drew her dagger and relieved the corpse of its eye before shouldering her pack once more and leading the way further down the hill. As they continued along the road, approaching the place where they would need to turn north, they heard a familiar roar that sent shivers up Bernadette's spine: they were being attacked by a dragon!

Looking up the side canyon where a tributary of the river they were following came in, Bernadette spotted Adalbert and Giselle. Adalbert *was* apparently a competent mage, and was hitting the dragon with weaves of fire and lightning from hundreds of feet away. She and Andrion kept low as they dashed toward them, anxious to join their companions in the fight to defeat the flying monster.

With Bernadette and Giselle raining arrows on the dragon while the men drained its health and stamina with battle spells, it was soon weakened enough that it could no longer fly. It crashed to the ground on the far side of the small tributary stream, bloody and tattered. Meanwhile, though, another threat had materialized: Hag's Needle was the site of an extensive Insurgent encampment. The savages, drawn by the dragon's roars, were now attacking the four companions instead.

Bernadette, confident that Andrion and her other companions would protect her from Insurgent attacks behind, walked forward and put another three arrows into the dragon. You needed to get them while they were down, or they might simply fly away and live to attack you another day. That taken care of, she whirled and began shooting arrows into several of the Insurgents as they fought with other members of her party. In moments, silence reigned.

Panting, her heart pounding, Bernadette slung her bow behind her back and picked her way across the shallow stream to the corpse of the dragon. She could not absorb its soul until she came within range, and if that was not done the creature might be resurrected yet again by Tarragin. Besides, she hoped it might yield gems that would power any new dragon spells she might learn. And then of course there would probably be loot to be found on the body – whatever indigestible treasures it had devoured while alive.

After raiding the dragon's carcass, and absorbing a glittering deep purple spell stone, Bernadette checked the bodies of the half dozen Insurgents lying here and there. They were an attractive people, the women especially beautiful in their skimpy fur armor and exotic war paint. She wished they were not so hostile to outsiders. It might be fun to spend some time with them, getting to know them and their culture. But that wasn't going to happen if every Insurgent in Iscandia wanted to kill her on sight.

Now that all of their adversaries had fallen, the four made their way up a trail on the hillside above the road, and into a cave opening. This, according to Giselle, was the actual Hag's Needle. They found two more Insurgents inside the cave, one of them a type of shaman. He had devastating battle spells, and was very hard to kill.

Four against two was not much of a contest, however, and the two defenders soon lay dead. This seemed to be a living area, with cooking and chemial facilities, sleeping pallets, and storage. Bernadette checked it all out before they continued deeper into the cave, following behind Adalbert and Giselle. She soon found herself in a large stone chamber, the two Guardians standing above her at the top of a nearby stone staircase. They were looking at three squat pillars.

The pillars were no more than thigh high, and rather than the animal symbols Bernadette had seen on other pillars in Iscandia, these were carved with sinuous, symmetrical geometric glyphs. "Ah, just as I expected," Adalbert said. "These are Sindelan symbols. The Guardians had their roots in the ancient Sindels, who followed the dragons to Agena from their land across the sea."

Even if these were not the same as other such puzzle keys she'd seen, Bernadette had a pretty good idea of how this should work. She didn't see any holes nearby from which arrows or spears might shoot if she guessed wrong; so she went ahead and rotated the pillar on the left one turn, until a new symbol was facing her. It looked vaguely like a circle with two tails at its top, or maybe a loop of ribbon with dangling ends. Adalbert approved of her action: "That's it! The symbol on the pillar to the left. Try turning all of them to that."

Scanning the three, Bernadette saw that the far right pillar already showed this same symbol. She rotated the center one twice, and as the desired symbol appeared a slab of stone abruptly fell down from their left to form a bridge across the ravine that had been preventing them from traveling further. Giselle said, "Good, it worked. Let's see what's up ahead." She led them across the bridge.

The four came to a dark opening in a stone wall, and entered it cautiously. On the other side of the opening, they found themselves in a medium-sized stone room with tiles on the floor, bearing various of the same Sindelan symbols that had appeared on the pillars. Adalbert warned, "Wait. Those tiles look like pressure plates."

Bernadette had seen something similar, in Grabentief near the chamber that had once held the Staff of Zauber. "I'm guessing we want the same symbol that worked on the bridge," she told them, and began trying to cross the floor, stepping only on the tiles with that odd eared circle showing. This seemed to be working. She was making her way across the floor, and nothing was bursting out to kill her. So far, so good. She wound her way back and forth, moving toward the far side of the room, where she was expecting to find a lever or something to disable the trap.

But as Bernadette reached the far side, the tiles she needed petered out. She executed a leap across two rows and made it to an area of smooth unbroken stone on the far side of the room, but there was no switch. Then she looked back the way she had come and spotted a pull chain, on a pillar in the center of the wall to her right. Mentally slapping her forehead, she leaped back to the last tile she'd been standing on. But she missed, skidding, and a gout of flame came up from the floor.

Nearly falling, Bernadette staggered to another safe tile then limped her way over to pull the chain, halting the flames before sinking to the floor in agony. "Berni!" Andrion shouted, hurrying to her. He scooped her up and carried her off of the tiled floor to safety.

"Put me down, I'm all right" she told him through the pain. Her arms were blistered and it hurt like hell. She used her healing spell and in moments the blisters had disappeared, the redness had faded, and she felt better than fine.

Andrion watched this with wonder and delight. "When did you learn that?" he asked.

"Oh, it was during that last trip with Erik," she replied. He gave her a quick kiss. Usually while questing they were all business, especially in the company of others; but his relief at her swift recovery demanded expression.

"I think we're through the last of the traps," Adalbert told them. He led the way through winding corridors, which soon spilled out into a stone courtyard. It was open to the sky, with a huge stone building at the back of it. Standing before them in the center of the courtyard was a large and ornate chest, which Bernadette of course immediately plundered. Then she approached the building for a closer look.

In the center of its façade was a tall and broad stone door with no handle or keyhole. Beside it was a recess in the wall, a dark hole around six inches in diameter. Adalbert joined her, pulling lore out of his memories. As the Guardians' archivist, he was full of useful information. "This is the keyhole," he told her, gesturing to the mysterious recess. "It will not open for just anyone, though. Put your hand within."

Bernadette gave him a look. You first, she thought – but did not say it out loud. Stifling her misgivings, she inserted her left hand into the hole. It was more than a foot deep, and she felt no mechanism inside. What?... Suddenly she felt a sharp pain, and when she tried to withdraw the hand it was stuck! But a moment later she was able to pull it out again. The middle finger was bleeding from a small cut on the pad.

"Ah!" Adalbert said. "I had read that the door would only open for the Fireblood, but I didn't know it would literally taste your blood. Let's see if…" Just then they heard a grinding sound and the stone door before them sank slowly out of the way to expose a doorway leading in.

"After you, Fireblood," said Giselle. "You should have the honor of being the first to enter the sanctuary." "Bloody" well right, Bernadette thought, her hand stinging. She engaged a moment's healing to restore the member to its former unblemished state, even as she strode through the doorway.

As she led her companions forward into the cavernous edifice and up a series of curving stone staircases, Adalbert said "I can't believe we're really here! I wonder what we'll find inside?"

Enchanted weapons, treasure, and the magic word that will make Tarragin go poof would work for me Bernadette thought, though she doubted any of these would appear. As they entered a large room with a couple of dining tables in the middle of it, they saw a massive wall carved in bas-relief, standing across the rear of the room from one side to the other. Adalbert approached it. "The Wall of the Ancients," he said in awed tones. "I've never seen such a fine example of ancient Sindelan carvings." He held up a torch, the better to examine the details.

Giselle was impatient. "Adalbert!" she said, "Cut to the chase, will you? We need to know how the ancients defeated Tarragin."

Moving toward the left side of the frieze Adalbert said, "Here you see him. This panel goes back to the time when the dragon worshipers ruled Iscandia." He moved to the right, holding his torch closer. "Here, the humans rebel against the dragon worshipers – the legendary Uprising." He moved further to the right. "Tarragin's defeat is the centerpiece of the wall. See, here he is falling from the sky. The Norse champions are arrayed against him."

Giselle strode closer. "So, does it show how they defeated him?" she asked. "Isn't that why we're here?"

Adalbert gave her a tolerant smile. "Ah, patience my dear. The Sindelans told their stories in symbolism. Here is the Sindelan symbol for the term 'dragon spell.' But there is no way to know what dragon spell is meant."

"You mean they used a dragon spell to defeat Tarragin?" Giselle asked. "You're sure?"

"Oh yes," Adalbert replied. Giselle looked annoyed.

"Damn it! I was hoping it would be something else." The woman stalked forward and addressed Bernadette: "Have you ever heard of such a thing? A dragon spell that can knock a dragon out of the sky?"

Bernadette considered the question. Gale could certainly affect a dragon on the ground, but she doubted it would have much effect on one from a distance greater than a few yards. "I only discovered I'm fireblood a few weeks ago," she pointed out. "So far I've only learned three spells, and none of them can do that. The Old Ones were willing to teach me the spells for the stones I had already absorbed, but I gather they guard their own horde of spell stones closely. They expect me to go out searching the countryside for additional spells and stones, I'm afraid. And that could take months."

Giselle seemed to get a grip on her ire at this point, and relented a bit. "I was hoping we wouldn't have to involve them in this. But it seems we have no choice."

"I'll talk to Aethelred and see what he has to say," Bernadette told her. "If they won't give me the stone, they could at least tell me the spell words and maybe give me some idea where to *search* for the stone."

Giselle's response was, "I'll be surprised if you can pry that much out of them, but I suppose you'd better try. It's our only hope." Meanwhile Adalbert was continuing his study of the wall and had moved to the far right side.

"Look!" he cried. "The prophecy that brought the Sindelans to Agena in the first place, searching for The Fireblood. Here are the Sindelans, the Guardians. You see their distinctive blades. Now they kneel, their mission fulfilled, as the last Fireblood contends with Tarragin at the end of time. …Are you paying attention, Giselle? You might learn something of our own history." Giselle shot him a look of annoyance. Uh oh, Bernadette thought. Time we were leaving.

"I guess Andrion and I will be off to Eberburg then," Bernadette said to Giselle and Adalbert. Adalbert seemed so entranced by his study of the ancient carvings that she doubted he'd even heard her. "I'll be back when I have something to report." Turning on her heel, Bernadette headed back down the stairs to the courtyard. As she'd hoped, this place was open enough to the sky that she was able to fast-travel from here right to their destination.

Chapter 31: A Visit with Ehrgeizig

Bernadette shivered as she and Andrion found themselves standing in the middle of a raging snowstorm before the front steps of the alpine monastery. Brrr! There were times when she thought she would almost rather walk, or maybe ride a horse, than undergo these instantaneous translocations. *Not* that she particularly hankered for a stroll up Hochstein's many steep, troll-and-bear-infested steps. But it would have been nice to have some time to talk with Andrion about the mission, or throw on a wool cloak. Maybe she ought to plan ahead a bit before touching the map.

As they approached the building's front door, Bernadette asked Andrion, "Is it just me, or is Giselle kind of a bitch?" Andrion stifled a smirk.

"I'm sure her motives are pure," he said, attempting a serious expression.

"Oh, I know," she sighed. "She just kind of rubs me the wrong way. She acts as if somebody appointed her my boss while I wasn't looking."

"Don't let it get to you," he replied, this time his seriousness unfeigned. He leaned over to give her a squeeze and a kiss on the cheek.

Bernadette smiled at him, thanking him silently for his support. Then she pushed open the door and they went inside. The entry area was empty, and she and Andrion had to trace a series of corridors, peering into rooms as they encountered them, before finally finding Aethelred.

The wizened but straight-backed old monk turned to regard her questioningly. "Fireblood. How goes your quest for mastery of the spells?" Bernadette got right to the point.

"I need to find the dragon spell that defeated Tarragin." Aethelred's expression hardened. "Where did you learn of that? Who have you been talking to?" he accused.

She hadn't expected this attitude, and replied in what she hoped was a conciliatory fashion: "It was recorded on the Wall of the Ancients."

Mouth set in lines of disapproval, Aethelred immediately knew what *that* meant. "The Guardians! Of course. They are always quick to meddle in affairs of which they know nothing. They believe The Fireblood to be theirs – to defend and to control. Would you simply be their tool, used for their own purposes?"

Bernadette was taken aback by his angry response. "And the Old Ones do not consider me theirs? Why did you teach me those spells, if it was not to prepare me for my destined role?"

Aethelred gave a disgusted sigh. "Have you considered," he said, "that this spell you seek was used before – yet Tarragin has returned? Perhaps it has always been fated that he would bring about the end of the world, so that a new one can be born."

Bernadette was horrified at this fatalism. All very well for a man older than dirt to lay down his burdens and let whatever came befall him. But she wasn't yet 23 years old, with most of her life still ahead of her. As was the case for millions of people all over Terris.

"I won't give up without a fight," she told him angrily. "And what exactly happened, anyway? Did the spell send Tarragin into the Netherworld or something? How could he be gone for all these thousands of years and then just suddenly return?"

In the midst of the argument, they all heard a deep, rumbling voice speaking in the dragon tongue – and Aethelred looked up, startled. Now he looked at Bernadette apologetically. "Forgive me, I have just received instructions from the master of our order. I cannot answer your questions, but he can."

Bernadette's heart leapt with renewed hope. "Ehrgeizig, right? The one who was mentioned on those plaques at the shrines along the way up the mountain?"

"Yes," Aethelred admitted. "It was he whose voice you heard a moment ago, and he has given us permission to open the way so that you can consult with him."

"You told me he doesn't live here, but at the top of the mountain?" Bernadette asked. The old monk nodded.

"The way between here and Ehrgeizig's abode is blocked by a magical barrier. Come, you and your companion, and I will open it for you." He led them through the back doors and out into the courtyard where Bernadette had learned the first word of the Stasis spell.

A chill wind was howling as Aethelred continued along the courtyard to a series of staircases leading upward, followed by Bernadette and Andrion. They halted as they came to a platform with a fire burning in the middle of it. Beyond the fire was a stone pavement, and beyond that an archway. As Bernadette stood watching, Aethelred walked to stand before the gate. He spoke the words, "tor-fried-ov." Only three words? And Bernadette had felt no resonance within her. But perhaps that only meant she lacked the gem for this particular spell.

"Was that a dragon spell, Aethelred?" she asked.

"Not exactly," he replied. "It is spoken like a dragon spell, but uses only one's native fund of magical energy to power it – no stones required. It was gifted to us by Ehrgeizig so that we might unlock the ward that guards his home from intruders. Follow the path and make haste, now! The ward will remain down for only half an hour, and you must reach the top ere then or be taken by it. It would not be pleasant."

Thanking the old man, Bernadette and Andrion scampered up the snow-packed trail. They encountered no bears or trolls, though mysteriously one of Iscandia's ubiquitous mountain goats was picking its way up the path ahead of them. Perhaps Ehrgeizig's ward was selective, keeping out only intruders with the capability to do harm?

Well before the half hour had elapsed they rounded a final bend and found they were at the very top of the peak. A small flat area lay before them, with a stone Spell Wall on one side of it. But where was Ehrgeizig? There did not seem to be so much as a cabin or a cave entrance in the vicinity, nothing to shelter even the most hermetic of ancient monks. As Bernadette peered around, the sound of enormous leathery wings beating the air sent fear into her heart. Dragon!

But this dragon was not roaring, spitting flames, or attacking them with its teeth. Looking beyond ancient, the enormous creature came to a landing before them and spoke in a deep, rumbling, yet somehow gentle voice: "Greetings, I am Ehrgeizig. Who are you? What brings you to my mountain?"

Bernadette was more than a little taken aback to learn that the Old Ones' ancient master was no human but an enormous being who could have her for lunch in around two bites. But she wasn't afraid to speak up. After all, it was he who had requested they come. "I think you know who I am," she said. "Did you not call me?"

The ancient one nodded, surprising her. Did dragons use the same gestures as humans? "I did," he replied ponderously. "But before we begin, there are social niceties that must be observed, at the first meeting of two of the *drachen*." *Drachen*, Bernadette thought. Dragons. He's acknowledging me as a dragon. If only my wings were longer…

Ehrgeizig continued. "By long tradition, the elder speaks first. Hear my *furml*! Feel it in your bones. Match it, if you are *fjurblut*!" He turned to his left, then, and directed a river of flame at the Spell Wall before continuing: "The word of power calls to you. Go to it." Knowing what to do now, Bernadette approached the wall and found a set of runes glowing high up on its surface. The word "fjur" became embedded in her mind. But though she understood it, and would not forget it, she sensed no quickening.

She turned back to the enormous old dragon. "I have not the stone, to use this spell," she told him. He performed a curious contraction, pulling his wings in to his sides, then bent his neck and deposited something at her feet. It was a glittering, bright red gem! Bernadette bent and gingerly picked it up. It was hot enough to burn her fingers, but as soon as she held it in the palm of her hand it melted away painlessly. *Now* the surge came, as the spell became part of her repertory.

"A gift," Ehrgeizig said. "Now, show me what you can do. Greet me not as a mortal, but as *drache*!" The beginning word of Holocaust now a part of her mind, Bernadette turned back to face the ancient creature and blasted him with flames. She felt sure that this was acceptable etiquette for the *drachen*, though it wouldn't win many friends at human gatherings.

Ehrgeizig seemed quite pleased. "Aaah… yes! The fireblood runs strong in you. It is long since I had the pleasure of speech with one of my own kind for longer than a moment or two." Bernadette was so astounded it took her a moment to speak.

"You just pulled that spell stone out of your own body!" she blurted at last. "Does that mean *you* can't use the spell now?"

The ancient *drache* seemed amused. "No, little one," he explained. "The magic of the *drachen* is inherent in us. Once we have learned a spell, we create the stone to power it as naturally as a human being grows hair – though faster. Another stone is already forming within me, though I doubt I will have much need of it for some time yet to come."

Both Bernadette and Andrion, two natural-born seekers after knowledge, were entranced. To be speaking with an ancient sentient creature, someone who had actually *been there* when the history that by now had become nothing but legends was taking place! But what topic to cover first?

Bernadette began with the mission that had brought them here. "You know, ancient Ehrgeizig, that Tarragin has returned to Iscandia?" He nodded again.

"I have not seen him, and would prefer not to. But others, *drachen* I knew when the world was young, have flown here to tell me the news. His return, and the resurrection of my kind from their ancient graves, portends the end of this world."

"You and Tarragin don't get along?" Bernadette asked. Something about what Adalbert had read on the Wall of the Ancients had given her an idea.

"It was I who conspired with the ancient Norse heroes, those who sought to rid the world of Tarragin," the old dragon admitted. "But how did they do it?" she asked. "And why is he back?"

The old one considered for a moment, framing his reply. Finally he began: "Tarragin is not as other *drachen.* He has always told us that he is the eldest, the very first created by our father Aderos. And among a race who live forever, none could contradict that claim. He had always been around, since long before my mother's mother had hatched from the egg. And he had powers beyond those of ordinary dragons as well."

Bernadette was looking at him questioningly, and after millennia with nobody to talk to but humans Ehrgeizig had become adept at reading their facial expressions. "Foremost among those powers," he explained, "is the ability to traverse at will between planes of existence."

"Like the planes of the Netherworld from which conjurers summon demons?" Andrion asked. He knew something of this art. It was difficult to master, and the summoned creatures could turn on the mage who had commanded them to appear if his will faltered.

"Those, and others," Ehrgeizig said. "He has the ability to take others with him to these other worlds, traveling back and forth at will. One I knew of old told me of Tarragin's own personal world, his retreat. It was an entire planet, rich in life; but without any sentient beings upon it. A place where a dragon could be at one with its nature, hunting and devouring whatever he wanted."

"I thought the dragons wanted humans to worship them as gods?" Bernadette asked. That was supposedly what had led to the Uprising all those millennia ago. The ancient creature made a chuckling sound.

"Worship of gods is a human thing," he said in his ponderous bass voice. "We honor our father Aderos as the creator of all, but we care little for human worship. It was the dragon worshipers themselves, their priesthood, who fostered their church as a way to gain power over their fellow humans. And we were the beneficiaries, as our worshipers brought us whatever we required and we could do as we pleased. Who would not accept such an arrangement, however foolish it seemed?"

Bernadette and Andrion exchanged glances. It made sense. "So this sanctuary of Tarragin's," she said, "How did you come to know of it?"

"I was just a young dragon in the time before Tarragin was banished," Ehrgeizig continued. "I was beneath his notice, as he

237

was considered to be a god among us 'lords,' as the humans called us. But one I spoke with bragged to me of being taken there. It was the ideal world for dragons, he thought."

"And is that what you thought?" Andrion asked, sensing an edge to the old dragon's comment.

"No, not for me. I was studious, hungry for knowledge, and I enjoyed the company of humans. We *drachen* are ancient, but the vitality of the short-lived humans gives you an advantage over us. You actively strive to learn more, to conquer your world – while we, in those days, were merely content to live in it despite the thinking minds gifted to us by our creator."

"You said Tarragin was banished?" Bernadette asked. "Banished where?"

"Why, to the very world he had made his own!" the old *drache* replied with a hint of amusement in his tone. "After the Uprising had begun, I cast my lot with the humans. That is to say, the humans who were opposed to the lordship of the dragons and their worshipers. I told them of Tarragin's personal world, and of his ability to translate himself between worlds. He also is known to visit the plane of Asengard, where the souls of the dead Norsemen go to feast for eternity in Valhaale."

Bernadette jumped on that immediately. "Adalbert called Tarragin the 'Soul-Devourer.' Can he actually consume people's souls?"

"Most assuredly," Ehrgeizig replied. "Souls, in the greatest part, are comprised of magical energy. And one of Tarragin's special powers, held by no other dragon, is the ability to absorb the souls of humankind. It is similar to what you, as *fjurblut,* can do when you are near a dragon who has recently died."

I guess that makes *me* a "Soul-Devourer" too, Bernadette thought bleakly. The idea was repellent, though it didn't seem as bad since it was dragons, not humans, whose souls were being stolen. "So how did the ancients banish Tarragin to this other world?" she asked. "Couldn't he just leave there whenever he wanted?"

"Many of the ancient Norse heroes were warriors," Ehrgeizig explained. "But there was among them one, Seimdal, whose magecraft went beyond anything that is known in this day. After learning what I could teach him, he and his colleagues crafted a spell and a potion precisely calculated to defeat Tarragin. For the third and most damaging of his special powers, the ability to call dead dragons back into life, was making it impossible for them to win the war."

"That's what I need!" Bernadette cried. "But I thought that dragons were resistant to ordinary magic?"

"Indeed we are," Ehrgeizig replied. "But this was a dragon spell, the only such spell ever created by man for use against dragons."

"Do you know it?" she asked excitedly. As fascinating as the old dragon's tale had been, it was not for that they had come.

"Alas, it is beyond my knowing," he said. "By its very nature, it is a spell that a dragon cannot absorb. Even if you were to speak it in my presence, I could not take it in – it would only harm me. And I cou

ld not create the stone to power it." Oh, that was a problem. "This Seimdal guy figured out how to make a stone linked to a spell he created?"

"Yes. None of them had the fireblood, so they could not recharge the stones. They were created in the *Edelmied*, the gem forge, and used in the same way the Old Ones do it – gems held against the skin to power the spell, then replaced when exhausted. They used the Dragonfall spell many times after Tarragin was gone – it was their greatest weapon in defeating the dragon lords. But once the dragons were gone, myself excepted, there was no need for it. Both the words of the spell and the means to forge the stones for it have long been lost."

Bernadette's inborn optimism let that last remark pass. She refused to believe there was no hope. If this man at her side couldn't help her to find what had been lost, she'd be damned surprised. "So the spell wasn't just for trapping Tarragin in his personal little universe?" she asked.

"Oh no," Ehrgeizig replied. "It was not intended to trap him there at all. It was only intended to weaken him, to bring him to ground. The potion they created was intended to wreak a permanent change in Tarragin, to rob him of his ability to move between worlds. The plan was to trap him *here*, where they could then kill him. He is much harder to kill than any ordinary dragon, but he is not completely immune to swords, axes, and arrows. They had been unable to kill him, only because whenever his enemies began to prevail he would simply vanish into some other plane of existence, leaving them behind."

"So, something went wrong with the potion," Bernadette said. It wasn't a question. "I conferred with Seimdal after the battle, though I was not there at the time," the old dragon said. "Once Dragonfall had brought Tarragin down, they planned to get him to ingest the potion, tossing the bottle into his mouth. But they failed, the bottle shattering harmlessly on his scales."

His audience was rapt now, and he continued. "They had but two bottles of the potion, it having been very difficult to make. Tarragin took to the air again, raining destruction on their heads. They brought him down once more, and the swordmaid Zenis, one of the foremost Norse heroes who stood beside Seimdal at that battle, dipped the tip of an arrow in the second bottle of potion. As her companion Boromund confronted the Soul-Devourer with sword and shield, she fired that arrow into the spot below the wing where Tarragin was less well armored – deep into the flesh."

"But... it didn't do the trick," Bernadette said in almost a murmur. Ehrgeizig might be ancient, but there was nothing wrong with his hearing.

"We can only speculate about what happened after Tarragin took to the air again and then vanished from sight," he said. "Clearly it must have had some effect, or he would have been back as soon as he'd recovered from his injuries. Instead, he was gone for millennia. We don't even know for sure if it was his personal plane of existence to which he fled, though it seems likely. And once there, the potion's effect must have prevented him from leaving. Yet somehow, after all this time, he has overcome it and returned."

It could have been almost anything, Andrion realized as he analyzed what the ancient *drache* had told them. Maybe Tarragin fled to the wrong world, one of the planes of the Netherworld where nastier things than he was lurked. Maybe some outside force took pity on the trapped monster and cured him of the potion's effects. The main point was he was back now, and they needed to stop him – once and for all.

"We need to learn that spell, and find this Edelmied you spoke of," Bernadette said. "The formula for that potion or poison would be good, too. Any idea where we can start looking?"

"*Enshul,* Pardon," the old *drache* said. "I have been hiding on this mountaintop for too many centuries. Without my ward in place, I fear I would become nothing but a trophy for some adventurer. Though now, at least, there are others of my kind to draw their attention away. I have not been in the world of men in so long I would not begin to know where to look – and my order, the Old Ones, have been as isolated. I assume you must have spoken with someone who suggested you come looking for the spell that defeated Tarragin?"

"Yes, an old archivist of the group known as the Guardians," Bernadette told him.

"They must have arisen since the last time I was out in the world," the old dragon replied. "But I can only suggest that you seek him out and tell him what I've told you. Perhaps with his resources he may find some ancient references to point you in the right direction. Fear not for the world. Though my brethren may be causing turmoil and destruction, it will likely be years yet before Tarragin unleashes his plan to end all life here."

The two puny humans looked at him with anxiety. "You know of this plan?" Bernadette asked. "It's not just a vague prophecy?" The dragon shuffled his wings, almost like a shrug. "I may be wrong," he said, "but I believe he intends to transport this planet and everyone on it into another universe – one without a sun."

Chapter 32: The Search Begins

Bernadette opened her map, and touched the sanctuary of the ancient Guardians. A few heartbeats later she and Andrion were standing in the courtyard before the entrance to the main building. Andrion hugged her, glad to have left the freezing mountaintop behind. "What an astonishing experience!" he said.

She smiled up at him. "Let's hope Adalbert can shed some light on the whereabouts of this spell."

Andrion nodded, and the two of them moved through the narrow opening and up a series of four stone staircases, each wider than the last. At the top, they looked around the dimly lit room but saw no signs of human occupation. "Drat," Bernadette muttered, and trotted off to check the living quarters on the floor above. Nobody there, either. She and Andrion next exited the building through doors at the back, and found themselves in a dirt-floored courtyard with archery butts at one side. Ahead under a stone canopy overlooking the river below, they finally spotted Adalbert and Giselle standing side by side, simply gazing out over the canyon.

Bernadette approached them, clearing her throat. He whirled, looking pleased to see her. "Ah, you're back!" he said, smiling. "Have you had any luck tracking down that dragon spell?" She filled him in on her visit with the Old Ones, and her conversation with Ehrgeizig.

"I need to find some ancient lore from the time of the Uprising, to pinpoint where this Edelmied, this Gem Forge, is located," she told him.

"And a wall with the spell on it too, I would assume," the old archivist replied. He seemed lost in thought for a moment. Then he said, "That's a pretty puzzle. You'll not find books that old in your local bookshop." He considered a moment longer. "Perhaps the Mages' Academy of Eisenstag… all the knowledge in Iscandia is gathered there. One of their mages might be able to put you on the trail of the spell."

Since her arrival in Iscandia, Bernadette had met several people who suggested she might want to travel to the Academy for instruction in magic. As spellbooks were available everywhere, and once a spell was learned only practice would improve its execution, it had not appeared worthwhile for her to make the trek to the far north of Iscandia or submit herself to the tutelage of the mages there. But now, it seemed, she had a reason to make the trip.

Likely, this would be a good opportunity to decide if the Academy truly had anything to offer her. Bernadette was in awe of Andrion's skills with battle magic, and wished she had his facility with it. But getting more practice was hard, when her current level of skills would soon see her killed before she'd had a chance to fry her adversaries.

Bernadette thanked Adalbert, then pulled out her map and examined it. Eisenstag was almost due north of Coldstein, which seemed to be its closest neighboring city. She was glad to find Coldstein Stables showing on the map, only a short walk from the city itself. Visiting there briefly after killing the dragon in Delvewood had been a smart maneuver. They fast-traveled there now, arriving in the midst of a blizzard as dusk settled on the land.

Bernadette turned to Andrion. "I don't think we want to be setting off on foot just now. Are you up for a visit to scenic Coldstein?"

"It's not my favorite place," he replied, "but it beats sleeping under an icefruit bush in this weather." Since their reunion, his manner seemed lighter. It was as if his whole attitude toward life had become happier, more easy-going. Bernadette liked it a lot.

They walked down the long, broad stone bridge leading across the river from the stables to the gates of the city itself. Those gates towered above them, and the walls certainly looked impressive. If those Norse partisans could invest this place with troops, the empire would never winkle them out, Bernadette thought. Inside, the buildings of Coldstein seemed to loom menacingly. The weather was miserable, the stone structures lacking in architectural charm. And ahead of them, an ugly scene was playing out between a pair of Norsemen and a pretty Nachtalfar woman.

The Norsemen were harassing her, implying that the nachtalfar were Reman spies or worse because they failed to support the Norse partisans. They issued veiled threats before skulking off as Bernadette and Andrion approached, and the woman turned to them. "How about you?" she asked angrily. "Do you hate my people?" Racial prejudice was not something Bernadette had often encountered, and it shocked her.

"No," she replied, "of course not."

"Then you've come to the wrong place," the Nachtalfar woman said bitterly. Evidently the former residents of Darkreach were relegated to a ghetto area of Coldstein, despised and persecuted by the Norsemen who shared the city with them. Yet another reason not to like this place, Bernadette thought as she and her companion continued on the short walk from the gates to the Drunken Oarsman inn a few yards away. Ah right, Bernadette realized. This city was a seaport.

Inside, though, they found no drunken sailors – just an attractive and extensive 2-story inn, timber-built and suffused with warm light. A bard could be heard singing a song on the floor above, melodious enough; though from its lyrics, Bernadette took it to be Norse partisan propaganda. She approached the woman standing behind the bar, a Norsewoman from the look of her, and had soon secured a room for them. The rooms were reasonably spacious, and well appointed.

After they'd dropped their packs and removed their armor, changing into more comfortable clothing, Bernadette and Andrion emerged from their room and went upstairs. In contrast with the snowstorm outside, the common room was cozy and lit with a pleasant golden light. Candles and lanterns were all around, and a cheery fire blazed at the far end. They took a table and enjoyed a meal of walrus stew (a "delicacy" Bernadette had not previously sampled, rich and slightly fishy tasting), with bread alongside and some apples and cheese to follow. They washed the supper down with wine, and enjoyed the entertainment while talking quietly between songs.

During and after the meal, they discussed the current quest. Was Ehrgeizig's theory of how Tarragin planned to end the world right? Wouldn't that kill him, and all the rest of the dragons, along with everyone he was mad at? Neither of them could entirely believe it, but the threat was real enough to drive them on.

In Andrion, Bernadette had found a lover with whom she could discuss the challenges of her life, somebody she could confide in and look to for advice. Not to mention he was gorgeous, even-tempered, and fantastic in the sack. As the wine relaxed her and made her feel increasingly more mellow, she found herself sitting closer to him, their chairs pushed together, her hand in his.

As the evening wore on Andrion leaned closer still and planted a kiss on her neck. Holding her right hand in his left, he raised it and traced the palm with the tip of his right forefinger, sending a little thrill through her. "What do you say," he murmured close to her ear, "we go back to our room now?"

"Sounds like a plan," Bernadette whispered, lifting her head to kiss him and insert her tongue into his mouth.

The pair walked only slightly unsteadily down the stairs and found their room again. After they had both stripped down and reclined on the bed, Andrion started by kissing her, gently at first, but with a great deal of concentration. Despite his focus on her mouth, somehow his fingers (strong, but not calloused) found their way to her full, firm breasts and he was gently massaging her deeply rose-hued nipples until they arose, throbbing with sensation.

His cock had stiffened by now and Bernadette laid hands on it eagerly, squeezing it as he continued to excite her with his mouth and hands. Gripping it with her fingers, she ran her right thumb up over the swollen, velvety head and was rewarded with a drop of slippery fluid. She used a circular motion to massage and spread this across the surface. He moaned slightly and bent to his ministrations with even more enthusiasm.

Andrion licked the first two fingers and thumb of his left hand before reapplying it to her right breast – where he soon had the nipple straining, standing at attention in a miniature emulation of his cock. His right hand he relocated to between her thighs and inserted the index and middle fingers between her inner labia. Bernadette was soaking wet, and the fingers slipped in with ease.

He pushed them in and out rhythmically, rubbing against her throbbing clit within its enshrouding hood as they emerged.

Bernadette was about ready to pop right then. "I want you inside me, now!" she moaned softly.

"We'll see about it," Andrion said. As she lay back against the pillows, he pressed the slippery head of his swollen cock against her equally swollen outer labia, and began working it inside ever so slightly. Using his hand to wield his stiff member like a tool in the hands of a master craftsman, he began moving it in circular motions around the entrance to her throbbing cunt, dipping inside just a bit and then coming back out, rubbing up against her clit.

"Ohhhhhh, yes…" Bernadette murmured, suspended in ecstasy.

Finally, when neither he nor she could stand it for another minute, Andrion plunged fully into her. All the way down, his prodigious length swallowed by her swollen and hungry cunt. Bernadette screamed almost immediately. But it was still another few minutes of increasingly furious pumping before they both cried out in the throes of orgasm. He lay across her, still encased, for some moments until his softening member had slipped from her and they rolled over to lie side by side on the bed.

They drifted into sleep, and after the tiring treks of the preceding day (Days? Fast-traveling made it hard to tell) they remained dead to the world for hours. Bernadette slept dreamlessly, warm and safe in her lover's arms.

Chapter 33: The Academy at Eisenstag

Even within the Oarsman's warm confines it was chilly in Coldstein, and morning found Bernadette and Andrion lying close together beneath the warm coverlet, sleeping soundly. It was only when the inn began to come awake around them and the sounds of people bustling about their business became noticeable, that the usually early-rising young adventuress finally cracked an eyelid.

Oh shit, she thought. Overslept. But it's so *warm* in bed, and Andrion is so delightfully solid and … Sigh. She rotated in his arms so she was facing him, and kissed his eyelids, then his mouth. "Awaken, my prince," she said softly. His warm brown eyes opened and regarded her, radiating love. She returned the loving gaze with her cool gray-blue ones. Then his eyes began to fill with hunger, and he clasped her to him for a kiss that had more passion to it. Body to body beneath the sheets with him, she felt him stiffen.

Whoops, that wasn't the idea. Not that it wasn't a *great* idea, but… "My love," she said, her heart still shining in her eyes, "we need to get on the road to Eisenstag." Andrion continued looking at her with a combination of love and desire, but sighed – acknowledging that now was probably not the time. Then he smiled and tweaked her left nipple with his right hand, as the tip of his still-stiffened cock sought the opening to her vestibule.

"Are you sure we don't have time for a quickie?" he asked. Bernadette gasped slightly and bit her lip, then rolled her eyes, pulling away.

"I'm sure. But definitely, check back with me later," she said as she wriggled out from between the covers and immediately went all-over goose bumps from the temperature in the room. "I hate this place! It's fucking cold!" she declared, searching for some underwear.

"Told you," Andrion replied lazily, still keeping the blanket tucked up around his chin. He was admiring the way the cold caused her nipples to stand up. They were lovely nipples, riding high and proud on one of the finest sets of breasts it had ever been his pleasure to fondle. Mmm! He bit his own lip, as his cock throbbed spontaneously at the thought. He gave it a stroke or two before resigning himself to leaving the bed. Ah, well…

Andrion climbed out of bed, his member jutting. Bernadette dug some long woolen underclothes out of her pack, but took a moment from putting them on to admire him in turn. What a superb specimen he was! Increasingly she loved him for his mind, his skills, and his steadfast devotion to her and her wellbeing. But there was no ignoring that, standing there naked with his stiff dick hanging out, he looked *way* beyond good enough to eat.

The two reluctantly continued their dressing, Andrion also finding some warmer underwear, and they were soon fully kitted up and ready to leave. They stopped briefly on their way out to take on a breakfast of hot pastries, apples and ale at the bar, then walked out the inn's front door, still munching.

Outside, looking at Coldstein's gates, Bernadette perused the map. It seemed to show a road heading north toward Eisenstag from the back side of Coldstein. They set off in that direction, through city streets wide and narrow, eventually coming up on what had to the eorl's palace. It was little more elegant than the rest of this cold, dreary-seeming city.

The road outside Coldstein's narrow back door proved to be no more than a snow-covered track in the middle of a snow-covered plain, with mountains in the distance on either side. Before Bernadette and Andrion had been traveling long, they were attacked by a pair of things that looked like a red-orange werewolf, more or less dog-like but the size of a small horse and bipedal, with clutching claws. "Shit, hellhounds!" Andrion exclaimed, his magical bolts sizzling as he fought furiously against them. Bernadette was able to knock one of them back with Gale, but the other had dodged out of her range.

She left that one to Andrion while she attacked the first one, which had not yet fully recovered from having been hurled yards away, with repeated shots from her bow. The thing was soon on its feet again, though, and Bernadette found herself knocked to the ground by a savage blow from its taloned forepaw. Meanwhile, Andrion had brought the other hellhound down and he turned to save her with more bolts of lightning before the creature could open her from belly to collarbone.

Moments later, he was at her side. "Are you all right?" he asked anxiously.

"Been better," Bernadette gritted, hurting. But with the immediate threat gone she had leisure to apply a healing spell once again, and was soon feeling fine. She felt as if she was getting better at healing magic, needing less magical power to repair even major damage. I should have bought those spellbooks weeks ago, she thought.

They went on their way again, finally striking the paved road Bernadette had seen marked on the map. She was halfway surprised the stones were even visible, given the apparent nonstop blizzard conditions in these parts. What a miserable place to live! About two hours' vigorous walk later, through the blowing snow, they could see stone buildings rising ahead of them.

Within a few more minutes they came into Eisenstag. *This* is the seat of Icemarch? Bernadette thought, looking around. At least half the buildings seemed to be abandoned, though an inn, a store, and the eorl's longhouse were still inhabited. But the whole place looked to be smaller than the village of Underhill, smaller even than Pied-de-Puce.

At the far end of town the road ended at a stone arch, with a sort of gazebo-like platform beyond it. And beyond that, perched on a rock that stood some distance north of the headland on which the town sat, the towers of the famous Academy rose. Did you have to know enough magic to be able to fly before you could even get there? That was going to put a hitch in their plans.

Inside the gazebo stood a lovely young elf maiden, dressed in typical mage robes. She barred their way, telling them that only those who were worthy would be admitted to the Academy. It was not enough that you had business with the Academy, or needed something from them – you could only get in if you had something to offer them in return. I'm not here to sign up for classes, fumed Bernadette silently. I need information! But aloud she said, "Would you let The Fireblood in?"

The woman didn't believe her claim to be The Fireblood, so Bernadette demonstrated by using the first word of Gale to shake her where she stood. Surprisingly, this still failed to impress the elf enough to effect passage. Eventually, Bernadette ended up paying the woman 30 guilders for the Frost Bolt spellbook, which enabled her to cast the spell on a seal embedded in the gazebo's floor at the center. It rimed over immediately, and the test had been passed.

Nonetheless, the young elf was now willing to allow them access. She silently cast a spell at the seal herself, and it transformed into a glowing blue pool of coruscating energy. Bernadette looked the gate guard in the eye, one eyebrow raised in question. "Just step into the portal," the young woman said with a trace of impatience. "You will be transported to the quad."

They did as she bade, stepping onto the blue circle, and the next moment found themselves in a broad central courtyard surrounded by 2-and-3-story stone buildings. Just ahead of them was a spry-looking older elf in ornate mage robes, who greeted them politely. He introduced himself as the Academy's Magister, and welcomed Bernadette as a new student. "We need to visit the library," she told him, and he directed her to enter the building ahead of them and go through the first door on the right.

Within, they came to a small entryway with wooden doors on either side and openwork double doors ahead leading to a large circular room. The door on the left was locked and no one seemed to be in the room ahead; so Bernadette tried the door on the right. It opened, and after mounting a short circular staircase carved from stone she and Andrion came to a large room that was obviously the Academy library.

On the far side of the room there was a U-shaped desk, and seated behind it was an elderly uruk. Bernadette guessed he must be the librarian. If anybody at the Academy had knowledge of where to start looking for the information they needed, it was likely this fellow. He looked at the approaching pair with what Bernadette hoped was an expression of benign curiosity – though with his protruding tusks, greenish complexion, and beetling brows he looked forbidding to say the least.

"Greetings, sir," she said with a slight bow, wishing now she'd had a chance to pursue the opportunity to become an uruk-friend. "I am Bernadette Bouchard, The Fireblood and incidentally a new student of the Academy, and this is my uh… colleague, Andrion Lamonte. We're hoping you can help us with some magical research."

He smiled slightly, no more reassuring than his frowns. "Welcome, young apprentice," he said in his deep gravelly voice. "The facilities of the library are available for the use of all students and faculty of the Academy. I am Mhyrzon din-Tzrek, and these books are my charge. As a student you are not permitted to remove books, but must do your studying here. And the gods defend you if any harm should come to them while they are in your possession!"

That last was said with such vehemence Bernadette found herself surreptitiously checking to see if he kept an axe behind that desk to deal with unruly library patrons. "Don't worry," she promised, "We'll take the utmost care with your treasured books. Could you please direct us to any that pertain to magic used during the Uprising?"

The old elf furrowed his brow, a frown of concentration. "There's not a lot actually from that period," he told them. "In that era printing and bookbinding as we know it today was unknown, and most knowledge was recorded by scribes on parchment scrolls. Over the centuries those deteriorated, some to be lost forever. Others were copied and recopied by hand, and it is from those that most of what we know about that time has come. Historians and scholars as far back as three thousand years ago wrote about the Uprising, but you must realize that even at that long-ago time, all who were actually there had been dead for thousands of years." Except Ehrgeizig, Bernadette thought with a feeling of smug satisfaction. What amazing good fortune that they had been able to talk with him!

Bernadette and Andrion exchanged a glance. This project might prove to be harder than they'd hoped. "Come on," the uruk said, stepping out from behind the desk and leading them into the stacks. He gestured to a shelf about halfway down from the top, in a bookcase four feet wide that ran from floor to ceiling. "What little we have, you'll find here."

With that he turned and went back to his desk, ready to serve other customers. "I guess eating lunch while studying these books is out of the question," Bernadette muttered *sotto voce* to Andrion. He grinned at her wryly.

"Why don't you let me get started, and you go talk to some of the Academy personnel and see if they've got a bed for their 'new apprentice,'" he suggested. "You can grab something out of your pack while you're out, and then you can switch places with me while I step out for a bite."

"It's a plan," she said with a smile.

Bernadette went back down the stairs and out into the courtyard again. As she was standing there looking around, wondering where to go, a youngish-looking woman in mage robes came up to her. "Are you lost, dear?" she asked kindly. Bernadette gave the woman her best "thanks, mom" sheepish grin, and said "I've just enrolled at the Academy as an apprentice. I met the Magister a little while ago, but I don't know where I'm supposed to go."

"Ah," the woman said with a smile. "You've come to the right person." She held out a hand. "I'm Lubelle Ondine, the Dean of Admissions. And you are… ?"

"Bernadette Bouchard."

"Recently from Auverne?" Lubelle asked conversationally, gesturing for the new student to follow her as she began walking toward a massive building on the east side of the quad.

"I was born in Iscandia myself," the woman went on without waiting for an answer, "but my parents emigrated here from Auverne. I've been with the Academy for more than thirty years." Thirty years! The woman didn't look a day over thirty. Maybe there were some real benefits to practicing magic…

Lubelle led Bernadette inside the building, which proved to be a dormitory for students. There were chemial and enchanting facilities, a small dining hall kept stocked with food, and individual rooms – simply furnished – for the apprentice mages. "This is amazing, Mistress Ondine," she told the older woman. "How can the Academy provide all this to its students without charging tuition?"

Lubelle smiled, gesturing to Bernadette to drop her pack in the room she'd been assigned. "The Academy exists to further the study and ethical practice of magic," she explained. "Our successful students will go on to become rich, using their powers to help others, and we thrive on their generous contributions. In addition, members of the public sometimes apply to us for magical services – and for those we charge. But we're always looking for new, talented students to teach."

Oh great, now I feel like a total fraud, Bernadette thought. After learning that she could wait until tomorrow to introduce herself to the faculty members and begin to take classes, she thanked the older woman and closed the room's door. Then she removed her armor and put on a warm woolen robe over her long underwear, before breaking out some apples and cheese for a belated lunch. Breakfast at the Drunken Oarsman seemed like it had taken place in another era.

Bernadette didn't linger exploring the dorm building or trying to meet her fellow students. As soon as the gnawing in her stomach had been satisfied she went back to the library to report to Andrion. He'd removed a stack of around six thick tomes from the shelf Mhyrzon had indicated, and had one open on a small round table in front of him. He had a small notebook out beside it, and was in the process of jotting something down.

He glanced up at her with a smile, seeing from her changed outfit that she must have managed to acquire them a place to sleep for the night. "I've started on this first one," he told her. "Why don't you start reading the next one in the stack?"

"Good idea," Bernadette replied. "Our room is in the north wing, bottom floor. It's the second door on the right as you come inside. Here's the key."

Andrion pocketed it and hopped up, kissing her on the cheek as he left her to it. Some time later he returned, now also dressed in warm woolen robes, and the two of them pored over the ancient tomes – or books *about* ancient tomes – until their eyes were beginning to cross. During that time Mhyrzon helped a few other customers, and spent some time re-shelving books. But he showed no sign of wanting them to leave so he could lock up.

They had made it through four of the original six books by the time both of them were starving again. So far, they had learned that much of what Ehrgeizig had told them had been written down. The nature of dragon spells was apparently known to the books' authors, though possibly this information had come to them from the same source. Had the old dragon really spent the past several thousand years hanging out on that mountaintop, teaching generations of old men in the Way of the Stones?

But they had yet to find any details about the human-created dragon spell, the gem forge, the potion that would rob Tarragin of his dimensional travel ability or even about the Fireblood. Despite the supposedly well-known prophecy of a fireblood arising to save the world – or not – the line of humans with this unique quality was scarcely mentioned at all.

"We've got to have something to eat before we faint," Bernadette said at last. "And I'd just as soon it were a little more substantial than apples and cheese. Maybe we could hop down to Eisenstein and get a bowl of something at that inn?"

"Good idea," Andrion replied. He stood up and went over to Mhyrzon, who appeared to be studying one of his books.

"Thanks for showing us where to find the books," he said. "Uh, when do you close?"

"Usually midnight," the old uruk replied. "And I open again at nine. You don't need much sleep at my age, and there's noplace I'd rather be."

"I thought we'd go get some dinner and come back, then," Andrion told him. "Fine, fine. I'll be here."

After a hot meal and a couple of ales in Eisenstag's inn, the Wavering Walrus, the two scholars (one born to it, the other quickly learning the trade) were back on the job until exhaustion sent them to their bed.

Chapter 34: Breakthroughs

Bernadette and Andrion slept the night squeezed up tight together in the narrow bed her dorm room provided. Considering the climate, it was all for the best. With no fireplace in the room, they piled their fur bedrolls over themselves for additional warmth. Her sleep was disturbed all night by an endless parade of words on paper, her mind regurgitating everything that had been crammed into it during most of the preceding day.

Andrion would have been happy to make love in the morning, but Bernadette was feeling too anxious and just wasn't in the mood. Ehrgeizig's remark that it would "probably" be years before Tarragin decided to carry the planet into another dimension and cleanse it of life had failed to ease her fears. She felt as if they needed to act swiftly. Once they had the spell and its required stones in hand, along with that potion, she would able to take a break.

They had made it through the rest of the half dozen books Andrion had started with last night. As soon as the library was open for business, after breakfast, they were back at the same table with a fresh stack. The histories were fascinating, in their way, and Andrion found himself getting so absorbed he almost lost track of their objective. Fortunately Bernadette was narrowly focused on anything that could point the way to what they needed.

It was nearing late morning when Bernadette looked up from the book she was studying: *Legends of the Uprising*, by Brydelion Avenyi. "Andrion!" she said in hushed, urgent tones. Mhyrzon had not specifically instructed them to remain quiet, but there was something about the atmosphere in this place that made you naturally lower your voice.

Her lover looked up at her, alert. Bernadette put her finger on a passage in the book, which was more a collection of tales than a history. "Seimdal is mentioned in this story," she said. "It talks of how he and others who were leaders of the forces of the Uprising built a mighty fortress from which they could launch their offensive against the dragons and their priesthood."

255

"That could be where they put their gem forge!" Andrion said excitedly. "Does it say any more about the place?"

"The name was Faastenberg," she said. "It was built in the mountains in the northeast quadrant of Iscandia, and apparently they built it completely underground – digging down like the dypalfar."

"That makes sense," Andrion mused. "With dragons arrayed against them any structures above ground would be at risk. Even stone can be knocked down."

"Anyway," Bernadette went on, "according to the legend Seimdal and his magical colleagues helped to build the place using their arts, and it was there they crafted their weapons to use against the dragons and their priests. There were generals for the regular troops, but the mages were an important part of the war effort."

Andrion nodded. "The dragon priests were masters of magic. And they're still out there, I'm afraid. The cult were really deep into the necromantic arts. The aptrgangr were interred with spells that would allow them to walk again millennia after death to act as defenders. But the undead priests mostly don't leave their tombs, thank the gods." A look of realization crossed his handsome features, and he picked up his notebook.

Bernadette looked at him questioningly. He smiled at her even as he began thumbing through the pages. He'd filled quite a few of them with notes since they'd begun their search. "That name, Faastenberg. I think I saw it in one of those books we looked at yesterday... Here it is. The book was *The Forgotten Cities of Iscandia.* I didn't write down the author. It's a list of a bunch of places that were famous in their day but are abandoned and forgotten now, including all the dypalfar cities."

He got up from his chair and hurried over to the shelf, returning a moment later with the book in hand. Bernadette watched him avidly as he flipped to the table of contents, then rifled through it looking for the page in question. "I wouldn't mind having a copy of that for myself," she remarked. "Think of the treasures you could find!"

"Think of the interesting ways in which you could be killed," Andrion replied with a grin. Then, "Here it is! It says that Faastenberg was an ancient Norse city that was built at an unknown date in the distant past. It was the only known Norse city in Iscandia built completely underground, not connected with a tomb or barrow. Supposedly it continued to be occupied by the Norse for millennia after the dragons were all gone."

"But I've never heard of it!" Bernadette said. "Did it collapse in an earthquake?" Andrion shook his head and kept reading. "Around 4,000 years ago, as the conflict between the Norse and the dypalfar was beginning to heat up, dypalfar tunneled into the city's lowest levels from the nearby dypalfar city of Alzhenten and caught their neighbors unaware. They slaughtered the inhabitants, and took over Faastenberg as an extension of their own city."

Bernadette's eyes were wide. She pulled out her magic map, and found a new arrow on it. Not that far from where they now stood, in the mountains south and west of Eisenstag, was a marker reading "Alzhenten." There was no nearby marker for Faastenberg, however. "So after the dypalfar vanished, what happened?" she asked. "Why didn't the Norse take back their city? I'd have thought an underground stronghold like that would be worth having, with all the wars in this region."

"According to this," Andrion said, getting to the end of the entry, "there *was* a massive earthquake there not too long after the disappearance of the dypalfar. At least the top level of Faastenberg collapsed, making access to it from the surface impossible. Alzhenten was damaged too, though not as severely. Those ancient dypalfar really knew how to build to last."

Bernadette stood up with a double armload of books, and began carrying them back to the shelf from which they'd come. "Come on, honey," she said. "The potion can wait until we find out whether the spell and the gem forge are lost forever. We're going to Alzhenten!"

Chapter 35: Lost Cities

"You know," Bernadette told Andrion as they found the trail leading to the southwest out of Eisenstag and began walking along it, "I think I might just make the next smilodon that attacks us into a fur cloak. At least if we're going to spend very much time in *this* part of Iscandia." He smiled fondly at her, then wriggled out of his pack and rummaged around inside it to come up with a heavy wool cloak, which he draped over her.

"It's not fur, but it's pretty warm," he said.

"*Thank* you, love" she murmured, standing on tiptoe to plant an affectionate kiss on his cold cheek. Her own must be glowing like a hearthfire, she thought. Cold *or* hot always turned her complexion ruddy. Drawing their weapons, they set off on a snowy trail that was just barely distinguishable from the white drifts blanketing the slopes to the west of town.

Bernadette was getting tired of being ambushed, and they could hardly make much speed in this muck in any case. Plus, she figured, with so little cover she ought to be able to spot any person or animal planning an attack from far enough away to do some good. So they crept along cautiously, her eyes constantly scanning the snowy hills for threats. She was delighted when this paid off a few minutes later, as she felled a smilodon with a couple of well-placed shots before it laid a claw on her.

Bernadette *did* skin the bastard, too; though tanning the hide and making a cloak would have to wait. They got a bit lost in the nearly trackless waste, but eventually found a well-trodden trail leading in the right general direction. Before long, though, it spilled out at what looked like some kind of archaeological dig site. There were wooden walkways erected here and there, and supplies scattered around. The met no one, though. After noting that "Gryndhaal" had appeared on her map, the two of them studied it to choose what path to take next.

A rocky mountain ridge stood almost due south of them, with smooth snowy slopes flanking it. Which would lead them to their goal? After some deliberation they took the left fork, and as

Bernadette continued to observe their progress toward the map marker it seemed they had chosen correctly.

About halfway up they were attacked by wolves, but once again their alertness paid off and the savage creatures fell dead before they'd had a chance to do much damage. Shortly after that, her eyes gazing upslope, Bernadette spotted what looked like a dypalfar tower ahead. As they drew closer, they saw they had reached their destination.

Bernadette climbed a snow-covered step and opened a pair of ornate doors that appeared to be cast, or perhaps carved, from the shimmering golden substance known as dypalfar metal. She didn't know what it consisted of, but it seemed impervious to rust and made good armor. Heavy, though.

As they went inside Andrion laid a hand on her arm, catching her eye. "Watch out. dypalfar ruins are usually full of leukalfar, mandimants, and hostile automatons." She raised her eyebrows at him and turned away. As if she needed to be cautioned… A couple of seconds later, as Bernadette started up one of two stone staircases in the room, a circular device on the wall at the top of the steps (which she had taken for a decorative medallion about two feet in diameter), suddenly irised open and disgorged a *thing* that appeared to resemble an enormous insect made all of gleaming dypalfar metal, with a glowing red gem in top of its head. It was… beautiful. And it was attacking her!

Bernadette hit it with several arrows, backing away. She tried Gale on it and it didn't seem to have any effect. Maybe the dragon spell only works on living things? Meanwhile a second unit had been spat out by a port on the opposite wall, and Andrion was blasting it with lightning bolts. They seemed to be particularly effective against the hard metal adversary, more so than arrows. But both of the things were stabbing at her with their spear-like legs, and by the time they had been reduced to scrap metal Bernadette was limping and bleeding.

Bernadette put up her bow and used her healing spell to close the wounds. Doing this, or drinking healing potions (which seemed to be the liquid equivalent of the spell), was not just a lifesaver. It made her feel *so* much better than she had a minute before, now not even bothered by the pervasive cold, that she had a moment of concern that the practice might be addictive. Well, she mused, sex with Andrion and/or Erik might be addictive too. But I'm *not* ready to kick the habit.

Recovered, Bernadette looked ruefully at Andrion. "Looks like you were right. Let's hope we don't meet too many more of them." Climbing another flight of stairs and opening another set of golden doors, they came into an intriguing corridor flanked by gates barred in that same burnished metal. Behind those gates, a series of enormous pipes ran here and there, and there was a loud rumble of machinery. Gigantic gears were turning furiously, though there was no sign of either a means of propulsion or the purpose of the activity.

Rounding a bend, Bernadette was in time to see another circular portal give birth to what looked for a moment like a shiny metal sphere perhaps three feet in diameter, composed of interleaved plates. In seconds, though, it unfolded itself into a metallic humanoid that moved around by rolling on a pair of metal wheels while wielding a sword. It was about as tall as she was, and one arrow was *not* enough to stop it. Bernadette swapped the bow for mace and shield, and began trying to bash it to bits. These things *did* seem to be somewhat fragile. And once again, Andrion's lightning bolts proved effective.

The automaton fell into pieces, scattering across the stone floor with a clatter of sheet metal. "That type's called a roller," Andrion told her. "The little guys with all the legs are called bugs. And we do *not* want to meet a robon."

"I'll take your word for it," Bernadette replied, panting. They'd barely gone 50 feet in this maze-like but strangely beautiful building, and they'd already nearly been killed twice.

Examining the wreckage, Bernadette salvaged some essence vials, dypalfar lubricant, and a few bits of useful-looking scrap metal. It could probably be melted down to make dypalfar ingots, which fetched a good price at smithies. They continued through the complex. Despite all the machine activity, it seemed (so far) to be devoid of flesh-and-blood inhabitants. Given that those inhabitants, if found, were likely to be the equally unpleasant leukalfar and mandimants, Bernadette felt she'd be happy to postpone meeting them.

They encountered several more of the smaller sort of automaton, all of them unremittingly hostile but relatively easy to deactivate once you'd found the right technique. Then the passage led around and up more stairs to a set of double doors, leading downward. It had been snowy on the slopes above, with an icy wind cutting through their garments; but here it was merely bone-chillingly cold.

"How do you feel, love?" Bernadette asked Andrion. "I'm thinking maybe we ought to camp here for the night before going on." The bread and cheese they'd munched on during their hike to the tower seemed to hav
e slid down hours ago, and they were both feeling a little footsore. "Good idea, my sweet," he replied. "Too bad there's not a double bed, though."

"We can put a couple of these bedrolls together and huddle for warmth," she responded.

There were bits of broken furniture scattered here and there, and they got a fire going in the corner of a cavernous stone hallway. Bernadette rigged a pot over it and simmered some dried beef with water, carrots, onions, and potatoes to make a hearty soup. While it cooked they removed their armor. In the long woolen knit shirts and leggings they'd put on beneath their armor in Coldstein, they were still fairly warm and a lot more comfortable with the heavy, stiff armor off. While the soup cooked they sat on a stack of their bedrolls, snuggled together under Andrion's wool cloak.

Bernadette was feeling a little troubled, weighed down by the perils they were facing as they headed down into the unknown depths of the dypalfar ruin. They'd already encountered much evidence of that long-ago earthquake, entire rooms and corridors buried under tons of fallen stone. What if they discovered that the tunnel between this place and Faastenberg had collapsed along with the Norse city's uppermost level? What if the chamber containing the gem forge, and (they hoped) the words to the Dragonfall spell, was part of a hundred-foot-deep stone sandwich? But with her love (one of them, anyway) at her side, his strong arm wrapped around her, her anxieties eased. She was not her usual ebullient self, perhaps, but she wasn't quivering in fear either.

Bernadette reached out to stir the pot, judging it needed a little more time for the beef to soften and the potatoes and carrots to cook. As she sat back down Andrion wrapped his left arm back around her shoulders, cupped her face in his other hand, and gave her a sweet, warm kiss. She melted into him, and they sat there huddled together kissing gently, stroking each other's bodies through the thick woolen garments.

When the soup was ready Bernadette ladled out a serving for each of them in thick earthenware mugs. It warmed them from their hands, cupped around their mugs, right down to their bellies. Dipping some stale bread into the soup, they devoured every bit of it and the bread as well. Bernadette hadn't realized how ravenous she was! It was easy to forget to eat, sometimes, when you were focused on a goal or busy fighting for your life. But it was sure to catch up with you. She'd become noticeably firmer and somewhat less rounded, these last few weeks.

After Andrion had cleaned up the pot and mugs, Bernadette meanwhile huddling alone under the cloak beside the fire, he added some wood to the fire and then helped her set up their bed for the night. They laid two of the ubiquitous fur sleeping pallets side by side, and spread another two out to form blankets for them as they lay down together – still wearing their woolies, their heads pillowed on spare clothing from their packs.

Andrion immediately enfolded Bernadette in his arms and pulled her close to him, shivering slightly. "Oh baby, keep me warm!" he said, pretending that his teeth were chattering.

"You're warmer than I am," she replied, smiling into his chest. "Ooh! Your hands are warm!" she said in surprise a moment later, as he slipped one up underneath her woolen jersey to fondle a breast. "Mine are freezing," she continued, putting both of hers up inside his shirt.

"Augh!" Andrion gave a muffled cry as Bernadette's little five-fingered ice cubes played over the warm skin of his back and chest.

"Ohhh, honey, that feels so good!" she purred, making him change his mind about evicting her hands from their new warm location. It wasn't her fault she was a smaller animal than he was and had a harder time conserving body heat.

"I'll bet I know one place you're not cold," he said softly, slipping a hand down past the waistband of her stretchy, woolen leggings. He cupped her crotch with his hand, his index and middle fingers slipping inside her.

Bernadette squirmed and moaned, and lifted her face for him to lock his mouth on hers. By now the hand she had slipped up between his jersey and his warm chest was thoroughly thawed, and she moved it down the front of his pants. His cock was stiffening, pressing out against the warm, soft fabric. She squeezed him rhythmically, and for a while the two of them writhed and moaned together. Ah, she wanted him so badly! And it was *way* too damn cold to get naked!

But their woolen underwear was quite stretchy. "I have an idea," Bernadette whispered. Andrion pricked his ears up in anticipation. When Berni got an idea during lovemaking, he'd learned, it was usually a good one. The inside of their double bedroll was pretty warm by now. She reached down with both hands, leaving his poor cock momentarily abandoned, and pulled her leggings down over her rump and about halfway down her thighs. Next she reached around his waist and grabbed the top of his, pulling them down past his buttocks in back and exposing his jutting cock in front. Then she rolled onto her side, her derriere jutting toward him so that he could enter her from behind as they lay spooning, still completely covered by the furs.

Andrion pushed into her eagerly. In this position she was particularly tight, her cunt hot and slippery, as he thrust in and out with firm, slow strokes. He pulled her jersey up in front so he

263

could cup and squeeze her breasts while they made love. Neither of them needed to expose much skin to the cold air this way; but though it felt wonderful to both of them Bernadette's clit wasn't getting enough stimulation. So she took Andrion's top hand off her right breast and moved it down, to rub against her from the front as he thrust into her from the rear. Oh yeah, *that* was it! She began moaning loudly, building to a climax, and as her vaginal spasms gripped him in waves he came too, hot and urgent.

Afterward, they continued to lie in the same position. When he slipped out, they pulled their leggings back up but stayed curled together. "I love you," he whispered, as they dropped into a warm and satisfied sleep. She was already unconscious.

Bernadette awoke when her internal clock told her she had had enough sleep. Here beneath the ground, the light remained unchanged. Their fire had long since burned down, but the corridor (like the rest of the ancient dypalfar ruin) glowed dimly with the ever-burning lamps the vanished dypalfar had left behind.

It took a moment before she remembered the details of their location and planned course of action. Aw, shit, she thought drowsily, humping a little closer to her deliciously warm and solid lover beneath the equally warm covers. But awakening was inevitable. Before long Bernadette's brain had kicked into gear and begun planning the next steps in their quest.

She rotated in Andrion's arms so she was facing him, and ran her hands down his chest to his belly. She'd been around men enough to realize that almost any young, healthy man was likely to awaken with an erection. And if you let them, they'd find something to do with it too. Not that that wasn't *fun*; but it didn't lead to a lot of early morning productivity.

Brushing her fingers lightly over Andrion's wooly leggings, feeling his hardness, Bernadette kissed him sweetly on the nose and then, feeling positively like a martyr, wriggled backwards out of the covers and got to her feet. Clothes! I need more clothes! And build up the fire… In surprisingly short order, in accordance with her status as the usual designated Morning Person, she had shrugged into her armor and the woolen cloak, and rekindled the barely-glowing embers of last night's fire into a cheery blaze. Then she toed her lover gently in the knee, where he still lay beneath the furs. "Time to get up!"

Andrion's eyebrows knit, and his eyes squeezed tighter shut. "Noooo!" he moaned piteously. "It's *cold* out there."

"Faastenberg beckons, my pet!" Bernadette chirped. "Up and at 'em!" Acknowledging the validity of her argument, he reluctantly crawled from the covers. Then he began feeling around for additional garments, until he had warmed up enough to stop shivering. He cast a baleful eye on her.

"I like you better at night," he said petulantly. Then, to take the sting out of it, he stepped close and enfolded her in an embrace. "Is there anything to eat?" he asked.

Already munching on a slightly stale sweet roll, Bernadette passed him one along with a couple of apples. Then she poured them both some herbal tea. The hot liquid, sweetened with honey, slid down their throats with a rush that, in this frigid place, seemed better than sex. Andrion began to look a little more cheerful. Before long they'd finished their minimalistic repast and broken their camp, taking little enough care to extinguish the fire where it lay on the stones. Then they shouldered their packs, weapons at the ready, and continued deeper into the ruins of Alzhenten.

Ahead, their way was barred by a slatted metal gate. Everything that was not carved stone in these dypalfar ruins seemed to be made of the same warmly glimmering dypalfar metal, save for the occasional piece of ruined wooden furniture. Making a left turn, Bernadette and Andrion came to a small stone plaza with a curious-looking structure in the middle of it. It seemed to be a light fixture, a glowing crystal caged within a metal openwork enclosure that was nearly as tall as a man.

And in the far corner of that plaza stood what looked like a knight armored all in golden dypalfar metal. Except that he stood about eight feet tall, and was clearly not human. Andrion hissed at her, "That… is a dypalfar robon!" Too late! It had already spotted them, and they had nowhere to run. Yet curiously, it seemed to lack agility and its enormous size was almost a handicap.

Bernadette ducked nimbly behind it and began raining blows on it with her mace, wishing she had a better weapon.

Meanwhile, one of those rollers had joined the fray and Andrion was busy fighting it off. And a couple of the medium-sized "bugs" were attacking as well! Holy crap! Bernadette figured her best bet was to dodge as much as possible to avoid the slow attacks of the robon, while lashing out at it and its smaller, faster cohorts as the opportunity presented itself.

A well-aimed blow or two from the heavy mace was enough to send the insectile mechanisms flying – in pieces, if Bernadette were lucky. The robon took quite a bit longer to wear down, but she was beginning to get a sense as to which were the most vulnerable parts of its running gear. After smashing a couple of those pistons that bent the legs, she had it down on the floor and was then able to obliterate its head (apparently the seat of its "intelligence") with a few more blows of the mace.

Gasping for breath, her arm feeling like a limp dishrag, Bernadette looked up to find Andrion collapsed on the floor. But his mechanical adversary was in pieces. "Andrion!" she ran to his side and helped him up. He was panting too, and bleeding from a dozen little cuts inflicted by the dypalfar automaton's weaponry. In need of healing herself, she readied a spell and kept it on Andrion until her magical power was nearly spent and her lover was standing there once again looking hale and hearty.

Not wanting to wait for her magical power to recover, Bernadette downed three or four minor healing potions, until her cuts and scrapes had faded and she was starting to feel better. Both of them were still panting, though. "So that was a robon, huh?" she asked him.

"One of the smaller ones," Andrion replied, still breathless. "They get up to about twenty feet tall." She just looked at him mutely. In another few minutes, rested and somewhat recovered, they pushed on.

A little further along in the labyrinthine corridors, the duo encountered some bigger members of the dypalfar bug class. These looked a lot like the larger sort of Chillmarrow spiders, though made all of metal and lacking the deadly poisonous bite of the originals. Feeling like they were starting to get the hang of this, Bernadette and Andrion attacked them with lightning and mace, soon leaving each a broken heap of scrap metal.

From time to time as they moved through the corridors, they would come upon dypalfar chests. Unlike the familiar box shape of chests elsewhere in Iscandia, these resembled a half-circle of stone and dypalfar metal, resting on a table or the floor. Each had a circular, carven metal lid that required the use of lockpicks to open. Bernadette was getting quite good at picking locks. At this rate, she thought, I'll be *required* to join the Guild of Thieves.

After several more turnings, leaving a trail of broken mechanical guardians in their wake, the pair came at last to a stone gallery. On its far side, another door opened into a corridor where the pair spotted their first signs of organic life. The walls on either side were encrusted here and there with shiny hemispherical bumps a couple of inches in diameter, dark red in color. Bernadette prodded one with a finger. It was leathery and yielding, and seemed to have somehow been cemented to the wall.

"Looks like we've found the part of this ruin that's infested with leukalfar and mandimants," Andrion warned Bernadette. "Those are mandimant eggs." She looked around in alarm, but the eggs seemed to be the only living things yet visible. Mandimant eggs! These were a useful and costly chemial ingredient, she knew, but she hadn't previously seen them "in the field." Given the level of peril associated with collecting them, she had a better appreciation of why the shops charged so much.

And of course, no longer afraid of mama mandimant showing up, Bernadette intended to harvest some. Approaching one, she poked the tip of her dagger into it. A gush of yellow ichor squirted out. Yeuch. Using the blade, she was able to carefully scrape a few of them off the walls without breaking them. Their "shells" were really quite tough.

The two pushed on with heightened caution, passing many areas where mysterious dypalfar machinery whirred beneath golden floor grates. Not very much after they'd left the eggs behind, Bernadette spotted a little creature scurrying across her path and pounced on it.

Gripping it firmly by the back, she held it up for closer inspection. It resembled an oversized ant, close to the size of a rat – covered in dark brown chitin and with eight legs frantically thrashing as it tried to escape her grasp. The head was outsized, and it had enormous mandibles that were snapping futilely at the air as it tried unsuccessfully to bite her.

Andrion leaned in for a closer look. "It's a mandimant nymph," he said. "After they hatch from those eggs we saw they go through a series of stages, shedding their skins until they're close to four feet long. Then they pupate and emerge as winged adults, or so I've heard. Haven't actually seen any, but the eggs would seem to be proof."

"Weird," Bernadette said. It looked so much like an insect, not really like a spider at all. But the number of legs was wrong. And now that she had it, what was she supposed to do with it? Suddenly Andrion cried, "Berni, look out!" She looked down and discovered a swarm of the things, coming down the corridor toward them at speed. She flung the one in her hand away, smashing into the horde of its fellows, and just then the entire swarm was engulfed in flames as Andrion wielded his battle magic.

There was a high-pitched chittering sound, and the smell of burning hair, as the little creatures crisped and fried. Andrion's spell had been broad enough to stop every one of them in their tracks, for which Bernadette was profoundly grateful. She picked up one of the small corpses, and the charred legs fell away. "I'll bet there's some good eating on one of those," she remarked. "But I'm not quite hungry enough to try it." They moved on.

Bernadette was trying hard to picture what this place must have been like when it was inhabited by the long-vanished dwelves, as the dypalfar were also called. She and Andrion had explored several living areas in their passage through the building, and apparently the ancient dypalfars' idea of jolly sleeping accommodations was a platform made out of solid metal. Either that, or their ancient mattresses were made of something that had crumbled to dust and blown away centuries ago.

They had mostly been traveling downward; but now they came to a stone ramp heading up, flanked on either side by steps. The ramp had a slot cut into it, stone lined with metal, and the square stone plates set here and there within it looked an awful lot like trap triggers. Bernadette could easily imagine something lethal emerging from that slot; and she motioned to Andrion, behind her, to follow her up the stairs – away from those triggers.

At the top of the stairs they fought and killed another roller, then turned to the left to find a large open doorway giving out onto a semicircular stone balcony. Looking down, Bernadette spotted a humanoid figure lying dead in a splash of old blood on the stone plaza below. It didn't look as though it had died from a fall, though. The plaza was only about fifteen feet down, and they seemed to be out of other directions to go in; so Bernadette crouched down facing Andrion, gripped the edge of balcony with both hands, and then let herself down to drop to the stones below. He followed her in a trice.

The corpse proved to be that of an Afran woman. She was clad in studded leather armor and riddled with long arrows. Bernadette had a sinking feeling these might be leukalfar arrows. After examining the dead woman, she looked at the room around them. They were about halfway up a broad stone chimney, and above them stone ramps wound upward, looking like sections of intestine. More led down.

"Up or down?" Bernadette asked Andrion.

"From what the book said, the tunnel through to Faastenberg was at the *bottom* of Alzhenten. So we ought to be heading down," he replied.

"Right you are," she said, and headed for the nearest curving stone ramp leading in a downward direction. They had not gone very far along this path when Andrion touched her arm, beckoning silently ahead. Bernadette looked where he was pointing and saw a scrawny, pale-skinned humanoid figure clad in skins, on guard but not yet noticing them, as it stood a few dozen yards further down the ramp.

"Leukalfar?" Bernadette whispered. Andrion nodded. Aha. She drew her bow and let fly, hitting the (beast, person?) squarely in the chest. It barely flinched, and began charging angrily up the ramp toward them. "Oh, fuck!" she exclaimed, launching another arrow. As Andrion began slowing its advance with lightning bolts it occurred to Bernadette that her Gale dragon spell might well work on this creature where it had not on the automatons; and she cut loose with a blast that blew it off the ramp and down into the darkness. Peering over the edge, she could see it lying down there, unmoving.

The two left the ramp and proceeded into another corridor, around a few corners and down a flight of steps. There were curious looking, more-or-less conical dwellings here and there, like yurts made out of some hard, leathery/scaly substance. Andrion said quietly, "Shhh... leukalfar dwellings. They make them out of mandimant chitin. All their armor and some of their weapons are made out of mandimant as well."

"I wonder if they eat, them, too?" Bernadette asked in hushed tones.

"I think what they eat are men and elves that wander into their caverns," he replied seriously. She shuddered and moved on, her caution redoubled.

They had to fight a trio of the creatures shortly, and after that fight Bernadette got her first close-up look at a leukalfar. They clearly were some kind of elf, with their pointed ears and slender bodies. But whereas ljosalfar, sylvalfar, and nachtalfar were all slim, these creatures looked emaciated. They had wispy-looking straight white hair, braided down their backs and held with clips of that same chitin. Their most strikingly horrific feature, though, was their eyes: they had none. Where the eyes should be, their faces were lined with wrinkles almost as if the eyes had been removed and the eyelids sewn shut. Their noses were tiny and flat, their mouths small and full of sharp-pointed teeth.

A thousand questions sprang to Bernadette's lips; and Andrion, for once, was short on answers. "They use bows. How do they see to shoot without eyes? Where are the women and babies?" He shook his head, smiling ruefully.

"I've never met anyone who knew how they can sense a target well enough to shoot. As for the women –you probably wouldn't even realize it when you saw one. They look almost exactly like the males, but they wear armor covering their chests. As to how and where they breed, maybe *you* will be the one to write the book on the subject!"

Bernadette sighed, and led the way further into the complex. On one side of the next room was a chamber ringed in dypalfar metal bars, with a circular stone floor and a large metal lever mounted in the center of it. "That's a dypalfar lift," Andrion informed her. "You pull the lever and the floor rises or falls and takes you to some other level."

"Maybe it'll be a way out," Bernadette replied, "later. But I think we need to go over there first." She pointed down another corridor.

Ahead, another staircase led upward to a dimly lit, airy natural cavern with a massive stone structure standing at its center. The entry to that structure was barred, and they could see leukalfar yurts scattered around on either side of it. Bernadette picked off a couple of wandering leukalfar with arrows, then she and Andrion had a furious fight on their hands as a larger, tougher member of the breed attacked them at close range.

When all was quiet once more, Bernadette and Andrion climbed a staircase and picked the lock on the gate. Stairs led from the gateway up to a platform, and there they found another dypalfar robon awaiting them. This time, both of them were free to attack it as it came lumbering forward, with Bernadette dodging around to hit at its legs from behind while Andrion attempted to disrupt its motive power with lightning blasts. In moments, the thing crashed to the ground and neither of them was even hurt. Bernadette gave Andrion a bright smile and threw her arms around his neck. "Brilliant work, sweetheart!" she exclaimed. He smiled back at her and gave her a kiss before getting back to the business at hand.

They found one of the largest known magical essence vials on the disabled automaton. As the vials were supposedly filled by capturing the souls of slain enemies, it seemed to Bernadette that the machine was haunted by the ghost of a former living being. Maybe that was what made them so hostile. One might well become cranky after death, to find one's soul pressed into service within an animated machine. More stairs led up from the platform, to another enclosure of metal bars.

They opened the gates and climbed some steps to find themselves looking at a small squared-off enclosure. The familiar golden bars surrounded it, while its base was flat stone. And on the far side, a stone pillar stood. "Uh oh," Andrion said, examining it. "This looks like one of the dypalfar's sonic locks."

Bernadette looked at him questioningly. "Among their many astonishing technological advances," Andrion explained, "they had ways of keying locks using sound. An attunement sphere was required to open the lock." Oh, crap.

"We don't have anything like that," she replied, feeling as if she had just run full tilt up against a stone wall.

"The dypalfar departed here thousands of years ago," Andrion assured her. "They had no further need of those keys, and many have been left behind. I've found them before, exploring these ruins. Let's look around." It seemed like the faintest of hopes to Bernadette, but Andrion's confidence buoyed her as they went on the hunt.

"The leukalfar are the dypalfar's heirs," he explained, as they began their search. "They were enslaved by them, millennia ago, and left behind when their masters vanished. They don't seem all that smart, but they are attracted by interesting artifacts. We should check the yurts in that last chamber." More concerned about finding the passageway to Faastenberg – and staying alive – they had not bothered to search either the bodies of their leukalfar adversaries or the chitin yurts where they'd lived.

The pair returned the way they'd come, and began a systematic search of the bodies of their fallen foes. They found many chemial ingredients and miscellaneous armaments – a sign to Bernadette that these curious creatures, however alien, were still human. But it wasn't until they began searching the yurts that they found what they were looking for.

From a curiously-constructed chitin chest in a yurt tucked far away in a corner of the room, Andrion pulled forth a spherical object all of dypalfar metal. It resembled, in miniature, the chests they had been plundering as they made their way through the ruins of Alzhenten.

Triumphantly, Andrion placed the sphere atop the pillar beside the barred enclosure. Bernadette had expected there to be sound, if this was supposed to be a "sonic lock"; but she heard nothing. "The sound is beyond the range of human hearing," Andrion explained as they heard a grinding sound and retrieved the sphere from the pillar.

A set of stone steps had appeared, sinking down into the floor. Quite a trick! Bernadette thought, as she eagerly stepped down them. They had been traveling for hours, stopping only briefly to relieve themselves and munch trail rations or drink from their water skins; but her excitement as it seemed they were approaching their goal drew her on.

At the bottom of the steps was another pair of those gleaming dypalfar metal doors. They pushed them open and stepped through onto a stone walkway that terminated in a panoramic vista. "By the gods!" Bernadette murmured, looking out on the cavernous space that confronted them. "Where do we go from here?"

Chapter 36: Faastenberg

Bernadette and Andrion were far underground. There was no daylight, the ceiling of this cavern far above them. Yet despite the overall darkness, everything was somehow illuminated. Below them was an underground lake, filling the bottom of the space. On all sides of that lake, dypalfar buildings stood. Like the one they had entered by, each overlooked the water. Stone ramps spiraled down, some of them terminating in more ruins that sat above the water level. Others vanished below the surface.

"The quake must have ruptured the foundations," Andrion said, gazing out at the scene. "Water has seeped in and flooded the very bottom levels of the city."

"Including the tunnel through to Faastenberg, I'd suspect," Bernadette said. Her hopes were hanging on desperately, but the winds of reality were threatening to tear them from their tenuous hold on her mind.

"Do you have any potions of water breathing?" Andrion asked. That they might find themselves needing to explore under water had not occurred to them, when they set off on this expedition.

"I brought along every potion I could think of crafting," Bernadette replied. "Invisibility, fire resistance… and some water breathing. But how are we supposed to know where to go?"

"Check your map," he said. She hadn't thought to pull it out once they reached their destination, but was surprised to find that it had narrowed its focus. It was now showing her a close-up view of the ruins of Alzhenten, sketchy gray outlines that provided no detail. But an arrow pointed clearly to the side of the lake opposite where they were standing. Amazing!

"This thing will even show me where I want to go when it's not actually on the map?" Bernadette asked.

"I haven't had all that much experience with the maps," Andrion admitted. "But anecdotal evidence would suggest that's the case." His casual, pragmatic acceptance of the astonishing situation they'd found themselves in filled her with deep love. What a man she had found, to stand by her side!

They moved down the curving ramp ahead of them, creeping silently along with weapons at the ready. Even here, in the remotest depths of the city its builders had abandoned so long ago, they found leukalfar sentries ready to contest their presence. One by one, they fell.

They reached water level and stepped into the water. It was surprisingly clear, and surprisingly warm – if anything, warmer than the air at this great depth. "We're never going to be able to swim in this armor once it gets too deep to wade in," Bernadette pointed out. The two of them studied the map one last time, before they were submerged beyond waist level.

"If we're able to get into Faastenberg through here," Andrion said, gazing into the dark waters, "we probably will have to come out the same way. It's likely that any other exits will be blocked."

"You're right," she said. "Might as well strip off for the swim, and leave our packs behind." They waded back up onto a stone platform, and began removing their armor. They seemed to have killed off the hostiles in the local area, so their belongings should be safe here. But Andrion was uneasy. Unarmored, and with few weapons, what would happen if there were more automatons, leukalfar, and mandimants on the other side of the tunnel?

"I've got my battle spells with me wherever I go," he told his lover. "I think you should wait here while I swim down there and check it out." Bernadette frowned at him. She was no more willing to see him in deadly danger than he was her. But what he said made sense. Without arms or armor, Andrion had a much better chance of prevailing than she did. And if it turned out the tunnel didn't go through, it made more sense if only one of them was down there to find that out.

"All right," she said. She handed over some potions – water breathing, healing, magical force regeneration – and he tucked the vials into the waistband of his underwear. Just before diving beneath the water, into the tunnel he could see opening below, Andrion downed a potion of water breathing. For several minutes, he would be able to breath as the fishes did. He hoped it would be long enough.

Bernadette decided to put some of her armor back on. It was chilly and dank down here, with steam rising from the water. Then, eyes constantly scanning for any signs of movement around her and bow at the ready, she stood guard. Inside she was silently praying to all the gods, "Let Andrion be all right." The thought of losing him was more than she could bear.

The tunnel had been closed off with heavy dypalfar metal doors, Andrion saw as he swam inside. But they had been left standing open when the inhabitants of this city had vanished. Fortunately the dypalfar lamps, which seemed to contain ever-glowing crystals, had been unaffected by their millennia-long immersion in water. They provided enough dim illumination for him to see as he swam along. His buoyancy wanted to plaster him against the tunnel's barrel-vaulted ceiling, and he was constantly having to dive down again to swim down the center.

The corridor was bare of the usual detritus one sees in dypalfar ruins, he realized. The deep elves had ruled here for many centuries after building the tunnel, but clearly it had only been intended as a passageway between their original city and the Norse one they had seized.

Ahead was darkness, and Andrion rested as he came up on an obstruction. How much longer would the potion's effects hold out? The ceiling of the tunnel had collapsed, blocks falling down to litter the floor of the passageway. But there was a hole above where the blocks had fallen from – raw dirt and stone. Andrion climbed the pile and swam up a little way, and found himself in pitch darkness – and air. It smelled of dampness and decay, and had probably not been breathed by any living thing since the pocket formed ages ago.

He didn't linger – soon he was traversing the blockage and swimming along the tunnel again. And in no more than another minute, he abruptly found himself swimming upward at an angle. Unless the dypalfar had had access to the lower levels of the Norse stronghold before they began digging their tunnel, Andrion realized – and that was hardly likely when they were at war with one another – the dypalfar would have had no way to know exactly what level they needed to be at when they arrived at their goal. They must have corrected after first finding themselves too low to connect with the underground installation's lowest level.

He came out into a large stone-lined room, built not in the dypalfar style but following the ancient Norse architectural conventions. Here there were no stone dragons, for the builders of this fortress were opposed to the dragon worshipers and all they stood for. And, he had reason to hope, there would be no aptrgangr here either. Even if some of the Norse dead had been interred here, likely the invading dypalfar would have removed the corpses.

Andrion climbed a staircase and found himself walking through a doorway. It had once been closed by an iron-bound wooden door, but in this close proximity to water the wood had rotted away and the iron was nothing but lumps of rust. Now he was standing in soaking wet underwear, in a room where the temperature was far below what would have been comfortable even if the underwear had been dry.

The corridor ahead of him was bare, with nothing stirring. It was lit by more of those dypalfar lamps. Could it be that the dypalfar had left no automatons behind here, and that the leukalfar had never taken up residence? It was a nice thought, but he decided he'd better check a little further. Teeth chattering, he stripped to the skin and wrung his underwear out. Then he downed a healing potion, which eliminated the worst effects of hypothermia, and used a minor fire spell to dry the underwear until it was only a little damp before putting it back on again. He wanted at least *some* protection, if it turned out there were hostiles here.

Feeling much better, Andrion headed down the corridor in his bare feet. At least, dressed like this, it was easy to move silently! There were rooms giving off the corridor, some of them with still-intact wooden doors and others with wide doorless openings. Inside, there was a curious mixture of Norse and dypalfar leavings – broken furniture, cups and plates, bits of scrap metal that looked like they might once have been housed in dypalfar automatons. The deep elves must have used this area for storage, after the Norse inhabitants had been driven out or killed.

At the corridor's end another set of stairs went up, and
Andrion found himself looking at a large chamber with many
doorways leading off of it. He sighed. It appeared that unless they
had Berni's map to guide them, they would be wandering lost in
here for a long time. He hoped the thing was waterproof.

As he turned, intending to go back through the tunnel to
collect his companion, there was a skittering sound and a dypalfar
bug came seemingly out of nowhere intent on attacking the
intruder. Twin bolts of lightning sprang from his hands, and the
little automaton flew through the air to smash against the far stone
wall – pieces flying.

Note to self, bring some more weaponry, Andrion thought as
he made his way back to the room the tunnel had come out in. He
downed another potion before diving under the water again.
Visions of dry clothing, a warm fire, and a hot meal were dancing
in his head as he swam back to the deeps of Alzhenten.

Shivering slightly, feeling chilled because she'd been standing
more or less motionless for what seemed like around ten minutes,
Bernadette's anxiety was growing. She was trying to suppress it,
knowing that it was just being all alone in this vast, creepy space
that was contributing to her fears. Andrion was strong, smart, and
skilled. He wouldn't just let himself drown, or be taken down by
some little automaton. He was probably already over in
Faastenberg, doing reconnaissance before coming back.
Everything was going to be fine…

When Andrion suddenly erupted from the water a dozen feet
from where she stood, Bernadette nearly jumped out of her skin.
Oh, thank the gods, he was all right! She slung her bow behind her
back and rushed over to him, hugging him tight until he winced.
Her armor was light, but he was dressed only in soaking wet
underwear.

She refrained from peppering him with questions, letting him
tell the tale in his own good time. But he didn't speak. Instead,
shivering, he began stripping naked on the spot! Bernadette
watched with interest. She was certainly not in the mood for sex at
this moment, but she was always ready to appreciate a naked man

– especially one as gorgeous as Andrion was – from an aesthetic standpoint.

Andrion repeated the maneuver he'd gone through on the other end of the tunnel, then began rummaging through his pack for some dry clothing. Finally, he spoke. "The tunnel's short enough to make it on one potion," he said, wrapping his cloak around him. "It's collapsed about three-quarters of the way down, but there's plenty of room to climb over the blockage. And at least the bottom couple of levels of the stronghold are reasonably intact."

"Any hostiles?" Bernadette asked. "I didn't see any signs of leukalfar or mandimants," he replied. "But there are definitely at least a few automatons still wandering around. If you think about it, there probably wouldn't have been enough air in there to support much of a population of breathing creatures. Likely some is seeping in through cracks from the surface, but with a cave-in above and water below, the vital gases would soon be exhausted."

Bernadette eyed him thoughtfully. "I guess we'd better keep our breathing down to a minimum while we're in there, then," she said.

"No hot sex sessions?" he asked, with an expression of disappointment. She grinned at him ruefully.

"Let's get this mission out of the way first, love," she said softly.

In the end they left their packs behind, but brought along armor for both of them, more potions, and some edged weapons. There was no way to keep their underclothing dry, but Andrion's fire spell worked well enough if given enough time. Within an hour they were dry, kitted up, and reasonably comfortable. The magic map had indeed proven to be waterproof.

As they moved through the labyrinthine rooms and corridors, they encountered mostly the smaller type of dypalfar bugs. The departed deep elves had not bothered retrofitting their captured Norse fortress with dispensers for mechanical guardians, and they found no rollers or robons – the gods be praised. And unlike the dypalfar ruin they had left behind, this place had no constant thrum of ever-running machinery. It was fortunate for the two intruders that the place had been fitted with those ever-glowing lamps, at least.

The map gave Bernadette a general idea what direction to take, but could not tell her on what floor they might find what they sought. They wandered back and forth searching for staircases to the next level, occasionally encountering dead ends where ceilings had collapsed or walls had fallen in. The fortress might have once been ten stories from top to bottom, they thought.

Finally, exhausted, they camped for the night in what seemed to have once been a dormitory for troops. Men were ever more numerous than elves, their ability to breed rapidly more than making up for the alfar's greater lifespans. Likely the dypalfar had occupied the captured fortress to assure no Norsemen would return to it; but they could never have been here in the numbers its builders had had, and some rooms appeared untouched.

They broke up some furniture for firewood and got a blaze going in the room's fireplace, used the iron cookpot that still sat beside it to make a sort of camp stew with dehydrated ingredients they'd carried in a waterproof pouch. The last of their bread was gone, but they had some pemmican for backup rations. Unsurprisingly, no edible foodstuffs were to be found in Faastenberg millennia after its last occupation.

The bedsteads still stood, but the mattresses had deteriorated. They threw their bedrolls down, extras piled on top for warmth, and slept in separate beds for the night. No dypalfar lamps had been added to this room, but they had found candles to light. After blowing them out, they lay drifting off to sleep and talking quietly. "Andrion," Bernadette murmured sleepily, "if the dypalfar were so much less numerous than the Norse, how did they manage to defeat them?"

"Ultimately," he said as quietly, "they didn't. Around three thousand years ago the entire race just vanished – there in their underground cities one day and gone the next. There were no bodies, not even skeletons, left behind. It's one of the great mysteries of Agenan history. But here, I think it was the element of surprise. I'd guess that the room they tunneled into was probably just a disused storeroom. The Norse wouldn't have wanted to be climbing a lot of stairs every day, so the bottom levels would have been used for things they didn't need very often. The elves probably brought a big armed force through, maybe with some robons for backup, and just overpowered the sentries before slaughtering the Norse troops in their beds."

"Sneaky bastards…" Bernadette said, so softly that he could barely hear her. She had drifted off to sleep, Andrion realized. A few minutes later, he did the same.

Chapter 37: The Edelmied

There was no day or night here, dozens or hundreds of feet below the ground. Bernadette was the first to wake, and she slipped out of bed to pad over to where her lover lay, snoring gently, in his own bedroll. Faint light came in through the room's door, from dypalfar lamps in the corridor outside.

"Andrion?" she murmured, stroking his face. She could barely see him in this dimness.

"Ungh," he grunted, and rolled over. Bernadette slipped under the top bedroll to lie beside him, pressed up against his back, and bit him gently on the neck. He started up, awake now, and rolled over to face her. "Morning?" he asked sleepily.

"Might as well be," his lover replied. "Could you give me some light, please?" He pulled an arm out of the covers and cast a globe of light about the size of a man's head skyward. It stopped when it got to the ceiling and floated there, its glaring brilliance forming dark shadows. "Thanks, sweetie," Bernadette said, and rolled back out of bed. Before the globe winked out she had blown the embers of last night's fire back into life and lit a few candles from the flames. She was getting back into her armor, munching on a block of pemmican, by the time Andrion sat up and began climbing out of bed.

"I don't see how you can just bounce right up like that," he complained. She smiled patiently at him.

"And I don't see how you can lie abed, when there are important things to do," she replied. "I guess it takes all kinds to make a world. But at least my kind takes care of business before lunchtime." He sighed.

Within half an hour they'd readied themselves, and moved on through the ruined stronghold. As they climbed higher, they saw more and more evidence of the underground facility's former use. After the dragon worshipers had been defeated and the last of the dragons killed, once Tarragin had been removed from the scene, this place had continued to be occupied for millennia as generation after generation of Norse found it to be a useful bastion in the wars they seemed to engage in constantly. Even today, many of

Iscandia's Norsemen would probably leap at the chance to start a shooting war with the Reman empire. They were a bloodthirsty lot.

Not that the history of Auverne had been one of great pacifism. A thousand years or more ago, the relatively small area had been broken up into more than a dozen little kingdoms – each ready to fight its neighbors at the drop of a hat. But while the Galise seemed to have mellowed in modern times, the Norse still reveled in the bloody arts. Even their afterlife was supposed to be a place much like Iscandia, with an enormous hall where the souls of fallen warriors could drink and feast for eternity.

There were barracks, armories, great dining halls – most of them little disturbed from the way they had presumably been at the time of the dypalfar takeover. The ever-burning lamps had been placed in most corridors, but many of the rooms themselves were in darkness and required Andrion to use his light globe spell as they searched them. "These people must have practiced chemia, if they were able to craft a potion to rob Tarragin of his trans-dimensional traveling ability," Bernadette said, "But I've seen no signs of any chemia stations or enchanting tables. Didn't the ancients learn how to apply permanent magic spells to arms and armor almost before they had learned how to forge steel?" So far, most of the weapons and armor they'd seen lying around in abandoned armories had been iron and leather.

"The modern chemia stations and enchanting tables are a recent invention," Andrion told her. "They basically assemble in one place the equipment that used to be scattered on tabletops or incorporated into vast laboratories. But I haven't seen anything magic-related yet. I sure hope it doesn't turn out Seimdal and his colleagues were working in the part of the stronghold that was destroyed in the earthquake."

"You and me both," she said, and they moved on. From the number of staircases they'd climbed, frequently having to zigzag back and forth across the entire complex in quest for the next set leading up (an annoying design feature, but perhaps one that would have slowed the invading dypalfar), Andrion thought that they must be getting very near the top. There was no reason to assume that the stories built by the Norse would match those built by the elves – dypalfar seemed to favor cavernously high ceilings in their underground structures, while what they'd seen here so far offered no more than ten to twelve feet between floors.

At last they came up another flight of stairs and into a long, broad corridor. Many rooms opened off of it, and peeking into each of them they saw what looked a lot like administrative offices. There were desks, conference tables, chairs, and some elements of décor that suggested the long-departed users of these facilities had been above the rank and file – generals, eorls, leaders. "I think we may be getting close!" Andrion said, a touch of excitement in his voice.

Bernadette pulled out her map and looked at it again, and found that the arrow marking their target lay straight ahead of them – at the end of this corridor, or perhaps at the end of a corridor on a floor above. Though surely, they should be getting near the top?

The stone corridor ended in a broad single door that was unlike any they had seen – here, or in any other ruin. It appeared to be made of solid iron, set into an iron frame that fit tightly into the stone surrounding it. It was blackened as if from great age, but there was no trace of rust. It had an ornate iron handle, but where you would expect to find a keyhole there was only a circle of smooth black metal, a little more than an inch in diameter. It was recessed slightly into the surface of the door.

"A magic lock!" Andrion gasped, his tone that of a child discovering that roasted nut confections were being served for breakfast. Bernadette smiled to herself. Her lover's enthusiasm for tidbits of ancient lore and forgotten magic was one of his most endearing qualities. He turned excitedly to her. "The ancient Norse had arts that have been lost for millennia!" he said. "It may well be that the dypalfar never passed this door."

"Didn't they have their own magical arts?" Bernadette asked.

"Yes, of course," Andrion replied. "But the dypalfar were much more focused on the mechanical arts. Their automatons, of course, are a blend of the mechanical with the magical. But it's unlikely they would have known how to open this door. It's magically warded against being battered down, though the ward has weakened over the millennia."

Bernadette considered. It seemed unlikely the two of them would have the ability to break down a door like this one by brute force, even if it *weren't* warded. "But you know how to work the lock?" she asked hopefully. Andrion put his hands on the door and closed his eyes, casting a spell of delving. It should give him some idea of what spells had been used here.

His lover waited, breath bated, for more than a minute. Then he turned to her and said, "Berni, can I borrow your dagger?" She handed it over, and he held out his left hand and drew the razor-sharp blade carefully across the ball of the thumb. Dark blood welled up at once, and he pressed it to the black circle. At once an aura of purple light burst out around the lock in a pulsating flash. As it subsided, the heard an audible "click." Andrion pulled on the handle, and the door swung outward. He had done it!

Bernadette was suitably impressed. It was so nice having a companion whose skills complemented her own! But a moment later he was asking her to heal the cut – seemingly, despite their age difference, she was already better at healing magic than he was.

They stepped inside, finding a large stone-lined room with some other rooms leading off of it. On the floor just inside the door lay a skeleton, clothed in the tattered remnants of what had once probably been mage robes. "He must have been locked in here when the dypalfar came!" Bernadette exclaimed, her heart welling up with pity. Had he died of starvation, or swallowed poison?

Against the far wall was a metal-topped wooden workbench the ran some twenty feet from side to side, and on it were a jumble of items – potion vials, gemstones, bowls of what looked like powdered rock or bone, apparatus that was probably the ancestor of today's chemia stations: mortar and pestle, retorts, flasks, and verdigrised copper tubing. The people working here had been almost as far advanced from the builders of Faastenberg as Andrion and Bernadette were beyond them, so this was probably not the original equipment.

Andrion walked over to the right side, where a large metal chest stood beside a small golden bowl. "An old-fashioned enchanting station!" he said. "You would put the item to be enchanted in the chest, fill the bowl with magical essence, and cast the spell. At that time only a mage who had mastered the spells could cast that spell as an enchantment. These days, almost anyone can become an enchanter and you scarcely even have to study magic – let alone possess a high enough supply of personal magical force."

Bernadette looked at the equipment, intrigued. She enjoyed having the ability to enchant weapons and armor, and looked forward to developing her skills to the point where she could produce items that matched the ones she found in ancient Norse barrows for potency. Clearly, the ancient enchanters must have been far above her in magical skill. And other than healing, she wasn't all that interested in learning magic.

On the wall behind the workbench was a shelf with several ancient-looking books on it, as well as pigeonholes in which scrolls were stored. Excitement flared as Bernadette realized that those scrolls must contain the original knowledge of the ancient Norse heroes, the men and women who had defeated Tarragin and brought down the rule of the dragons and their vicious cult.

"Andrion, look!" she said. "Do we dare try to unroll them?" He eyed the scrolls thoughtfully. They didn't *look* like parchment… Gingerly, he reached for one and rubbed the material between thumb and forefinger.

"Berni! Let me see your map!" he said excitedly. She brought it out, eyes questioning, and handed it to him. He made the same gesture with it, then handed it back to her. "I'm almost sure it's the same material!" he said, and pulled the scroll he'd touched earlier out of its pigeonhole. He carefully rolled it out onto the surface of the workbench, and it lay flat as if it were made of cloth.

Bernadette squeezed in behind him so that they both could read what the scroll had to say – assuming it was written in characters they could understand. It was! Astonishingly, though the handwriting had a trace of the antique about it and there were some spellings that were not in accordance with modern usage, it appeared to have been written in the same common tongue used throughout Agena today.

"I... I'd have thought it would be in ancient Norse," Bernadette said, trailing off in disbelief. How old *was* the common tongue, and why had it not undergone so many changes in the past several thousand years as to render it incomprehensible to modern speakers?

"I detect a magic about this scroll," Andrion said. After more than a decade of practicing magic his sensibilities were finely attuned. "Not only is it made from the same seemingly indestructible material as your map, but it seems to possess another magic as well. I'd suspect that if you were to carry it to the other side of the world, the people there would be able to read and understand it as easily as we can."

"Andrion, that's wonderful!" Bernadette said, her excitement rising. "The ancient Norse heroes left us a treasure trove!"

"Indeed they did," Andrion said calmly. But she could detect his own excitement. What incredible knowledge would be found in these scrolls – and he was one of two people to get the chance to read them in the past four thousand years!

This particular scroll, which was too long for all of it to be unrolled at once on the space available, was titled "A Lyst of the Dragonne Spells, and the Stones Whych Power Them." Holy shit! The very document Bernadette had been itching to get her hands on!

Below the title was a notation: "This lyst hath been supplied by the dragonne Ehrgeizig, who hath earned the eternal gratitude of the Norse people for his assistance in our struggle against the cult of the dragonnes. See Stone Formulae for the ingredients required for each stone."

Proof, beyond doubt, that somewhere in this room lay the Edelmied, the gem forge that could create gems to power dragon spells just as the dragons themselves did naturally within their own bodies! No wonder the ancient Norse heroes had triumphed – with Ehrgeizig's help, they had stolen the secrets of their enemies.

"This is solid gold, Andrion!" Bernadette said in triumph. The spells she'd already learned, and the missing words from the Stasis spell, were all laid out in simple text. As long as she possessed the spell's gem within her, learning the spell was as simple as reading it on the scroll. She supposed that carving spell words into stone walls, in runes only the ancient dragon priests could read, was not something the ancient Norse heroes had bothered with. Why should they?

"It's amazing!" Andrion declared, and began looking around for the scroll titled "Stone Formulae." There were more than a dozen scrolls, and they were all intriguing. But it took him several tries to find the one he was looking for. It listed each stone (gem) by spell, but gave no further instructions. Each seemed to have magical essence, as was used in enchanting, as a basic ingredient. The other ingredients were chemical compounds, or sometimes powdered ores.

The Dragonfall spell had not been on the "Lyst of Dragonne Spells." But the formula for producing its stone in the Gem Forge was shown. Andrion glanced around, and saw an apparatus off to their right that must surely be the forge itself. An enormously thick, circular metal tabletop held an inner bowl of some kind of thick ceramic. And a gigantic lever was attached to a matching top, hinged at the back.

"Keep looking for the Dragonfall spell, Berni," Andrion told his companion, as he walked over for a look at the apparatus. He seized the lever and brought it down, though without any contents in the bowl he assumed that it would not activate. The lever had a locking position, as if designed to hold the top down while great forces were applied to the ingredients contained within the ceramic bowl halves.

The eagerness to try it seized him, and he began looking around for ingredients. They could try making a gem for one of the other spells, while Berni was searching for the one they'd come for. "Got it!" she cried, before he'd identified anything to put into the forge. As she read the scroll, the words penetrated into her being though she had not yet absorbed the gem that would power them: Alt-Wach-Sterb-Tot. Something about her Fireblood heritage seemed to make her able to understand the meaning of the words in the dragon tongue: age, weakness, mortal, death. They should be powerful concepts to the immortal *drachen*!

"Great, love!" Andrion said. "Let's explore these other rooms, shall we? I think I've figured out how to use the Edelmied, but I need to try it with some gem ingredients." She smiled at him, as alive with excitement as he was. Getting in here had been a royal pain in the butt, but had it been ten times as difficult it was worth it all.

There were three rooms giving off the main chamber. They started on the left, and found what was obviously a sleeping chamber. Another skeleton lay amid the crumbled remains of a mattress, as if the person had died in bed. There was no sign of any gem components in the room, and they turned to the room that opened off of a small chamber behind the wall on which the workbench had been set.

This room was more promising. It was not all that big, but completely lined with shelves on which sat neatly labeled, sealed glass jars containing what appeared to be chemial ingredients. Most of them, those that were biological, had withered over the past millennia until they were unrecognizable. Dried, plant and animal ingredients might last for years – but not for millennia.

Andrion and Bernadette gathered up everything that seemed like it might still be useful. Many of the ingredients were unfamiliar to them, as he had never studied chemia and she was still learning the discipline. They carried their finds back and arrayed them on the workbench, before trying the third room – over on the right side, beyond the Edelmied.

Jackpot! As with the previous room, this one was lined with shelves bearing neatly labeled substances. But these substances were mostly mineral, not biologic – the ingredients needed for creating spell gems, and vials of the magical essence needed to infuse them with power for the spells.

"The Old Ones said that the supply of spell gems dried up after the dragons were gone," Bernadette said. "But it was probably a few thousand years later, when the dypalfar overran Faastenberg, that there were no more gems being produced."

"I have to assume the Old Ones are mortal men," Andrion replied. "I'd guess Ehrgeizig has trained countless generations up there atop Hochstein. So probably Aethelred and his cohorts are clueless that there was once another source of the gems, one that lasted for thousands of years."

"And now it's back!" she crowed. "Well, I suppose it'd be good if we could figure out how to excavate the top layers of Faastenberg and burrow down to this lab. But the Old Ones, and anybody willing to put in a little effort and study, should now be able to cast dragon spells to their hearts' content! This might be just what we need to keep dragons from overrunning Iscandia and making life a living hell for its inhabitants!"

She was right, Andrion realized. The Firebloods' special power was the ability to incorporate dragon spells into their bodies, and use them for the rest of their lives – recharging the gems that powered them from within their beings, just as dragons did. But there was no reason someone else, a mage like himself for instance, couldn't use those spells – as long as a ready supply of the gems existed.

Bernadette had carried along the scroll enumerating the ingredients for the Dragonfall spell stone, and luckily they found them among those on the shelves. The spell, so critical to the ancient Norse heroes' defeat of the dragons and their cult, would have become nothing but a curious historical footnote once they had triumphed. None alive in that time would have believed that Tarragin would return, that dragons would once again threaten Iscandia.

Most of the spell stone recipes had been fairly simple: the magical essence common to all of them, plus at most three additional ingredients. But the recipe for the Dragonfall spell stone required a total of five minerals as well as the basic magical essence. Andrion and Bernadette carried the jars from the storage room, and she left it to him to measure out the small quantities of powdered minerals. Spell gems were usually no larger than the end of your thumb, so they didn't require bulk quantities.

Following the recipe precisely, using a measuring spoon he had found on the workbench, Andrion placed the five mineral ingredients in the ceramic crucible at the center of the Gem Forge. Last, he added the vial of magical essence. The glass comprising the vial would be incorporated into the makeup of the gem, its size and spiritual content precisely calculated with the other ingredients. As Bernadette watched avidly, he pulled the lever down on the top and locked it into place.

Andrion had expected that some spell of quickening might be required. After all, this entire setup had been created by a fellow mage. But in the presence of the right ingredients for the creation of a spell stone, the forge acted on its own. A blaze of light and heat radiated from its center, driving him and Bernadette back. It went on for far longer than they'd expected; but after a couple of minutes it began to fade.

When the Gem Forge had lost any trace of glow, Andrion gingerly released the lever from its locked position. The top of the mechanism rose up easily, as if counter-weighted, and he and Bernadette stared at the glowing gem that sat within the lower chamber. Only a faint layer of ash coated the bowl, a remnant of waste products generated in the forging of the spell stone.

Andrion put a hand over it, feeling to see if it was cool enough to touch. The thing was amazing! Newly created, and without a mold to shape it, it yet seemed as if it had been cut and faceted. A thousand colors sparkled in it, from the brightest to nearly black, depending on the angle at which one viewed the gem. That this was something special, something unique, was beyond doubt.

"Go ahead Berni," he said in tones of awe. "It should be safe to pick up." Eagerly Bernadette reached into the extremely warm lower half of the Forge, and plucked up the spell gem. As soon as she had cradled it in her palm, it melted away – vanishing in a trice. And the voices chorused in her head, filling her soul with exaltation. Dragonfall, I have you!

"Got it?" Andrion asked, though he could tell from her expression she had.

"Yeah."

"What about the potion?"

"I guess we'd better search the rest of these scrolls to see if there's a formula for it," she replied. Coming back to reality after the transportation of obtaining that spell was like a bath of cold water. They studied the remaining scrolls, most of which were histories describing the ancient Norse heroes' battles to defeat the dragons. No mention of the potion!

No reference to any potions, actually, which was strange considering the room full of outdated chemial ingredients. They moved from the scrolls to the modern-style bound books, and encountered some chemial formulae; but of the potion the ancient Norse heroes had used to poison Tarragin and keep him from returning to this universe for thousands of years, there was no mention.

"That was a potion that was used once, to nullify the powers of a unique being who'd vanished eons ago," Bernadette said after their search had led to nothing. "Maybe nobody thought it was worth discussing. They had to have assumed, after uncounted generations, that Tarragin was never coming back."

"You're probably right," Andrion said. Then he added, "Are you tired? Because I'm about ready to fall over." She leaned into him and fell into his arms. The intense excitement of their discovery had driven both of them far beyond the point where they should have taken a break.

They munched some more pemmican and drank some water, which was about it for their remaining stores. Anything down here had turned to dust long before they were born, and they would soon need to leave. Bernadette and Andrion bedded down on the stone floor of the lab, unwilling to move too far from their discovery.

When they had rested enough for Bernadette to awaken, which was to say about an hour short of when Andrion would have begun to think about getting up, they ate yet more pemmican and drank nearly the last of their water. "We'd better get back out of here," she said.

"I've been thinking about that," her lover replied. "As much as I'd like to carry off these scrolls, I think that the ones related to the Gem Forge should stay in place. Why separate them from the unique device that can make use of the knowledge they contain?" Bernadette considered.

"You're probably right," she admitted. "But what should we do? We need to get out of here soon, before we run out of food and water."

"Let's get you all the rest of the dragon spells," Andrion proposed. "At least, all the ones we have ingredients for. Who knows when we'll have this chance again?" Bernadette considered, and knew he was right. A concentrated effort to excavate the top entrance to Faastenberg could eventually provide a "normal" way to reach this chamber. But who knew how long that might take? She needed to fortify herself with all of the dragon spells she could take in!

Hours later, Bernadette fairly reeled from all that had assailed her being since they had begun. She now knew the spells to bind an animal as an ally, to rip the weapons from an opponent's hands, to still an attacking animal's animosity, to turn an opponent into a solid block of ice – and so much more. Many of these spells made her wonder if they had truly originated with dragons. Why would such a creature need to fend off the aggression of a bear, when it could kill one with a single blow and turn it into lunch? Perhaps these spells had been a collaborative effort between dragons and the cult who had worshiped them?

Andrion patted her shoulder. It was time for them to leave. They'd brought along extra stones for the Dragonfall spell, and a few others as well. But hunger gnawed their bellies, and there was no more food. He used his blood again to lock the door to the laboratory behind them, before they retraced their steps down through the many levels of Faastenberg to the room where they'd entered. Now that they knew where they were going, the trip went much faster.

Back in Alzhenten, cold and wet and on the verge of exhaustion, the two changed out of wet underwear into dry, removed the water from their armor, and shouldered their packs. These had remained undisturbed in their absence, thank the gods. They had a long uphill hike ahead of them, Bernadette thought. But when they reached the dypalfar lift they'd passed earlier, Andrion had a surprise in store for her. Pulling the central lever, they rode up and up to find themselves looking through metal bars at a snowy landscape. Another lever let them out onto the mountainside. They were almost home!

Chapter 38: Home Sweet Home

In the Bathing Maiden's basement bedroom Erik Johannessohn slipped from the bed, careful not to awaken the pretty blonde woman he'd been sharing it with. Some noblewoman she was, with a rich old husband back in Sylvanian no doubt. She'd been a lively enough lay, certainly more fun than Lifa; but nothing special. In his time as an employee of the Maiden, Erik had acted as bed-warmer for dozens of such. It was harmless fun, the amulet he always wore ensuring that neither fatherhood nor disease resulted from these romps. He loved women and they loved him, though some few were frightened of his size.

Yet lately, Erik had found that his enjoyment of life at the Maiden was missing something. Alas, he knew exactly *what* was missing: one smallish, red-haired minx of a Fireblood adventuress named Bernadette. He found himself thinking of her while he was fucking other women, while he was soaking in the bathing pool, while he was eating his supper. He missed her especially in the evenings, when the gaiety of the place seemed muted without her exuberant participation.

Just thinking about Berni caused a stiffening between Erik's legs. She seemed to have some near-magical power to arouse him. But the longer she was gone with Andrion, the more Erik became convinced that he was second in her affections. After all, Andrion had her first. Even when Berni had discovered that Andrion had met her, shared her bed, and accompanied her on her adventures initially as part of his job duties – which had made her angry enough that she had almost dumped him (and given Erik his opportunity to get next to her at last) – it had not been enough to drive a permanent wedge between them.

Well, he didn't know what to do about it. Berni was the kind of woman who did things her own way, and if she had changed her mind and only wanted to be with Andrion in the future, Erik was probably out of luck. If only he didn't want her so badly! In his 25 years, Erik had never met anyone like her – never been so troubled by the absence of one particular woman. They had all seemed about the same to him before, like candies in a dish. Each delicious and delightful in her own way; but after being enjoyed for a moment, soon forgotten. This one, he could not get out of his mind.

Erik sighed, slipping on a robe, and climbed the ladder to the trap door behind the Maiden's main floor bar. He felt like having a soak before breakfast. Dropping his robe on a table near the central bathing pool, he sighed more pleasurably as he sank into the hot, clear water. At this hour, he had the pool to himself. He closed his eyes for a moment as he relaxed, the water up to his armpits. Then he opened them again, as he heard the Maiden's front door open. His heart leapt as he beheld none other than that selfsame red-haired minx, coming into the hall. She was bloodstained and smudged, her hair was a mess, and she looked absolutely wonderful.

Bernadette's eyes fell on Erik almost at once as she and Andrion walked into the Maiden's central room. Her heart beat faster and a huge smile spread across her face as she hesitated for a moment, taking him in. *Damn* that man looked fine. His face was wreathed in a smile too, his warm blue eyes radiating delight at seeing her, and his enormous, perfectly sculpted body was on display in the bathing pool's clear water – nothing hidden.

The moment having passed, Bernadette dropped her pack and weapons with a clank, and rushed to poolside. She knelt beside Erik where he sat there in the water and threw her arms around his neck, planting a big kiss on his lips. Mmm! Then she released him, sitting back on her haunches to just beam at him some more. Her eyes looked huge, dilated with excitement and (dare he imagine?) desire.

Erik couldn't stop grinning. "You're back!" he exclaimed, stating the obvious. "I've missed you…" Looking down at him through the water, Bernadette could see that his claim was not a false one. Just her proximity had already set his finely-formed manhood on the rise. She returned his grin. "I've missed you, too, lover," she replied. "And I've missed this hot water!" Jumping to another subject, she exclaimed "Wait'll we tell you everything that's happened!"

Getting back on her feet, Bernadette turned to Andrion. He'd been standing back a bit, watching his lover's reunion with her *other* lover. Maybe, he thought, he was lucky there was just the one – and that one a friend of his. He felt a pang, but he was hanging on firmly to his reactions. Berni loving Erik did not mean she would stop loving him. Andrion getting into a fight with Erik over Berni's affections might, though. She was the flame that sparked his desire, not to mention the likely savior of the world; but he could not hold onto her by locking her in a cage.

"Undo my straps, please?" Bernadette asked him, giving him a light kiss and hug. He helped her get the armor off. Standing in her long woolen underclothes, which were now far too warm, Bernadette helped Andrion remove his own armor. Then she stripped to the skin, and in moments, had splashed into the pool beside Erik.

"Ahhh!" she exclaimed, delighted. Bernadette knew of no magic spell that would cause a large pool of hot water to appear on demand, but she vowed (only half seriously) that should she succeed in saving the world from Tarragin she would go back to the Mages' Academy at Eisenstag and make the discovery of such a spell her life's work. Turning to her golden godling, she reached for him through the water to give him a much closer hug, now she was naked and sitting beside him.

Erik enjoyed this immensely; but it was a little embarrassing, too. His cock was half-hard just from her proximity, let alone having her nearly crawling into his lap! For her part, Bernadette would have liked to take him right there – if propriety had allowed. She'd missed his combination of tenderness and animal magnetism, not that Andrion wasn't also a wonderful lover. The two were just… different. Each had his own unique approach to lovemaking, and she found each of them irresistible.

Realizing Erik's discomfort at sporting a huge erection in full view of anybody who might be walking through the inn's central common room, Bernadette sat back down and let him have a little space – after kissing him thoroughly. Andrion joined them, sitting on Berni's other side, and that helped Erik to tear his mind away from thoughts of ravishing her on the spot.

Bernadette was soon chattering away at Erik, filling him in on all of their adventures since she and Andrion had left to meet with Giselle and Adalbert in search of the sanctuary of the ancient Guardians and the Wall of the Ancients. Andrion had his own perspectives to add to the story, doing a passable imitation of Adalbert's scholarly maunderings.

Meanwhile, beginning to wrinkle after their long soak, the three friends climbed out of the pool and toweled off. The elf who worked as innkeeper when Lev was not on duty, Drelos Elendion, asked Bernadette if she needed anything. Tucking the towel around herself, she responded "Could you scramble us about a dozen eggs? I'd also like some bacon, cheese, apples, bread, and maybe some sausages if you've got 'em." It felt like an age since they'd last eaten.

"And another thing," Bernadette added as an afterthought. "Could you please take our underclothes to get washed, and bring us some clean linen ones?" Drelos smiled and said "right away!" before running off to do her bidding. It's good to be "queen" Bernadette thought, pleased. Erik donned the clothing he'd brought up with him from the basement and joined Berni and Andrion, still swathed in towels while they waited for underwear to arrive, at a poolside table.

The linens appeared shortly, allowing both Bernadette and Andrion to get dressed. They'd barely managed that when their enormous breakfast arrived, and for a while all conversation ceased as the three of them began shoveling food into their mouths. The pair just returned from questing appeared to be half starved, whereas Erik – as a very large, very healthy young man – could always eat enough for two. His eyes widened slightly, though, as he witnessed how much food his small, lithe lover was capable of putting away. He guessed meals on their journey must have been irregular at best.

Bernadette finally felt as if she had eaten enough to make up for the deficit of the past few days and subsided, sitting back in her chair and taking a healthy swig of herbal tea. Ahhh, that was better! There was another hunger lurking at the back of her mind as she looked at Erik, but she needed to let her breakfast settle before getting involved in anything athletic. Besides, they had not yet finished telling him about Tarragin, and the possibility that ancient dragon might bring about the end of the world.

As Bernadette and Andrion wrapped up the discussion, Erik's face took on a more serious look. Except for his near-berserk ferocity in battle, his disposition was usually so sunny that this expression of quiet concern seemed absurdly out of place. "But you got the spell, right?" he asked Bernadette. She nodded, smiling. "And every other dragon spell we could find ingredients for," she confirmed.

"But we still haven't found the formula for the potion, the one that the ancient Norse heroes used to trap Tarragin in his pocket universe," she went on. "Until we can prevent him from just fleeing to some other, unreachable place, there's no way we can kill him."

Erik put his hand on Berni's arm. He hadn't a clue what to do about the situation, but was determined that he would stand by his Fireblood lover to the death, if need be, to help her in whatever fight she chose. "Don't worry, Berni," he said softly. "We'll figure something out. Right?" he added, looking his older and usually wiser friend Andrion in the eye. Andrion nodded, his mouth set in a look of determination.

Bernadette turned to Erik, then to Andrion, and smiled. "How could I not triumph, with you two by my side?" she said half-jokingly. She stood up and hugged the still-seated Erik around the head, inadvertently pressing her full breasts into his ear and making his member leap once again – this time, safely hidden by his trousers.

Turning, Bernadette hugged Andrion as well and planted a kiss on his forehead. Then she grabbed her pack and headed for the upstairs sleeping loft. "I need to take a nap," she said, and he seconded the motion. They climbed the stairs together, as Erik watched them wistfully. After everything they'd been through it was no wonder they were tired; but he ached for Berni, could think of nothing he wanted more than to hold her in his arms again.

A couple of hours later, after taking care of some personal business of his own, Erik was at the bar shooting the breeze with Lev when Bernadette appeared at his elbow. She looked much refreshed. "Andrion's still sleeping," she said cheerfully, "But I'm going to do some crafting. Why don't you come down with me?" A smile lighting his face, he was at her side in a heartbeat.

In the basement, Bernadette dumped out her pack and surveyed her collection. During the excursion through that dypalfar ruin, before going through the tunnel into Faastenberg, she'd picked up a mall pile of jewels, essence vials, and a considerable amount of cash – and some arms and armor that she could improve.

There were quite a few pieces of dypalfar scrap metal she had scavenged, and she pumped up the smelter fire and set it to melting. Then she pulled out an elven-crafted bow, and worked it over before applying the fire damage enchantment to it. I'm really starting to get the hang of this, Bernadette thought, elated. Life held many joys for her; and one of them, she was coming to understand, was the ability to create something beautiful, useful, and valuable with her own two hands.

Erik watched her, fascinated. As much as he hungered for her body, he was entranced by the skill and concentration with which she worked. Soon he was pitching in, helping her rework his dypalfar heavy armor to make it stronger and lighter. Hours passed, and abruptly they both realized that they were starving.

They went upstairs again, and found Andrion up and just starting on lunch. "How are you feeling?" Bernadette asked him, as she and Erik joined him at the table and signaled Lev to bring some more food.

"Better," he replied cheerfully. "Still a little sleepy. I think my internal clock got clobbered by all the time we spent underground."

"Any ideas about tracking down the potion formula?" Erik asked. Andrion shook his head.

Food arrived, and as they dug in he said, "If only we knew exactly what the potion was supposed to do. Ehrgeizig said the ancient Norse heroes had intended it to permanently destroy Tarragin's inter-dimensional travel ability, and it appears that it worked – only not permanently. The only thing I can think of for us to do is return to the Academy library and hit the books again."

"You know," Bernadette said, "I'm thinking I would like to take a little break from all this. I thought maybe I would see if the eorl's steward has another bandit gang to root out or something like that, and I could take Erik along with me. Then when we get back from that you and I can go back to Eisenstag."

Andrion knew what she really wanted – a chance to knock it out in private with Erik before heading north to freeze her ass off again. He couldn't blame her. "Sure," he said. "That'd be fine. I'll stay here and see whether there are any chemia books in the Waterdon area. But don't be gone too long, okay?"

She grinned at him, and finished with her meal she stood up and gave Andrion a hug and a kiss. "I'll just run up to Wyrmshalla, then," she told Erik. "Why don't you get ready while I'm gone?" He grinned at her, jumping to his feet and heading for the trap door behind the bar. They'd left his armor cooling downstairs.

By the time Erik had finished getting into his armor and assembling his pack and weapons, Bernadette was walking in through the front door with a big smile on her face. She was waving a sheet of paper. "There's a bandit gang down near Forestville," she said. "And we're going to do them in."

Chapter 39: A Little Excursion

Bernadette and Erik soon found themselves standing outside the gates of Forestville. Instead of going into town, though, they turned and went east along a barely-visible road that wound through the forest of mixed pines and oaks to the north and south.

As they walked along the road, Bernadette kept glancing over at Erik. He looked so damn *hot* in that dypalfar armor she'd fitted for him. All she *really* wanted to do was jump his bones right here in the road. But good sense prevailed. You might as well start making love in the middle of a full-fledged battle as try to knock off a little nooky in the wilds of Iscandia. Things out here wanted to eat you, and *not* in a good way.

The afternoon was young, and there were hours of daylight left. Following the map, they turned to the south and began trying to find a way up to the overlook where the bandits were supposed to have their camp. They forded a medium-sized stream, picking their way across at a spot below a little waterfall.

Eventually they picked up what looked like a decent trail on the other side of it, heading in the right direction. At last! Bernadette was always eager to close with the enemy, and time spent floundering around in the wilderness looking for a trail just filled her with impatience.

The bandit encampment proved to be miniscule, hardly worth the effort of the walk it had taken to get here. Good thing it was just an excuse to get them away from the Maiden awhile, alone together. They found one lone bandit, standing in a tent working at a crafting table, as they sneaked in past the tiny campsite's hide screens. A couple of shots with the fiery elven bow dropped him in his tracks. A second bandit, hearing the noise of the first one's death throes, came up the hill through the brush and was swiftly dispatched by Erik's warhammer.

Bernadette raided the corpses and picked the lock on a small chest to come up with a handful of valuables. "Well that was a disappointment," she remarked to Erik. "I was hoping for half a dozen bandits and some serious gold, at least. It makes you wonder why the eorl bothered to post a bounty."

Erik came up beside her and put a hand to the side of her face, tilting her chin so she was looking into his eyes. "Who cares about gold?" he asked. "It's a nice afternoon, and there's a bed of sorts right over there…" he gestured to one of the bandits' tents, within which lay a couple of the familiar fur bedrolls. It *was* a nice afternoon…

Bernadette's eyes lit. Who cares about gold, indeed? The gold she sought now was the gold on this godlike young man's head, his warm skin flecked with golden hairs. Any other treasure could wait. Continuing to gaze into those bottomless blue eyes, she stepped closer to him, as close as she could get before locking her mouth on his.

Their armor provided a barrier that did not deter them for long. Underclothes were gone in another few moments. Now naked, they stood there squeezed together for a little while, skin to skin. Erik's cock was hard and throbbing, pressed between them as he bent to kiss Bernadette deeply. But at 6'5" to her 5'6", the height disparity was giving them both a crick in the neck. He reached down to seize her by the buttocks, two rounded and delightful handfuls, and lifted her up to him. Then, as he lowered her slightly, his cock pierced her vulva and found it warm, wet, and ready to receive him. Oh yes!

Erik drank Bernadette's mouth, his tongue probing hungrily within, as he used the immense power of his arms and shoulders to move her up and down on his steely shaft. She wrapped her legs around his hips, helping to support herself as she bounced on him, engulfing his full length with every stroke. Breaking the kiss, Bernadette threw her head back in wild abandon, screaming out his name as he continued to raise and lower her rapidly on his pulsing member. "Erik! Oh yes, Erik! Augh! Fuck me!" While she was often fairly noisy, he had never heard her cut loose in quite this fashion before. He found it a huge turn-on, and in moments the sensations in his eyes, his ears, his cock were driving him on like a missile to a climax he could not hold back.

Their bodies forming a V joined at the crotch, the two of them gasped, groaned, screamed and shuddered as he pulled her down to bury his spurting cock as deeply as it would go within her quivering, clutching depths. As the wave passed and left them gasping, still standing on the leaf-strewn forest floor, Bernadette leaned forward to rest her upper body against Erik's chest, her legs feeling too rubbery to maintain their grip around his hips for long.

Her feet returned to the ground in another moment, his cock slipping from within her while still half-rigid – twin streams of his seed running down her inner thighs. Bernadette gripped Erik around the middle with her arms, her face turned to the side and buried in his muscular chest, gasping for breath as he panted above her. His powerful arms enfolded her in turn, his lips pressed to the top of her head.

"You got me again," she murmured to him between gasps for breath. There was something almost magical about his desire, at times. Here she would be, having organized plans and businesslike thoughts, and he would just come along and blow her mind to bits with the hurricane-force winds of his astonishing sexuality.

"Come," Erik said softly, and stepped aside to guide her to the tent they hadn't quite made it to earlier.

The pair lay down together on the fur bedrolls. Erik found a random bit of some bandit's clothing lying inside the tent, and handed it to Bernadette so she could wipe up the amazing quantity of semen that was now coating her inner thighs. With a murmur of thanks she soon took care of that chore, then tossed the rag aside and surged toward him, eager to resume full body contact.

Despite the fact that Erik had been getting laid on a regular basis in Bernadette's absence, and had just had an earth-shaking orgasm with this woman who had been the subject of so many fantasies for him over the past few days, he found his hunger for her not yet slaked. Within moments, he had begun kissing and stroking her once again. Her response was eager. He had been in her thoughts as well, and now that he was in her arms she couldn't get enough.

They lay there sheltered by the bandit's tent, fondling, licking, and kissing, for several minutes. It felt wonderful, and all other thoughts were driven from Bernadette's mind as she immersed herself in the pleasure of Erik's body. Before long, Erik's powerful cock had returned to towering hardness and he slipped inside her once again. He was so big! But she was so wet, so completely ready, that his size was not a problem.

They made love for a long time, now, enjoying the warm breezes blowing through the woods, the quiet sounds of birdsong, and the delicious sensations of cock within cunt, mouth on mouth, skin on skin. Erik brought Bernadette to climax again and again, until she was so weak she felt as if she could barely move; then he rolled her over, helped her to kneel with her rump in the air, her head pillowed on her arms, and carried them both over the edge one last time with a fierce pounding from behind.

Bernadette's body felt utterly drained, her mind exploding in sparks of red and white. It occurred to her, as she struggled for any semblance of conscious thought, that she could not remember when she had last slept a full night. Was it yesterday? Two days before? The time distortions of fast-travel, coupled with their time spend underground, made it impossible to tell. Even as a flash of annoyance came over her at this realization, her mind snuffed out like a guttering candle and she slept. Her virile young lover, now blissfully satisfied, kissed her tenderly on the neck and then, throwing an arm over her body, dropped off to sleep himself.

Some time later, Bernadette awoke. How long had she been asleep? Peeking out of the tent, she judged from the angle and color of the light slanting down through the trees that the afternoon was well advanced. At this season in the north, sunset was still hours away. The sun would not go down until past nine, and it was still very warm out. She felt a little wrung out, still, delightfully content if a tiny bit sore physically. But her few hours of sleep had re-energized her mind, and she didn't really want to camp here, with the corpses of the dead bandits, for the coming night.

Erik lay beside her snoring softly, but he soon roused as Bernadette began stirring. She leaned in and gave him a deep kiss. Such efforts as he had put in recently deserved a reward. Then she crawled out of the hide tent and began gathering up her clothing. Erik sat up and watched her for a while, simply feeling happy.

Berni was back, she had spent the afternoon in his arms, she loved him! What more could he possibly want?

Well, another couple of hours' sleep and some supper, probably. But Erik was content enough. Regretfully, he crawled out of the tent and began gathering up the clothing and armor he'd shed with such eagerness a few hours past. "I suppose we ought to be getting back to the Maiden?" he suggested with a touch of regret.

"I think I'd like to take a swim first," Bernadette replied. "Remember that waterfall we passed on the way up here?"

The pair, still enveloped in the joy of their passionate reunion, began picking their way down the trail to the west. By the time Bernadette had led them back down to the stream she was feeling sweaty on top of the stickiness that surrounded her as a consequence of the fun she and Erik had been having. They eagerly shed their armor again, laying it on the ground near the ford where they'd crossed a few hours earlier.

Above the waterfall was a pool no more than four feet deep. The water was cold and exhilarating, and Bernadette whooped and laughed delightedly as she splashed and swam, teasing Erik by diving beneath the crystalline waters to nibble at him where he stood. Astonishingly, this activity had his cock on the rise again – even though his scrotum was squeezed tight against the cold.

Bernadette couldn't resist diving down and taking him in her mouth briefly, while holding her breath. Then she burst to the surface, grinning, and slipped away as he tried to grab her. She led him on a merry chase back and forth across the little swimming hole, splashing and giggling at his frustrated efforts to catch her. He was pretty fast for a man his size, but she was faster. Finally she let him catch her, and he clutched her to him for a deep kiss; but by then they were both starting to shiver from the cold.

Erik's erection had ebbed during the pursuit, though it was rising again as he held her. But Bernadette fended him off. "We just don't have *time*, love!" she protested. "We need to get back to the Maiden and check in with Andrion." He looked abashed. Truth to tell, he felt as if he'd had every drop of semen extracted from

306

him already today, and he'd be surprised if he could even come again. Not that it wouldn't be fun trying…

They donned their clothing and armor again, and Bernadette fast-travelled them back to the inn. They found Andrion awaiting them in the common room, chatting with Lev at the bar. He spun on his stool to greet them, giving Berni's armored form a slight hug. He looked them both over and remarked mildly, "My, you both certainly look… clean, for having just come back from killing bandits." Bernadette gave him a fond smile.

"It's a long story, my love. What do you say we get some supper, and we can talk about our next move?"

Bernadette ordered some food to be brought to them by Lev, then the three friends took their usual table on the mezzanine overlooking the pool. "Did you have any luck finding books on chemia while we were gone?" she asked.

"I checked with Adele, and also with Garimund up at Wyrmshalla," Andrion replied. "No luck. I think we're going to have to make that trip to Eisenstag, so you'd better pack your woolies."

Chapter 40: Destroyer of Magic

The old uruk librarian, Mhyrzon, favored Bernadette with his fearsome grin when she and Andrion walked in, asking this time for books on chemia. "Heard you haven't shown up for any classes yet," he remarked.

"Um, I got sidetracked," Bernadette said. It was true, in a way. "I really would like to study magic, but I have some kind-of important errands to run first."

"Just don't take off with any of my books!" he warned.

Soon Bernadette and Andrion were back at the same table again, with books stacked up and notebooks out. There were many more on this popular and practical subject, two whole shelves' worth, and they had a lot of ground to cover. Additionally, she was eager for the opportunity to learn how to prepare some of the potions she most liked having on hand – potions to recoup one's health, magical essence, and stamina, potions to enhance one's skills at a dozen different sorts of endeavor, ones with special tricks like the water-breathing potions they'd exhausted on their recent expedition.

Faastenberg had now appeared on Bernadette's map, around a mile to the southwest of the marker for Alzhenten. She and Andrion were sure that with that as a guide, they would be able to find where the ancient Norse stronghold's exterior entrance had once been. Even if they had to hire a dozen workers, excavating that site would be a profitable endeavor.

Page after page of Bernadette's notebook was being filled, and she could hardly wait to get to the chemial station back home at the Bathing Maiden and try out what she'd learned. Not that she had all these ingredients, but she felt certain she could obtain them – from Adele at The Potent Potion, or by gathering them in the wild.

They had to scan every page of every book, but Andrion – who was *not* trying to learn new potions, and skimmed past any formulae that weren't to the point – was making much better time than she was. He'd searched four books in the time it had taken her to get through two, though he hadn't taken any notes beyond jotting down the titles he'd already searched.

They hadn't picked and chosen from among the books, doing
as they had previously and simply removing every book from one
end of the shelf until they had a reasonable-sized stack. In any
case, many of these books were ancient and the spines worn
beyond legibility. The interiors, not exposed as much, were often
in much better condition. Bernadette noted that the one she'd been
taking most of her notes from showed signs of having been used
like a cookbook – several of the pages were stained with what she
judged to be chemial ingredients.

Andrion set the book he'd just scanned aside, and picked up
the next one from the stack. This was a slim, small volume, the
cover a faded red and the gold-stamped title completely worn away
from both the spine and the front cover. He carefully opened it to
the title page, and remarked "Now this looks promising!"
Bernadette glanced up from the notes she was making, and he went
on "*Permanent Poisons: The Deadly Dozen*, by Garethion
Nightpool."

"Sounds elvish," she replied. "Nachtalfar, I think," Andrion
confirmed. The nachtalfar, and the leukalfar as well, created some
of the most virulent poisons known. The book listed only twelve of
the most harmful potions, otherwise known as poisons, with a
couple of pages of information on each – the ingredients, method
of preparation, origin if known, and the expected effects. Several
would kill you in nasty ways, others only cripple you for life.

Although a healing potion's effects were permanent, as were
those that restored your energies, most other potions – especially
the harmful ones – had a relatively short duration. A poison would
sicken you for a minute or two, and it would take you more
minutes to recoup the damage that had been done. Some poisons
could even impact one's magical energy so severely that a
powerful mage would be utterly unable to cast spells for however
long the effects lasted.

Bernadette had set down the book she'd been studying and
had walked around the table to read over Andrion's shoulder. "The
Destroyer of Magic," she read, scanning down the page. This
poison, it claimed, would make a person completely unable to cast

spells –ever again. It permanently prevented one's magical energies from recharging themselves.

"This looks like it might do the trick!" Andrion said excitedly. Bernadette wasn't so sure.

"I suppose you could cast one good spell after you'd been poisoned," she mused. "And after that a potion of magical energy might give you the temporary ability to cast more spells, but you'd have to take a potion every time you ran out. You wouldn't be able to generate your own magical energy anymore."

"And what about the dragon spells?" he asked, following her thought. "Would this mean you couldn't recharge your spell stones?"

"I'm not entirely sure, and I don't think I want to experiment to find out," she said. "From what Aethelred told me, the stones draw on my mana – all three parts of my life force – to recharge. So probably if I no longer had the ability to generate magical force within me, I'd only be able to cast the dragon spell once and then the stone would be just lying there inside me, useless."

"We have to assume that, even though Tarragin's unique ability to pass between planes of existence is inborn, it still requires energy. A gateway to one of the planes of the Netherworld can be created and has been in the past, but I doubt there's a mage living on Terris today with enough magical energy to make one," Andrion said. Bernadette pulled her chair around and sat down beside him, the better to continue the discussion.

"That would totally make sense," she said. "I'd been assuming that the potion the ancient Norse heroes used on Tarragin was something of their own devising, but we found no formula for it there in the lab. They probably just used this, or something with the same effects. After Tarragin had been hit with a dose of the poison, he might not even have realized what had happened. But he was getting the worst of the fight, so he just fled like he always had done – and after he got to his personal planet, he found out he couldn't leave!"

"But then how did he get back again?" Andrion asked. "According to Ehrgeizig, there were no sentient beings on that planet of his. And clearly, a dragon can't do chemia – their forepaws may resemble hands, but they can't be used like them. The claws are too long, and they have no opposable thumbs."

Bernadette furrowed her brow. "Maybe… What if the dose wasn't enough to permanently destroy Tarragin's ability to recoup his magical essence? Perhaps slowly, bit by bit over the millennia, it was coming back. Maybe he didn't even notice it. He might have given up trying when he'd been without magic for a few hundred years and there was no need for him to *use* magic because, there was nothing for him to do but fly around and eat creatures. He'd have been the top predator on that world, with nothing to challenge him."

"We'll never know for sure unless we can ask Tarragin himself," Andrion concluded. "And I don't think he's going to offer to do an interview. But I think this potion will be the closest we're likely to get." He set to work transcribing the entry on The Destroyer of Magic word for word, putting archaic spellings into modern usage as he went.

"Here, it says that three drams of the potion are required per hundred pounds of body weight in order to assure that the ability to regenerate magical energy is completely and permanently destroyed," Andrion remarked as he was copying.

"I assume Tarragin was a little smaller all those millennia ago than he is now," Bernadette said. "But he surely must have weighed more than a ton even then. They would have needed to get more than a cupful into him – you could never deliver that much by dipping arrowheads, unless he was going to hold still while you emptied a few dozen quivers into him. And in that case, the potion would have been moot."

"You're right, Andrion said. "Unless we can manufacture this potion in large quantities, and then get Tarragin to drink it down, we're not going to be able to do the permanent damage we want."
"How about if we get a goat and stake it out," Bernadette suggested. "We could string small vials of the potion all over its body, hidden by the wool. Tarragin decides it's time for a little snack, snaps it up in one bite, and we've got him! Maybe we could

even include some vials of an ordinary potion that takes magical energy away, so that he'd be left without enough to flee. Then we could just keep attacking until we can kill him for good."

They were dressed in ordinary clothing, and Andrion reached over and gave Bernadette a hug. "Great idea, sweetie!" he said enthusiastically. "I think that could really work. Dragons are so hot inside they've got to be going around hungry all the time. And if we can make enough of the potion, you could still put some on your arrows for backup. Let's see what the ingredients are."

Their joy at the discovery of the potion they were searching for subsided when they took a look at the ingredients list: refined thorium salts, freshly extracted juice of the Demon's Fire mushroom, and Chymera Venom. "Andrion," Bernadette said in despair, "I've never even heard of these ingredients let alone seen them for sale."

"It's not your fault, honey," he told her and patted her arm. "You've been learning the chemial arts for less than a month. We need to find us an expert." He stood and approached the desk, where Mhyrzon stood going over a stack of books. The uruk looked up questioningly. "I'm hoping you might be able to tell me," Andrion said with what he hoped was a winning smile, "Who the best chemiast is here at the Academy."

"Chemia, huh," the librarian said. "You found the potion you were looking for, then?"

"Sort of," Andrion admitted, "but we have no idea where to find the ingredients.

"There's not much call for that here at the Academy," Mhyrzon said with a touch of asperity. "Not really magic, is it? Most here can craft a few potions, and that's about it. But if you're looking for a real expert in chemia, you'd probably want to go talk with Lemba Sanderion in Coldstein."

Chapter 41: The Chemiast of Coldstein

They stopped by at the inn in Eisenstag, and lingered long enough to sit down for bowls of hot stew with fresh bread. If they were lucky, this Lemba person would just whip the necessary ingredients out of her back storage room and cook them up a pint of Destroyer of Magic without any further effort. But Bernadette doubted it would happen that way. They had copied every word of the potion book's entry on the subject, and even the preparation seemed trickier than anything she had ever tried. One didn't just toss all one's ingredients into a mortar and bash away – things must be added in the right order and at the right time, or failure would result.

On their first trip to Eisenstag it had taken Bernadette and Andrion a few hours to walk from Coldstein. Now, with the magic map, they were spared hours of slogging through snow. But it was still after dark by the time they arrived. Despite that, and the fact that snow was swirling through the air, they found many of Coldstein's citizens out and about.

Bernadette approached a nachtalfar man she spotted moving in the direction of the quarter of the city where most of his race lived. "Greetings, brother," she said with a friendly smile. The elf looked down at her with a trace of suspicion on his angular, elongated features.

"What can I do for you?" the elf asked politely enough, despite his air of wariness. "We're seeking a chemiast, need to get a potion crafted," Bernadette explained. "Fellow up in Eisenstag told us that the best chemiast in all of Iscandia, maybe in all of Agena, is right here in Coldstein."

Now she got a smile in return. The nachtalfar of Coldstein might be an oppressed minority, but they had their ethnic pride. "He told you true," the elf replied. "Our own Lemba Sanderion is a mistress of the chemial arts. You want a love potion, or a poison to send your enemies into a permanent sleep? She'll do it. But her work doesn't come cheap. You have gold to pay?"

Bernadette grinned at him and patted her pocket. "No problem," she said. "Can you tell me how to find her shop, and what time she opens in the morning?"

"I can do better than that," the elf replied. "Come with me, and I'll lead you to her door. She's open most of the night."

They were called the night elves, after all. And perhaps not just for their dark skins? Bernadette and Andrion trailed behind their guide as he led them through a maze of dimly-lit, winding alleyways. The squalor of Coldstein seemed still worse in this part of town; but for the nachtalfar, it was home.

When he delivered them to a narrow shop with the familiar chemiast's shingle hung outside, Bernadette thanked him and slipped him some guilders for his trouble. He didn't refuse them. If the xenophobic Norse partisans here in this chilly place didn't want to hire anyone but Norsemen, it might be that the nachtalfar here found it hard to make a living.

They crowded into the small shop, which was no more than eight feet wide though it appeared to go quite a way in from the street. Unlike other chemiasts' establishments Bernadette had visited, there was no chemia station out front where visitors could craft their own potions.

Lemba Sanderion proved to be far shorter and far broader than any elf woman Bernadette had seen before – only a few inches taller than she herself was. And she looked old, which for an elf probably meant she was *very* old. She eyed them questioningly, waving to their guide as he took his leave, and then looked from one to the other of her unlikely visitors.

Bernadette stepped forward, clutching the paper on which Andrion had transcribed the information about The Destroyer of Magic in his neat, clean hand. The chemiast took the paper and her eyes narrowed as she read it. "The Destroyer, eh?" she said after looking it over. "Why you wish to make this? It is an evil potion."

She was familiar with it! Bernadette decided to come clean. "We believe the ancient Norse heroes used this potion to banish Tarragin during the Uprising," she explained. "You're aware that he has returned, and has been raising dragons from the dead?" The old elf woman nodded.

"We had a little green dragon here in Coldstein a few days ago. Killed a horse down at the stables, but the guards drove it off."

Sensing that the woman was now sympathetic to their cause, Bernadette pushed on. "I make a few potions myself, but I have never heard of these ingredients before. Do you have them?"

"Let me go see what I have," Lemba said, and turned on her heel. She disappeared behind a door at the rear of the shop, and returned after a few minutes carrying an ancient-looking jar with some kind of powder in it.

"The salts I have," she said in a no-nonsense voice. "They keep indefinitely. But the mushrooms must be picked fresh, the juice extracted right before making the potion. I can tell you where to get some. The hard part is going to be coming up with the venom."

Bernadette nodded. "I thought that might be the case," she said. "What *is* a chymera, and where do they live?" An expression that was almost a smile came across the old elf woman's face.

"I hope that one may still live in Iscandia," she said. "They were never common here, though the annals of my people say there were many of them in our homeland of Darkreach once. They are not the sort of creature you would want in your back yard."

Both visitors were staring at Lemba, waiting for more details. Andrion had been in Iscandia for nearly a decade, and was a scholar – but *he* had never heard of this creature. "The chymera," Lemba said seriously, "is something of a mismatched monster. I have never actually seen a live one myself, mind you, though I have spoken to a man who claimed to have seen one. He had climbed a tall tree at the time, and felt lucky to have escaped with his life."

She was enjoying herself now, drawing out the suspense. Bernadette hoped the nachtalfar woman wasn't just yanking their chains. "As he described it, the head and shoulders of the beast seemed similar to those of a smilodon, but without the dagger teeth

315

and of a tawny color – closer in shape to the catamounts of Remus, I believe, though far larger. The fur gradually thinned out to be replaced by scales as the body narrowed toward the hindquarters, and it had a long, segmented tail like that of a gigantic scorpion, which it held over its back when it walked. It was apparently too large to climb trees, which is how my informant came to survive and tell his tale."

"And it's about the size of a mammoth?" Andrion asked, as if Lemba's description had sparked some memory. She nodded.

"You know it, then?" He looked dubious.

"The description matches something I read in a book about Agenan mythology," he said. "It was called an arachnogryffe, supposedly the result of mischief by one of the demonic masters of the Netherworld. He forced a lion, a dragon, and a scorpion to mate, and the result was this legendary creature. There was just one of them though, and it was slain by the ancient Reman hero Tyrenius."

Bernadette felt a stab of disappointment. *Was* the chemiast just having them on? "Your arachnogryffe was probably a myth, but based on sightings of the genuine chymera," Lemba responded. "They are real enough, though as I say I do not know for sure if any yet live in Iscandia. I have seen the skeleton of one. They are not really part lion, part dragon, and part scorpion, but some kind of mammal. In any case, if you have a map, I can mark for you the area where my informant spotted one. That was more than thirty years ago; but where there was one, perhaps there are others."

The mountainous region where the hunter had spied the beast was some distance from Normarsh – south and east of there, in the same range Bernadette, Andrion, and Lifa had crossed when searching for the Staff of Zauber for the Old Ones. "They den in caves, coming out to hunt at night," Lemba told them. "You will no doubt have no trouble killing one, but you must be very careful handling it. You will need to cut off the tip of the tail, with its stinger and twin venom sacks, and put it in a tightly sealed, waterproof bag. You do not want to get the venom on your skin as it is very corrosive."

"And what about the mushrooms?" Bernadette asked.

"Those should be considerably easier to bag," Lemba told her with a smile. "I recommend you go after those after getting the chymera venom, as they should be picked and delivered as fresh as possible."

She marked another spot on the map, in the same mountain range where it petered out not far from Iscandia's west coast. "That's Drakespire Cave," Andrion said, noting the location.

"You've been there before?" Bernadette asked, and he nodded.

"Past it, but I didn't go inside. The Drakespire is an active volcano, and though bandits have often used the cave's outer reaches as a hideout, it's said you can move through tunnels in there down to where lava is flowing."

"That is correct," Lemba said. "The demon's fire mushroom is a thin, waving fungus that comes up out of volcanic soil like a little red tongue of flame. It grows only in volcanic caverns, dark or lit only by the glow of molten lava, feeding on the minerals in the soil. The mushrooms themselves glow with a dull red light, not like the blue light of the more common sort of phosphorescent fungus. Pick plenty of them, then bring them back to me as quickly as you can. They must be squeezed freshly in the making of the potion. Now get on with you, and good luck."

Chapter 42: An Accommodation

"We need to go home and pick up Erik, along with some supplies and equipment," Bernadette told Andrion, and she got no arguments. Despite the nachtalfar chemiast's assumption they would have "no trouble" taking down a predator the size of a mammoth, both of them wanted as much help as they could get.

They arrived outside the Bathing Maiden in the early evening, local time, and found Erik in the common room. "Did you find it already?" he asked eagerly.

"We're not sure if this is what the ancient Norse heroes used," Bernadette admitted. "But I think it will do the job if we can get enough of it into Tarragin. We have to go hunting ingredients tomorrow, and you're coming along."

"Great!" he replied. The powerful young man's appetites for sex, food, and fighting were *all* prodigious.

Bernadette decided to drop her things in the master bedroom before slipping into her robe and returning downstairs for a bath. Her two guardians were right on her heels. Pulling out her robe first, Bernadette tossed her pack and weapons into the room's large trunk, then asked Andrion for some assistance in removing her armor. She threw that into the trunk on top of her pack.

Bernadette now stood in her underwear, and as she began removing it both men watched her with a rising interest. Andrion's gaze was particularly intent, as she stood there revealed in her naked splendor and reached for her robe. He couldn't stand it any longer, and stepped forward to embrace her carefully, mindful of his armor against her bare skin. Kissing her fervently, he then took a step back and looked her in the eyes. "I believe it's my turn to sleep here tonight?" he asked.

Bernadette was startled. This direct approach, coming from Andrion, was a surprise to her. But she liked the idea. Might this be the way they could handle their three-way relationship without awkwardness and resentment? She was certainly eager to be back in bed with Andrion, having spent the night after their bandit-hunting excursion sleeping here with Erik. And it would be nice to be able to move back and forth between her lovers without having to leave town.

"Um," Bernadette hesitated while her mind raced to think through the implications, "I believe you're right, my love." She looked questioningly at Erik. A brief shadow may have crossed his eyes, but his slight smile didn't waver.

"I'll see you downstairs, then," he said cheerfully, and took his leave. Bernadette's eyes lit, and she gave Andrion the full benefit of a loving smile.

"You're a genius!" she told Andrion. "Now, let's get you out of that armor so I can give you a hug!"

Andrion didn't really need her help to get out of the less-bulky elven armor, but Bernadette was eager to assist him anyway. Still naked, she ran her hands up his torso, savoring the feel of the hard muscles beneath supple skin. After the top section of the armor had come off, she hooked a finger into the "waistband" of the bottom section, between the armor and his flat belly, before working the mechanism that would release the buckle.

In moments both pieces of armor had fallen to the carpet beside the bed, and Andrion stood there in only his underdrawers. They resembled a tent pitched on its side, the pole jutting straight out. He looked so adorable that way, Bernadette was torn between gazing at him in avid admiration and devouring him on the spot. She chose a third option – stepping into his arms, pinning that "pole" between their bodies.

After squeezing Andrion tight, Bernadette licked salt sweat from his chest and then raised her head for a deep kiss. "Bath first?" he asked her, nuzzling her neck.

"Yes, please…" They stepped apart, and Bernadette resumed putting on her robe. Andrion stepped out of his drawers, his cock still standing mostly at attention, and threw on a robe of his own. Then, hand in hand, they descended the steps to the ground floor and the central bathing pool. By the time they got there, he had subsided to an acceptable level.

Dropping their robes at poolside and getting into the water the pair joined Erik, who'd already been soaking for a while. He looked relaxed and happy, and was having a friendly conversation with a stunning, statuesque brunette who appeared to be in her late thirties. From her commanding bearing and polished appearance, she was probably from one of Iscandia's elite families and used to having her way.

As Bernadette and Andrion sat down in the pool, Erik greeted them before introducing them to his companion. Bernadette was polite, but forgot the woman's name as soon as it was spoken. She didn't tend to make many women friends. Most of tomboy Bernadette's friends throughout her life had been male, whether she'd slept with them or not.

Rather than interrupting Erik's conversation, Bernadette and Andrion sat soaking and talking quietly between themselves. The pool wasn't too crowded, so Bernadette lay back and floated for a moment atop the water, soaking her hair. Andrion was entranced at the way her full breasts bobbed on the surface, and having a hard time maintaining decorum.

After resting like this for a short time, Bernadette executed a backward somersault, swimming underwater to come up beside Andrion once again. She was grinning and shaking the excess water out of her long, auburn locks. Then she squeezed up beside him and gave him a sweet, more-or-less chaste, kiss. Sitting there just relaxing, she picked up a little of Erik's conversation with the black-haired beauty. Bernadette had noticed that, while Erik was a magnet for all women, it was the older ones that went after him particularly. They were probably less intimidated by his size, she mused.

Just then, Bernadette heard the woman say to Erik, "I am in need of a bed-warmer." "Let's go, then," he replied, and the two of them stood up and walked to the steps, picking up towels as they exited the pool and walked off toward the trap door to the basement. Bernadette watched Erik's finely chiseled behind walking away, thinking ruefully that the taste of her own medicine was not so sweet. Then she sighed, snuggling closer to Andrion, and said to herself, get over it, girl. You can't have your own freedom and then deny it to everybody else.

"Her" golden god wasn't really hers, any more than she was his. But they cared deeply for each other, and their lovemaking was so sweet, so powerfully exciting, that Bernadette hoped she never had to give it up. The same went for this beautiful man beside her, though she suspected that in Andrion's case there had been no substitute women for him while they were apart. She turned to him, drinking in the look of love she found in his warm brown eyes, and said softly, "I feel pretty clean now. How about you?"

He gave her a gentle smile and murmured, "I thought you'd never ask." They arose and, holding hands, climbed up the pool steps. After toweling off, they put their robes back on then walked side by side, each with an arm around the other, toward the staircase leading to the sleeping loft. In the bedroom, the robes were off in seconds and they stood, glowing pink from the hot water, just gazing at each other. Andrion's cock was swollen and stiff once more, straining toward her.

Smiling radiantly, Bernadette took him by the hand and led him to the bed, beckoning him to sit on the edge. Then she knelt beside it and took his member in her mouth – licking, sucking, and squeezing until pre-cum was oozing from the tip and it looked as if it were quivering, about to explode. Andrion was gasping, eyes closed, swimming in the sensations. But as he felt his balls screaming for release, he held back.

He cupped Berni's chin and lifted her face, tilting her head back to kiss her, then said in a hoarse whisper, "My turn." Drawing her onto the bed, he had her scoot up until she was lying with her head on the pillow, her legs wide apart. He knelt between her legs, dipping into her glistening sex with his tongue like a hummingbird sucking nectar from an exotic blossom. She didn't taste like nectar, of course. She tasted like Berni. Clean, wonderful Berni. The throbbing in Andrion's cock eased slightly now that she was not rubbing and sucking it, but it still stood rigid, an arrow pointing the way home.

Bernadette loved the things this man could do with his mouth. She writhed and moaned as he filled her entire crotch with tingling sensations, then bucked wildly, her hands pressing down on his head, as her orgasm surged over her. When her quivering had subsided he crawled up her body, hands fondling her breasts for a moment, tongue tweaking her nipples. Then he found her mouth, his own slightly salty with her juices, and as his tongue went between her lips his thick, hard cock pushed in between her nether lips – dripping wet and eager to receive him.

Though she had just come, Bernadette gave a stifled moan of pleasure as he pushed inside her. Not quite as enormous as Erik, Andrion was still a very well-endowed man; and he filled her with an aching sweetness that made her want to hit the ceiling again only moments after he had entered her. While claiming her mouth with deep soul kisses he began stroking in and out, lingering to press up a little on the out-stroke, stimulating her clit. As she responded to this with a rhythmic keening, rising higher with each set of strokes, his thrusts became stronger and faster. *Now* he could contain himself no longer, and with a groan and a shudder, legs straight and toes curling, he shot a hot gush of cum deep inside her while her vaginal muscles locked around him, rippling in spasms as her own climax engulfed them both.

Bernadette wrapped her legs tight around his middle, her pelvis still thrusting up to meet his, gasping, her heart pounding like a galloping horse. "Oh, Andrion! My love!" She smothered his face with kisses before slowly subsiding, just trying to catch her breath. Clasping her tight, he rotated them around so that his weight was not pressing on her. She let her bottom leg come down, his still partly stiffened cock pinned within her, her other leg thrown up over his hip. Andrion kissed her more tenderly, now, stroking her face, then drew her head into the shelter of his arms and just hugged her to him.

They lay there like that for some time, as he slowly slipped out and they both began breathing normally. Then they talked in murmurs, of inconsequential things, just savoring their closeness with one another. Andrion rolled over on his back and lay there, one arm behind his head, while the other was cradling Berni where she lay resting her head on his shoulder. After a long while she said, "Are you hungry? 'Cause I'm *starving*!" That's my girl, he thought, a smile wreathing his lips.

Bernadette wriggled out of bed and he joined her, both of them choosing to slip back into their robes rather than get fully dressed. Downstairs they found the Maiden beginning to come alive for the evening, with many chattering inn guests at tables here and there, the clink of tableware, Lev playing his lute.

Drelos was on duty at the bar, and it appeared the inn now had a couple of female employees filling the customers' needs, as well as the men that had been employed there before her arrival. Bernadette and Andrion took seats at the owner's usual table, with a good view of the common room and pool. She ordered up some food and they were soon served bowls of a savory stew, rich with beef, vegetables, and mushrooms. There was plenty of warm, fresh bread to go along with it, and the two ate with good appetite. It had, after all, been a long day.

Bernadette looked around, but there was no sign of Erik. That middle-aged beauty was giving him a run for his money, she'd bet. Bernadette had been told once or twice that a woman's sexual appetites only increased in the middle years, though she was hard put to imagine how that was possible. As far as she was concerned, she'd become randy as hell from about the age of 13, and had spent two years developing her technique for self-pleasuring before getting that amulet from Selene along with the confidence to go out there and start taking what she wanted. If she was like this now, at 22, what would it be like in ten years? Would she need a whole stable of men like Erik and Andrion to keep her satisfied?

Bernadette grinned around her mouthful of stew, her eyes twinkling with amusement at the thought. Right now, at least, two men like Erik and Andrion were plenty – all she could handle. Not that she wouldn't *consider* a roll in the hay with somebody else, if somebody irresistibly sexy should happen to cross her path; but there was no way she was getting into any deep relationships with another man while these two were in her life. She loved them both to distraction, distraction from what she saw as her duties to mankind.

Well, that was a sobering thought. Time to lighten the mood a little. Eat, drink, and be merry, for tomorrow we must march up the mountain and beard the legendary chymera in his den! Gee, I hope he's home...

Chapter 43: The Hunt

Making the requisite waterproof container for holding the venom sacks they hoped to be obtaining took quite a bit of the next morning. Leaving all of her surplus gear behind to lighten her pack, Bernadette laid on thick, insulated gloves for all of them and some dypalfar metal jars with tightly fitted lids, which she hoped would preserve whatever they found and prevent it from eating holes in her pack – or her back – while they were traveling.

They'd found Erik armored up and sitting at the bar, eating some eggs and bacon, when they came downstairs in the morning. There was no sign of his erstwhile bed partner, and Bernadette didn't mention her. Bernadette and Andrion ate some breakfast before leaving, and she mused that she now had a fund of eighteen dragon spells at her command – each one at its full four-word strength. As she considered what eighteen spell stones would look like in a bowl, and then imagined ingesting that quantity of solid, crystalline stone, she wondered why she didn't feel bloated. Where, exactly, did those stones reside? And why hadn't she gained weight? She was as light and lithe as ever, though she did truly feel more powerful. Wouldn't the Old Ones be astounded to learn what she had done!

She reasoned that, since each spell was powered by a different stone, she could use one spell while another's stone was recharging. And another, and another, so that she could attack her foes with a barrage of spells and not have to wait between them. But, recharging the stone took life energy – her mana would automatically be diverted to recharge a stone once its spell had been cast. Might that leave her too weak to move, if she suddenly found herself trying to recharge four or five stones at once? Better, she concluded, to rely on her bow and her other weapons and use the dragon spells sparingly.

They fast-traveled by map to Normarsh, and though the journey had taken some time that city was far enough to the west of Waterdon that it was still only around midday. They set off on the road leading east with snow falling lightly, turning the woods into a white fairyland.

One full of wolves, bears, and the odd highwayman though. They had not gone more than a mile before they were attacked, as a trio of hungry wolves made the classic blunder of mistaking them for lunch. Bernadette would ordinarily have taken time to skin them out for their pelts; but she was becoming increasingly focused on their mission. She just retrieved her arrows, and they went on their way.

Bernadette was keeping one eye on the map and the other on the mountains to their right, looking for any sign of a path up. As their goal was the hunting ground of a legendary monster, and not a current or former human habitation, there was no reason to assume that a path would be available. But she was hoping! Iscandia's mountains were far younger than those in Auverne, steep and craggy and nearly impossible to get across unless you could find a pass.

Her attention was suddenly wrenched back to the road ahead of them as Erik drew his bow and began firing, and Andrion unleashed a bolt of lightning that struck with a fearsome crash. An overturned cart lay by the side of the road, two corpses beside it, and three bandits were in the process of rifling it – and its former owners – for valuables. They'd turned their attention to the party of travelers as they came into view, and for a minute there was a furious fight in the middle of the road.

Almost before Bernadette could get her bow drawn Erik had brought down one of the bandits with his own bow, setting the man on fire. Then he had rushed in to go toe-to-toe with the remaining cutthroat, battle axe swinging. He'd admitted that he preferred an axe to the blunt warhammer, and she'd crafted him a beaut. It was all of gleaming steel in the ancient Norse style, but half again as big and with a shaft tightly wrapped in leather to give a better grip. It was enchanted to steal an enemy's life force, actually taking health away from whoever you struck with it and transferring that health to the wielder.

Bernadette released the draw on her bow and slung it over her back, tucking the arrow back into her quiver. The three bandits lay dead in the road beside their victims, and she found herself feeling a little disappointed that she hadn't gotten to contribute to their deaths. Ah, but who could complain at two such valiant warriors guarding her back?

They rifled their dead foes' bodies and came away with some gold and other small loot. Then they left them lying and continued on the way. Another mile or so down the road Bernadette spotted what looked like a goat track leading off to the south, winding its way up the slopes, and led them onto it. This looked like their best chance to reach what they hoped would be the chymera's hunting ground.

It was damned cold here, and though the snow had stopped falling it only got colder as they climbed higher. Luckily they were on the move, and had dressed appropriately. The goat trail wound back and forth, climbing the peak ahead of them in switchbacks, and then circled the mountain's upper slopes to come around to the south side. They hadn't seen another human being in hours, not since the bandits, and the snow-covered slope above them was glowing golden in the rays of the westering sun.

"Shit, I was really hoping to come on this critter in the daytime, when it's supposedly napping in its den," Bernadette remarked. Puffing up into the mountains with their heavy packs and armor, there hadn't been all that much conversation during the hike. By unspoken agreement, they all stopped at a halfway-level spot to take a breather, looking upslope for any signs of life.

"Leb-Such-Jag-Fun," Bernadette said softly, and the Finder dragon spell triggered and began searching the area for anything living (or undead). Tiny glowing trails formed in the air, visible only to her eyes, and pinpointed birds in the trees, mice tunneling beneath the snow, a fox curled up asleep beneath some fallen pine boughs. And a bundle of much thicker, brighter trails wound up the slope above them and dived to earth about halfway between the level on which they stood and the peak. Whatever had been detected was hidden from view, though.

Neither man had seen anything, but Andrion knew what Bernadette had done. "What's out there?" he asked.

"Little critters, mostly," she replied lightly. "But there's a big something, or maybe several somethings, up there around to the south side of the peak. I think we have to go investigate before the sun starts going down."

Erik grinned and hefted his axe, and Bernadette unslung her bow and held it ready for use, an arrow clasped in the same hand that held it. The track they were on offered the best footing, and they continued on it until they'd come around to the south side. There they found a small brook rushing down the mountainside, and the goat track turned away south to follow it downslope.

Andrion bent to the stream and cupped up some water in his hands, taking an icy drink. Brrr! Then his eyes fell to the mud and rocks beside the water and he bent for a closer look. By the gods! "Berni, Erik, look at this," he said pointing. There on the muddy stream bank, perfectly outlined and probably not a full day old, was an enormous pug mark – as if a cat the size of two smilodons put together had stopped here for a drink.

Bernadette felt a shiver run through her, one that had nothing to do with the temperature out here. But was she not The Fireblood, a fierce and intrepid fighter? Uh, sure... They began walking up beside the stream. Snow covered the rocky slopes in most places, but it was melted away for a space on either side of the rivulet. This was, after all the southern slope – and full summer as well.

As they climbed toward the peak, they could see that the stream was flowing out of a cavernous opening in the mountainside. And there was increasing evidence that something very big indeed hunted here. Enormous tracks ran across the snow here and there, and they began to see the bloody remains of deer, goats – and even a couple of cave bears. They were hunting a creature that had cave bears on the dinner menu!

Going out to beard this legendary creature in its den had sounded perfectly reasonable to Bernadette when they were discussing it at the Maiden. After all, if a few puny humans could bring down a fire-breathing dragon, a lion the size of a mammoth hardly seemed like any challenge at all. But as they approached the cave entrance, she felt ice running down her spine.

They were now moving with the uttermost caution, creeping up the last of the slope. The creek flowed from within the cave, along the east side of the opening. On the west a broad stone ledge spread. It was littered with cracked bones and blood smears, where the chymera (and its family?) had feasted. Fortunately, in these icy conditions, there was no smell.

At least, not until they had actually made their way inside the cave. Then a sharp musky scent with a hint of the reptilian about it (despite Lemba's claim that the creatures were mammals) assailed their nostrils. It was much warmer within the cavern, and growing warmer still the further they advanced.

The cave was broadest at the entrance, narrowing as it went in further toward the mountain's core. The creek originated in a spring, flowing out of a crack in the cavern's east wall. Bernadette supposed that this wonderful nearby water source (which, downstream, would also attract prey animals) must make the cave an ideal denning site.

Most of the light was coming from behind them, and their eyes were not yet adjusted to the dimness. Was that some huge, sleeping shape thirty feet ahead of them? "Andrion," Bernadette whispered in his ear, "do you have some spell that could get us a little more light in here?"

He smiled down at her, and raised a hand. A globe of light formed, but instead of hovering above his head it flew from his hand to stick to the cavern's ceiling – at this point, no more than twenty feet above their heads – another forty feet further in. In its coruscating light, they beheld the chymera – lying curled up with its scorpion tail wrapped around its body and snoring.

Gods save us! Bernadette thought. Even rolled up in a compact ball, the thing was enormous. And it surely must be immune to its own venom, she guessed. Creeping carefully around to the side, she looked beyond to see what was behind it. How much room did they have for maneuvering, here? She really, really didn't want to back such a creature into a corner.

Oh, fuuuck. In the narrower confines of the cave beyond the sleeping creature was a much smaller one – only about one and a half times the size of a smilodon, overall. She (and surely, it could only be she) was lying on her side, also asleep, and beside her lay three cubs. They had been nursing, but had apparently fallen asleep.

Bernadette felt a pang. She needed that venom, was determined to get it. But she didn't want to slaughter this little family, and certainly didn't want to render the species extinct in Iscandia. If these were the only chymeras in the province, killing them all might make it impossible to make the Destroyer of Magic potion in the future. Lemba hadn't said how long the venom would keep, but most biological ingredients were perishable over time.

Beyond the mother and her brood was the rear wall of the cavern, and in that wall was a dark hole – another cave opening. From here, it looked as if it might be small enough to admit the mother chymera, or at least the cubs. It was a defensible space where she might hold off any attacker. But would she take it? Bernadette had no idea how ferocious these creatures were. But maybe she could hit them with something that would put the wind up them.

She didn't get a chance to discuss her plan with Andrion and Erik, though. As she was creeping back to where the men waited, staring in horrified fascination at the father chymera, a pebble rolled beneath her booted foot. One of the cubs, who had probably only been drowsing, roused immediately. Only a little bigger than a wolf though much different in shape, it got onto its feet, looking around for the source of the sound as its scorpion tail (more like the hairless tail of a large rat, except for that stinger on the end) lashed. It opened its kitten mouth and roared, "Meerow!"

The jig was up! The biggest monster was stirring already, getting onto his feet, and the mother and remaining two cubs had gone on the alert as well. There was no way, from where she was standing, that Bernadette could hit all of them with the spell. She moved back until she had the female and the three cubs in full view, and shouted "Ang-Los-Scher-Flieg!"

The Terror spell took the four smallest chymeras and sent them cowering – roaring, spitting, claws out and ears back, those deadly tails lashing – but they were all retreating backward toward the hole at the back of the cavern. Now if only they would stay there for a while!

Meanwhile Andrion and Erik had launched a frontal assault on the huge male, arrows and battle spells flying as they backed slowly away from him. He must have stood seven or eight feet tall at the shoulder, tapering to scaled back legs with taloned feet. There was barely room inside the cavern for his tail to come over his head to threaten them, and they were trying to stand their ground. In the open, they would be dead meat.

Staying way out of the range of that tail, Bernadette dashed around to the front side so she was facing the chymera side-by-side with her men. From the front it did look, she realized, quite a bit like the pictures of the lions of Zahar she'd seen pictured in books. Except she was pretty sure they weren't this big. Now, to put her theory to the test. "Fjur-Bruns-Zon-Ens!" she shouted (pitching the spell words loudly and forcefully seemed to help the strength of the results, somehow – except for that Finder spell).

A roaring holocaust erupted as if the not-very-large woman had truly been a fire-breathing dragon. The chymera howled in pain as the heavy ruff of fur around his head caught fire, eyelids blistered. He went down onto his haunches, screaming, and behind him the mother and her cubs squeezed into the smaller cave at the back. In moments she had returned to the entrance, blocking it with her body and prepared to defend her babies to her last breath.

Bernadette's life force had been going into the recharging of the Terror spell stone, and now she felt an additional draw on it as the Holocaust spell stone began to recharge. She sagged momentarily, staggering on her feet, and Erik took her by the elbow. She clawed a couple of potion bottles out her armor, and downed them hastily. Health, magical energy, and stamina came flooding back. These potions would increase her life energies' regeneration rate as well –giving her, she hoped, enough power to continue using dragon spells for a while without collapsing.

331

Andrion hit the damaged beast with dual streams of his own fire – the spell not nearly as hot and devastating as the dragon spell had been, but still effective – and the singed beast cringed away, rolling on the cave floor and covering its face with its paws as if trying to hide from the pain. The deadly tail was thrashing wildly.

Seeing Berni was all right now Erik made to start shooting again; but she touched his elbow. "Don't shoot anymore, Erik!" she cried. "His mate and three babies are hiding at the back of the cave, and I'd really rather not kill him. Get your axe ready, and if I can get him to hold still maybe you could just lop off the tip of his tail." She saw he was wearing the gloves she'd given him.

He nodded at her, his usually sweet features set in an expression of ferocity that made Bernadette glad they were friends. Hanging the bow behind his back, he pulled forth the enormous axe from where it hung at his belt. "Andrion! Hold your fire for a second!" she called, and he stopped shooting his firebolts. The chymera was still lying on the cave floor pawing at his face, emitting a bone-chilling keening.

"Eiz-Nehm-Bild-Stalz!" Bernadette cried, and in an instant the great beast was still. He had turned into a statue, a chymera-shaped block of ice. But the effect would last only for a few moments, nor would it permanently harm the creature. She hoped. "Come on, Erik!" she urged, as they dashed around to the back where the beast's tail lay. The bulbous tip containing the venom glands was lifted a little above the cave floor, the stinger frosted over.

As Erik raised his axe to sever the frozen member at its base, Bernadette stood guard. The cubs were still hidden inside the inner cave, invisible behind their crouching mother. She stood with her hindquarters inside the cave, facing outward with claws out and sharp-toothed mouth roaring defiance. But she seemed more concerned about guarding her babies than fighting to protect her mate.

"Got it!" Erik cried, hanging the axe on its belt loop and gingerly lifting the watermelon-sized tail tip in both hands. It was already beginning to thaw out. "Let's get out of here!" Bernadette responded, and they backed hastily out. Turning tail and running from predators wasn't usually a good idea.

By the time they'd gotten almost all the way back out of the cave the male chymera was fully thawed and extremely pissed off. He was singed, blistered, punctured by at least half a dozen arrows – and he was missing a very important part of his anatomy. But as he got to his feet and began moving toward the trio, Bernadette felt the Terror spell stone return to full power.

"Ang-Los-Scher-Flieg!" again, and the recovering monster reeled backwards. Stumbling, mewling, he retreated all the way to the back wall to where his mate guarded their cubs. She snarled at him. On the ledge outside, Bernadette pulled out her map. And in an instant, the three attackers were gone.

Chapter 44: Drakespire Cave

Andrion steadied Bernadette as they arrived at their destination. That last dragon spell had nearly sucked her dry, despite the earlier potions! The men looked around in the darkness and recognized the Dancing Rabbit over to their left. "Sylvanian?" Andrion asked, somewhat surprised. This was many miles away from the volcanic cave where they needed to go to find the mushrooms.

Sucking down a couple more potions, Bernadette grimaced. The notes she'd taken during their most recent study session at the Academy had enabled her to craft dozens of vials of the ones she most cared about. But the flavor of some of them was less than delicious. I wonder if I could add fruit syrup to the potion without harming the effect, she thought idly.

"We need to regroup," she said, "And I for one am about dead on my feet. I wish they had hot baths here, but it'll have to do." Turning to Erik, who was still gingerly clutching the severed tip of the big chymera's tail, she added "Let's get that into the container before somebody gets hurt."

The tail tip, which Erik had removed just one vertebra back from where the twin venom sacs swelled, had a slightly curved talon protruding from the end like a cat's claw, with grooves on either side. Small openings released venom from the glands to run into those grooves, and anything the chymera pierced with that claw would be dead or paralyzed within seconds. When attacked, it had squeezed out some venom and the claw was glistening with it. Ew!

They got the thing into the container they'd brought, and heaved a sigh of relief. Erik was inspecting his gloves in the torchlight to make sure no trace of the venom had gotten onto them. Andrion smiled at Bernadette. "Berni, I had no idea how tender-hearted you were!" Always before when they were fighting foes together, she had never hesitated to kill.

They began walking into the Rabbit. "I don't know," she replied, trying to plumb her own motivations. It just hadn't seemed right, somehow, to slaughter the little family – even if they *were* monsters. "They were just creatures minding their own business," she said at last. "And those might be the only chymeras on this part of the continent. It didn't seem right to come into their home and kill them, just so we could get some of their venom."

Andrion patted her on the arm. "You're right, love. Besides, we might need more venom later on."

"I wonder if he can grow back the part of his tail we cut off," she mused. "There are lizards that can regrow their tails."

"I don't know of any mammals that can," he replied. "But even if he can't, he's still got claws and teeth aplenty."

She grinned at him. They seated themselves at a table and ordered some supper, though the hour was late. Then, replete, they rented two rooms and slept for the night. Bernadette volunteered to sleep alone, disappointing both her lovers. But she was exhausted and just wanted to sleep.

In the morning over breakfast, much refreshed, they studied the map. "I'm afraid where we are is probably the closest," Bernadette said. "And it's going to be a long walk. I wish we could fly like dragons!" Erik grinned at her.

"We'd better pick up some more food and water before we leave," he remarked.

Two days later, and long departed from any paved road, the bedraggled trio found themselves looking up at the Drakespire. "It hasn't actually erupted in hundreds of years," Andrion reassured them. During some long-ago eruption a section of the volcanic cone had broken off, leaving a rocky spire rising off to one side and a trail of ash and rock on the other. A few miles away was the continent's ice-ringed northwestern shore. A thin plume of smoke rose from the crater, as if from a small cookfire.

"Let's hope it minds its manners for a while longer," Bernadette said. She, like the men, was caked with dirt and dried perspiration and spotted here and there with the blood of the several wild animals and one misguided group of highwaymen who'd attacked them during the walk here from Sylvanian. "So, where's this cave we're going to?"

Andrion had been their guide on the long walking trip, having been this way years before. Now he led them up a well-worn dirt path. "It's not very far up the mountain, and goes down from there," he told them. "But get ready for a fight. There's almost bound to be someone – or some *thing* laired up here."

Unlike the cave where the chymera family had lived, this cave seemed to have begun as a volcanic tube – uncounted millennia in the past. It was well worn, and frequent earthquakes had changed the shape – but basically it was a nearly circular opening, a hundred feet or so up the slope from the mountain's base. A stake with a deer skull on it sat outside, a signpost for visitors. All three of them had their weapons at the ready.

As their best archer, Bernadette took the lead. Her small size and light weight helped her to move almost silently, bringing down enemies with her bow before they were even aware of her presence. This band was probably making a living preying on traffic along the coast road a few miles to the northwest, she guessed. They hadn't bothered to post a sentry, and as she and her companions followed the slightly winding tunnel into the mountainside it was nearly two minutes before they saw anyone.

A well-armed bandit was standing beside a fire pit, stirring something in a cast iron cookpot. He was facing to the side, and easily spotted them in the flickering torchlight as the invading party came into view. In a split second he'd dropped the spoon and drawn his sword. And in another, he was lying supine on the cave floor with an arrow protruding slightly from his chest. He hadn't made a sound.

The tunnel had opened out into a broad cave with a ceiling ranging in height from ten to twenty feet, a wooden platform built over to one side. There were half a dozen sleeping pallets, so there must be another five bandits at least. But where were they? Out lying in wait for travelers, or deeper in the cave? Bernadette pocketed a few small items from the bandit's corpse, and from a chest over against one wall. Then they moved on. Lugging that chymera venom sack all this way was no picnic, and she wished they'd gone back to Coldstein and dropped it off before coming here. But fast traveling still took time, and she was anxious that as little as possible should elapse before they had the potion in their hands.

A tunnel led down out of the main cavern, and in a smaller space below they found the rest of the bandit gang. There were minerals to be gathered here, apparently, and two of them were working with pickaxes against the far wall as another three sat around a table drinking ale and throwing dice.

All five of the bandits were busy about their own pursuits, and hadn't noticed the party who had just arrived. Holding her bow, Bernadette communicated in sign language with Erik. The two about the serious business of mining were probably the main threat, as the others had been drinking and were feeling relaxed.

The three intruders spread out across the side of the cave where the tunnel entered it. Bernadette and Erik wielding their bows, each took out one of the miners with a shot in the back as Andrion, putting all his magical strength into it, fired a blast of lightning – not at the dicing bandits, but at the center of the table they were sitting around.

Flaming splinters flew, and the three around the table were hurled back – chairs tipping over, occupants bleeding from dozens of little cuts. They milled in confusion, struggling to get back to their feet and grab weapons that had been left sitting nearby. Bernadette put one down with an arrow, while Andrion and Erik waded in with blade and axe to dispatch the remaining two. Thanks to the element of surprise, the bandits hadn't stood a chance.

"Whoo!" Bernadette crowed, slapping hands with her men. "Good job, guys!" A feeling of relief surged through them all. They'd endured days of cold trail rations, miles of walking every day, and no sex at all – but now all they needed to do was find those mushrooms, and they'd be on their way home. Via Coldstein, of course…

"Come on, let's find those damned mushrooms and get out of here," Bernadette told her companions. The urge to have hot water around her, followed closely by a hot cock inside her, was building into a constant ache. They found another opening at the rear of the cavern, one barely big enough for Erik to stand upright in, and followed it as it wound back and forth and while dropping deeper into the Drakespire's bowels.

With every few feet deeper they went, the temperature increased. "By the gods, I hope there's no more fighting to do," Bernadette swore. "Because I have *got* to get out of this armor!" Andrion and Erik, as starved for sex as she was, looked on with interest as their lover peeled off her armor and stood there in her underwear. Hey, not a bad idea! Soon they'd left their packs behind as well, and Bernadette carried only two of the containers in which they meant to store the mushrooms they'd come to collect – and her dagger.

The tunnel continued on and on without coming to any more caverns. There were still torches burning every few yards, lighting their way; but those abruptly petered out and they found themselves entering a low-ceilinged, irregularly-shaped space that felt as hot as Bernadette imagined the air must be in far-off Zahar. It was not dark, though – a dim red glow pervaded everything.

The tunnel seemed to end here. On the far side of the space, a deep crack ran. Bernadette was stunned, and fascinated, to discover on peering down into it that a glowing orange river of lava was running along at its bottom. She quickly backed away, an image of what would happen if she fell into that crack coupling with the searing heat coming off of it, to convince her she'd seen enough.

At the furthest remove from the crack, though, were areas that looked like glowing, motionless red flames – the mushrooms! Figuring they would survive better if she took some of the roots as well as the top, Bernadette set to work with her dagger digging a little chunk of the soil out as well as the mushroom itself. The soil was surprisingly damp, and she realized when a hot trickle went down her neck that water was dripping into this cavern from above. It must seep all the way down from the summit, where snow cloaked the slopes, to water these little fungi!

When they had two good-sized, tight containers full of the mushrooms, they declared their mission accomplished and began walking back up the tunnel. Bernadette put her pack back on, after transferring the containers of mushrooms to it, but was still carrying her armor. Better to get into it when they got back to cavern where they'd killed all the bandits. The men followed her lead.

They were sweating and taking no care for stealth as they climbed the last few yards to the cavern. Andrion and Erik, more heavily laden than she was, were lagging a few steps behind Bernadette and as she saw the opening ahead she turned to say, "We're almost there, troops!"

With a "whsssh!" sound an arrow flew from the cavern ahead, tearing a bloody furrow in Bernadette's right arm as it passed her and then struck Erik in the chest. He was clad only in his underdrawers, but enough of the missile's force had been dissipated that it only penetrated his pectoral muscles and embedded itself about a quarter of an inch into one of his ribs.

Shit! Bernadette plastered herself against the tunnel mouth, peering out into the dimness of the cavern, and saw a pair of armed bandits – who had apparently been lying in wait for them – standing side by side in the center of the room. The one with the bow was drawing for another shot, while his companion swung a nasty-looking sword.

"Kraf-Luft-Struung-Wund!" The Fireblood cried, and the bandits were blown off their feet to slam hard again against the far wall of the cavern. Before they could pick themselves up, the three intruders had left the tunnel and fanned out into the room.

Andrion raked them with a battle spell that caused lightning to jump from one target to another, and as they were reeling from the effects of that Bernadette put an arrow into the sword-wielding bandit. Erik rushed the other, his face a mask of fury as the bowman's arrow still protruded from his bare chest, and took off the man's head with a sweep of his axe. After which he furiously ripped the arrow from his flesh and hurled it down onto the body of his fallen foe. "Ow shit, that hurt!" he complained.

Relief flooding her, Bernadette hurried to him and applied her healing spell. Much practice was making it more and more effective, and it seemed to require less of her magical energy each time. When Erik's wound had closed nicely, she kissed him on the nipple and then turned her attentions inward. Before she ran out of magical energy, the bleeding gash on her arm had vanished.

Andrion had escaped unscathed, and he rushed to enfold Bernadette in his arms. He, too, was only wearing underdrawers – and, she could feel, sporting a rising erection. She looked over at Erik and saw that he was getting turgid as well. Must be the adrenaline?

"It won't be very much longer," Bernadette promised them. "But for now, let's just put our armor on and get out of here! They took a few small, valuable items off of the dead bandits before exiting the cave. The day was getting on into late afternoon by now, and the weather was almost pleasant.

"Berni, did I mention you could get a hot bath here?" Andrion asked.

She turned and stared at him, eyes burning. "Seriously?" she gasped.

"There's a series of hot pools a little further toward the coast on the trail we were following," he assured her. "The snowmelt water mixes with water boiling up from beneath the mountain, and the temperature of the largest pool is just about the same as the hot pool at the Maiden. It's got a bit of a sulfur whiff to it, but it's really pretty nice. I used it when I came past here before."

"Those mushrooms had damned well better be able to keep another hour or two," Bernadette declared. "*We* are having a bath!"

"Can't argue with that," Erik remarked with a grin. They continued along the trail and soon found the pools, a larger one followed by a series of smaller ones spread along a single mountain stream like pearls on a string.

Lying stretched out beneath the water (nowhere more than about four feet deep), Bernadette moaned. "Gods take me now," she breathed, "because life is never going to get any better than this." Andrion and Erik exchanged glances, and they slid across the pool until they were flanking her. As Erik gently massaged a breast, Andrion put his left hand down between her legs and said, "Do you want to bet?"

340

Chapter 45: Battle Plans

"There you go," Lemba Sanderion said, handing over the tightly sealed bottle of potion. There had been enough ingredients to produce slightly more than a pint of the stuff, which they hoped would be enough. "That will be a thousand guilders," she added. Pretty steep, considering they'd had to do all the hard work of gathering the ingredients. But on the other hand, the old nachtalfar chemiast's expertise had enabled them to create a potion that might save the world from destruction. It was worth it.

As Bernadette was paying over the money, Lemba gave her last-minute instructions. "Be very careful with the potion," she warned. "It will not penetrate the skin, but should you get some into your mouth or into a cut or abrasion, it could make it impossible for you ever to regenerate your magical energy. You would never be able to cast spells again, except by first taking potions."

"We will, and thank you," Bernadette said, and they took their leave of the old elf. She, Andrion, and Erik exited the shop feeling triumphant. They were clean, relaxed, and looking forward to a trip home before returning to Ehrgeizig and finding out what to do next. They still thought that staking out a potion-laden goat was a good idea, but how would they get Tarragin and not some *other* dragon – or even a random smilodon – to come to the bait? Iscandia was a big place, with a lot of predators in it.

Moments later their eyes were treated to the sight of the Bathing Maiden standing in front of them, and they hurried inside. They had no idea what day it might be, but it seemed from the position of the sun that it was mid-morning. Bernadette carefully removed the dypalfar metal jar of potion from her pack and set it on the chemia station near the master bed. They would need to decant the potion into a number of small glass vials, such as were used for magical essence.

Lemba had told them that the potion, once made, would keep indefinitely if kept sealed away from air and light and at constant cool temperatures. She had also promised them that she could make more of the potion with the quantity of chymera venom they'd brought her, once she had been able to replenish her supply of the thorium salts. However, if it took very long to get more of the salts they'd be needing to make another trip for fresh mushrooms. Bernadette hoped that more potion would not be necessary. Why would you want it, except for stopping Tarragin?

Andrion had followed her up the stairs, and dropped his pack on one of the beds in the sleeping loft. Over their days of search for potion ingredients, they'd all lost track of whose "turn" it was to share the master bed with Bernadette. And she herself was undecided. She loved each of them in their own way, and making love with both of them together was amazing; but the bed here was awfully small for the three of them to share.

Andrion wandered in to wrap his arms around her from behind and kiss the nape of her neck, as she was taking things out of her pack and arranging them on the bed. "What do you think should be our next move, love?" he asked lightly. Dropping her burdens, Bernadette rotated in his arms and gave him a tight squeeze. Then she pulled back.

"I've been considering it, and I think I should go up to Hochstein and confer with Ehrgeizig. We're going to need all this potion decanted into little bottles, and maybe you and Erik could deal with that while I'm gone." She looked up at him questioningly.

A trace of disappointment passed across Andrion's face, but he said "That sounds like a plan. Where do you suppose we can get a goat?" She giggled.

"I hadn't considered goat logistics, yet. I suppose it would be better to get a tame one from one of the farms hereabouts, something we can lead on a leash, instead of trying to capture one of the wild ones and get it to hold still while we give it a makeover." He grinned back at her.

"I'll have Erik see what he can do about that," he promised. "He knows everybody in town, I think."

Bernadette kept her lightweight armor on, brought along a few weapons and her much-lightened pack, and fast-traveled up to Hochstein. As the crow (or perhaps, the dragon) flies it was not that far from the Bathing Maiden, and not much more of the day had elapsed by the time she found herself standing on the snowy mountaintop.

Ehrgeizig was as she had seen him the first time, perched like a patient vulture atop the Spell Wall perhaps fifty feet from the spot where the map had deposited her. "*Einkliin,* you have returned!" He rumbled in his deep, ancient voice as she approached. "You have found what you sought?"

Bernadette looked up at him, half amazed at how unafraid she felt conversing with this gigantic creature. "I got the Dragonfall spell, and pretty nearly all the other dragon spells as well!" she said proudly. The old dragon seemed taken aback for a moment.

Finally he said, "You found the forge, then? I had thought it destroyed millennia ago."

"It was perfectly intact," she replied, "buried beneath stone but warded so that it remained untouched after the fortress that contained it was taken. We were able to make enough spell stones so that Andrion will be able to help me with the Dragonfall spell, holding a stone against his skin." Ehrgeizig seemed impressed.

"It is best to mount the stone on a cord around the neck," he informed her. "Closer to the body's core."

"Thanks for the tip," Bernadette said politely. "We got what we think must also be the potion the ancient Norse heroes used on Tarragin. Their plan was that he would be unable to escape by translating himself between dimensions. But while the potion destroyed his ability to regenerate magical energy, he still had enough of a charge for one more trip. Then, we think, his regeneration ability must have healed itself over time."

"Hmm," Ehrgeizig rumbled. "You may be right. That would explain why he did not return for thousands of years. But how do you plan to get Tarragin to take this potion?" Suddenly Bernadette felt embarrassed. Here she was, a tiny upstart mortal who'd been on the planet for what must seem an eyeblink to the old *drache*. Yet she was supposed to give him advice? The goat idea seemed silly, now. But she bit her lip and explained.

"We thought we could tie a bunch of vials of the potion, along with a potion to take away magical energy, underneath the wool of a long-haired goat," she said. "The goat might look like a tempting snack, and it would just be a bite for a dragon the size of Tarragin. But we haven't figured out how to call him to eat it."

The old dragon chuckled. "An amusing picture," he said. "But I fear it would not work. We *drachen* prefer our meals cooked, at least a little. Should Tarragin decide he wanted your 'small snack,' he would be likely to singe away the wool first with his Holocaust spell. That might cause your vials to shatter, or at least to fall to the ground when their strings were burned off. But as to bringing him to battle, that will be no problem. Can you imagine another way to deliver the poison?"

How could she not have realized that? Feeling like an idiot child, Bernadette cast around for other options. "Do dragons ever eat animals that are just lying there dead?" she asked.

"Sometimes, if the meat is freshly killed," Ehrgeizig replied. "But I am thinking if you were to stuff a goat's corpse with potion vials, it would have been dead for too long to be appealing by the time you could present it to Tarragin. And he might be suspicious, as well. A dragon is not a dumb beast, like some predators."

One more goat-themed idea came to Bernadette, and when she explained it to her scaly mentor he nodded. "That might very well work," he said. "But I would recommend that you bring along some arrows dipped in the potion as well. If the plan does not work, you'll need a backup. Supposedly the ancient Norse heroes only managed to deliver a very small dose, yet that saved many generations of men and elves from the depredations of Tarragin and his worshipers. It was true, that might only be passing the problem along to future generations – but it would certainly postpone the day of doom."

"That's what we're going to do, then," Bernadette said positively. "Now how and where do we get Tarragin to come to our surprise party?"

"As for where," the ancient *drache* replied, "I think right here would be best. I can aid you in the fight. And it was here that the

344

Norse heroes defeated Tarragin in ancient times – a fitting venue for his final defeat."

"And how?" she asked, wishing he'd get to the point a little faster.

"Nothing easier," he replied. "You may not realize it, but not every spell used by dragonkind is four words powered by a stone. In addition, there are certain spells made with three words of power, that draw directly on the caster's magical energy alone – leaving the life force and stamina alone."

"Aethelred cast a three-word spell to bring down the ward around the mountaintop, before the first time we came here," Bernadette said.

"Exactly," the ancient dragon replied. "Likewise, the spell with which the ward was set also contains three words. And each dragon's name is in itself a spell, made up of three syllables. By speaking the name of a dragon using the voice with which you speak the stone spells, the dragon so Called will hear you and know who you are and where you stand."

"Is the dragon compelled to come when Called?" Bernadette asked.

"Oh no, not at all," Ehrgeizig replied. "But should the Called one desire to answer the call, they have only to will it and, no matter how far away they were, in moments they will be within a short distance of the one who Called them."

Amazing! Boy, that would be a handy thing for getting around the province. "But why should Tarragin come to my Call?" she wondered. "Doesn't he know I'm prophesied to defeat him? You'd think he would want to steer clear." Again, the low rumble that was dragon laughter.

"Do you imagine he fears you?" Ehrgeizig asked in surprise. "The prophecy says only that there is a *chance* the Fireblood may stop him. It's in direct opposition to the prophecy that says the Soul-Devourer will destroy the world. One or the other may be right, but not both. And naturally, he assumes that *he* will defeat *you*."

Bernadette stood silent for a moment, considering the dragon's words. They weren't as reassuring as she might have liked. He continued, "But in any case, I plan that it will be *I* who Calls Tarragin. It was I who helped his enemies defeat him all those years ago, and I am sure he has long wanted my blood. I think he will be unable to resist the chance to seek his revenge. When you are ready, bring your goat and your battle companions. We will have it out with him, once and for all."

Chapter 46: Tarragin's Bane

"Are you ready for this?" Andrion asked. The goat, the long wool from her belly having been shaved away for this procedure, was being held in place on the smithing table in the Bathing Maiden's basement. She was not a happy camper.

"Mmmmaaa!" she complained, squirming as Erik kept a tight grip.

"Go ahead, give her the sleeping potion," Bernadette told her assistant, and he forced the jaws open and trickled the bottle of potion into the animal's mouth before squeezing the jaws shut and massaging her throat. Eyes rolling, she continued her struggles for another minute – and then relaxed.

"She should be asleep for at least fifteen minutes," Andrion said. Bernadette grinned at him.

"Roll her over so her belly's facing straight up," she instructed Erik. He did so, holding the animal's limp legs out of the way. The "doctor" brought up the steel dagger she had ground to a thin razor edge, and carefully made an incision – cutting through the she-goat's hide and the thin layer of fat beneath it, but leaving the peritoneum intact.

Andrion was beside her with the tray of tightly-sealed vials. They had been thoroughly washed after being filled and the stoppers inserted, so should be safe for handling and would not, they hoped, cause the noble volunteer for this suicide mission undue discomfort. Bernadette began gently inserting the potion vials (both the Destroyer of Magic potion and a good quantity of Drain Magic potions she herself had crafted) into the goat's body cavity beneath the skin.

No one, not even Ehrgeizig, knew how to quantify the amount of magical energy a fully charged-up dragon might have. Certainly they had a lot more mana just because they were so big. But all Bernadette and her crew could do was put in as many of the potions as would fit, and hope they would do the job. If they failed, the world would be right back in the same situation as before – at the mercy of an enemy who would return long after anyone alive remembered how to defeat him.

When the poor nanny was stuffed to the gills, Andrion held the goat in its unnatural position on the bench while Erik pulled and stretched the skin on either side of the incision – forcing the edges close together. Using a curved needle and some gut fiber, Bernadette did a quick and crude sewing job – closing the incision. It would only need to hold for a little while. As soon as she had taken her last stitch, she began to cast a healing spell on the "patient."

Before their eyes, the edges of the incision knit together and welled up a bead of pink proud flesh. The goat stirred slightly, beginning to come out of her drugged sleep. "Give her another dose, Andrion!" Bernadette urged. The vials were fairly tough, but not *that* tough. She didn't want the goat banging around and ending up with broken glass inside. Cutting her stitches and pulling them out, she cast the healing spell again until the skin had become unblemished – only a faint scar remaining. The goat looked awfully... lumpy, but when she was standing on her feet her long wool should hang down to hide the anomaly – especially when seen from above.

Now, they needed to scramble. They put the goat into a large canvas carrying sack, only her head protruding, and set her gently down on the nearby bed while they all hurried into their armor. Packs loaded with potions, and weapons for all of them, sat ready. Before the goat had begun to stir again they were outside the Maiden, Bernadette placing a finger on the marker for Hochstein and wishing them there.

Not a lot of time had passed since they left, but it was long enough for the goat to have awakened from her slumber. "There, there," Erik rumbled soothingly, stroking her forehead, and her struggles subsided. While Erik held her horns Andrion pulled the bag off of her, then they got the rope they'd brought attached to her collar and staked her out, with about five feet of rope, in the center of a flat area near the summit. It was cold up here, but the snow was only a few inches deep.

Ehrgeizig looked on, fascinated, as the Fireblood and her companions arrayed what they hoped would be a tempting tidbit for their adversary. The goat seemed to be a little unsteady on her feet at first, eyes rolling as she looked around and nostrils flaring with the scent of dragon. But the dragon was not attacking her; and a short while after being staked out she began to nibble at some low-growing plants that were poking out through the snow cover. Goats are nearly imperturbable, nature's survivors.

Bernadette looked at Andrion, then at Erik. "Ready?" she asked, and they each gave her a thumbs-up. All three fearless dragon hunters had brought bows to the party, and each had a supply of arrows specially fletched for the occasion. Their hollow tips held a little bit of the Destroyer of Magic potion, designed to separate from the shafts when they penetrated flesh and release their cargo. It had taken them days to get ready for this, but they now felt confident they could succeed.

"Ready, Ehrgeizig!" Bernadette called, and the old dragon lifted up his head and called "TAR-RA-GIN!" in a voice that made her own puny efforts seen like the barest whisper. The humans had spread out around the edges of the central summit facing the Spell Wall, giving the goat plenty of room and hoping to obtain some shelter from the nearby rocks.

The moment dragged on for what seemed like an eternity. Where was Tarragin? Would he come? Then suddenly he was there! "Ehrgeizig!" he boomed, flapping in midair and facing his old enemy – then shooting out a gout of flame. Bernadette and her companions were shocked to see, close up, how much bigger he was than Ehrgeizig.

"Long did I languish, trapped in Ekelvelt with nothing to eat but the flesh and souls of beasts," Tarragin said. "Such tiny souls cannot nourish the *machteh* of a *drache*. And scarcely did a day go past, as I waited for my strength to return, that I did not think of the revenge I would take on Ehrgeizig – traitor to all the *drachen*!" The tattered old dragon, a lighter shade of gray than his adversary, heaved himself up to hover in mid-air and shot his own flames. Polite greeting, or deadly insult?

"Can you not see, Tarragin," he said in his ponderous growl, "The time of the *drachen* is over? It is men who rule *Erte* now.

Even should you succeed in raising all who died in those days, it would not be enough. Already they fall again, and those killed by the Fireblood are gone forever."

Tarragin flapped sharply and rose in the air, circling the clearing. He quickly spotted the three armored warriors arrayed against him. "Fireblood?" he roared. "Is it to be the Norse heroes all over again?" He hovered now facing Bernadette. Evidently the first-born's supernatural senses could tell what she was just by looking at her.

"My belly is full of the souls of your fellow mortals, *Fjurblut*," Tarragin taunted her as he approached on the wing. Bernadette considered retorting, "Well, *my* belly is full of the souls of your fellow *im*mortals, *drache*" but inasmuch as she'd only actually consumed a couple of them so far, she felt the boast was exaggerated. And she thought it better not make him any madder than he already was.

Tarragin continued, "Die now and await your fate in Asengard!" But as the Soul-Devourer swooped to the attack, Ehrgeizig launched himself into the air to add his efforts to the battle. Bernadette wanted to use the Dragonfall spell, but she didn't want to cripple their strongest ally. Instead, she took careful aim with her bow and sent an arrow – one that did *not* bear the Destroyer potion – flying toward the larger dragon as he turned in air to meet Ehrgeizig's attack.

The range was too far, and though the arrow hit it bounced off of Tarragin's scales and fell to the ground – as Bernadette had feared it would. That was why she'd used an ordinary arrow, not wanting the poisoned ones falling on their own heads. "We need to hold our attack until we can get him on the ground!" she yelled to Andrion and Erik, whose shots had also failed.

Both dragons were wheeling above the summit, roaring and flaming at each other, and too far away for a shot. So far, the hapless goat had been completely ignored though she was bleating in terror. Tarragin roared, "Stin-Ful-Fjur-Toet!" and suddenly the humans found themselves under bombardment. That spell was Rain of Death, Bernadette realized, instantly memorizing the words. But it had not been among the spells on the list at the gem forge. Maybe this one was Tarragin's own?

Flaming rocks the size of hen's eggs were falling all around them, bouncing off their armor and sizzling in the snow as they hit the ground. Injured by dragonfire and flying rocks, Bernadette downed a couple of health potions and drew her bow again, as Tarragin circled lower. He had temporarily driven off Ehrgeizig and was now turning his attention to The Fireblood.

When he halted to hover in midair above them, flapping his huge wings and readying a blast of dragonfire that would obliterate them all, she gathered her power and roared out "Alt-Wach-Sterb-Tot!" as loudly as she could. The effect on Tarragin was dramatic. A multi-colored shockwave seemed to ripple through and past him as Bernadette's words left her throat, and he glowed momentarily. Then he backpedaled as if slapped, wheeled away, and in moments came down to the ground near where she stood, her men by her side.

Ehrgeizig was back, wheeling above them. "Now!" he shouted. "Attack him while he is on the ground!" Squinting up at him through the swirling snow and rain of fiery stones, Bernadette grinned wryly and thought, no sooner said than done old fellow. She fired one of the poisoned arrows at Tarragin from a few yards away, managing to place the shot in the relatively unprotected, flexible hide beneath the wing. The men, too, were firing their poisoned arrows. Erik risked fire and the enormous jaws (the same ones that had killed Gunnar back in Plainview, she recalled with a pang) to fire an arrow up into the monster's mouth.

Erik rolled out of the way as Tarragin shot an enormous gout of flame – incinerating the arrow shaft and dislodging the point, but not before it had deposited its tiny dose of poison. We must have hit him four or five times with the potion, Bernadette realized, but he was completely ignoring the goat! Would that dose be enough, if he decided he'd had enough and tried to leave?

The Soul-Devourer soon launched himself into the sky again, raining death and destruction on them from above. Bernadette and her companions took cover in among the rock spires dotting the summit, where the dragon's missiles were less likely to strike them.

She had to drink another couple of health potions before she got another chance to bring Tarragin down again. Despite the freezing conditions on the mountaintop she was running with sweat, her chest heaving and heart pounding as she whirled in place, trying to keep the dragon in view and ready to strike him with arrows if the moment came. Then, once more he tried to hover for a shot at them with fire – and once again she staggered him with "Alt-Wach-Sterb-Tot!"

This time, as Tarragin came in for a landing, he fell heavily – as if he had been drained of the energy to stay aloft, not merely staggered by the dragon spell. Once again Ehrgeizig, who seemed to be gleeful at seeing his old adversary in trouble, exhorted them to attack. All three puny humans gave it their best shot. It was working, too! At least another three of the poisoned arrows drew blood, and as Erik charged in from the side to swing his axe Andrion hit the dragon in the face with a burst of concentrated lightning.

But dragons had a natural resistance to ordinary spells. Creatures of magic themselves, spells seemed to roll off them. He snarled and snapped at Erik as the axe cut deep into the scales along the leading edge of one wing. The graceful giant leaped back out of the way, and Tarragin followed.

Though many times larger and heavier, dragons were essentially big lizards with wings added on – the only such six-limbed vertebrates known on Terris. And they could move across the ground as well, if with less agility. As Tarragin lunged toward Andrion, roaring his anger, Erik stood on his right and Bernadette on his left as they fired arrow after arrow into him.

Andrion, dodging blasts of flame and answering with his battle magic, was almost beside the goat and the dragon was coming on. "Maaaugh!" the terrified animal screamed. She had had enough, and so had the rope with which she'd been tethered. It parted with a jerk, and she got her hindquarters under her for a dash to freedom.

The movement caught Tarragin's eye, and his enormous head snaked out faster than an eyeblink. He didn't swallow the goat whole, as they'd hoped. Instead he caught her in his jaws – snapping her spine and piercing her abdomen with each of his many teeth. The shattered vials released their poison, and as it ran out into his mouth Tarragin realized he had been tricked.

Andrion dashed out of the way, moving off to the side, and the enormous dragon shot out a gout of flame still larger than before. He was trying to incinerate the poisons, rather than swallowing them. But some of it had already trickled down his throat, and more of it was already in his bloodstream.

"No!" Tarragin raged, infuriated. "You will not trap me again!" He lifted himself from the ground with an effort, flapping heavily, and as he rose into the sky there was a pulse of light. The dragon was gone. Damn! Bernadette stood there panting, her bow hanging at arm's length. Had they just handed the dragon problem to their thousand-times-great grandchildren?

Ehrgeizig, seemingly little more tattered than before, came flapping in for a landing. "It appears that the potions did not rob Tarragin of enough of his magical energy," he said. "He was able to escape us once more."

"But he took in a lot of the potion!" Bernadette said. "That has to have been four or five times as much as what the ancient Norse heroes were able to dose him with."

The old dragon nodded. "True," he said. "It is a victory of sorts, and I think Tarragin's followers will take note of it."

"So has he gone back to his private planet, his 'Ekelvelt,' as he called it?" Andrion asked.

"I do not think so," Ehrgeizig replied. "You heard what he said, the souls of the non-sentient beasts there lacked the nourishment he needed to recover his powers. He will have fled elsewhere, to some other plane of existence."

Bernadette downed a healing potion and passed some to Erik and Andrion. All of them were bruised, blistered, and bloodied by the rain of flaming rocks. Then she said, "He mentioned Asengard, the plane of the Norse afterlife. Might he have gone there?"

353

"It's likely," Ehrgeizig replied. "He has always reserved for himself the privilege of feasting on the souls of the departed. And they can replenish his powers like nothing else. He boasted that he had been there but recently, did he not?"

"And is there a way that we can chase him down there?" Bernadette asked. "Uh, without dying I mean? If we could catch him there before he's recouped all of his powers, and I have to think that's going to take some time, we could finish him off!" Ehrgeizig considered.

"I have heard that in the time before the Uprising the priests among the dragon worshipers had many secret powers. It might be they had a way for a living man to pass between the worlds and enter Asengard. But I was not privy to much of this information. It's possible that one of Tarragin's followers, one who was among his adherents in that time, would know how it could be done."

She grinned, her buoyant spirit rising again. "What'll we do, twist his arm and give him noogies until he blabs?" she asked. The old dragon sounded as if his dignity was affronted.

"I know not of these 'noogies.' Some sort of potion? But there is another way. You know, do you not, that the palace in Waterdon, Wyrmshalla, was originally built to house a captive *drache*? A fine place to trap one of Tarragin's allies, I would think."

Bernadette recalled having heard something of this history. There was a broad space on the palace's second floor, with an enormous balcony looking off to the north. It was certainly large enough to lend credence to the tale of a dragon having been held captive there in ages past. She tried to envision how Ormund would react to the suggestion that he turn over his hall for the purposes of dragon-catching. To Ehrgeizig she said, "The eorl of Waterdon might not think so."

"Hmm, yes," he replied. "But I do not doubt that you can convince him of the need."

"All right," she told him. "I'll try. Do you have the name of one such, a dragon who's been resurrected and is available as a subject?" Ehrgeizig gazed sightlessly past her, lost in memories.

"There was one from the old times who was ever a supporter of Tarragin," he said at last. "And I know that he is alive again, for he came to talk with me – to taunt me, really – a few days ago. After you've convinced the eorl of the wisdom of your plan, go out on the balcony and Call Sneyagflug. He was ever arrogant, and he is sure to be curious about your powers once he hears of Tarragin's defeat. Call him, and I am sure he will rise to the challenge."

Bernadette turned away, looking at her lovely men. They were still kind of grimy, but no longer injured. "Well, team," she told them. "We did it. Sort of. I'm so glad I had your help! But now we have to go talk Ormund into letting us use his place for a dragon trap. And I, for one, could use a bath and probably a night's sleep first."

Erik dazzled her with his angelic smile, saying "You, my darling, are the boss."

Chapter 47: Wyrmshalla and Diplomacy

Less early than usual, Bernadette's eyes fluttered open. She could hear people stirring in the Maiden below, and knew she should be getting up; but it seemed to her as if each step in her journey to fulfill her "destiny" was becoming more daunting. I'm getting good at killing dragons and aptrgangr and bandits, she thought. But what on Terris is supposed to make me qualified to bend eorls to my will?

So instead of leaping right out of bed, she rolled over in Andrion's warm arms and reached down between his legs to squeeze his member where it lay, already semi-turgid. Her touch soon had it rising more, and he woke to look at her with a mixture of delight and bleary puzzlement. His Berni, initiating sex in the morning instead of jumping out of bed and cracking the whip over him to get up as well? Hmm, he recalled. It *had* happened at least once before.

Why argue? He gathered her to him and fondled her breasts, thumbing her nipples to stiffness, as he kissed her deeply. What's a little morning breath amongst friends? When a gentle probing with two fingers between her legs told Andrion that she was ready for him, he pressed the now-quivering tip of his engorged member into the folds of her swollen vulva and slowly worked it inside.

She threw a leg up over his hip, the better to allow him access, and they made love in this position, lying on their sides, until both of them were fully awake and getting more and more excited. Bernadette always found morning sex to be delicious but somnolent, no mind-blowing explosions; yet as Andrion's thrusts became more urgent she felt her desire rising.

"Wait!" she told him. Pulling away from him and throwing off the covers, she crouched on hands and knees with her back to him. "Take me from behind!" Oh yeah, thought Andrion. The sight of her rounded buttocks, her swollen and glistening sex nestled below them, caused his already rock-hard member to stiffen even more, pointing the way. In a moment he had entered her, and her screams told him that he had hit the spot. He pumped away furiously, sinking his shaft to its full length with each stroke, and soon they were both coming hard.

Bernadette flattened on the bed, Andrion atop her, his cock ensheathed, as the pulsations of her climax still surged through her. More sensitive about such things than Erik, he soon rolled off of her and they lay face to face for a moment as he cupped her head in his hands and deposited sweet kisses on her forehead, her chin, her eyelids. When their panting had subsided she opened her eyes and said softly, "It's no use. We really need to get up and get on with it."

They put on robes and hit the bathing pool, then returned upstairs to get dressed. Bernadette, returning to her usual cheerful self despite the weight of her responsibilities, grinned at Andrion. "I almost forgot – I have a present for you, love." She dug into the chest and came out with a complete set of fine clothing: a tunic in fine embroidered wool with velvet sleeves, woolen hose, a fur mantle, and jeweled embellishments. A stylish fur hat and a pair of gleaming leather boots completed the ensemble.

Andrion was touched, and surprised. "For me?" he asked, running his fingers over the soft wool. "Why...?"

"You, my dear," she replied with a fond look that melted him, "are going to accompany me to impress the eorl with the urgency of our need to use his residence as a dragon trap. Erik looks too much like a Norse warrior, but I think that in these clothes you'll do nicely as a nobly-born counselor to the young yet also nobly-born and Very Important Fireblood." What could he do but smile, and put on the clothes?

Meanwhile, further rummaging in the trunk produced a similarly fine set of clothing for Bernadette. She felt that while heavily armed and dressed in battered armor she had a certain hard-bitten authority, it seemed (and what did she know? She was nothing but a Galise lass from a remote rural village) that the eorl would be more likely to take her seriously if she were dressed as a member of his own exalted class.

Thus splendidly attired, the two returned to the Maiden's main floor and found Erik, wearing casual clothing, sitting alone at their usual table. He'd gone off with another of the inn's patrons last night, but there was no sign of her. She was probably sleeping off the effects of a night spent with Erik, Bernadette thought cattily. He goggled at them, a half-eaten bread roll suspended in midair on its way to his mouth. "What...?"

Bernadette grinned at him and stepped over to give him a hug, her breasts pressing against his ear, filling his nose with her scent. She smelled clean and... determined? Dropping into the chair beside him as Andrion took the one on her other side, Bernadette squeezed Erik's enormous hands in her little ones and gave him a peck on the lips. "We're going to Wyrmshalla to get Ormund to let us trap the dragon there," she reminded him. "Do we not look magnificent?"

Erik smiled his lazy grin, understanding. "Going to impress him with your upper-class ways, huh?" She nodded sagely. He had a whole plate of bread rolls and some honeycomb on the table before him, and Bernadette reached over to help herself. A little light breakfast would be good, to fortify herself before approaching the eorl in his palace.

Munching away, and passing a roll to Andrion as well, Bernadette asked slyly, "Erik, where's your friend?" He flushed. Despite the arrangement between them, it still embarrassed him somehow that she knew of his other activities.

"Sleeping," he replied shortly.

She rolled her eyes and murmured, "I'll bet..." Preferring to drop the subject, he bent to his interrupted breakfast.

Bernadette and Andrion soon washed their abbreviated meal down with some tea and then took their leave. "Wish us luck," she told Erik. "I suppose we should be back within a couple of hours."

"I'll be here if you need me," he responded, standing to give her a hug before the pair departed. They fast-travelled to the gates of Wyrmshalla from the Maiden's front porch, not wanting to get any road dust on their fine clothing.

At the palace, Bernadette strode in the front doors unopposed and up the long hall to the dais – Andrion flanking her. He looked remarkably sober and important in his unusual outfit. The eorl, who knew her well and had been the first person in Iscandia to accord her respect as The Fireblood, blinked as if he did not recognize her at first. Then he greeted her with a nod, and waited for her to state her business.

I'm not a diplomat! Bernadette thought. Might as well just spit it out… "I need your help, sir. We have successfully routed Tarragin, but he has escaped us and we must coerce one of his dragon supporters into helping us go after him. I need to trap a dragon in your palace," she told him bluntly.

Ormund looked concerned. "The Soul-Devourer?" he asked. "That is what we are facing?" It was Ormund who had sent her to the Old Ones in the first place.

"I thought you had realized that," Bernadette told him. "Since you commanded me to seek out the Old Ones I have learned much. The dragons are returning because they are being resurrected by none other than Tarragin, returned from exile as prophesied. And he means to carry our world into a sunless universe where all life on it will be destroyed – unless my companions and I can stop him."

The old man, seeming older still at her words, looked from Bernadette to Andrion and back again. Maybe full armor would have been the better choice, she thought, as she realized how little she looked like a formidable champion in this outfit. "But how… how *can* you stop him?" Ormund asked. "Is he not immortal, invincible?"

Bernadette lifted her chin, a sly smile curving her lips. "Not so immortal or invincible as all that," she drawled. Ormund looked at her hopefully, and she explained. "Andrion and I found Faastenberg, the legendary stronghold of the ancient Norse heroes. We now have both the dragon spell they created and the potion they used, and we have already poisoned the Soul-Devourer with it."

"But… you said he had escaped you?" the eorl asked, confused. He was being asked to absorb a lot of shocks in a short period of time.

359

"Tarragin has, or had, the ability to instantly translate himself between worlds," Bernadette explained. "No one has been able to kill him, because whenever he was close to losing a battle he would simply flee – far out of reach, to rest until his wounds were healed."

"I thought that the ancient Norse heroes banished him millennia ago," Ormund said uncertainly.

"They did, poisoning him with a potion that stole his ability to regenerate magical energy," she replied. "He fled to another plane, but found that though his health returned he no longer had the ability to move between worlds. He was stuck there from the day he fled until just a few days before I first came to Iscandia."

The eorl gathered himself. He was a man of prominence and power, and it ill befitted him to seem weak in front of this so-very-young woman – Fireblood or not. "So you poisoned him again and he fled again. But are we not back where we were before? Surely you and I will both be nothing but dust before Tarragin troubles the world again."

Andrion had mostly been window dressing until this point, but now he added his voice to the argument. A mature male voice, one that might carry more weight with the eorl. "We believe he has fled to Asengard, where he builds his strength by devouring the souls of the honored Norse dead," he said. "If we do not act quickly, find a way to seek him out there and kill him before he regains his powers, he will be back far sooner than we'd like. And next time, he is not going to let us trick him as we did before. He may decide to move up his schedule, cleansing Terris of all life within the next few weeks."

Andrion had no idea what was in Tarragin's mind, or what he planned for the time when he was able to depart Asengard. But he thought it would make a good argument, and it seemed to have impressed Ormund. The old man appeared to be racked with indecision. "But what you're asking for is insane. The mechanism above is ancient, and has not been used for millennia. If you try to trap a dragon it will likely smash it to pieces before running rampant through my city."

"But the mechanism still exists?" Bernadette pounced. "It wasn't taken apart and lost, or anything?" Ormund lowered his eyes.

"It's… sort of a historical relic. Part of the ancient heritage of Iscandia. But you can't subject it to such strains. It would be sure to fail!"

"My eorl," Andrion said commandingly. Though Ormund had twenty years on him, he could do "commandingly" in a pinch. And the fate of the world might be on the line. "Would you do us the courtesy of coming up with us to inspect the device? Time is of the essence!"

"Very well," Ormund said. He led the way, his nachtalfar body servant Miralis at his side, and the four of them climbed the stairs near the dais to the palace's second floor. Then they went out the double doors to the enormous space where once, in an era long past, the ruler of Waterdon (at that time a city-state, the ruler a king not an eorl) had held a dragon captive and subject to his will. It was an act that had not gone over well with the dragon priesthood.

They walked out into the center of the space, and Ormund gestured to the ceiling forty feet above their heads. A gigantic wooden yoke, bound with iron, was suspended there from a complicated arrangement of pulleys and thick black chains. Bernadette and Andrion gazed up at it in wonder. At this distance, it didn't look big enough to restrain a dragon.

"The yoke is operated from a mechanism on the balcony over there," Ormund explained – gesturing to their right. "It weighs close to a ton, yet the mechanism is so cunningly crafted that a single man on the crank can raise it by himself. He has only to pull a lever to drop it, of course…"

"You've actually seen it in action?" Bernadette asked, surprised. She'd thought he said it hadn't been used for thousands of years.

"When I was a child, my father had the mechanism brought down onto a table to show me my heritage. It destroyed the table."

361

"Perhaps not as fragile as all that, then," Andrion suggested. "Shall we go up for a closer look?" The party took a stairway to their right and went up to take a look at the mechanism by which the yoke could be dropped and raised. The chains were thicker than those one might see attached to the anchor of the largest seagoing vessel, and there was no sign of rust or corrosion on them. The metal was a matte black.

Andrion ran his hands over the chain where it came into the cranking mechanism. "There is an enchantment on this chain," he said. "The iron is imbued with something similar to a magical ward, making it proof against breakage and oxidation. And for it to remain strong after all this time, whoever cast the enchantment must have had power beyond anything we know in modern times."

Ormund looked suitably impressed. Andrion was older, and quite probably deeper in the magical arts, than his own court wizard. "The mechanism has not been operated for more than forty years?" Andrion asked, and the eorl nodded. "Do you have a quantity of dypalfar oil available?" This amazing lubricant, which enabled the automatons in dypalfar ruins to keep moving millennia after their builders had departed, was a prized ingredient in chemial potions.

"I can obtain some," the eorl replied uncertainly.

"Good," Andrion replied. "And I think that a few mattresses might be more appropriate than a table as a stand-in for our dragon. After the mechanism and its chains have been oiled, we need to bring the yoke down so it can be inspected."

Somewhat to his astonishment, Ormund found himself commanding that oil and a stack of mattresses be brought. There was something about the Galise mage's sense of urgency, and of decisiveness, that made him want to go along with whatever he said. Bernadette smiled to herself, thinking "I *knew* there was more than one reason I love him."

Within the hour the yoke had been dropped, hitting the stack of mattresses with a resounding thump. They had been placed along an inch-wide groove carved across the stone floor of the space, a visual guide for whoever was operating the mechanism.

362

When the dragon's neck crossed that line, time to pull the lever! The iron with which the yoke had been bound was still in perfect condition, the wood ancient solid oak nearly as black and as hard as the iron. "As I suspected, the same enchantment was placed on the yoke," Andrion said in tones of satisfaction. "I am sure, now that we've lubricated it, this mechanism should work as well as it did in the time before the Uprising."

Bernadette didn't want to be a voice of negativity, but she had to ask. "It's very large and impressive, but is it really enough to imprison a full grown dragon?"

Ormund answered her, "According to the lore of Waterdon, a dragon's neck is its weakest part. Pinned by the neck, the creature is unable to rise onto its feet, flap its wings, or move either forward or back." He spoke with a tinge of pride in his voice. The kings of Waterdon were nothing but appointed provincial officials these days, yet once they had conquered dragons!

Bernadette and Andrion eyed him, waiting for him to acknowledge that there was no reason to refuse their scheme. He looked back at them, then sighed. "All right, we'll do it. I'll need some time to prepare, to make sure that we have enough guards to fight this beast if it somehow eludes the trap. But we will be ready by tomorrow at ten, if you feel you must do this thing."

Chapter 48: Erik's Turn

Bernadette and Andrion walked in through the front door of the Bathing Maiden as evening was coming on. There'd been more discussions of logistics with the eorl's men, that had gone on longer than anticipated. Both of them were fairly anxious to change into more comfortable clothing; but as what they were wearing was both presentable and free from the bloodstains, arrow holes, and grime more usual when returning from a quest, they decided to eat first.

Bernadette was delighted to find Erik sitting at their usual table, right where they'd left him. Presumably he'd been elsewhere in the interim, but there he was again – and once again, with food on the table in front of him. He was no longer wearing the same clothes, at least. Her spirits soaring, Bernadette hurried over to the table as Andrion sauntered behind her.

He sat down on one of the other chairs, but Bernadette seated herself on Erik's lap, throwing her arms around his neck and giving him a hot kiss. Then she pulled back a bit and beamed at him. "So it worked?" he asked. "You got the eorl to say yes to using Wyrmshalla for a dragon trap?"

"It wasn't easy," she replied, putting one arm across his broad shoulders while reaching down with her free hand to steal a morsel off his plate. "Really, it was all Andrion's doing…" She devoured another bite of Erik's meal, and before it was completely chewed up she said indistinctly, "Eat first! Talk later!"

Andrion motioned to Lev, who was doing innkeeper duty at the moment, and in a few minutes plates of food began appearing on their table. Erik resumed eating his own supper, while Bernadette (having relocated to a chair) and Andrion bent to their own meals with determination. After the immediate yawning hunger had been sated, she continued eating at a more measured pace, actually chewing the food and swallowing it before trying to talk.

The three friends sat at the table for some time, as Erik was given all the details of their conference with the eorl, and the discovery that the mechanism used to trap dragons was still in perfect working order thousands of years since it had last seen use.

Bernadette ordered a bottle of wine for the three of them to share, nicely washing down the huge meal and taking the edge off her anxieties a little more. Just being in company with Erik and Andrion, relaxing in the Maiden over a good meal, was balm to her soul. And she was already starting to think of something else that would take her mind off her troubles. Erik was looking at her in a way that suggested he, too, was thinking of that; and Andrion was studiously ignoring the situation.

Sighing, Bernadette stood up. "Time to get out of these clothes," she said, heading for the stairs. "I'll be down in a minute – I'm going to have a soak." She hoisted her skirts one more time to negotiate the steep stairs up to the loft, and the two men watched her go.

Andrion gazed at the tabletop for a moment, then looked up at Erik again. "I'll clear my gear out of the master bedroom for the night…"

Erik returned the slight smile, interrupting him to say "You don't have to do that. I've taken over the bedroom down in the basement. Berni and I can sleep down there tonight, so you don't need to move your stuff." Andrion looked Erik in the eyes, a certain amount of pain showing in his own.

"Thanks, buddy," he said. He thought wryly that if he got any more noble, he'd have to start wearing clothes like this all the time.

After another couple of breaths Andrion sighed slightly and stood up, giving Erik a bigger smile. "That bath sounds like a good idea. I'm going to go get out of these clothes." As he started to walk away he said, "Oh – Berni says she wants us both with her when we go up to Wyrmshalla tomorrow to try to trap the dragon."

Erik grinned, a wolfish expression that suggested he was mentally sharpening his axe. Dragons, beware! "Thanks," he said.

While his friend and his lover were gone upstairs, Erik nipped down to the basement and put on his own robe, a tent-like affair that fitted him nicely and would have completely obscured Bernadette had she tried to wear it. When he returned to the main floor, he found Berni and Andrion already soaking in the pool. She gave him a huge grin as she spotted him approaching them in his robe, and beckoned him into the water.

Immediately, Erik discovered a familiar problem. This woman who haunted his dreams seemed to cause his cock to swell at the mere thought of her, let alone her touch or the sight of her in a fetching pose. He'd been stiffening while she sat in his lap, stealing food from his plate. Now he was standing in the middle of the Maiden's ground floor common room, about to climb into the clear water of the bathing pool; and there sat his Berni, *their* Berni, glowing pink from the hot water, utterly naked save for that amulet she always wore. Her slender waist and flat belly were set off by the curve of her delicious hips and her full, shapely breasts bobbed on the surface of the water, nipples rosy.

Argh. Erik hadn't even gotten into the water yet and already his cock was so hard he imagined he could use it to pound armor on the crafting table downstairs. He felt like a 15-year-old getting his first look at a naked woman. He turned as pink as Berni and, clutching his robe around him, he said "I'll be back in a little while." Then he dashed back to the trap door and returned to the basement.

Letting his robe fall open, with a towel to hand, Erik seized his recalcitrant member in one huge hand, and began stroking it firmly. He hadn't done bedwarmer duty with any of the Maiden's clientele since that insatiable woman a couple of days ago, and he was horny. He let his mind run back a few days to that time away from the inn with Berni, making love in the woods, pumping into her from behind. In moments his cock exploded in his hand, soaking the towel, and he felt a great sense of relief. This was nothing like the transport of an orgasm with his lover, but it went a long way toward easing the pressure he'd been feeling.

Cleaning himself up, tying the robe around his midsection again, Erik hurried back upstairs. He was now able to climb into the hot pool beside Bernadette, naked but not rampant. Andrion seemed oblivious. At seven years Erik's senior he no doubt had all such things nicely under control. Bernadette eyed him a bit curiously, however, and scooted over slightly to touch hips with him. Then she put her hand on his thigh, and when this too failed to elicit the expected response her eyes widened. She cast an analytical gaze at him, and then burst out laughing.

Andrion looked at Berni in curiosity. Had there been a joke he missed? Still chuckling, Bernadette threw her arms around Erik's neck and kissed him. Her voice bubbling with laughter, she said "I love you, Erik Johannessohn!" His face reddened. Andrion was quizzically looking from Berni to Erik as he tried to figure out what just happened, which triggered another peal of laughter from Bernadette. She repeated her actions with Andrion now, saying "And I love *you*, too, Andrion Lamonte." Well, *that* was alright then…

The three sat soaking and talking quietly about nothing much until they were starting to prune. Erik put an arm around Berni and murmured in her ear, "We're sleeping in the basement tonight. Okay?" The basement? Sure, why not. The bedroom down there was often more private than the master suite actually, certainly quieter. And if you woke up early, as she was wont to do, you could get in a little smithing without leaving the room.

They all climbed out, drying off with towels and donning their robes. Bernadette stood on tiptoe to give Andrion a hug and a kiss, then she and Erik made their way to the trapdoor and their subterranean boudoir. On reaching it, she was surprised to see that some changes had been made to the décor. "Have you been fixing this place up, Erik?" she asked. "I like it!"

He grinned somewhat shyly. "I picked up a few things in town. I wanted to make it nice for you… when it's my turn to…" he trailed off, embarrassed. Bernadette was touched. How could this huge, deadly warrior be so *sweet*?

"Oh, Erik! Thank you! It's wonderful! I especially like the embroidered coverlet…" His confidence returning, Erik gestured around the room.

"I kind of like this place as a bedroom, you know. It has so many… accessories available."

Taking Bernadette by the hand, he led her over to the forge area at the far end of the room. "See, it's even got an enchanting table…" Erik had stood right here in this room watching her work at that enchanting table, creating some of the magically-enhanced armor and weapons he'd been using in their recent quests. What was he getting at… Oh! Bernadette's memory suddenly returned to the first time she had made love with Erik, in that bandit stronghold… *on the enchanting table*! A hot thrill shot through her from her crotch, up through the center of her body, and became a warm glow rising in her cheeks.

Erik was looking at her expectantly, and Bernadette could tell that he knew she had remembered. Her eyes were alight with desire, her face flushed, as she approached him and picked at his robe, pushing it off his shoulders to lie crumpled on the floor. "Are you bleeding?" she asked him, stepping close to run her fingers over his torso, his chest, his nipples. Those were stiffening now, as they had then. His cock, so recently quelled, had recovered its enthusiasm and was now standing at attention once again.

Bernadette dropped her own robe and fell into his arms, bent back with her breasts pressed into his belly, reaching to have her mouth engulfed by his. His tongue down her throat, he clutched her to him, his powerful arms holding her as if he never planned to let her go. Then he released her mouth and, slipping his hands down lower, he grasped her by the buttocks and carried her over to the enchanting table.

This time, Erik had control. Masturbation less than an hour past had left him feeling like he could make love to this woman, this beautiful, maddening woman, for the rest of the night. Perching her at the edge of the table he entered her carefully, making sure she was ready for him. His size could be an issue with some women, but with Berni he always found her wet, eager to receive his full length and girth.

On this occasion Bernadette was ready to soar to the skies, almost at once. Though she and Andrion had made love before leaving on their visit to Wyrmshalla, it somehow felt as if it had been a long time since then. And the excitement of reliving that first red-hot encounter with Erik had her passion surging even before he pushed that giant hot cock inside her.

Berni bucked and screamed as Erik pumped into her, bumping against her clit on each stroke. Her legs were spread wide as her buttocks perched on the edge of the table, allowing him full access and a good height for thrusting, his powerful legs bent slightly at the knees. After she came the first time he cradled her in his arms for a while, but didn't cease his strokes. He just slowed down a little, savoring the way it felt in there. So hot, so wet, her vaginal muscles clutching him as she climaxed. If he hadn't taken some of the pressure off earlier, he'd have been a goner just like that.

After an indefinite time on the table, Erik eased off his strokes for a moment, still inside her but moving less as he cupped her face in his hands and kissed her tenderly. Then he gestured to the other side of the room. "There's other accessories, too," he pointed out. Bernadette's mind was nearly gone at this point, but she followed his gaze and spotted… the crafting table?!

"Erik Johannessohn, you are wicked! And I like that in a man…"

Pulling out, his cock still jutting skyward and now reddened and glistening, Erik helped Berni down off the enchanting table and the two of them padded over, barefoot, to the crafting table. This workbench, used for improving everything from boots and breastplates to greaves and shields, was just about the right height to support her as she bent over it, allowing him access to her from behind. As he surged inside her, she cried out "Oh!" Followed by "Yes, yessss!" Berni *did* like those rear-entry positions. She was soon screaming again, as he fucked her harder and harder. Despite his earlier release of tension, the passionate reunion under exotic conditions was starting to get to him, and his control was beginning to slip away from him.

Easing his rhythm once again, Erik bent over Berni where she rested against the crafting bench, to murmur in her ear. "I think the grindstone, forge, and smelter are right out, love. How about the bed? I want to see your face."

"Okay," she murmured hoarsely. She had come so many times she could barely walk, let alone think. Observing that he'd put her in such a state, Erik smiled with satisfaction. Then he scooped her up in his arms as easily as if she were a small kitten, and carried her over to the bed – his cock still sticking out in front of him like a lance, bobbing slightly as he walked.

Erik laid his lover gently on the bed, face up, then climbed onto it beside her. He looked into her eyes, letting his love shine naked in his gaze, and she looked back at him with the slightly glazed expression of somebody who has nearly had her brains fucked out. And with love, too. A surge of emotion welled up inside of Erik. "Augh, Berni!" he groaned. "I can't get enough of you!" He buried his face in the flesh between her neck and shoulder and began kissing her passionately, sending renewed thrills through her.

She grinned weakly and opened her legs to him. "Well," she said softly, "you can try…"

Some time later Erik shuddered and gave a prolonged groan, as he spent his seed at last. Bernadette rocketed with him to orgasm one last time as he did so, feeling as if her mind were ready to disintegrate under the repeated waves of pleasure that had assaulted her for the last… hour? For a change, her gigantic lover was sensitive to his mass atop her, and after collapsing briefly he quickly rolled over so they could face one another. She covered his face with kisses, hands stroking his cheeks. Then she gave a sigh as if all the air had been let out of her at once, and melted into his arms. Before long, both of them had dropped off to sleep.

Chapter 49: To Trap a Dragon

Bernadette awoke to the dim light of a candle on the nightstand, wondering what time it was. Down here in the basement there were no windows, and one could not even really hear if people were stirring in the Maiden's common room above. Somehow, though, she sensed it was morning and time to get back to work. But oh! Her mind played back over her evening of passion with Erik, and the throb that went through her as she recalled it was accompanied by a less-than-pleasant ache. It's possible, she thought, that we may have overdone it.

She was lying nestled against Erik's chest, and as she stirred against him Bernadette noticed that his cock remained quiescent. Even *he's* fucked out, she thought. Squeezing into him, she kissed his nose and his eyes opened, looking sleepy but lighting with love as he beheld her. He was usually a little quicker to shift out of bed in the morning than Andrion was, though neither of her lovers was the sort of guy to spring up at dawn with a song on his lips.

"We'd better get up, love," Bernadette told him yawning. "Dragons to trap and all that…" He hugged her to him and kissed her firmly, then released her so she could crawl out of bed. As she got up, she realized that she was standing bowlegged. Ow. "Oh shit, Erik, you've ruined me!" she cried. "How am I supposed to trap dragons if I can barely walk?"

He looked at her with concern. "I'm sorry, love. You just inspire me, I guess… Hey! Why don't you use your healing spell?"

Bernadette mentally slapped her forehead. Erik was no dummy, but sometimes *she* was. "Of course!" she said, and in moments the glow that marked the spell's triggering took form around her right hand. Compared with being raked by bear claws, blistered by dragon fire, or sliced up by broadswords, the results of being shagged ragged by an enthusiastic Norseman with a cock of heroic proportions were a snap to heal.

"Would you like a little too, dear?" Bernadette asked Erik tenderly. Now sitting up in the bed, admiring her as she glowed with wellbeing from the application of the spell, he stroked his cock thoughtfully. It *was* a bit sore, and oh how Berni inspired him. Sometimes he felt as if he'd like to make love to her until it fell off.

Having plenty of magical power left over after her brief self-treatment, Bernadette applied the healing spell to Erik. The result was less spectacular than the closing of wounds and vanishing of bruises the spell could produce when treating someone with severe injuries; but it was still fascinating to behold – his cock immediately rose to rigidity, and an expression of surprise and delight suffused his perfect features.

Bernadette was grinning at him now, a powerful surge of affection washing over her but not much desire. She had stored up enough orgasms to last her until the other side of Asengard, she felt, and their pressing business pushed all thoughts of romance aside for the moment. "Not right now dear," she told him. "We've got work to do." Erik smiled back at her a little wistfully. He knew her well enough by now to realize that once she got into go-ahead mode, there'd be no luring her back into the sack.

Erik rose from the bed, his cock subsiding, and began getting into some underdrawers. As Bernadette put on her robe, kissed him, and headed up the ladder to go retrieve her gear from the master bedroom, he put on his armor and gathered his weapons. This expedition should be fun, or so he hoped. Upstairs, Bernadette saw that light was coming in through the Maiden's amber glass windows. Daylight was burning!

She continued up the stairs and found Andrion still in bed, lying on his back with his mouth open and snoring gently. True love is willing to make allowances, and Bernadette thought he looked cute that way. Not to mention, lazy. She set her robe down, then pounced on him naked, which very quickly got his attention. His eyes lit up to see her looming above him, and he grabbed for her breasts.

Grinning, Bernadette dodged him, backing down the bed. Come and get me, she seemed to be saying, and he started up from between the covers, his manhood on the rise, and caught her before she could put a foot on the floor. Both of them kneeling on the bed, he pressed her to his chest and kissed her enthusiastically. Feeling his stiffening, Bernadette had a moment of regret. Both of her men had the power to fill her with lust at a moment's notice, it seemed, even after a session like last night's with Erik. But no.

Bernadette slipped out of Andrion's embrace and walked to the chest, digging for her underclothes and armor. "Sorry, love!" she told him. "We're off to save the world today, remember?" Oh right, he thought ruefully. Save the world. At least, once he'd helped his beloved perform that feat, he had hopes of a happy reward. Andrion sat on the side of the bed, trying to get his brain in motion; then stood up, his stiffness ebbing, and began gathering up his own armor.

When the two of them were completely equipped, they trooped down the stairs and met Erik in the common room. Rather than take their usual table the three sat at the bar, where Drelos served them room-temperature ale and sweet rolls for breakfast. An odd combination, but Bernadette was focused on the mission ahead and filled her stomach without paying much attention as the food passed her mouth.

Everyone was counting on *her* to come up with a plan to force this Sneyagflug to cooperate with them, and Bernadette had only the foggiest, general idea of what she was going to do. Trap the dragon, and then what? If he knew of a way for her to travel to Asengard without dying first, would it even still be possible for her to use it? It was likely that this recently-revived dragon's knowledge of such things was thousands of years out of date.

Her eternal optimism returning, Bernadette told herself that things would, somehow, work out. What 22-year-old is not convinced of his or her own immortality? The companions had finished their meal, and they now climbed off their barstools and headed for the door. Bernadette could see that both Andrion and Erik were excited, looking forward to the adventure ahead of them. Onward!

It was a lovely morning in the Waterdon region, blue sky and puffy clouds extending to the horizon. Bernadette briefly considered walking instead of fast-traveling, but concluded that time was of the essence. In moments they were standing outside the doors of Wyrmshalla, and headed inside. She hurried past the long dining table, anxious to talk with Eorl Ormund.

As Bernadette and her companions approached the eorl's throne, Ormund greeted her respectfully. "We're ready, Fireblood," he told her. "Just say the word."

She replied, "Thank you. Let's go trap a dragon." The eorl, accompanied by Bernadette and her companions, climbed the stairs again. Miralis was already there, arraying the complement of city guards who would help with the dragon-trapping.

After double-checking that everything was in readiness, Bernadette walked out onto the semicircular balcony. With Andrion and Erik flanking her, she put power into her voice and cried "Sne-Yag-Flug!" The guards sharing the balcony with them stared at her, then out into the sky beyond the balcony, then back – waiting for something to happen.

It soon did. Only a few moments after Bernadette's Call they saw a dragon winging toward them and heard its deep, chilling voice calling out in challenge. By the gods, Bernadette thought, Sneyagflug was enormous! Smaller than Tarragin or Ehrgeizig certainly, but bigger than any other dragon she had seen.

The dragon came flapping in, raking the balcony with the Holocaust spell as she and the rest of the defenders scattered for cover. Running into the space beyond, Bernadette began firing arrows from her enchanted bow, even as Waterdon guards attacked the dragon at closer range. Andrion was by her side, hurling bolts of battle magic, while Erik shot his fire-damage bow.

Sneyagflug lifted and ponderously flew away again, calling taunts and threats in a mix of dragon tongue and the common speech. Bernadette hit him with the Dragonfall spell, rocking him in midair. In moments he came down, landing heavily on the balcony. "Your *furml* is strong, *Fjurblut*!" he declared in his deep voice. As Andrion and Erik got closer to attack the dragon with their bladed weapons, he lumbered forward – snapping at them with his enormous jaws. Those teeth were half the size of her forearm!

Convinced her guys knew what they were doing and were safe, Bernadette kept approaching Sneyagflug and then running back to the shelter of the space inside, trying to lure him to follow her as she stood pelting him with arrows. She was beginning to think it had been a mistake bringing Andrion and Erik with her for this stage of the operation. She loved having them by her side, but as guardians they were almost *too* effective. Their close-up attacks were preventing Sneyagflug from moving from the balcony to the location where the trap was set to spring.

Finally, after Sneyagflug was beginning to look much the worse for wear, he flew off again. Bernadette and her fellow defenders stood there panting, mostly unhurt, and waited. In moments he was back and she yelled at Andrion and Erik, "Run! Inside! We need him to follow us!" As the huge reptile came crashing down behind them they sprinted into the dim recesses, and Sneyagflug chased them – only to have the yoke drop like a stone from above, pinning him helpless to the floor.

Success! Bernadette exulted, followed by "now what?" She approached the gigantic, trapped dragon leerily, staying a little off to the side lest he decide to toast her with his flames in payment for her trick. Sneyagflug rumbled, "*Zu ind schlees, Fjurblut,*" then added "Ah, I forget. You do not have the *drache* speech."

Andrion and Erik hung back, panting, letting their hurts mend themselves while their fireblood lover did the negotiating. Sneyagflug went on, "My... eagerness to meet you in battle was ill-considered, *Fjurblut*. Your trick has caught me." Speaking as though it pained him, he added "No doubt you want to know where to find Tarragin?"

Despite the size difference, it appeared that Bernadette had the upper hand here. And she seized it firmly. "That's right," she demanded. "Has he fled to Ekelvelt?"

The revenant monster replied, "Ah, so you know of his private world. That which became his private prison!" She stared him down. "No, he would not return there. Where else would he go, but to Asengard? Of all the available universes, it is there that he will find the sustenance to regain his strength."

"I thought you were one of Tarragin's supporters," Bernadette replied. "How is it that you are willing to speak so freely?"

"Many of us have begun to question Tarragin's lordship," the red dragon replied. "Among ourselves, of course," he demurred. "None were yet ready to openly defy him. He is the first-born, the eldest and therefore largest among us."

"Ah, so it's time for a regime change?" Bernadette asked. Sneyagflug nodded slightly. "Ehrgeizig suggested that there might be a way for humans, or others who lack Tarragin's ability, to travel in physical form to Asengard. Is that true?"

Sneyagflug replied, "The traitor spoke truly, though I am surprised he knows of it. The secret was guarded closely by the dragon priesthood, and rarely shared even with us they claimed to worship."

"And how might I travel there, then?" she asked him. He was being a lot more cooperative than she'd feared, but was still taking longer than she'd have liked to get to the point.

"You are more versed in lore than I expected, *Fjurblut,*" the dragon said. "Therefore you may know that Tarragin has the ability to take others with him when he travels between planes of existence. I myself visited Ekelvelt with him, there to feast on the prey animals that fill its plains in numbers beyond counting."

"I do know that," Bernadette said, her patience beginning to fray.

Sneyagflug went on, "At the request of the dragon priesthood, Tarragin created a magical gateway, a portal through which the living could travel to the world of the dead without needing to be accompanied by him. None age there, and a time spent feasting in Valhaale is said to be as good as a hundred healing potions. That door to Asengard is at Todenstor, one of the dragon cult's strongholds high in the eastern mountains."

The dragon continued in a warning tone, "He will certainly have marshaled his remaining supporters to guard the gate. And the portal opens only to the key of a *Drachansstab,* the staff given to a dragon priest on initiation in the highest ranks of the priesthood." Andrion's ears pricked up at this. Those staffs could often be found in ancient Norse tombs, along with the magical masks that were also part of a dragon priest's regalia. Of course, one usually had to wrest them from the undead original owners, first.

Concluding, Sneyagflug asked, "Now that I have answered your question, will you allow me to go free?" Sure, Bernadette thought. Thanks for the info, ta-ta now. Not without some guarantees, first.

"Do you promise to serve me?" she asked.

Sneyagflug replied, "I don't think so. If and when you defeat Tarragin, I will reconsider." The battered monster seemed to searching for something he could offer her instead. "Hmm… There is one… detail about Todenstor I neglected to mention." Which would have remained unmentioned, Bernadette knew, if she'd simply let him fly away.

"Tell me what you know, then," she demanded.

"Only this," the dragon replied. "You have the *furml* of a *drache*, but without the wings of one, you will never set foot in Todenstor." He continued wheedlingly, "Of course… I could fly you there. But not while I'm imprisoned like this." Bernadette didn't know what to think. Could she really trust this… creature? If not, it would be insane to let him go. But if the only reason she had trapped him was to get to Tarragin, and the only way she could get to Tarragin was to trust Sneyagflug, then trust him she must. Unless there was another way?

It seemed they were at an impasse, but there was no time to lose. "How about this?" Bernadette suggested. "You agree not to harm me or my friends, and to stop helping Tarragin. And you promise to take me to Todenstor. Then I'll set you free."

He replied, "I see there is only one choice."

Sneyagflug continued, "And you can trust me. Tarragin has proven himself unworthy to rule. I go my own way now."

"Done," Bernadette replied. She climbed the steps at the back of the hall to the balcony where one of the Waterdon Guards manned the yoke mechanism, telling him "Open the trap." He looked at her questioningly, or so she assumed though his uniform's helmet made it impossible to see his face.

"You sure about that?" he asked.

"Just do it," she replied, turning on her heel and hurrying back down the stairs.

The bar lifted. Sneyagflug, tattered and dripping blood from their earlier battle, wheeled and made his way across the floor to the balcony. There he stood, awaiting her command to carry her away to the ill-omened Todenstor. It suddenly struck Bernadette, with a sensation like an icy hand grasping her heart, what she was getting into. She had just signed up to have the dragon fly her, alone, to do battle with "all of Tarragin's remaining supporters," in order that she might enter the land of the dead and challenge the Soul-Devourer there. There was a good chance she would never see Andrion or Erik again.

They were hanging back, watching in awe, as she prepared to climb aboard the enormous beast and take to the skies. Bernadette ran to them, pale-faced, tears starting from her eyes. They drew together, and she hugged both of them. "If I don't come back... I love you both!" she declared, struggling to keep from breaking down sobbing on the spot. Not the sort of image you want to project as The Fireblood, savior of the world.

Bernadette took Andrion's face in her hands and kissed him, as he clasped her lightly. Then she did the same for Erik. If she didn't come back, she realized, they wouldn't miss her for long because with nobody to stop Tarragin, the world would be destroyed and everybody she had ever known and loved would be dead. This realization hardened her resolve, and with a grim smile she told Sneyagflug, "Let's go." Then she climbed up his scaly shoulder to perch on his neck, just forward of the wings.

Sneyagflug seemed a lot happier now he was no longer trapped. For a creature used to the freedom of the skies, imprisonment would be a hard burden indeed. "I warn you," he rumbled, "once you've flown the skies of Agena, your envy of the *drachen* will only increase." That's assuming I can bring myself to open my eyes, thought Bernadette, as the dragon walked forward a little further onto the balcony before flapping his wings and leaping into the sky.

Bernadette surprised herself by being exhilarated as they soared above the mountains, valleys, and streams of Iscandia. The view was so breathtaking (though, she had to admit, the smell of dragon in such close proximity to her nose was a little breathtaking as well), that it was as if she forgot to be terrified. "This is wonderful, Sneyagflug!" she whooped. "You were right!" Ah, to have wings and be able to travel like this whenever you wanted!

All too soon, Bernadette's mount alit on an area of flat stone before a chasm, surrounded by steep mountains. On the far side of a narrow stone bridge loomed an ominous-looking stone fortress, its gate open. Soon, she would find out what "all Tarragin's remaining supporters" really meant. After she climbed down from his neck, Sneyagflug turned to her and said, "This is as far as I can take you. I will look for your return, or Tarragin's." With that he launched himself into the air and was gone.

Chapter 50: Todenstor

Bernadette felt woefully alone and afraid, but took a deep breath and stiffened her resolve. She drew her bow and nocked an arrow. Creeping carefully toward the bridge she had her eyes wide open, searching for enemies. Just then an arrow whizzed past her head, coming from one of the walls of the fortress on the far side of the bridge. An aptrgangr, she realized; and as she took aim, she was utterly astounded when the undead warrior was suddenly hurled from its perch into the chasm below by dual bolts of lightning streaming from behind her left shoulder.

Bernadette whirled, dumbfounded. "Andrion! You're here! And Erik... how?" She was almost crying again, so strong was her joy to see her two lovers, her protectors, her boon companions here beside her. Andrion smiled at her, and came close to give her a little squeeze, saying.

"While you were climbing onto the dragon, we just sneaked up onto his back in between the spines. I don't think they have much feeling in that scaly hide of theirs. He didn't even seem to notice we were there."

"Yeah," Erik added, delivering one of his famous grins and a second brief hug. "You didn't think we were going to let you save the world all by yourself, did you?"

Bernadette reached out to draw them close, hugging them as much as was possible in heavy armor. "Oh, you two! I love you so much! I can't believe you're here – thank you!" At that point, a roar from the sky alerted them to a smallish dragon, which had just spotted them and was wheeling in for an attack. The three instantly scattered into a defensive formation. Bernadette readied Dragonfall and her bow, and between that and the combined efforts of her two champions, the beast had soon fallen to the stones of the bridge. Its flesh disintegrated almost immediately, as she quickly absorbed its life essence. There were no spell stones left behind, but that hardly mattered now.

For once, Bernadette was so distracted by the imminent peril all around that she passed through the exalting experience of the soul capture without paying any attention to it. The three of them moved on, up a flight of stairs, and were soon attacked by a trio of aptrgangr. These were the first such undead guardians she had ever seen wandering around in daylight rather than down in the corridors of some tomb, but they were no less effective in the open. Staeven's explanation that some thought the aptrgangr to be servants of the dragon worshipers was evidently borne out, if these were the "supporters" Sneyagflug had spoken of.

Across a broad concourse stood another massive building, carved double doors set in the side. As the trio were deciding what direction to go they were attacked by another dragon. With three experienced dragon-killers arrayed against it, it was down and giving up its soul to The Fireblood in under a minute. After that, Bernadette decided to check the nearer building first and they ventured up a long, broad stone staircase at the front.

Before long more aptrgangr began to appear, each attacking as soon as it sighted them. These seemed to be mostly of the middle-range type, whose weaponry and toughness made them a challenge to stop. Some of these had *furml*, and Bernadette found herself staggered and nearly thrown down the stairs even from 50 feet away. Hmm, she wondered. She had never found any dragon spell stones on the bodies of defeated aptrgangr. How was it they could use the spells?

Not wanting to use her own dragon spells with Erik and Andrion in the way, Bernadette settled for trying to make arrow shots on the walking corpses, even as her companions attacked them at close range. Erik was a demon with his axe, hurling himself at his adversaries and shouting out curses. "I'll see you dead! Victory or Asengard!" His fierceness thrilled her to the marrow even as she feared for his safety. He was not invincible... was he?

They fought their way up a series of staircases and went around a few corners, to find themselves at another pair of carved double doors similar to those across the courtyard. Now this, Bernadette thought, looked more like the entrance to a typical aptrgangr den. She was not disappointed. Soon she, Andrion and Erik found themselves moving stealthily through a labyrinthine barrow, fraught with traps and aptrgangr guardians. The aptrgangr never knew what hit them.

There were puzzles, as well, and both Andrion and Erik stood in awe of Bernadette's knack for these things. After the first puzzle gate, Bernadette had to swap her bow for a mace as she found her passage blocked by a thick net of spider webs. As soon as the way was clear, she switched back to the bow, quickly dispatching a Chillmarrow spider the size of a large dog that had not yet noticed her approach.

That one's death triggered the attack of three more, and Bernadette began dropping them one by one as they raced nearer and nearer. The last, and largest, almost had its fangs in her before her last arrow struck it, but a blast of lightning hurled by Andrion dropped it at her feet. Bernadette, panting, took a moment to assess herself and decided she had not been poisoned.

The trio killed a few more spiders as they wound their way through a maze of corridors, then came into a second puzzle room. As Bernadette was approaching to inspect the situation, a pair of aptrgangr burst from vertical sarcophagi on either side of the room. Erik had chopped one into kindling almost before she got her bow up, and the other soon fell to blasts of Andrion's battle magic. My heroes, Bernadette thought with a wave of gratitude. She was so glad they were here!

The walls began opening out after they passed the second set of gates. They were attacked by a small pack of aptrgangr all at once, keeping all three of them busy in a dizzying melee. Bernadette felt as if she wasn't holding up her end, here. Bowshots from hiding were her best killing skill, and in these situations with friends and enemies all jumbled up together she could neither shoot nor cast dragon spells. Still, the men seemed to be handling their foes with ease, and enjoying it a great deal as well. Polishing off the latest round of undead foes, she found them grinning fiercely and looking to her to lead the way to the next batch. Perhaps she should just assume a management role and leave the killing to her staff?

Shortly they came to a series of unpopulated halls lined with
bas-relief scenes, which reminded Bernadette a lot of the Room of
Legends in Deadfall Barrow. And sure enough, at the far end was
one of those doors that was operated by a dragon statuette. It was
guarded by an aptrgangr, but three against one was tough odds for
him and he soon lay at their feet. Bernadette was immensely
pleased to discover a dragon statuette, its hind claws tipped with
what appeared to be diamonds, among other items on his person. It
opened the puzzle door in short order.

A little further up, they came to a cavernous hall, with a
catafalque lying in a central position up a broad flight of steps.
Bernadette was relieved to find the platform littered with burial
urns and embalming tools, rather than inhabited by an aptrgangr
overlord or some such. As they went along, she had of course been
helping herself to a handful of gold there, a few gems or a potion
there. The Fireblood's got to eat…

There seemed to be no enemies at all here, and as they moved
beyond the catafalque Bernadette spotted a Spell Wall. Nothing lit
when she approached it, though. If there were any dragon spells
recorded on it that she had not already acquired, the stones for
them must not be present. And she suspected, there were not many
dragon spells left that she didn't have. She led them on – up a
flight of steps, and through a door that opened onto a raised
courtyard.

As she came through the door Bernadette was immediately
attacked by an aptrgangr archer, shooting at her from a dozen yards
off. For a change, she was able to drop the foe before Erik got
there with his axe. But no fear – there were plenty more
adversaries for her homicidal honeys to play with. Bernadette
moved around as they fought, getting in a shot whenever the
opportunity presented itself without hitting either of her
companions.

In a minute or less, all of the undead had been returned to dead
status, and Bernadette checked their motionless corpses for
valuables before exploring further. Next they headed along the
raised courtyard, around a corner of the building. Her heart already

beating fast, Bernadette nearly jumped out of her skin when a pair of aptrgangr appeared from around the corner and began attacking them at close range.

Andrion fought the one nearer at hand, and after getting out of its range Bernadette focused her attention on the far one, with which Erik was contending. He looked well on the way to defeating it, and she added her two guilders' worth with a well-aimed arrow shot. But just as the aptrgangr fell, a swing of its war axe pitched Erik over the edge of the courtyard, into a recess that plunged down to ground level some thirty feet below!

"Erik!" she screamed, rushing to the edge. He had just vanished from sight! But as she approached the edge and looked down, she saw him, looking quite unhurt, clinging to a projection about halfway to the ground. "Are you all right?" Bernadette cried anxiously, though she could see that he was. Her heart was still in her throat. Were her golden warrior to be snatched from her life, it would be worse than losing a limb.

He looked up, grinning at her, and said "I'm fine. Just hanging around…" with that he dropped the rest of the way to the ground, muscular legs flexing to absorb the shock. In moments he had run around to a staircase and climbed back up to join them.

Bernadette rushed to him and clasped him briefly. "Don't *do* that!" she scolded him. "You just gave me a heart attack."

"Won't happen again," he rumbled, kissing her forehead. They shouldered their weapons and pushed on. Around another bend and up a flight of stairs, their eyes were suddenly drawn to a column made of scintillating arrows of light, rising from what appeared to be a stone pillar at the top of a short, narrow flight of steps ahead of them.

Bernadette turned to Andrion questioningly. She'd come to rely on him as an encyclopedia of facts, but in this case he drew a blank. Shrugging, he said "My bet is that's Tarragin's portal to Asengard. What else could it be?"

"Good point," she replied. While they'd been speaking, a curiously emaciated figure in what looked like a ragged brown robe began climbing the steps, approaching the column of darting light streaks. And Erik, having decided that figure was hostile, was already most of the way up those steps and attacking it with his axe!

Bernadette and Andrion broke off their conversation and ran to assist. Erik's battle with the strange figure had now pushed back out of the light column, and the two were fighting fiercely on the courtyard nearby. Now the light had vanished, but the two fought on. Bernadette saw a chance at a bowshot, and as her arrow struck home the thing vanished into a pile of ash. Erik, once again, seemed unhurt.

Exploring the ash pile Bernadette came up with a twisted staff. Could this be their key? If so, meeting this fellow had been remarkably fortuitous. Could it be that the gods of Agena were looking out for them? There was also an odd-looking metal mask. Andrion was watching over her shoulder as she sifted through the ashes, looking excited. "Let me see those!" he said, reaching for the staff and mask. She certainly had no idea what to do with them. Andrion pointed the staff at the ground at the foot of the stairs, and a sheet of lightning shot out to engulf the stones. Whoa!

Next, Andrion put the mask on his face. It rather spoiled his looks, but when he turned and blasted a nearby ornamental carving with fireballs, the "attack" seemed to go on for much longer than what he was usually capable of. Removing the mask to smile broadly at Bernadette and Erik, he said "I knew it! That thing you just killed was a dragon priest!"

Calming down a bit, he explained further. "Sneyagflug mentioned we needed a dragon priest's staff to open the portal. They also had special enchanted masks. This one" – beckoning to the mask in his hand – "Is *Raachen*. It boosts your magical power and gives you battle spells for less power usage. Kind of ugly, though. Anyhow, it's worth a fortune. Good score, love."

Bernadette and Erik goggled at him for a moment. When Andrion got going on bits of obscure lore he'd managed to pick up in his magical studies and/or his years wandering Iscandia, it was hard to remember he was the same guy who had just slaughtered half a dozen aptrgangr, almost without breaking a sweat. The three resumed their progress up the steps to where the portal had been; but there was nothing there but a stone circle, now. Andrion spotted a small hole in that circle, and inserted the staff into it. Immediately the column of light reappeared, as a broad circle of swirling chunks of stone formed before them.

Chapter 51: Asengard

It looked hazardous, but Bernadette bit her lip and just stepped off into the light. Moments later all three of them were standing at the top of a series of stone staircases that ran down a hill. The walkway was flanked on either side by tall, worn statues – too ruinous to be able to tell whom they portrayed. Around them, the land looked just like parts of Iscandia. Even the vegetation seemed the same, though the light was an odd color and the sky looked as if the aurora borealis had taken it over from one side to the other.

They left the staircases behind and headed along a path, seeing a building in the distance that Bernadette assumed must be Valhaale, the legendary mead hall where the dead heroes of Iscandia feasted throughout eternity. They had barely set their feet on the trail when Bernadette spotted a dragon that could only be Tarragin, riding the air currents above a rock promontory some distance away and roaring out his hunger. She and her companions ducked down, not wanting him to see them. He very likely held a grudge against these three.

A few dozen more yards down the trail Bernadette saw a figure garbed as a soldier coming their way, and she stood erect so that he would see her. This must be one of the dead, she guessed. The man spoke, saying "Turn back, traveler! The Soul-Devourer is abroad!" He went on, his diction antique enough to suggest it had been many years since he was last alive. "None may now pass through to Valhaale. Tarragin, his hunger insatiable, hunts the lost souls wandering within this shadowed valley."

This was monstrous, Bernadette thought. To die in battle, only to find one's soul devoured by a dragon instead of the reward one had been promised? "We are here to stop him once and for all," she promised. "Come with us, and we'll lead you to Valhaale."

The former soldier answered sadly, "I'll try, but I fear the Soul-Devourer will have us all!" He was unable to see that his three companions were not disembodied souls, but living men.

They forged on, but before they had gone any great distance Tarragin swooped down and snatched the soldier like a hawk catching a running rabbit. Bernadette was stricken, watching as the

Soul-Devourer flew away again; but there was nothing she could do. Except to get to Valhaale as quickly as possible, before Tarragin ate any more mortal souls – his strength, they could presume, growing greater with each such meal.

The three followed a barely-visible stone-paved path across the valley, keeping to the shadows and staying low lest Tarragin attack before they were ready for them. Andrion now wore a stone for the Dragonfall spell on a cord around his neck, and he and Erik were doughty warriors; but Bernadette hoped they might find some helpers on this mission. Wasn't the hall ahead packed full of Iscandia's finest?

They rounded a rock spire and Valhaale sprawled massive before them, taller in the middle and with stylized dragon carvings decorating the eaves. In front of it, a staircase flanked by massive bones, which must surely be dragon ribs, led to a bridge formed from an enormous dragon's spine. And before this bridge stood an impressive warrior with dark shoulder-length hair. Irrepressible even in the midst of deadly peril, Bernadette couldn't help admiring his massive chest and shoulders. Ah, if only you weren't dead, she thought. Then wondered, can the dead get it up?

The faintest of smiles curved Bernadette's lips, thankfully unseen by her two stalwart companions, as she approached the warrior. "What brings you, wayfarer grim, to wander here?" he asked ponderously. Whoo, they *do* talk funny around here...

"I pursue Tarragin, the Soul-Devourer," she told him.

"A fateful errand," he replied. "Many have charged to face the wyrm since he came once more to Asengard. But none can prevail, it seems."

Bernadette needed to get into the hall and try to recruit some some help within. She had visions of going into battle against Tarragin backed by every Norse hero from the stories she'd read as a child. "I seek entrance to Valhaale," she told the magnificent doorman.

"No shade are you, as usually here passes, but living, you dare the land of the dead" he replied. Uh huh, you hit the nail right on the head, she thought. Now… He went on, "By what right do you request entry?"

Time to play the *Fjurblut* card. "By the right of birth," she declared in her best approximation of hauteur. "I am fireblood." This seemed, finally, to make an impression.

"Ah!" he exclaimed. "It's been too long since last I faced a doom-driven hero of the dragon blood. Yet living or dead, none may pass this perilous bridge 'til I judge them worthy by the warrior's test."

Uh oh. Bernadette grabbed her mace and shield, prepared to do battle with this guy who couldn't be much more than twice her size. After all, dragons are a lot bigger than that and she'd brought *them* down a time or two. She motioned to Andrion and Erik to stand back, though they were quivering with the desire to go to her aid. But as the doorman raised his massive sword, as long as Bernadette was tall, she cried "Kraf-Luft-Struung-Wund!" and blew him into the ravine beneath the bridge.

The dead warrior, crawling back out to return to his station, acknowledged her the victor. "Pass, Fireblood," he said. "It is long since one of the living has entered here. May the gods' favor follow you and your errand." Nodding to him in thanks, Bernadette led her troop across the bridge. The spinous processes on this side were tall, requiring you to pick your way carefully along the short ribs lest you slip and find yourself in the chasm below.

On the far side of the bridge they stepped up onto the porch and entered through one of the tall, narrow doors. Inside, Bernadette saw that the hall of valor was constructed of stone. The space inside the doors was forty or fifty feet high, with feasting tables and an enormous, raised fire pit in the center. Two spitted whole oxen were roasting over the coals. There seemed to be surprisingly few people there, considering that this was supposed to be the eternal home of all the heroes of antiquity. Could Tarragin have eaten that many?

As the trio descended the steps to the central hall, a tall, bearded Norse warrior dressed in antique armor approached them. He spoke, saying "Welcome, Fireblood! Our door has stood empty since Tarragin returned to trouble us again. But three await your word to loose their fury upon the perilous foe. Zenis the fearless, maiden of valor; Boromund the strong, fierce warrior; and Seimdal the wise, far-seeing and grim."

Zenis, Boromund, and Seimdal! The three ancient Norse heroes who had exiled Tarragin during the Uprising, according to Ehrgeizig! If anybody could help Bernadette fight Tarragin, it was those three. Though she'd put her money on Andrion and Erik, if it came to that. She moved a little closer to the impressive fellow with his long dark-blond hair, thanking him. Then she stepped further into the room, looking around. She had no idea what the legendary trio looked like.

As she did so, Andrion caught her arm and hissed, "Sigrandil! That was Sigrandil!"

"Really?" She whispered back at him. Even in Auverne, the deeds of Sigrandil were legendary. He was said to be the ancestor from whom all Norse kings were descended.

"Absolutely. I recognized him from his statue. Wow, Sigrandil…" Andrion would probably like to stay here interviewing all the ancient heroes and pumping them for lore, Bernadette thought affectionately. But she just wanted to kill the damn dragon and go home.

She shortly spotted a woman and two men on the far side of the fire pit, and they were looking at her expectantly. The woman, armor-clad, spoke urgently: "At long last! Tarragin's doom is now ours to seal – just speak the word and with high hearts we'll hasten forth to smite the wyrm wherever he lurks."

A gray-bearded man wearing mage robes, who must be Seimdal, said "Hold, comrades – let us counsel take before battle is blindly joined. Tarragin's might is great. But with four voices joined, our valor combined, we can bring him down." Bernadette then turned to a grim and fierce-looking warrior, surely Boromund, as he put in, "Seimdal speaks wisdom, Fireblood. Casting Dragonfall together we shall force him to the ground, and then unsheathe our blades in desperate battle with our black-winged foe."

"Make that *five* voices," Bernadette said. "My companion Andrion has learned the spell and has the stone at his throat. Erik, my other companion, knows no magic – but he is as mighty with an axe as any living or dead." To her astonishment, she saw that Erik's ears were turning pink. He was always so calm and cheerful – except when he went near-berserk in battle – that it was strange to realize there were some situations that would awe even him. For a Norseman, apparently hobnobbing with heroes out of legend was such a situation.

There was a chorus of "Well met, Andrion and Erik," and clasping of hands. "Let us forth then," Seimdal said, "and confront the foe." Bernadette noted that all three bore pendants with the Dragonfall stone at their throats, and wondered how these useful items had translated to the plane of the afterlife. Well, they had armor and weapons, didn't they? Why not the stones needed to cast the spell they had created?

The six of them headed for the doors. Interesting, Bernadette thought, how the configuration of her, Andrion, and Erik reflected the group of Zenis, Seimdal, and Boromund. Except she was really in the mage camp with her dragon spells, rather than a super-swordmaiden. She suspected Zenis could probably kick her ass with one hand tied behind her back.

They filed across the bone bridge to stand on the slope below the promontory that rose beyond the hall. "Why don't you Call Tarragin, and see if he will come to us?" Bernadette suggested to Seimdal. She figured that the ancient *drache* had a longstanding grudge against these three, in addition to which they were souls he could devour to fortify his powers. That should be inducement enough. If he knew he was confronting the Fireblood and her companions, he might not be so eager to put in an appearance.

"We three will Call him, and tempt him near," the legendary mage replied. "Do you and your companions wait in hiding, to take him unawares when he draws nigh." There were piles of stone here and there in the area between the bluff and the ravine that fronted Valhaale; and Bernadette, Andrion, and Erik took cover.

"As soon as he shows up, we blast him with Dragonfall," she murmured to Andrion as they slipped into their hiding places.

The three ancient Norse heroes, as one, raised their voices and Called "Tar-Ra-Gin!" This pocket universe wasn't all that extensive, and it was no more than a couple of heartbeats before Tarragin came roaring forth – eager to devour those who had eluded him for so long.

"Seimdal, you are mine!" he growled. As he hovered to deliver these words, Bernadette and her companions stepped forth from among the rock shadows. As she and Andrion declaimed, "Alt-Wach-Sterb-Tot!" in unison, the other three chimed in scarcely a beat behind.

A coruscating pulse of purple and green light exploded around Tarragin, and he twisted in the air with wings flailing and tail lashing, all four limbs clawing for purchase as he fell thirty feet to the ground and landed with a crash in the road directly in front of Valhaale.

As soon as the old monster was on the ground, he was under attack with bow, blade, and spell from a half dozen champions. But oh, he was strong! Much stronger here than he had been at Hochstein, Bernadette thought, or perhaps it was just that Ehrgeizig's contribution to that battle had been greater than she realized.

He drove them back with Holocaust, which seemed not to hurt the three ancient Norse heroes but was deadly – and extremely painful – to the three living warriors who beset him. Fireballs were dropping around her, and Bernadette didn't even realize that she was badly hurt until she suddenly staggered and almost fell to the ground, bleeding and battered. In an instant Erik was at her elbow, handing her a health potion. As it took effect and her thinking became clearer, Bernadette realized that he and Andrion had come better prepared than she had – and that they were keeping an eye on her.

A powerful wave of love and gratitude swept through her, before her attention was wrenched away again by Tarragin. He seemed unable to rise again after that quintuple blast of Dragonfall,

but his four clawed feet could carry him thirty feet in an eyeblink.
They scattered, dodging out of the way of his lunges. Once those
jaws closed on you, Bernadette knew too well, you were done for.

Erik came in from behind as Tarragin's attention was
distracted by the attackers in front of him, risking the lashing,
spiked tail to leap up onto the dragon's back. He sank his axe blade
deep into the old monster's right shoulder, cutting deep into the
muscle that attached to the wing on that side.

With an earsplitting, *basso* howl of pain and rage, Tarragin
spun and bucked – throwing Erik off to skid in the dirt some
twenty feet away. The right wing hung limp, twitching but no
longer capable of flight. They had him now! But the furious dragon
had turned to find the man who had maimed him. Erik was only
stunned, and was already picking himself up as his foe unleashed a
blast of fire that blistered the back of his legs.

No, Erik! In a panic, fearing she was about to see her beloved
devoured, Bernadette cried "Steh-Mag-Zund-Leb!" This spell was
among the deadliest of the *furml,* robbing its target of mana.
Tarragin pulled in on himself as if cringing, and turned from where
Erik was scrambling away to safety to face The Fireblood, his
doom-driven nemesis. She pulled her bow one last time and
released it, the arrow driving deep into the flesh along his side and
passing between two of his ribs. It buried itself to the fletchings;
and the first-born, most ancient of dragons, gave out a cry of
mortal agony.

"*I'in ewiche! I'nst enze!*" he screamed. As Tarragin sagged to
the ground, his life force ebbing to nothing, his scaly hide became
crisscrossed with glowing dark orange lines. Then he began to
disintegrate before their eyes, his outer form flaking and flying
apart to reveal a darker dragon-shape within. It coiled like a
serpent made of ink-drops, writhing in the air. And then it just…
faded away.

Bernadette was watching avidly, her chest heaving. Tarragin
was gone! The three ancient heroes were jubilant, and she herself
was as pleased to find Andrion and Erik still breathing as she was
at the defeat of their relentless foe. The hall's gate guardian

approached her as she stood, still taking it all in. "This was a mighty deed!" he declared. "They will sing of this battle in Valhaale forever. But your fate lies elsewhere. When you have completed your count of days, I may welcome you again, with glad friendship, and bid you join the blessed feasting."

Bernadette appreciated the thought, but while it did look as if they might get a pretty good party going in there, it didn't seem like the way she wanted to spend the rest of eternity. Or even the next couple of days. There *was* that unresolved question about the virility, or lack thereof, of the honored dead. And she had two men at her elbow whose virility was beyond question. She approached the warrior.

"When you are ready to rejoin the living, just bid me so, and I will send you back," he said.

"Right now, please," she replied. They had done it! And now she was free to go adventuring for fun and profit, spend days just enjoying herself at the Maiden with her beautiful lovers, or whatever else she wanted to do. Nobody to try to tell her what to do. Giselle and Adalbert could go their own way, but they would have no more influence over her life!

"Return now to Terris," the ancient warrior said. Immediately the landscape around her faded to white. She had half expected he would return them to the point in Todenstor where they'd entered Asengard in the first place. But instead, she found herself and her companions standing on a snowy expanse surrounded by rocky peaks.

Chapter 52: Aftermath

Bernadette jumped, reaching for her bow. That was a dragon, flying down to land on the low peak in front of her. And there was another, and another – they were all around! Andrion and Erik were on the alert too, ready to do battle against insurmountable odds; but Bernadette soon realized these dragons were not attacking them. Turning around, she spotted a Spell Wall, with ancient Ehrgeizig perched upon it. They were atop the Hochstein, and the dragons had gathered – to mourn?

One spoke: "*Moch obher zwichen.*" Then he took to the air. Others came and went, all around them, as Ehrgeizig yet rested atop the Spell Wall. Bernadette approached him, hoping for some explanation. "*Fjurblut est zihn mordren,*" he said in his deep, ponderous voice. And again, "*Tarragin est stilde.*" She might be *Fjurblut*, kin to the *drache*, but Bernadette felt profoundly out of place at this gathering of dragonkind. If her soul was the soul of a dragon, her human heart and mind could not comprehend what passed here.

Finally, Ehrgeizig spoke to Bernadette in Common speech. "So, it is done. Tarragin is dead. The Eldest is no more, he who came before all others, and has always been." She sensed a deep sadness there, and understood the reason for it – but she felt a need to justify what she had done.

"Tarragin brought this on himself," she said.

"Indeed," he replied. "His doom was written when he claimed for himself the lordship that properly belongs to *Vaterhiin* – our father Aderos. But I cannot celebrate his fall. This world will never be the same."

It'll be better, Bernadette thought, somewhat stung. Though why she should expect dragons to thank her for killing one of their own, she couldn't explain. "I was just fulfilling my destiny as The Fireblood," she said.

Ehrgeizig seemed to acknowledge her justification. "I understand. You were driven by your doom just as Tarragin was."

Bernadette had nothing to say to this. She was troubled by the weight of Ehrgeizig's words, and the import of her deeds. She, a

22-year-old snip of a girl, had ended the life of a being ancient beyond belief. Ehrgeizig continued, "But I forget myself. The time for melancholy is over. You have won a mighty victory, one that will echo through all the ages of this world. Enjoy your triumph, *Fjurblut*. This will not be the last of your great deeds, I am sure."

With that the ancient *drache* shook himself, declaring "By Aderos! I feel younger than I have in many an age." Sad he might be over the passing of an icon of his people, but he seemed to be getting over his grief pretty quickly. As he took to the air, his words could still be clearly heard. "Many of the *drachen* are now scattered across Agena. They may yet bow to my leadership, as I have lived longer now than any other. Fare thee well, *Fjurblut*!"

And with that he was gone. Bernadette stood as if spellbound, watching him fly away. The thought crossed her mind that his motives in helping her against Tarragin might not have been so altruistic as she'd assumed. Had all that he had done to help humankind defeat the Soul-Devourer been intended to create a power vacuum into which he might step? The thought bothered her, but she brushed it aside. He wasn't likely to become the problem Tarragin had been, and without his help they never could have triumphed.

As Bernadette turned to her companions, another huge dragon came down to land at her feet. Sneyagflug! "I wish the old one luck in his efforts," he said. "But I doubt many will wish to exchange Tarragin's lordship for the tyranny of Ehrgeizig's disciplines." He went on, "As for myself, you've proven your mastery twice over. I gladly acknowledge the power of your *furml*. Call me when you have need, and I'll come to fight at your side if I can."

"Thank you, Sneyagflug," Bernadette said as the huge dragon gathered himself and then flew away. Now she and her companions found themselves alone on the snowy mountaintop. Andrion and Erik stood on either side of her, their arms crossed across her back. Shaking off the pall of sadness the dragons' melancholy had cast on her, she turned her head to look at first one then the other – joy bubbling up within her like the purest spring water. "You did it," Andrion said, his eyes glowing. "What are you going to do for an encore?"

Bernadette beamed at him and Erik in turn, as if the sun shone from within her soul. To them, it did. "I want to go back to the Academy and learn more magic," she said. Then, picking up speed, "and spend some time in Sylvanian, visit Alfenstein…" She began ticking things off on her fingers as her lovers watched in amusement. "Take a sea voyage, raid some tombs… we'll be rich!" She stopped for a heartbeat, eyes sparkling and breath coming faster. "But first," she continued, "I think we could all use a bath."

Andrion's and Erik's eyes met across the top of Bernadette's head, and they grinned at each other. Then they said, in unison, "How can I argue with that?"

The End (for now)

www.ingramcontent.com/pod-product-compliance
Lightning Source LLC
Chambersburg PA
CBHW071155250626
47159CB00001B/102